Victoria Routledge worked [...]
her first novel, *Friends Like* [...]
in the Lake District and no[...]
time as a novelist and a jou[...]

Also by Victoria Routledge

Friends Like These
Kiss Him Goodbye
. . . And For Starters
Swansong
Constance & Faith

THE SECRETS
OF ST DEE

VICTORIA ROUTLEDGE

POCKET
BOOKS

LONDON • SYDNEY • NEW YORK • TORONTO

First published in Great Britain by Pocket Books, 2006
An imprint of Simon & Schuster UK Ltd
A CBS COMPANY

1 3 5 7 9 10 8 6 4 2

Simon & Schuster UK Ltd
Africa House
64–78 Kingsway
London WC2B 6AH

www.simonsays.co.uk

Simon & Schuster Australia
Sydney

A CIP catalogue for this book is available
from the British Library

ISBN: 1-4165-0214-9
EAN: 9781416502142

Typeset in Garamond by M Rules
Printed and bound in Great Britain by
Cox & Wyman Ltd, Reading, Berkshire

For Lizzy Kremer, with love and thanks

Author's note

St Dee was inspired by the ghost village of Imber on Salisbury Plain, evacuated at short notice in December 1943 when the War Office requisitioned the land for training purposes. Despite a long and impassioned campaign, the villagers weren't allowed to return when the war ended, and the Army has continued to use what remains of the houses for urban combat training ever since. However, after an appeal to the House of Lords, it was decided that Imber's beautiful church with its medieval murals should be maintained, and its doors opened once a year to celebrate the Feast of St Giles, allowing old residents and curious visitors into the shell of the silent, ghostly village.

The Army currently allows access to the rest of Imber throughout August and for shorter periods over Easter and Christmas.

Chapter One

As a child, moving from one diplomatic residence to another, Carrie had dreamed of living in her own little house in the countryside with a thatched roof and an attic stuffed full of her own junk that she'd never have to sort out and pack up if she didn't want to. And a husband too, who'd mow the lawn, and be there for dinner. When she was old enough to wonder more seriously about that sort of thing, a psychic helpfully told her that her future husband would be tall, dark, handsome and have some kind of connection with mice. Which was reassuring and worrying in equal measure.

Carrie was a romantic, and she wanted to believe that Fate would deliver the right man to her, even if he turned out to be a Spanish rat-catcher, but Fate didn't seem to be on her side, and by the time she was thirty Time was ganging up with it. She'd spent her twenties attending hopeful parties, looking hopefully in the face of random strangers on the bus, searching hopefully for positive points (and mouse connections) in numerous blind dates. She wasn't so romantic that she felt her life would be over if she didn't get the lawn-mowing husband, but she felt a certain hollowness at her core as the years went on, and she started to buy moisturisers that promised wrinkle-treating qualities, even though she didn't believe they'd work.

The day after her thirty-second birthday, spurred on by half a bottle of wine and news of her cousin's third baby, Carrie fed her details into an Internet dating agency and, to her astonishment, met the man of her dreams at first click. After that, she really did believe in Fate. Because not only had Fate managed to keep her and Mark Armstrong single for each other till that moment, but he was an IT consultant. With a mouse at his fingertips all day.

As the computer had helpfully noticed, she and Mark were strikingly compatible: both had travelled (Mark through choice, Carrie during a childhood of being carted around the globe), both worked freelance (Mark fixing systems, Carrie as a children's book illustrator), neither had baggage to declare, both were ready to settle down – although naturally neither had opted to declare that in the questionnaire, for fear of seeming desperate. It was something they both confessed, after a few drinks, much, much later, on their third date.

It was refreshing, too, that they could offer up the aspects of their life that each thought most relevant, not dig up and cling to the tenuous links between friends or shared work experiences. Carrie was secretly delighted that Mark seemed to share her own rootlessness, part of her background she'd found almost embarrassing to admit to family-centric friends, who reacted to her self-contained life with something approaching pity; half-American, half-English, not many friends in London, Carrie didn't have a 'home'. 'Home' was somewhere she'd have to make for herself.

And though the way they met was very modern, their courtship was really quite old-fashioned. It took weeks of emailing before Carrie and Mark allowed themselves to arrange a proper meeting, not least because their flirty emails set such high expectations. Though she wouldn't have admitted it, Carrie had fancied Mark from his first witty, well-punctuated email. He had a casual, easy way of writing that made her feel as if she'd known him for years, and the intimacy of email let them punt questions back and forth in a way that would have felt far too cheesy in some wine bar.

'Who would play you in a film of your life?' she'd asked, in an early late-night exchange.

'John Cusack,' he'd replied straight away. 'You?'

Carrie had thought carefully, not wanting to disappoint him when they met. 'Drew Barrymore,' she replied. 'But not in *Charlie's Angels*. In something with less make-up. One of those character roles.'

And when they finally did meet, Carrie wondered if he hadn't done himself an injustice. Mark was the best-looking IT geek she'd ever seen: short dark hair, bright blue eyes half-hidden by the regulation Clerkenwell IT dark-framed glasses everyone seemed to wear. He looked younger than thirty-four in a long-sleeved T-shirt and subtle jeans, comfortable in himself, and confident in a way she'd always envied in other people.

'Hey, Drew,' he'd said, throwing his hands up into a *Charlie's Angels* gun pose. 'You're prettier than you look on screen.'

Mark wasn't just funny when he could type his anecdotes, and Carrie loved the nerves beneath his coolly delivered stories – the hand in his hair, the quick glances to see if she was looking. Whatever she felt, she could tell he was feeling exactly the same; an intuitive connection she'd never had before. He confessed he'd been worried that after their easy online conversations there'd be no real-life chemistry, but there was more than enough chemistry to get them thrown out of the cab on the way back to his flat, where they talked for nineteen hours (on and off), and when Carrie finally left, dazed and sore and completely in love, Mark ran after her to bring her back.

After that, Mark and Carrie saw each other every day.

Without the traditional barriers of mutual friends to cause politics, or office-romance limitations, there didn't seem much point in following the normal route of testing the relationship to breaking point with DIY and Christmases before getting engaged, so they didn't bother waiting.

'I don't want to waste any more time,' said Mark, going down on one knee in the Starbucks by Smithfield Market, ignoring the stares from other IT geeks. 'You're perfect. The computer has spoken. I don't argue with computer authority. Let's get married.'

Ninety-two days after opening his first email, Carrie became Mrs Mark Armstrong. Two and a half years later, she still didn't share Mark's love of technology, but she was eternally grateful to it for finding her a man who ticked pretty much every logical box she could think of, and still fitted in with psychics' predictions. That had to be Fate.

Mark was already packing his laptop bag when Carrie came into the kitchen, three days after Boxing Day. He was fitting his daily needs into the padded slots with the practised air of a bomb-disposal expert: iPod, phone, laptop, an assortment of leads and plugs. Carrie didn't know what they did, but according to Mark, they could induce spontaneous outbreaks of grateful weeping. It might have been the dead time between Christmas and New Year, but Mark's phone never stopped ringing with new office crises to soothe and smooth over.

His expertise was one of the sexiest things about him, Carrie thought.

She looked at him through sleepy eyes, and wondered how she'd managed to end up with someone who could programme any electronic device without reference to the manual and still look so cute, first thing.

'Will you be back for dinner?' she asked. 'I still have four or five new turkey recipes to try.'

'Can we throw the turkey away now, please?' Mark swilled back the quadruple espresso he'd made for himself and blinked several times as the bitterness hit his throat. 'You're my domestic goddess – you don't have to keep proving it with stir-fries.'

Carrie pulled an apologetic face. Their kitchen was only marginally bigger than the bathroom, and the hacked-up Christmas turkey was making its presence felt. 'Well, I guess we could, but it seems a shame to . . .'

Mark looked up from his bag. 'We could always eat out. Run away from it altogether?'

'That would be nice,' she sighed. 'You know, I've been working here, all through Christmas on this deadline . . .' She rolled her eyes. 'We should cut back on the takeaways, save up and go away somewhere proper.'

'I know, I've been working late too.' He paused and cocked his head, giving her his amused look. 'Go on. Do your spiel.'

Carrie looked innocent. 'What?'

'Your country-house spiel.'

It was a running joke between them because he'd never been able to take more than a few days off since they'd met. Carrie sighed and clasped her hands together. 'Why don't we treat ourselves to a mini-break in a country-house hotel! Please, Mark. Take me away to a baronial lodge with full English breakfasts and maids who snoop around your luggage. It'll be cheaper after New Year!'

'Yeah, yeah.' He rolled his eyes and put his coffee cup into the sink. 'I think you'll find the English countryside isn't quite as magical as you've been brought up to believe. It's all cow shit and feuds. And out-of-town supermarkets and multiplexes.'

'Not on the Internet sites I've been looking at.'

'Don't trust the Internet. I don't.' Mark started looking round for his jacket. 'Have you called your agent to tell her you're going to need another month on your deadline?'

Carrie's smile faltered, and she wrapped her dressing gown tighter around her. 'It's in hand.'

'So you keep saying. There's no need to lie to me, honey, I'm not your editor.' Mark swung his bag over his shoulder. 'I'll ring you – we can go out after. Now come here and give me a goodbye kiss.'

She slid into his arms and lifted her face as Mark curled one hand round the small of her back and pulled her into his thick jacket, so their noses touched and they breathed each other's breath for a few seconds before their lips met. His jumper felt scratchy against her chest and he smelled of shampoo and deodorant – his fresh morning smell before cigarettes and coffee and office air conditioning hung around him.

She was glad he still kissed her like a girlfriend, and not like a wife, even first thing in the morning.

'Hey,' he said, pulling away from her enthusiasm. 'Stop, or you'll make me want to come back to bed.'

'Go on,' said Carrie. She wound her bare leg around his calf and slid it up and down like a bad lap dancer. 'Who'll know? I'll phone in sick for you.'

'Carrie, I have to go. Servers don't stop breaking down just because it's Christmas. No rest for the geeks.' He rolled his eyes. 'Oh, listen, meant to say last night – I'm expecting a letter from the building management people about the outstanding service charge. If it comes, will you open it, and phone them and tell them we've put a cheque in the post?'

'And have we?'

'No, but there's a postal strike coming up and that buys us a good fortnight.'

'Mark!' Carrie's heart sank. She'd been brought up to have a morbid fear of debt; Mark, on the other hand, never even looked at bills until the red final demands arrived. It was one of the hardest things she'd had to work at in the two years they'd been married. 'We've got to pay it. They can send bailiffs round.'

He was already nearly at the door. Carrie followed him, clenching her fists. She'd made a promise to herself that she wouldn't ever be a nag like her mother. 'Mark, just tell me – do we have the money to pay it?'

'No, we don't,' he admitted. 'Not until one of us gets paid. Let's not talk about it. See you tonight. We'll go out for sushi. Cheer you up.'

'We'll watch a DVD,' said Carrie, resentfully. 'And boil some eggs.'

He kissed her on the nose, his warm lips engulfing the cold tip of her nose. A draught of his morning smell flooded her nostrils.

'Later.' And he was gone.

Carrie leaned against the door and looked back into the flat. It felt even smaller without Mark in it. She turned on the radio and began to tidy up the kitchen, as she did every morning to put off the moment when she'd have to go into their tiny study – the theoretical 'second bedroom' – and begin work on the book that refused to end.

Out of the big window above the sink she watched the buses and rain-slicked taxis crawling along Old Street, like giant red snails and black beetles. The roadworks had started again, and the traffic was passing in broken streams, first one way, then the other. The grumble of white noise seeped into the huge picture windows, but Carrie had almost grown used to it, along with the distorted graffiti that scarred the sides of their building, and the twenty-four-hour police sirens.

It had been Mark's flat before it had been Mark and Carrie's flat. She'd loved it when she moved in; glossy fitted kitchen and huge windows with a view of the Gherkin, and the steely City buildings around it. Since she and Mark bathed together, cooked with his arms wrapped round her waist, and spent most of their free time in bed, it didn't matter that it was tiny. Everything about it had made her feel like a proper Londoner, until she'd realised there was a darker flipside to cosmopolitan hustle and bustle: the grime, the suspicion, the way everyone was cramped in the same space while they pretended not to notice one another.

To live in London had been all Carrie had wanted during her nomadic childhood, as her father's postings criss-crossed the globe in disorientating lurches. That, while she was young, then a little house in the countryside. Still, she thought, staring out of the window, life doesn't always work out the way you think it will when you're a child. Which wasn't necessarily a bad thing.

Carrie was several weeks behind her own conscientious deadline for delivering the artwork for her new book – the second she had written about a mouse called Morris. *Two books was getting towards being a series!* as her mother pointed out to their friends and relations in her word-processed Christmas letters.

Mark was banking on Morris turning into a publishing sensation and frequently texted her with suggestions as to how she could infiltrate the nation's pre-schoolers: product placement was a particular obsession of his. Mark insisted she should morph Morris from a cuddly dancer into a computer mouse who delivered educational lessons about word processing, so she could get him onto the National Curriculum in primary schools, and from there, into Sainsbury's, Boots and PC World and, in ten years' time, into Knickerbox on ironic thongs.

Today Morris was learning to dance in a badly fitting tutu and Carrie was beginning to wish she'd thought of a less complicated way of earning some money. A creature with fewer spindly parts, for one thing. She pinned the preliminary sketches she'd done at the toddlers' ballet class in Hampstead around her easel. Luckily for her, the little girls weren't unlike tubby little Morris, with their rounded tummies and chubby fingers splayed out into straining pink starfishes as they stretched valiantly for the teacher's poses. Babies, really, in tutus, and tiny shell-pink slippers.

No room for a baby here, she thought as her pencil skimmed the paper. It would have to have a pull-down cot, like their pull-down bed. A pull-down baby for their pull-down life. Looks like a traditional family unit, but folds back into trendy London couple at night! Mark would love that. Room for a baby and his trainer collection.

Stop it, she chided herself, you're happy enough as you are. But she knew deep down that she wasn't. What she did have, though, was a grown-up, modern arrangement that contented her more than she'd ever thought possible. For the time being, maintaining that was the most important thing.

When the post arrived at eleven, Carrie gladly abandoned her work and sorted through the bills – Visa, phone bill, council tax, all accusingly red inside – and set aside a card from her mother, complete with Christmas photographs of her cousin's kids in St Paul, and another thicker letter for Mark. For a moment, she considered opening it, in case it was some final warning from the flat management people, but one of the unspoken rules of their marriage was that private post was private post. They'd both lived alone too long to give up that sort of independence now.

Carrie sighed and tucked it with the rest of the letter.

Mark was back by five, earlier than she expected, his eyes shiny with several post-work beers and carrying a bag of sushi.

'Did the estate managers write?' he asked, as he laid out the little bowls of soy sauce and wasabi paste and the ebony chopsticks on the breakfast bar.

'Oh, I guess so.' Carrie spotted a red carrier bag by the door, which Mark had unsuccessfully tried to disguise with his jacket. Another pair of trainers. Her good mood contracted a little. 'I didn't open the letter. It's behind you . . . on the windowsill. Along with the bills.'

'The bills, the bills . . .' Mark pulled a Hunchback of Notre Dame face. 'Oh, go on, laugh, Carrie, even the Men from Visa won't kill us.'

'Yeah, but they might evict us. Go on, open it.'

'They can't evict us,' he said, slitting the envelope with a knife. 'We pay our rent on time.'

'Most months.'

'How's Morris?'

'Dancing like a very fat mouse. Don't change the subject.' Carrie looked up when Mark didn't reply. He was staring at the letter with a strange expression over his face. 'What is it?' She put her glass of wine down. 'What? They *are* going to evict us, aren't they?'

Mark pushed a hand into his hair. 'No, no. No, quite the opposite.' He shook his head. 'You might get your weekend in the countryside sooner than you think.'

'What are you on about?' Carrie put out her hand and he passed her the letter.

It was from his solicitors in Northampton, where he'd grown up. Mark was reticent about his family background, but Carrie had seen the Sanderson & Spears letterhead before; Mark's parents had both died in a car crash when he was at school and the compensation battles with the insurance companies had wrangled on for years. Mark refused to talk about it, and, seeing the badly disguised hurt that sprang into his face, Carrie had never pushed him for details.

She studied the letter, her eye skimming through the legalese. It wasn't about insurance liabilities. It was about some property, in Wiltshire.

'Oak Cottage, St Dee?' she said, looking up curiously. 'I thought your parents' house was sold after they died?'

'It was.' Mark's brow was furrowed, as if he couldn't remember what he was meant to remember. 'This is my grandparents' house. Well, according to the solicitors – I wouldn't know, to be honest.'

'Your grandparents?' Carrie probed gently. 'On which side?'

Mark shook his head and started opening his sushi boxes. 'Dad's side. They both died years ago. I never met either of them.'

'I don't understand.' Carrie re-read the letter. 'If this cottage belonged to your grandparents and they died ages ago, why didn't your parents have it? Is it one of those funny English family will things? Who's been living there since?'

'Oh, it's complicated. I don't know much about it, really.' Mark began to play with his maki rolls, dipping them carefully in soy sauce. Mark the world traveller was ostentatiously good with chopsticks. 'Dad's parents used to live in some village near Salisbury Plain that was evacuated during the war, for missile testing or something. The Ministry of Defence acquired the land and made everyone move out while the war was on, but they weren't allowed to go back. Grandad and Granny took the compensation and went to live in Northampton. I think that was the story. Well, it tells you that much in the letter if you read it. Dressed up with some sort of bollocks about official secrets acts – whatever.'

'Poor things!' said Carrie. 'They didn't campaign after the war to get their houses back?'

Mark shook his head. 'Well, yeah, I guess so. They were all tenants, so they didn't own the houses as such. I don't know the ins and outs. Dad didn't really talk about his parents much. They weren't what you'd call close.'

'Really?' asked Carrie. 'How do you mean?'

Mark raised his eyebrow at her. 'The way some families aren't. I don't know – there was some problem with my granny, I think. The usual family stuff. Not very happy.'

'But this cottage – it's yours now, right?' Carrie felt a thrill of excitement, doubly exciting after the dull day-long panic brought on by the service-charge issue. 'After all these years? That's so weird! You're a homeowner! In . . . St Dee. Wherever that is.'

'Wiltshire.'

'Where's that?'

'The middle of nowhere. Not far from Stonehenge? Remember?'

Stonehenge had been on Carrie's list of places to see in England when she and Mark had first got together; to her surprise, he'd never been there either.

'Of course I remember Stonehenge,' she said. It hadn't been quite as she'd thought it would be, but she hadn't said so at the time.

'Well, it's more rural than that.' Mark was concentrating a little too hard on his maki, but Carrie was too excited to notice.

'Don't you think it sounds just like something out of Agatha Christie? We *have* to go.' Carrie pushed back her bar stool and went to look for the road atlas. It still had the crumpled Post-it notes she'd attached to sights they'd driven to see: Ely Cathedral, Beatrix Potter's house, Blenheim Palace. Mark had added his own, including 'the best service station in the country' and a famous fish and chip shop. 'Phone the solicitor in the morning and get them to have the keys ready for a viewing!'

'I'm not sure I *want* to,' said Mark. 'I think I just want to sell it. We could buy a bigger flat in London. Clerkenwell, maybe. Or go travelling.' He put his chopsticks down. 'Come on, Carrie – think of the money! Isn't it better not to see it, than end up getting all attached?'

'Mark! Come on, are you kidding? Our own house!' Carrie traced down the index of places until she came to St Dee, then flicked to the right page. There were barely roads, let alone villages on the page. She ignored the sulky note entering Mark's voice. 'Wouldn't you like to live out of town for a while? Think about it – why throw rent away on this place, when we could be living somewhere for free? It would solve all our problems!'

'No,' said Mark. 'It wouldn't. Anyway, there's something weird about this place. No one's lived there for sixty years as far as I know. God alone knows what sort of state the house'll be in, Carrie. And I am not Handy Andy, you know that. So don't get excited and then make me the bad guy when you're disappointed.' He rounded his eyes. 'Let's just take the cash, OK?'

Carrie put down the map and gave him a reproachful glare. 'I don't expect *anything*. It just sounds so pretty – a real country cottage. Anyway, if it is run-down, surely it's better for us to do it up *then* sell it? Wouldn't we get more for it then? At least let's go and see.'

Testiness overtook the sulky tone, and to her surprise, Carrie saw Mark's jaw jut, something she'd never witnessed in the three years she'd known him.

'Oh, just look at the map, Carrie!' he snapped. 'There's a bloody great firing range over the other side! We're not talking about Bourton-on-the-bloody-Water! I don't want to trek halfway across the country, at a really busy time, just to see some old cottage!'

They faced each other over the breakfast bar, the sushi sitting between them, and Carrie realised they were having their first marital argument. A proper one, with some kind of subtext she wasn't sure about.

'And anyway, it's not that simple,' he added quietly.

She swallowed. Mark was incredibly touchy about his family – not surprisingly, she chided herself. Most of his childhood was miserable, and what happiness there had been was made even more bittersweet by its scarcity. And here she was, coming across like all it meant to her was a free house.

Carrie hated upsetting Mark. The happiness they had was still so fresh, and so precious, that she hated doing anything to spoil it.

'Mark, I didn't mean to sound . . . I don't know. Grabby,' she said, stretching a hand over the table to take his. It wasn't a big table. There wasn't enough room in the flat to bear bad moods.

After a moment's pause, he uncurled his fingers and took hers. His hands were very dry, and stained with printer ink.

'I know,' he sighed. 'I know you're not grabby.'

'Don't you want to see where you came from?' she asked, softly. 'Where your roots are? I do.'

'Well, I *don't*,' said Mark. He was making an effort to sound reasonable, and the effort showed. 'Why should I? I never met these people, I don't know much about them, and even my dad didn't grow up in this house. It's just a house. In a place I don't want to live.' He tried a half-grin. 'Come on. There won't be a Tesco, you know. No bagels.'

Carrie smiled sympathetically. 'Well, I'd hope not. Please, Mark, I'd like to see it. I'd like to know more about you, where you come from. We don't have to have the house.' When he didn't reply, she took it as a positive sign, and pushed a little further. 'Do you have pictures? Of your grandparents? You know, I don't even know what they're called? Isn't that weird?'

Mark gave her a hard look, and seeing that she wasn't going to give up, pushed his chair away from the table and walked out of the room. When he came back, he was carrying the big shoebox he stored his photographs in.

Mark had lots of photos – of his travels, of the people he'd met, of his time at university – but he didn't put them up in frames around the house the way she liked to, and though Carrie had often hinted at how much she'd love to go through them with him, putting some faces to his stories, he'd never taken her up on it. 'It's the past,' he usually said. 'Over.'

He still kept the photographs, though, Carrie noted, even if he didn't look at them. When she'd asked if she could flick through them, he'd smiled and said no, because she wouldn't know who anyone was, and what was more boring than other people's holiday pics? Carrie had pointed out that your own husband wasn't just 'other people' but he'd laughed off her interest. And though he hadn't made a big deal about it, there was something in his expression that stopped her asking again.

'It's all about you and me now, Carrie,' he'd said, and the vulnerable note in his voice, she knew, was something he didn't let slip to many people.

While she held her breath, Mark piled bulging packets of holiday snaps on the table, propping them up with soy sauce bottles, until he came to a thin brown envelope, worn around the edges.

Carefully, he took out the pictures from inside, and sorted through them until he came to the one he wanted.

'Lily and Jack.' Mark put the photograph down in front of her, and Carrie lifted it by the scalloped edges. 'Their wedding day, in St Dee, I guess.'

Lily and Jack. Mark's grandparents. An awkward couple, standing outside a country church door, beneath a simple stone arch that framed them with reassuring solidity. Which was as well, since the bride in particular looked about as nervous as it was possible to be without actually stopping the service. Although the stone looked austere and plain, directly above them at the apex of the arch was a striking carved man's head, with snake-like tendrils of hair radiating around, and huge staring eyes. Carrie suppressed an instinctive shudder and turned her attention back to the bride.

'She looks so young,' said Carrie, searching the sepia-tinted image for clues to Lily's personality. It was difficult with brides, since they were expected to look a certain way. This bride was slight, and blonde, and rosy-cheeked, which should have added up to devastating radiance, but instead Lily seemed cowed by the huge bouquet of summer flowers she carried like a shield in front of her, and ill at ease in a simple white frock and short veil. Her shoes, Carrie noted, were beautiful, though – dancing shoes, with pearl buttons across the strap. Were they new for the day, or being worn for the last time?

'She was about seventeen, I think,' replied Mark. His attention was somewhere else, somewhere amongst the small stack of photographs in his hand.

Carrie gazed into the photograph, willing it to tell her something more than the bare bones of the image. Jack seemed older than Lily, nearer her and Mark's age, and he was tall and dark-haired, with round spectacles and a straightforward look into the camera. He, at least, seemed more at ease in his suit, as if he was used to being smart. One arm was slightly behind Lily, in a protective gesture that Carrie guessed said a lot about their relationship. Lily, though, was standing upright. Independent, despite her tense expression.

'How old was Jack?' she asked.

'Er, late twenties?'

Not as old as us then, thought Carrie, with surprise. Is it that people looked older in those days, or just that I can't accept I'm getting on a bit?

Both.

'And what did he do?'

'I think he was a teacher,' said Mark.

'Yes,' said Carrie. 'He looks like a teacher.'

There were no bridesmaids, no parents, no children, no vicar. Just Lily and Jack framed in the ancient stone arch of the church door. Carrie's eyes slid back to the intricately carved stone face, with round lidded eyes and thick hanks of hair, and she wondered, with a shiver, whether this church would still be there, abandoned in the village. Would it still be a holy place, if there was no one there to worship in it?

'They make a handsome couple,' she said, because they did. Not a happy one though. Not like the riotous wedding snaps of their ecstatic register office do, where only her and Mark's broad smiles were visible through the clouds of confetti and freshly blown soap bubbles. 'When did people start smiling in wedding pictures? Is it a recent development? Only I've never seen an old wedding picture that doesn't look like they were running a funeral at the same time to save money.'

She was joking, but when Mark looked up, his face was serious. 'I don't think it was a happy wedding.'

'Oh? Why?'

He shrugged, and Carrie spotted a forced lack of interest. 'I'm not sure. It was one of those family stories I never got the full version of. There was something not quite right about it – I think she was pregnant.'

'Really?' Carrie looked more closely at the defensive bouquet. That would make sense. It would also explain the absence of well-wishers in the picture. 'And she's seventeen?'

'Look, I don't know the exact details,' said Mark. 'It wasn't something I ever asked about, know what I mean?'

'No, guess not. Sorry.' But Carrie was intrigued. 'Are there any more? Photographs?'

'Just these.' Mark passed across a snapshot of Lily taken a few years, Carrie guessed, before the wedding picture. It was taken near a forest in summer, and Lily, fresh-faced and laughing, looked like a model for a railway poster advertising the benefits of countryside holidays: her long, untied hair lifted in the breeze, while a wide smile lit up her face, and her long round limbs stretched out in guileless enjoyment of the obvious good weather. Someone had coloured in the black-and-white photograph with a set of watercolour paints, making her hair a luminous honey blonde, and matching her blue eyes to the kingfisher blue of her sprigged dress. The effect was gorgeous, but quite eerie.

'She's beautiful!' exclaimed Carrie. 'Pass me the other?'

Mark pushed a photograph towards her with a wry expression.

Carrie's brow creased when she saw the bitter-looking woman leaning against a back door. 'I don't get it,' she said. 'This isn't Lily, surely?'

She turned it over. '1947' was written on the back in Biro. The brightness had gone, to be replaced with a pinched look: not just in the face, but over Lily's whole body, which seemed prematurely dessicated in the drab checked housecoat she wore. She looked years older. 'What happened?'

Mark shrugged. 'Well, they lost their home, didn't they? And she'd had a kid, and the war . . . Children, you see,' he added, wagging a finger at her, 'look what they do to a pretty woman.'

'Stop that,' said Carrie, unable to stop comparing the two pictures. 'I don't get it. The poor woman. She must have had a terrible time.'

'Yeah. The only thing I remember my dad saying about his parents was that when my grandad was on the way out, he'd go on about how a bit of Lily died in St Dee. That was after she died, mind. Never really talked about her much otherwise. I suppose when you've grown up with fields, and the same people round you all your life, the city must be pretty grim. Sad, really,' he said, as if he'd never thought about it like that before.

Carrie gazed again at the snaps, trying to see Mark's face in theirs. There seemed to be nothing of Jack's solid dependability in him, but the amused light in Lily's eyes seemed familiar. The tilt of the head, maybe.

'Doesn't that make you want to see the house, though?' she asked.

Mark let out a sigh. 'Not really. What's to see? No one's lived there for sixty years. It's just a house.'

Carrie looked pleadingly at him. 'Mark, you know, I don't have any real roots in this country.' She paused, then risked it. 'But I want *our* family to have roots.'

The words hung in the air, and she held her breath.

Mark was an expert at not talking about things he didn't want to talk about, even if it meant sacrificing a lesser evil. 'Fine,' he said now, deflating. 'Fine, we'll go, we'll have a nose around, you can take lots of pictures, OK? Happy?' And he started stuffing the packets back in the box.

'Mark, have I upset you? I really didn't mean to,' said Carrie. 'Please . . .'

She put out a hand to soothe him and her eye caught the photograph he'd been looking at. It was his mum and dad, on their own wedding day. Ten years younger than she and Mark were now, kitted out in flares and surrounded by cheery faces, blissfully unaware of the short time they'd have to be so smily and in love.

'Oh, Mark,' she said, 'I'm sorry.'

'Don't be sorry for me,' said Mark, and swept the box off the table. Carrie could almost hear the doors closing on that side of himself that he usually defended not with aggression but with glibness and jokes.

'Mark, this is something we need to talk about,' she tried. 'I mean, I know so little about your family.' Ridiculously little, in fact. At the time, the lack of in-law dinners had seemed very modern and mature – it was just her and Mark against the world – but as time wore on, Carrie was beginning to wonder if a little background help might not be such a bad thing.

'But I don't *want* to talk about it, OK?' Mark interrupted her. 'Listen, if it makes you happy, phone the man, make the appointment. We'll go and look at the house. Yes, it's great to have inherited something. Very exciting. But I can't promise you a rose-covered English cottage life, if that's what you're after.' He tried a wry smile, but it came out twisted. 'It doesn't work like that.' Then he swept out, bearing his shoebox of neatly contained history with him.

Carrie looked at his retreating back, numbed with the unexpected turn the mood had taken. This was the first time she'd really seen into the murky branches of Mark's disconnected family, looming in darkness over him. OK, she'd guessed that there were some problems there because he'd never wanted to talk about it, but now she could see shapes moving around in the shadows, and it bothered her.

Her eyes dropped back down to Lily and Jack, standing awkwardly at the first day of their married life. A married life that would eventually lead to Mark himself. They were as much strangers to him as they were to her, even though he had their blood running through his veins, and now they were giving them a house, and a chance to live a village life they hadn't been allowed themselves.

Carrie bit her lip. Should she let him walk away from this, if it was going to give him so much pain? But then she didn't see the point in ignoring the past. The past was too much part of who you were to be ignored, and when a chance like this came up – the chance to see some past that *no one* had been allowed to see for sixty years – then surely it was too ridiculous to pass it up?

He's behaving like a child, said her mother's voice in her head. *And if you let him, there'll be no room for any more children.*

Carrie took a deep breath, and jotted down the solicitor's number.

Chapter Two

The drive to Wiltshire took rather longer than the two hours Carrie expected; irritatingly, it took exactly as long as Mark had predicted gloomily while they sat in traffic, inching their way past the Old Street roadworks. She tried valiantly to chat the whole way, to counteract the endless motorway speeding them away from London and sushi and work, but once they were into the countryside, her attention was entirely absorbed by the green hills rolling down into valleys around her, and the dappled fall of sunlight through the thick-leaved trees.

Conversation faltered and then stopped altogether as they sank into their own thoughts.

'What time did you arrange to meet this bloke about the house?' Mark was chewing the nails on his left hand, one after the other in quick succession: an indication that he was irritated, which, in turn, also irritated Carrie.

'His name is Paul Jenkins, and he said about twelve.' Carrie squinted at the map through her sunglasses. There seemed to be an amazing amount of green space between the villages around St

Dee, not to mention dense forests – something she'd never really seen in England before. 'I can't quite work out who he's representing, but he's going to have the keys to the cottage and all the legal details.'

'And we're meeting him there?' Mark started on his right-hand nails, making hard clicking noises as tooth met tooth.

'Yes, we are. Come on, Mark, it's an amazing thing – just to be able to see the place, after all this time. Aren't you even slightly curious? Don't you think it's like something out of *Scooby-Doo*? The spooky ghost village? Isn't that worth half a day off work?'

Mark's grudging agreement to humour Carrie and her curiosity hadn't improved when he'd heard that the only day available for the viewing had been a Tuesday, a day when he had 'an uncancellable meeting at five'.

He was checking his phone now, muttering under his breath about reception.

'And will you stop checking your phone and concentrate on keeping on-road, please?' demanded Carrie. 'It's single lane, practically.'

'Well, I hope you're noting that,' said Mark. 'For when it's snowed up and there's no way out and you're trapped with the Wicker Man and all his in-bred, violent cousins.'

'*Your* in-bred, violent cousins, you mean,' she said without thinking, but when he only cut her a wry look, she knew he was getting interested, despite himself.

They were getting closer to St Dee. Carrie's pulse sped up with excitement as the road narrowed and twisted like a ribbon through the valley, the green slopes of which were pocked with sheep, rather than the burned-out tanks she'd expected. She checked the map again. They'd just gone through Deeting Magna, so they were nearly there.

'Look at that!' Mark said, suddenly. He slammed on the brakes and pulled the car into the side of the road.

Carrie's head jerked up from the map. He was pointing at something on the hillside and she had to shade her eyes to make it out against the sharp wintry sunlight. She wasn't even sure what she was looking at.

'It's a chalk horse!' said Mark. 'Wow! I didn't know there was a chalk horse here. They're amazing. Look – there's the head, and the tail . . . It's been really well kept, this one.'

Carrie watched Mark's face light up as his ragged fingers pointed back and forth along the line of the huge horse, while he babbled nuggets of *Boy's Own* manual information: history, Druids, chalk deposits, Victorian restoration, schools sent out onto hillsides with brushes to scrub enormous chalk penises. His blue eyes gleamed with a childlike excitement she hadn't seen in him for months – since he bought his video iPod, in fact.

'And of course the figures all have these massive cocks because they're basically pagan fertility symbols. Can you believe that they were organised enough to create something so big, without any kind of mapping or computer design or . . .'

She caught Mark's chin with her fingers and turned his face round so she could look right into his dark eyes.

'Shut up,' she said, and kissed him. Her heart thumped with relief as he responded eagerly, snaking his arm around her waist and pulling her close over the handbrake.

More than anything she wanted this to be the beginning of a new life for the pair of them, and if it was in a valley dominated with a giant fertility symbol, so much the better.

After a series of pretty villages with solid churches and the last vestiges of Christmas decorations still jollying up the houses, the road became narrower and the surrounding countryside sparser.

'Is that the sign?' asked Mark for the ninth time as they shot past another unpromising side track.

Carrie looked up from the map and the letter from the administrator. 'It's down a side road,' she said. 'They haven't put new signs up for security reasons, apparently. I think we've missed it.'

Mark sighed, then laughed, and turned the car round.

'What's this sign coming up?' he asked, as they passed an ominous heap of rusting metal, abandoned by the side of the road. Carrie ignored it, and stared at the flaking road sign which was leaning to one side with age.

'That's it!' yelled Carrie. 'St Dee one mile!' And he swerved down a pot-holed side road that rattled the suspension so hard the CDs fell out of the side pockets.

'Are these tank tracks?' demanded Mark above the clattering noise.

Carrie looked. They did look like caterpillar tracks, extending up and over the road. Then suddenly, they were driving on smooth new tarmac, and the rattling stopped, as if by magic.

They turned to look at each other, and giggled nervously.

Next to some neatly rolled barbed-wire fencing was a brand new roadsign. 'Welcome to St Dee,' it said. 'Please drive carefully.'

'Now if they'd put that nearer the main road, it wouldn't have taken us twenty minutes to find the place,' he said.

'Maybe they don't *want* people to find it,' said Carrie. 'Not if it's been shut off for all this time. Maybe they don't want people snooping about.'

'Carrie, I know what you're doing – you're turning this into a story, aren't you?' Mark wagged a finger at her. 'For one of your books? Well, stop it. You're making it more interesting than it is.'

'Do you want to concentrate on driving, please?' Carrie tried to sound stern, but she was cheered by Mark's improved mood.

Despite the chilly air, she buzzed her window down and gazed out into the bright morning. The greens and blues of the landscape around them were stunning in their intensity, but shards of twisted metal, wrenched into delicate origami by the force of a massive explosion, gave a hint of the military neighbours over the valley.

Carrie tried to imagine the explosions that had caused such damage – target practice for inflicting the same damage on vulnerable human flesh. She'd seen battlefields in Normandy, and the Somme, and tried to envisage the blood and stench and groans of human agony, but there, as here, it was hard to remove the rolling greenery and peaceful birdsong and overlay it with urgency and violence.

They drove past the rusting shell of a tank lurking some way back from the road, like the discarded carapace of a giant beetle, and Carrie shuddered.

It was the silence that made it hard to imagine. The air was like glass: clean, silent, fresh. There was something in the atmosphere that she couldn't put her finger on and while she was marvelling at the gorgeousness of it all, she couldn't help feeling unnerved at the same time.

'OK. We're here,' said Mark as they rounded the corner and saw St Dee ahead of them.

The first house stood alone: a good-sized two-storey stone cottage with fresh thatching and a curious new-old appearance. Its red-brown walls were weather-worn, but the dark green paint on the windows and the door was new. Its gardens were marked out with large pebbles, overgrown with moss between, and the beds themselves were empty and exhausted. It was called Abbey Side, and was built in 1828, according to the carved slate by the wall, but there were no roses in the garden or curtains in the windows.

Mark drove past slowly so they could peer inside without getting out. The sun flashed on the windows, making it hard to see past the clean panes. Carrie thought she could make out bare floorboards and the shadow of a fireplace, with more windows beyond. Even though there was no one to stare back, she felt nervous, as if she were spying on someone asleep and unsuspecting. The woman who had locked the door last, before moving out in good faith, sixty years ago, never to fumble for her keys on the doorstep again. Was her spirit still hovering at the step, waiting to see who would open the door and let her back in?

'Don't get out,' she said quickly, as Mark seemed about to stop.

'Why?' he said. He turned to her with a teasing smile, letting the car glide in neutral.

'I don't know,' she said truthfully. 'I don't want to . . . look nosy.'

'This is a village, Carrie. Nosiness is the whole point. Anyway, who's here to notice?' But he put the car back in gear and drove off.

The next houses were two little rows of stone cottages, banked slightly on each side of the road; they were neat and simple, with clean stone steps, but with the same curious air of forgery about them.

'You know, it's like a film set.' Mark peered out of his window. 'All a bit too clean? Like one of those Jane Austen costume dramas on television. It all looks old, but there's something not quite convincing about it, don't you think?'

Carrie murmured in agreement. There was something quite creepy about the place, he was right about that. But it wasn't just the cleanness of the thatch, where you'd expect grown-in mould, or the lack of litter. There was something else. A sort of hovering atmosphere about the houses that seemed empty one moment and curtain-twitching the next. Even though there were no curtains in any of the blank-eyed windows. Empty doll's houses, ready for occupation, but not fresh, not quite new.

They drove past a deserted village green, bordered by pretty little cottages, each window frame painted a different shade of green or blue. The gloss of the paint stood out against the weathered old stone.

'Where is everyone?' she murmured, half to herself.

'Is that a maypole or a phone mast!' spluttered Mark. 'Oh my God, it is a maypole! Come on, this is just an old Poirot set they've decided to sell off to the general public, isn't it? No, no, it's more like *Big Brother*! They're going to move us all in here, then watch how we go about turning it back into a gossip-ridden village!'

'Stop,' said Carrie. Mark pulled over, but she meant him to stop talking in that rude way as much as she meant him to stop the car. She tried to compose herself while he was turning off the engine and buzzing up the windows. Excitement was bubbling up in her, but it was tinged with nervousness. All these front doors, all these interrupted lives, all about to start again with traces of the last owner's blood still running through their veins. What could be silently passed down in flesh and blood? Memories? Old loves? Old grievances?

'Look,' said Mark. 'That must be Paul Jenkins over there, on the bench.'

They parked in front of a tiny pub, not yet renovated to the same standard as the cottages they'd seen, and got out, buttoning up their coats against the chill January wind. Carrie would have liked to peer into its shadowy windows to see if there were still cobwebbed old optics inside or tarnished horse brasses around the fireplace, but Paul Jenkins was waiting for them on the other side of the village green.

Mark polished a little spyhole into the glass, made a quick joke about real ale, then stopped abruptly, seeing her nervous expression. They walked self-consciously towards the man now shading his eyes with his hand to see them better.

'Calm down, Carrie.' Mark slung an arm around her shoulders and squeezed her. 'We're just having a look at some old house. It's not like there'll be a test. And for God's sake, don't get carried away. I know it looks like something off a shortbread tin, but . . .' His voice trailed off. 'No bagels, remember?'

Carrie knew he was trying to humour her, but she sensed a stiffness in his arm that suggested it was all more of an effort than he was making out.

She squeezed him back. 'I know, I know,' she said brightly, 'I'm just excited. It's like the perfect English village that time forgot. Mom would be in hysterics by now.'

'Well, we can send her photos. "Greetings from the Firing Range!" Are you going to tell her the bit about being a mile down a single-lane cart track?'

Carrie's heels sank into the soft grass of the village green as she hurried to keep up with Mark's long strides. 'Should we really be walking on this?' she asked. 'The grass, I mean.'

'You are so equipped for village life already,' he said.

From a distance, Carrie couldn't see the man's face. The incongruity of the vision in front of her reminded her of a Magritte painting: a man in a dark city suit, sitting on a bench in the middle of a silent, deserted village green.

He rose as they approached and held out his hand.

'Good morning,' he said in neutral British tones. 'Paul Jenkins.' He was very neutrally British altogether, thought Carrie: mid-brown hair, mid-brown eyes, any age between twenty-five and forty. Nothing there to pick out to identify him from the next middle manager at all. Did they breed these people somewhere?

'Hello,' she said, offering her hand. 'Carrie Armstrong.' She wasn't sure why she suddenly felt so formal; his dark suit, perhaps?

'Delighted to meet you.' The handshake was a little limp.

'Mark Armstrong,' said Mark. He held out his hand, and a worn leather bracelet slipped out from under his sleeve.

There was a momentary awkward pause. Paul Jenkins clearly wasn't an estate agent – no stream of easy patter emerged. The distant chatter of birdsong broke the silence, and Carrie was beginning to feel uneasy about the solitude, as though the empty houses were sucking the sound from the air.

'So, where's this cottage then?' said Mark, briskly. 'I don't mean to be rude, but we've got to get back to London for an appointment later today.'

'Absolutely.' Paul Jenkins flipped his leather portfolio and extracted some papers. 'Oak Cottage. Armstrongs. Fine. If you'd like to follow me, it's really very close indeed.'

Carrie and Mark followed him as he strode past the green, past an old Victorian postbox, now gleaming ladybird red again, and down a narrow road, heavily bordered with thick hawthorn bushes.

'Is it always this quiet?' she asked, not wanting to seem rude.

'No, it's not, actually.' He seemed relieved to talk. 'The builders aren't working today – it's normally like being in the middle of London, with all the crashing and banging going on.'

Carrie tried hard to imagine the tranquillity shattered by workmen, but she couldn't. She had to look hard to see even one or two machines in evidence. 'They're the tidiest builders I've ever seen,' she remarked. 'Not a cement mixer in sight!'

Paul Jenkins cracked a smile at last. 'Ah, well, we've tried to utilise traditional craftsmen as much as possible. All the work is taking place within heritage guidelines, you understand. And I do ask them to store their tools in one of the unrestored houses. Keeps the place looking nice.'

'Mmm,' said Carrie. She flashed a look at Mark, to nudge him to contribute, but he was staring at his feet, concentrating on his trainers – grey and expensive with dull pewter-coloured stripes banding the sides.

And new, Carrie noted, her heart sinking at the thought of the red bills at home.

Mark was anal about his trainers, and was obviously trying not to get them muddy. But there was no mud on the road, and the hedges had been trimmed recently; tiny new spearmint-green leaves were budding among white-tipped branches.

'Right then, this is Oak Cottage,' announced Paul Jenkins, as they approached a semi-detached cottage, set back a little from the road. He stopped at the gate and checked his papers, discreetly offering them the moment to themselves.

Carrie knew at that instant that she would fight tooth and nail to make Mark keep the house. It was exactly like her nursery drawings of the perfect home brought to life: five small-ish square windows set around a red front door, surrounded by the flaking remnants of a rose trellis, and topped by a newly tiled roof. The old red-brown brick was weathered into an inviting warmness, and to add to the sense of bucolic plenty, a huge tree spread over the back garden – the oak, she presumed – with smaller fruit trees round the sides. The house next door was a mirror image, shaded by more trees and some gnarly rose bushes, with an old wrought-iron bench still standing in the front garden.

'Oh, Mark,' she breathed, forgetting his instructions to look like she wasn't that interested. 'It's like a fairy-tale cottage!'

'If I had a pound for every time I've heard that this month,' said Paul Jenkins with a knowing smile at Mark. He pushed open the gate, which creaked and swung back dangerously on its top hinge. 'Basic structural repairs have been made,' he said apologetically, wiping the flakes of rust off his hands, 'so the building is sound, but there's some work still to be done to bring it completely up to modern standards, of course. This gate, for instance . . .'

Carrie ignored Mark's warning grumbles and walked up the path feeling like Snow White. There was a well in next door's garden, covered over with a stone circle, stained red where the iron chain had corroded. How far down into the chalky ground would that go? How pure would the water be? And what might be at the bottom?

Fairies? Trolls?

'I don't like the look of that,' muttered Mark in her ear. 'Rats.'

'Quiet, will you?' Her heart skipped with anticipation as Paul Jenkins tried a series of keys before finding the right one.

'So, here we are.' He swung open the door and moved aside to consult his notes, bowing his head to let them in first. Carrie guessed he'd done that for all the families, coming back to take up the threads of their grandparents' lives – stepping into halls and front rooms already familiar from stories or well-handled photos. How much emotion had that stirred up? Could he tell that she and Mark knew nothing more than the names of the previous owners? Did that make their claim less valid?

She thought of Lily – the fresh young bride, not the dried-up old lady – as she followed Mark into the house, and concentrated as hard as she could on imprinting the first instinctive feelings about the house on her brain for later, reaching out to the spirit of the house.

The threshold stone was worn in the middle from thousands of feet scuffing the mud off their boots, and she stepped over it into the empty hall. Mark was already inspecting the front parlour on the other side of the staircase, but Carrie felt drawn to the kitchen, down the hall, through the house to where bright sunlight was falling in thick streams through the windows.

A smell of cold earth and stone and damp rushed out at her as she walked in, and she caught her breath, wondering what the view from the garden window had been the last time Lily had stood at the big white sink. Apple blossom? Snow? Aside from the wooden racks above the sink, there was no furniture and the room seemed huge. Dusty footprints, presumably made by the recent workmen, led across the stone flags, towards the door that led down to the cellar. There was a key sticking out of the lock, as if someone already wanted to keep visitors out. Or in.

The cellar. A funny feeling gripped her stomach. Carrie had spent most of her life in airy, self-contained flats, without dark cellars or dusty attics. None of her childhood homes had had any hiding places at all. And here there would be space for all the creepy things she sometimes drew in her own books: spiders, and mice, and cobwebs . . .

Don't be silly, she told herself, surprised by her own childishness. Think of the storage space. Plenty of room for boxes. And laundry.

Still, she moved quickly away from the door, back towards the hall. The front parlour seemed to take up most of the front right side of the house, and there was a wooden staircase leading up to the first floor. Carrie put a hand on the banister and looked upstairs. This should be a happy house, she thought, with cooking in the kitchen and kids running around. And yet it felt so empty, beyond its lack of furniture and carpets.

It's been waiting for us, she thought. Waiting for us to come back and fill it.

Mark stamped hard on the floor behind her and made her jump. 'Floorboards seem OK.'

Paul Jenkins was quick with an answer. 'They've been checked and replaced where necessary. All the houses have been surveyed by an independent surveyor to confirm they meet project safety standards – I've got the report here if you want to go over it.'

While Mark grilled Paul Jenkins about foundations and damp courses, Carrie drifted back into the kitchen towards the sink, imagining how warm this room would feel if they installed an Aga, and put a cat basket in the corner. She could paint the walls a sunny yellow like daffodils or primroses, and find an old pine table, and invite the neighbours round for coffee. Surely there would be lots of people just like them moving back, taking the opportunity of this fresh air and purer light?

She tried to imagine how Lily would have had it. Had she invited her friends over for tea? Had she *had* lots of friends?

Carrie leaned forward to look out of the window into the thick vegetation of the untended garden and her hand made contact with the edge of the sink. Despite the clean sunshine streaming down onto it, the stone was freezing cold, and the deep chill sent a shiver up her arm, through her whole body. At the same time, out of nowhere, she felt a powerful rush of unspeakable melancholy, that punched then bloomed in her heart.

She stepped back from the sink with an audible gasp.

'Carrie?'

She spun round. Mark and Paul Jenkins were looking at her in surprise.

'Cold,' she said with a weak smile. 'The sink.'

'That's the problem with some of these cottages,' said Paul Jenkins. 'Stone built. Chilly. And you have to remember that at the time of the evacuation, there was pretty much no electricity in the village, with it being so isolated. In many ways conditions here were still Victorian.'

Mark's concern was abruptly diverted. 'Are we talking about outside loos?'

'Some of the houses, yes.'

'This one?'

Paul Jenkins allowed himself a little smile. 'No, I'm happy to say that the previous owner had installed a very modern lavatory system. And central heating has been installed as part of the modernisation, as well as complete rewiring.'

The previous tenant, thought Carrie, not listening to the rest of the spiel about what had been done. He means Jack. Jack, who might have had Mark's eyes or Mark's funny smile, but someone he knows practically nothing about.

Out of the corner of her eye, Carrie thought she saw something move in the overgrown garden. And that was another project. Taming that wilderness into a pretty garden again, so they could sit in it, eat their breakfast in the summer.

She stepped away from the sink and moved nearer Mark's side. His new trainers now seemed comforting, rather than annoying.

'So, in a nutshell, what's the story?' asked Mark. He leaned back against the cellar door. 'Why've we got this back now?'

'Well, it's very simple.' Paul Jenkins coughed and launched into an uninflected speech Carrie sensed he'd rattled through several times that week already. 'The Crown acquired the land before the Second World War for MoD training purposes, and then evacuated the village completely in 1941. But since they're working now on scaling down some of their operations locally, this working group has been set up to return St Dee to habitation. By that I mean we're tracing the direct descendants of the original tenants and offering them first refusal on the properties.'

'Why's it taken so long to give back?' asked Carrie. 'What sort of training was it?'

Paul Jenkins opened his mouth then closed it again quickly. 'Ah, now if you're about to give me a list of conspiracy theories, I can assure you I've heard them already!' he said with a short laugh. 'Nonsense, all of them!'

Carrie looked at Mark, confused, but he was staring at Paul Jenkins. 'No, sorry. What do you mean?'

For a split second, Paul Jenkins looked almost wrong-footed, but he recovered quickly. 'Oh, there are all sorts of ridiculous stories about secret testing sheds and what have you. But I can assure you that the simple reason the Ministry acquired the land was nothing more sinister than a significant expansion of shell-testing a few miles away. It wouldn't have been safe.'

As if on cue, a dull boom echoed in the distance, the sound mushrooming, then fading back into the silence.

'Does that happen a lot?' asked Mark. 'Because that could get very old very fast,' he added with a significant look at Carrie.

'Oh, very rarely. You might see the odd tank on the road, maybe the occasional shelling, but nothing much. The Army tend to let us know if there's going to be anything serious. But, anyway, to get back to the matter in hand,' he went on swiftly, sorting through his notes, 'what we're offering is the tenancy to the cottage, for a nominal yearly ground rent. You could move in within the month if you decided to take it.'

'And if we didn't? Is the property ours to sell?'

'No – your grandfather wasn't a freeholder. Oak Cottage was built on land belonging to the manor estate.' Paul Jenkins looked up from his file with a neutral expression. 'We did anticipate that not everyone would be at liberty to take up the offer, so there has been some provision made for retrospective compensation, which you can apply for if you decide not to take the tenancy. There's nothing to stop you keeping it as a holiday home. Although,' he added, 'off the record, we're hoping that most people will opt to make a permanent move here and re-establish a community. It would be a shame if St Dee turned into a weekend place.'

'Absolutely,' agreed Carrie. 'It deserves to come back to life.'

Mark flicked his eyes towards her, surprised by the fervour in her voice.

'Is it practical to live here?' he said instead. 'Being realistic for a moment.'

'Well, perhaps after London . . .' Paul Jenkins shrugged, again with the same wry inclusive grin and almost imperceptible glance at Mark's trainers. 'It's as practical as any other small village. There's no school any more, but there's one in Deeting Magna, and of course one in Devizes. The new owners of the pub will be moving in at the end of this week, there'll be a small post office and shop, there's electricity, we've installed phone lines, you've got all modern amenities and the houses just need decorating. And it's maybe two hours back to London, on a good day? There are worse commutes.'

'We're both self-employed,' said Carrie immediately. 'So the commute's not an issue.'

Mark glared at her.

Paul Jenkins tucked his notes back into the leather case. 'In that case, if you want a peaceful life, it's one of those relocation shows come true. Shall we have a look upstairs?'

Carrie led the way, conscious of the loud noise her shoes made on the bare stairs.

I'll get thick tapestry stair-runners, she thought, and I'll stain the treads deep oak. Her hand slid up the banister, letting the smooth grain of the wood trickle under her palm. The colours started returning to the house in her mind's eye, spreading vividly across the walls and tiles, like the coloured-in photograph of Lily.

Behind her, Mark was asking questions about the Army's comings and goings, but though she knew she should be listening, her attention was caught by the room that faced the top of the stairs.

The door was open, inviting her in, and she knew as she stepped over the threshold that this was the studio she'd imagined in her head all her life. Her steps across the bare floorboards slowed, then stopped as she reached the centre of the room, bathed in crisp wintry sunlight from the big window. A little wrought-iron fireplace, surrounded by original old tiles, was the only splash of colour in the unpainted walls, and the bare beams, cut from thick oak, crossed the ceiling with sturdy assurance.

But best of all, the view out of the window took in the whole village: the side road they'd just walked down, the village green with the maypole at the centre, the church off towards the right, the crumbling ruins of the abbey beyond . . .

Carrie leaned on the windowsill and gazed out, letting the colours burn into her imagination.

And she knew they were going to move in here.

Mark was quiet on the drive back to London, as he always was when he was thinking hard about something. He sucked his teeth, chewed his nails and only grunted in response to Carrie's attempts at conversation. The more he thought, the faster he drove, until he was flashed by a speed camera doing 105 mph, which at least broke the silence.

In the end she turned on the radio, just to fill up the space between them with something.

Since they were both clearly thinking about the same thing, it was frustrating not to be able to roll out her ideas and examine them in detail. Carrie preferred to talk her concerns through, out loud, to a mirror if necessary. She liked to be persuaded one way, then the other, so she could decide which side felt right. Mark's protracted silences inevitably ended up with him informing her of an unshakeable position, but for once, she felt just as certain as he did.

If she was honest, Carrie was taken aback by her longing to move into what she could see rationally was a chilly house. But the airy space and huge potential made their flat seem cramped and sterile by comparison: a holding container for two people waiting to move on somewhere else, not a home. A chronic lack of storage space might be OK for trendy twenty-somethings in sitcoms, but they didn't have to live with an ironing board and two drying racks permanently shoved behind the kitchen door.

The vision of a proper laundry room floated seductively into her mind. Warm and comforting, with clean sheets and blankets stacked up in fitted cupboards, and shelves for starch and linen sprays, and bunches of lavender hanging from the old drying racks . . .

She glanced over at Mark. He was chewing his nails again, popping them in and out of his mouth in quick succession, his eyes fixed on the road ahead, although she was sure getting back in time for his meeting wasn't really what he was concentrating on.

He doesn't want to leave London, she guessed instinctively. He doesn't want to be stuck out there. But he knows I loved that cottage and he's working out ways of letting me down gently. It wasn't just the house she'd be losing. It was the connection with Mark's family. The glowing farm girl who'd shrivelled and dried when she'd been uprooted from her village. What had happened there?

Lily isn't your family, Carrie reminded herself. And she isn't some kind of research project either.

She chewed her lip, thinking how best to open up conversation.

'Are you going to be on time?' she asked, adding, 'For your meeting?' when Mark looked blank.

He seemed to snap back to attention at the sound of her voice. 'What? Er, yeah. Listen, do you mind if I drop you off at the tube station?' he said, changing lanes too late and cutting up a black cab. 'Haven't got time to go all the way to Old Street and back again.'

'No, no, that's fine. I don't want to go back to the flat straight away anyway. It'll feel so small after having so much open space around.'

Mark sighed. 'Carrie, I know it's a lovely house, but . . .'

'Can't we at least talk about it? Please?'

'Later?'

'Later you'll have worked out two hundred reasons to say no.' Carrie kept her voice light, but her eyes had gone steely grey. 'Mark, did you see that room upstairs? The one I could have as a studio? Just think how much easier it would be for me to work if I had more space . . .'

'Oh, for God's sake . . .' Mark shoved his left hand into his hair and scratched his head distractedly. 'What do you want me to say? It was a nice run out, nice to see where my grandparents lived, but . . . Look, it's just impractical, honey. They don't even have broadband – I asked him while you were upstairs. I work in the city, so do you, we can't afford to run two houses, and especially not one that's miles from anywhere and right next to a bloody firing range.'

'I don't work in the city,' she replied stubbornly. 'And I can't carry on working in that tiny cupboard of a study. It's just not big enough and I feel completely cramped. It's affecting my work! Anyway, you could do a lot of what you do from home on the Internet. And don't tell me there wouldn't be plenty of freelance business for you in Bristol or Swindon or any of those IT companies based out on the M4 corridor.'

'Maybe I like being in London.'

'Maybe I do too, but not in that flat.'

There. She'd said it.

Mark swerved, and pulled over into a parking space by Gloucester Road tube station with scant regard for the traffic behind him. 'What's wrong with the flat?'

'It's a great flat – for a single man living on his own.' Carrie knew she might be going too far, but couldn't stop herself. 'But isn't it time we got somewhere proper? There isn't enough room for us both. Especially when I have to work there during the day too.'

She didn't add: and while it's a single man's flat, you'll carry on behaving like a single man with no pension and a live-in girlfriend, and we won't make any decisions about what it means to be married because neither of us will want to seem boring to the other, and suddenly we'll both be forty and I'll be too old to have kids anyway.

Until that moment, she hadn't actually realised that that was how she saw it too.

Mark turned off the engine, leaned back in his seat and shut his eyes. The car suddenly seemed very quiet. 'Is this about babies again? Because it's a big topic, Carrie, a really big topic, and it's not that I don't want to talk about it, but I just *don't* want to start it now, after driving all day and with a big meeting in half an hour.'

'It's not *just* about babies,' said Carrie. 'It's about us. We need somewhere where we can live together and build a proper life as a couple.'

'OK, so we need to think about getting somewhere bigger. I hear that, it's fine. But why does it have to be out of town? There are plenty of houses in London, and we need to stay on the property ladder here.'

'We're not *on* the property ladder, Mark!' snapped Carrie in exasperation. 'We're *renting*! And we're getting behind on that rent! Oak Cottage, on the other hand, is free accommodation. Listen, if you're so desperate for some tiny house in Hackney, we might as well live in St Dee while we save up some deposit. And,' she went on, seeing his eyes roll, 'it's about time we got serious about money. Like, how come we can't afford the service charge but you've just spent two hundred pounds on those trainers? Don't deny it, I saw them in the *Observer* magazine.'

'Carrie, I'm sorry,' said Mark, starting up the engine. 'I don't have time to have a big scene about this right now. I've got to get to this meeting, I've got to focus my brain to explain the magic of the Internet to some people who don't even understand how to send a text, so please don't start giving me a load of grief about how we should pack it all in and become farmers, all right?'

'It's a perfect house!' said Carrie. 'It's a dream come true! Why are you behaving like this, Mark?'

'Behaving like what? You're the one yelling.'

Carrie opened her door and got out. She didn't want the day to end like this, in a flurry of gritted teeth. It was as if London had cast a dark net of tension back over them, pinning them back into this half-conversation where both of them shied away from actually saying too much.

Mark leaned over from the driver's side. 'We'll talk about this later, yeah?'

'Talk about what?' said Carrie. Because what they needed to discuss wasn't just about whether they should move, it was about everything else trailing underneath that problem: babies, their careers, money – things that neither of them actually wanted to drag into the light.

'Your dream house?' Mark smiled hopefully up at her, and as usual, his smile melted something in Carrie's heart.

'Our dream house,' she reminded him.

'Later,' said Mark, and pulled away.

Carrie strode off towards Starbucks, nearly treading in a discarded Big Mac carton in her haste.

Up until this week, she and Mark had never had a cross word, sailing along in blissful ease, not needing to speak for hours some nights. But the last few days seemed to be littered with cross words, like screwed-up bits of rubbish messing up their living space.

Carrie went into the coffee shop and ordered a soya latte. She stood holding the fake wood of the delivery counter, trying to make sense of her jumbled feelings.

You're being unfair, she told herself. You're taking out your frustrations with Morris Bloody Mouse on Mark. Just because you can't draw comedy mice to order in a cupboard. It's not Mark's fault.

But at the same time she knew that wasn't it.

Carrie wound her fingers around the hot mug and took it over to the window where she could watch the traffic crawl down Gloucester Road, narrowly missing the tourists who wandered naïvely between the cars like bemused sheep.

Her mind drifted to the large bedroom next to her studio. It was a gorgeous, light room, and had exposed beams too. Carrie loved the idea of exposed beams. When she was ten, her father, who was keen to instruct his half-English children in their native history, had rented a cottage in the Cotswolds for their family summer holiday; since they were living in a very modern condo in Berlin at the time, the idea of a house held up by trees that were already hundreds of years old at the time the roof was thatched was fascinating to Carrie. She chose the room under the eaves and lay awake at night, listening to the unfamiliar countryside noises and watching the moonlight fall on the ridges and furrows of the ancient wood.

Mark had rapped his knuckles briskly along the beams in Oak Cottage, trying to find a weak spot. There wasn't one.

Best of all, there was a clear view of the chalk horse from the bedroom window, stretching its long white legs out along the valley.

You could really sleep in that room, she thought, and cupped her hands around her latte.

Sleep, and lie in, and read the papers, and make love on Sunday mornings. In a huge iron bedstead, filled with cloud-white duvets and pillows, where we could shut out the world and vanish into ourselves for days and days, the way we did when we first met.

Carrie stared at a traffic warden stalking along the line of meters outside to distract herself from the involuntary crawling of her scalp as she recalled their last disinterested manoeuvrings: Mark's excuses, his snores, her own ringing emptiness.

It wasn't just that there wasn't space for a child in their flat; finding the time and energy to have sex was getting to be a problem too. There was something very enervating about living and working in the same place for her, and as for Mark . . . He seemed preoccupied. Even more than usual.

'Enough,' she said aloud. 'Bad sex is not a reason to move into the middle of nowhere.'

The woman at the table opposite stopped quacking into her mobile phone about her cliff-top wedding plans and stared at Carrie, frosty-pink lips momentarily stilled.

Carrie stared away, out of the window. Maybe I should get a therapist to listen to all this crap, she thought. Or maybe I just need to get out more.

Mark got back at eleven, throwing out only a few thick words about 'stupid bastards', and went straight into their bedroom.

From the sofa, where she was reading the paper, Carrie watched him cross the room in a trance, gave him ten minutes to snap out of it, and when he didn't, went in to see what was wrong.

Mark was lying on his back, staring up at the ceiling. He had taken off his shirt, but had given up at his jeans. One arm was flung over his eyes and the other was tucked under his left side for comfort.

She lay down on the bed next to him. 'Honey?' She put her hand on his chest. He was cold and smelled of pubs. So she'd been right to guess that was where the 'meeting' had been. 'Are you all right?'

'No,' he said flatly. Soberly.

'What happened at the meeting? Didn't it go well?'

'No,' he said. 'No, it didn't.'

'Why?' Carrie probed gently.

Mark's mouth twitched but there wasn't any humour in it. The cheap willow blinds let in enough moonlight for Carrie to see the beginnings of worry lines on his face and the washed-out weariness in his expression. She could see his thirties beginning to shadow his boyish face, but somehow it only made her feel more protective of him, more determined to throw herself between him and the stress.

'Why didn't it go well? Oh God,' he said, half to himself, 'where would I start?'

Carrie waited for him to explain further, but he didn't. They lay there breathing quietly in the darkness, while an ambulance siren approached, then hurtled past the building.

Carrie twisted her gold wedding band around on her finger.

'It's been a bit of a headfuck day,' he said eventually, rubbing his forehead. 'One way and another.'

Immediately, Carrie felt bad. 'I'm sorry about earlier,' she said. 'I didn't mean to slam the car door like that. I didn't break it, did I?'

'No.' Mark made a small noise of despair, and twisted himself around her warm body, hiding his head in the curve of her waist and wrapping his arms around her legs.

Carrie's nerves tingled at the urgency of Mark's sudden grip, but she stroked his hair and his shoulders calmly, trying to spread comfort over his cold skin. 'You don't have to tell me what went wrong, honey. But you know I love you, and we can fix anything together,' she said softly. 'We can make it right, I promise you.'

She could feel Mark's breath on her stomach, and the prickle of his stubble through her T-shirt. She churned inside. More than anything she wanted to make things better for him. He'd suffered more in his life than anyone deserved to, and when his guard dropped as it had now, the self-assured Hoxton techie vanished, and all she could see was a scared little boy, with no mom to turn to for reassurance.

'It'll be OK,' she said, pressing her lips to his head, soothing the words into his hair. 'Don't worry.'

'I'm sorry, Carrie,' he murmured eventually. 'I'm just a screw-up. I don't deserve you. We need some space of our own. Start again.' He sighed heavily, a gust of hot breath onto her skin. 'I don't know about St Dee, but let's talk about it in the morning.'

It was always like this with Mark: everything fine, fine, fine, then total, unbearable disaster, then fine, fine, fine again.

Carrie stroked his hair, seeing the first few strands of silver picked out by the moonlight, and carried on stroking until Mark pretended to be asleep.

Chapter Three

After Mark's moment of panic on Tuesday night, Carrie felt a distinct change in their relationship, as if the planets had suddenly shifted or a tide had turned, sweeping them along in a whole new direction. Wednesday felt strange, like the dragging hours before a thunderstorm breaks, and on Thursday morning, Mark got up early, made Carrie tea in bed, and confessed that the contract he'd been working on four days a week for the past six months hadn't been renewed, as he'd assumed it would be.

'Don't overreact,' he said, as she tried not to look as horrified as she felt. 'There's plenty of work out there for IT specialists who don't have bad breath.'

Carrie got the distinct impression, though, that he wasn't telling her the full story. That was the thing with Mark; he didn't actually lie, but she'd slowly begun to realise that sometimes he was rather selective about what he told her. Yes, he'd bought new trainers; no, he didn't mention a price. Right now she wasn't sure she had the strength to ask for the missing pieces. But, not wanting to add to the stress he was already feeling, she kept her thoughts to herself and tried not to let her panic about the rent show through.

Mark went out as normal on Friday morning, precision-packing his laptop bag with all the usual paraphernalia and avoiding the post as if it were just a normal day. His initial, painful despair had given way to a gleam that Carrie wasn't sure she recognised: he looked focused and determined, and muttered agreement when she suggested selling their unused mountain bikes to pay the service charge. This bothered Carrie, since she'd only mentioned it to provoke him into a response.

On Friday night he came home with a spiky new haircut and then spent an evening sorting through his trainers in his wardrobe while she watched television and listened in amazement through the thin wall to the sounds of Mark tidying up. Mark never tidied up. He never threw anything away, either. But now he was asking for black bin bags and she handed them over, dumbstruck.

During the advert break, Carrie peered into the bedroom and was horrified by the wall of boxes separating her from her husband. The only thing more astonishing than the small fortune Mark had spent on making sure his feet were ageing slower than the rest of him was the mystery of where he'd managed to secrete them in their tiny flat.

Mark was acting busy but Carrie suspected he was actually doing very little apart from colour-coding his trainers, like a squirrel obsessively counting its hoard before a long winter. Clearly, she was going to be the one to take the reins, before the bailiffs came round. So she started making lists. Lists that would drag them out of this crisis.

Now Morris Mouse had turned hard-nosed sole financial provider for her marriage with his much-needed delivery payment, he was somehow much easier to draw than when he was Morris Mouse, artistic vision. The grey of London January didn't keep Carrie pinned down with lethargy in bed any more, and she was drinking coffee at her easel before Mark was even awake. She scrapped the marshmallowy tutus and lovingly detailed backgrounds of wobbling Hampstead ballerinas, photocopied Mark's computer magazines and collaged them into a blinking, flashing cyberworld, where Morris danced up and down keyboards, sending terse communiqués to his international mouse pals with a click of his spindly paws.

Carrie realised that she liked Morris a lot more when he was actually doing something. She also realised that she had made his wrinkled nose and squinting concentration look a bit like Mark when he was hunched over his laptop, downloading obscure indie music from the Internet.

Morris's computer odyssey was done within days. Carrie bundled him up in tissue paper and delivered the pages to her agent. 'If they need Morris this month, here he is,' she said. 'If they want him in a tutu, they'll have to wait.'

'I think this will be fine,' replied Gina, her agent, doubtfully.

Now she had some money coming, next on the list was St Dee.

Even there, the tide was moving in unexpected directions.

'I've been thinking about working from St Dee,' Mark mused, peeling his fourth orange of the evening. Carrie was trying to cure him of his nail-biting by keeping his hands occupied; recently it had intensified to the point where his chapped and raw fingers looked like those of a serial killer. 'I could set up on my own, checking people's hard drives before they hand their PC over to PC World for mending. Mark Armstrong: Discreet Disc Doctor.'

'You think there's a market for that?'

'I know there is.' Mark twisted his mouth into a meaningful leer. 'You want to see some of the stuff I see. Or rather, you don't. *Or* I could set up a business teaching mothers how to send emails. Laptop Lessons. Does that sound too much like a *Carry On* film?'

'The *rent*, Mark,' said Carrie patiently. 'We have no income. I have enough in the bank to cover next month. Then we're stuffed, unless you plan to find another job very quickly.'

Mark thought for a moment, then said, 'OK. When did Paul Jenkins say we could move into St Dee? If we wanted it?'

Carrie stared at him over the kitchen counter. He hadn't even asked where she'd stashed the emergency rent money. 'Just like that?'

'Just like what?' Mark began systematically separating his orange segments, peeling off the white pith.

'Just like that. One moment you'd rather walk over broken glass than move to the sticks and now you can't wait!' Carrie was too surprised to be tactical. 'You're not even suggesting we both get bar jobs for a month until something turns up. What's changed?'

'Circumstances change,' said Mark easily, as if he'd wanted to move all along. He popped an orange segment in his mouth. 'You've got to be practical about these things. I'm not earning right now and you are. And you say you can't work in this flat, so fair enough – we need to go where you can work. I mean, I can always find something to do until I get a proper job sorted. Actually,' he said airily, 'it's probably a good time for me to take a career break, think about where I'm going. If we can save money by moving out to Wiltshire for a while, then yeah, let's do it.'

Carrie stared at him. She had a whole portfolio of persuasive reasons prepared – the extra space, the cheap living, the chance to experience something quite weird, and her final, dicey card – children. She'd been resigned to a long campaign.

Mark grinned and winked at her. 'You never know, country air and all that. Haystacks, empty barns, secluded woodland nooks and crannies. There's a reason yokels always have red faces.'

Carrie leaned back in her chair until it touched the sink unit – not very far. 'You'd really just go? Leave London?' She tried to keep the incredulity out of her voice, and failed. The delight bubbling up inside her struggled against her instinctive concern. There had to be far more to the job situation than he was letting on. 'You haven't destroyed an entire server or something? Compromised a whole company?'

Mark shrugged and laid out the orange segments in a sun shape on his plate. 'Course not. I mean, who really belongs in a warehouse-loft conversion, for God's sake? Maybe it's just time to move on. I suppose my grandfather just had to move out and get on with it when they kicked him out in 1941.'

Carrie waited a moment to be sure he meant it, and wasn't just waiting for her to dissuade him. 'Really?' she asked cautiously.

'Yeah, really. Well, come on,' said Mark, 'aren't you going to fling your arms around me and tell me how happy you are?'

She shoved her chair back and got up so she could wrap her arms around his neck. 'Thank you,' she said, into the warmth of his neck. 'Thank you! Oh, Mark, I know we're going to be so happy there!'

'I hope so,' said Mark, and though he dropped his lips to her arms and kissed her bare skin, Carrie was aware that she couldn't see his face.

Mark and Carrie were in Oak Cottage within three weeks.

First of all, Paul Jenkins called Carrie to let her know that the specialist team of restoration decorators had a gap coming up in their schedule, if they wanted to go ahead and sign a tenancy agreement for Oak Cottage. Mark's offer to pitch in with the roller brushes was politely refused. The cottages, Paul Jenkins explained, fell under some heritage guidelines and any work had to be supervised by the project team, although Mark and Carrie were welcome to discuss the specifics of the decoration.

Mark, predictably, wasn't bothered, but for Carrie the idea of decorating the cottage as Lily would have had it became something of an obsession. She stacked her study with reference books and pored over the material Paul Jenkins sent, trying to imagine the rooms through Lily's eyes. She even stuck the wedding picture and the snapshot of young Lily on her easel for inspiration. It would have been wrong, she felt, to have imposed crashing modernity on the place. Rude, almost.

The cost of this work, including an approved Aga, was 'commensurate with the level of experience involved': astronomical. Fortunately – the second stroke of luck – Carrie's parents were so enchanted by the idea of their daughter living in a genuine pre-war ghost town that they sent her some money to cover the moving expenses. 'Call it a late wedding present,' wrote her mother in a flurry of exclamation marks, 'and make sure you decorate a spare room for me!' Carrie hadn't told her about the single-track road, or the tanks.

The other part of this miracle was that Carrie's editor loved Morris's new computer-nerd direction and wanted to commission more books in the series. 'Can I be honest? She was going to dump you both, darling,' Gina confided breezily, 'but apparently this is exactly the right direction for him to take. Marketing, you know. How many more do you feel comfortable agreeing to?'

'It's a sign,' said Mark. 'The mouse wants you to go to the countryside. With my computer. It's so symbolic.'

But what made the abrupt decision to give up their London life and move to St Dee seem obvious and right was a strange new feeling of actually starting their marriage properly. Carrie and Mark were both loners by nature; though Mark had plenty of easy acquaintances, he could take or leave company, and since they'd met, it had really only been Mark and Carrie, in their own little bubble. It had been fun, and they'd had some amazing evenings doing fairly irresponsible but fun things, but suddenly Carrie really sensed Mark was her partner, not just her boyfriend. For the first time, they were making decisions for their life together, for their marriage, not merely adapting their old single lives to fit the new circumstances.

It felt like they were riding a high wave together, and when Carrie caught Mark ordering the exact same fairy-tale brass bed as she wanted off the Internet, she knew it would all be fine. A fresh start, no secrets – just the two of them.

They moved to St Dee in the last week of January. There was no sign of activity round the maypole other than a fresh coat of white paint, but several of the other houses in the village had curtains, and there were six or seven cars parked around the green.

They'd gone back twice to supervise the decoration and to sign for the Aga, Mark complaining about the slush-filled craters in the road all the way home, but even so, Carrie couldn't stop herself tingling with fresh pleasure as they drove into St Dee. The trees were bare of leaves, but the sky was a soft china blue, and a big black cat stalked across the village green, winding itself around the benches, as if it had been there for years.

'Do you think Paul Jenkins got that cat from Central Animal Casting?' observed Mark. 'Don't you think it's all a bit too perfect?'

'It'll feel different when there are people in the houses,' said Carrie. 'We must be one of the first to move in.'

She looked around and tried to superimpose images of army training she'd seen on television over the neat little houses: squaddies in camouflage gear, leaping through the exposed uncurtained windows with guns spewing bullets, hiding behind the low walls to snipe at each other. Had they driven tanks across the green? It was too hard to picture now. They must have been incredibly careful, or else how would the houses be in a good enough state to be renovated?

Carrie blinked and the violent mental images vanished. The renovation team had worked quickly and discreetly: the little post office was finished – and occupied, by the look of the car outside – but the derelict tithe barn had been left crumbling into the grass like a half-eaten cake. There was something so clear and pure about the light in the valley that the bright reds and yellows of the flowers already stuffing the window boxes seemed too vivid to be real.

'Oh my God! Look at the pub!' breathed Carrie. 'They've even got hanging baskets outside already!'

'Thank God there's a pub,' said Mark. He squeezed their Golf between a decorators' van and a very battered Land Rover to get up the narrow lane to their house. 'Let's hope it serves real beer. Are you noticing how narrow this lane is, by the way?'

'As soon as we've unpacked and checked that the movers have left the right stuff, we'll go and have a pint.' Carrie searched in her bag for the keys, too impatient to wait for Mark to park. 'But let's get in.' She held up the bunch triumphantly. 'The keys to the door!'

'Ah, stop there,' said Mark, 'I've got something for you.' He leaned over her to open the glove compartment and took out a blue Tiffany's bag. 'Call it a moving-house present.'

'Mark!' said Carrie, eyeing the box with a mixture of longing and guilt. 'Whatever it is, you know we can't afford it.'

'What do you mean, we can't afford it?' demanded Mark. 'I'm married to Morris Mouse's mother. He's going to be a one-mouse goldmine. Go on, open it.'

Carrie's hands trembled with excitement as she undid the ribbon and opened the little box. Inside was a silver Tiffany keyring: a little house dangling expensively from the thick circle.

'Mark . . .' she said.

'Turn it over.'

Carrie turned over the house and read, 'Home & heart. M&CA'.

'I could only afford three words,' he explained. 'And I have to tell you there was some haggling about the ampersands.'

Tears filled up Carrie's eyes and she leaned over the handbrake to kiss him. 'I love you,' she murmured into his stubbly cheek. 'I just want this to be . . .'

'I know. Now, let me.' He slipped the front-door key off her old bunch, hooked it on the silver circle and handed it back to her. 'You going to let me carry you over the threshold?'

Carrie laughed. 'Not until I know where the nearest A&E is!'

They got their overnight bags out of the boot, along with the emergency box Carrie had packed, containing the kettle, mugs, coffee, radio, candles and bottle of champagne for celebrating.

The creaky gate had been replaced with a new iron one which swung open easily as Mark pushed it with his knee, and they crunched down the gravelled path.

'Still no one in next door, I see,' he observed. 'What time did you say the delivery men were going to arrive?'

'Which delivery men?' Carrie stepped into the bare hall. 'The auction furniture's already here.'

'I meant the removal men. The guys with all our stuff.'

Carrie braced herself to savour the thrill of stepping into her own house, and was disappointed to feel instead a twinge of anti-climax. The house smelled of new wood and old damp, with an overhanging fustiness she hadn't noticed before. The ceilings seemed much lower than she remembered. And there were no boxes.

'Lunchtime? They were meant to be here by one, they said.' She put her bag down on the stairs and went into the kitchen in search of boxes.

What looked solid and plain next to the gaudy repro Georgiana in the sale room looked perfectly at home against the kitchen walls. In fact, thought Carrie, with a shiver, all this stuff could easily have been there for the last sixty years, waiting for the evacuated owners to return. It could have slowly materialised against the bare walls, fading up like a developing photograph. Only the lack of dust gave it away. The dark dresser stood next to the stone sink, its shelves empty and shadowy, while the big pine table almost filled the area in front of the range.

'Looks all right, doesn't it?' she said to Mark, but more to the house in general.

'Looks fine! Maybe it'll look different once we've put everything in,' he replied, and she could tell he was making an effort to be cheery. 'More like home. Um, I'll just go and check upstairs.'

He'd cheer up with a cup of hot tea and a biscuit. Carrie went to the sink and tried one of the big brass taps. There was a gurgle from the pipes, then a trickle of brackish water, which petered out into nothing. She turned it off, then turned it on again. Nothing.

Mark's footsteps thundered up the bare stairs, over her head, and she heard him striding across the landing. Her own breathing seemed echoey in the empty kitchen and a quick shiver of something passed over her skin. A feeling of intrusion, as though the house had woken up, but wasn't quite ready for them yet. Suddenly Carrie didn't feel alone in the kitchen.

The footsteps thundered back down the stairs.

'Are they in here?' Mark strode in, one hand in his hair.

'Are what in here?' she replied jumpily.

Calm down, she told herself. It's just an old house. You know too much about it to be rational.

'Our things. Our worldly possessions. The stereo. My Bridget Riley prints. My trainers . . .'

'No,' said Carrie. 'They're not in here.' Seeing Mark's fingernails return to his mouth for the first time in weeks, she decided not to tell him about the water. Instead, she went over and put her arms around his wiry waist. 'Don't get stressed. They're probably stuck on the motorway somewhere. Or down a lane. Have you got their number?'

'Somewhere.' Mark looked strained and checked his mobile. 'No reception. Have you got reception on yours?'

Carrie checked, and shook her head. 'Oh no! We're in a horror movie.'

Mark returned her pretend-panic expression. 'But where are they? They set off at six o'clock this morning! That's why we were up at the crack of dawn to let them in. That's why we gave them our spare bloody key!' He shoved his chewed fingers back in his hair. 'What if they've gone to the wrong place?'

Carrie held on doggedly. 'Which wrong place? Salisbury Plain training camp?'

'I don't know, do I? They could be in France by now with all my stuff! And none of it's insured!'

'What?' demanded Carrie. 'You didn't renew the contents insurance?'

Their voices were bouncing around the walls, which had been painted an authentic shade of sludgy yellow, not the daffodil yellow Carrie had originally wanted. She could feel irritation building up inside her chest and knew it was because whenever she had fondly imagined Oak Cottage it had been with a full complement of furniture and fresh linen, not this damp and echoing shell which smelled of holiday cottages. She released Mark from her grip and walked towards the window, as if she might suddenly see the van outside.

'And anyway,' she added, 'it's not just your *trainers*, it's our bed linen and blankets for tonight, and my painting gear.'

Mark stopped chewing his nails and looked guilty. 'Sorry,' he said. 'Sorry, I know. I'm just . . . kind of on edge.' He pulled a self-deprecating face. 'I've never been so far from a Pad Thai before. Maybe I'm in shock.'

Carrie stood up and felt in her pockets for some cash.

'Look, we're overreacting,' she said. 'Plan B. Let's go to the pub, use their phone, and have that drink now, and I bet you by the time we come back, the removal people will be here. And if we have a couple of drinks first, we won't even be mad at them.'

Mark shrugged. 'I guess we'll be able to see them arrive from the pub,' he sighed. 'If they're not in there already themselves.'

'Exactly. I've been watching *Emmerdale* for research. We're meant to go straight to the pub, so we can find out who's sleeping with who. They announce things like that in pubs in the countryside. And we'll see the removal men drive past from the window. You can go and bawl them out in front of the whole village, if you want. That should get us known nice and quickly.'

'Good plan, Mrs Armstrong,' said Mark, and wrapped her up in a tight hug. 'We haven't been here more than ten minutes, and already you're insisting we go down to the pub. What a star wife you are.'

OK, it wasn't what she'd planned. In her head, the cottage had been completely furnished, even down to plump ranunculas in a jug by the window and the new white duvet smoothed out on the bed, all ready for them to start as they meant to go on with an evening of champagne-fuelled country passion. She wanted it to be perfect, to prove to Mark that they'd made the right choice, that he'd be safe there with her.

'Well, yeah,' she said. 'Even if they were here, we'd only be having a row about setting up cables and broken plates. Hey?'

'Guess so.' Mark sighed. 'Sorry for shouting. I just wanted it to be . . . perfect for you.'

She put her arms around his waist, tucking her thumbs in his empty belt loops. It meant more to him than her, this house. 'It doesn't have to be perfect straight away. We've got each other, haven't we? We'll make it perfect.'

Mark was looking out over her head towards the green and she couldn't read his expression. 'Let's go to the pub,' he said.

They hesitated like underage school kids outside the studded door of the Rose and Thorn.

Despite her brave words, Carrie baulked at the thought of opening the door to a sea of curious eyes, and she pretended to examine the multi-coloured hanging baskets on each side of the door. The eye-wateringly bright flowers were, indeed, real. 'Ooh,' she said. 'Look. The licensees are called Tony and Judith Williams. Make a note of that.'

'I have. Now, ladies first,' said Mark.

'No, you go first. Ladies don't go into pubs first.'

Mark nudged her playfully. 'You scared it'll be like something out of a spaghetti Western? Big silence when the city folk walk in?'

'Mark, probably everyone in this village is city folk right now.'

He grinned and pulled his 'hey, you're funny' face. 'That's very true. So the sooner we're in, the sooner we can blend into the wallpaper and stare at newcomers like we've been here for ages.'

Carrie looked up at him. Mark looked exactly like a caricature of a Hoxton IT consultant: sludgy grey cargo pants, expensive trainers, long-sleeved T-shirt under a fleece, hair artfully tousled. 'Blend in how exactly? This is a pub, not a Prêt à Manger.'

Mark brushed his cowlicks flatter with his hands. 'Less city folk?'

'Not with those trainers.' Carrie shook her head in pretend sorrow and a trickle of relief spread through her veins. Maybe it would all be fine. They were just off-balance. 'OK, let's go in. You're right.'

'I'm always right.' Mark pushed open the door and Carrie followed him in, hovering slightly behind the broad expanse of green fleece.

Inside the pub was cosy, with low ceilings, crossed with dark beams that made it seem lower still. A large fireplace dominated one side of the room, a gaping, blackened arch in the whitewashed walls, surrounded by gleaming horse brasses. Old photographs were hung everywhere – cricket teams, school groups, wedding shots, formal portraits of men in high-necked collars and women with hair piled up like cottage loaves around their head.

Carrie peered more closely at the school group. A jumbled class of twenty or so children in smocks and shorts, ranging from angelic tots to gangling young boys on the tricky verge of adolescence, were lined up in front of the maypole. All the St Dee children in 1939. There was Jack, standing at one side, his glasses reflecting the sun, long academic gown settled round his shoulders like a bat's wings. Carrie's pulse quickened. Standing at the other side was a tall blonde teenager – Lily. Her hair was rolled into two buns on each side of her head, to differentiate her from the younger girls, but she still had a curious half-girl, half-woman look. An awkward kind of grace, as if she was still surprised at no longer being one of the children in pinafores leaning shyly against her leg.

Despite the bright light streaming in through the lead windows, Carrie felt a shiver run across her skin – what had happened while that photograph had been taken? What had the weather been like? Had the children fidgeted? Had it taken long?

There was something quite strange about the pub being decorated with photographs of its old regulars. Sixty years later they were all back in the bar, watching the incomers from behind the picture glass.

'Look, Mark,' she said, touching his arm, 'have you seen this picture of Lily and Jack?'

'Where?' Mark came nearer.

'Here. Look, she must have been one of those assistant teachers. How old do you think she is there?'

Mark made a non-committal noise. 'Dunno. Fifteen? Still, good that we've got some proof of ownership, right here in the pub, eh? That is definitely my grandparents.'

Carrie opened her mouth to protest at his lack of interest, but as she did so a friendly voice boomed out, 'Good day to you!', and the pair of them spun round.

The sturdy, middle-aged man behind the bar beamed up at them from the cash-register instruction manual he was studying, dimpling his ruddy cheeks in a fetching Hogarthian manner.

'Good morning,' said Mark. 'Are you open?'

'If you like orange juice and can pay in cash.' The man rubbed his hand thoughtfully over his bald spot and gestured at the till, which sat resolutely silent on the bar counter. 'Beyond me, I'm afraid.'

'Do you want a hand?' Mark leaned over to read the manual. 'I know a bit about this sort of thing.'

His eyes lit up with relief. 'I'd be much obliged.'

As Mark and the barman mumbled and prodded, Carrie wandered to the wall with the most photographs, not sure what she was looking for. The maypole and the green and the view of the crumbling abbey were all spookily familiar already. It was harder to tell which individual houses were which yet – here was a very grand-looking house Carrie didn't remember seeing, with an army of staff lined up outside on the pristine lawn, the maids in starched white aprons, footmen in livery uniform, a severe butler, a round cook, awkward gamekeepers in tweeds, looking as if they'd been called in from the woods.

And next to it the church, with the vicar and his wife. From her tea dress, Carrie guessed it to be around 1935. Or earlier? He looked long-suffering in his dog collar; she, with her flowery hat and not-quite-sober-enough shoes seemed to be itching to tell him off. She looked closer to see if she could make out that weird face on the church door – there it was. Looming over the entrance.

And here was the pub, full of cheery faces packed together in the snug. She peered closer. Someone had written 'May Day 1936', just along the bottom of the frame. Everyone seemed very drunk, but in a shiny-faced, healthy way, smoke wreathing around their heads, tankards of beer on every surface. She searched for Lily's face among the younger people: was that her? It was: tucked into the corner of the photograph with two other girls, definitely a girl here, with baby-round cheeks and a giggling look in her eyes. Carrie felt a sudden twinge of intrusion, as if the people in the photograph disapproved of her nosiness.

She stepped back and sniffed discreetly. It didn't quite smell like a pub yet: there was a pleasant mixture of wood and beeswax furniture polish and pipe smoke, but the smells were new, and had none of the ingrained beery staleness she associated with London pubs. In fact, there wasn't any beery aroma at all.

'Ah, I see you've spotted our little gallery!' boomed the landlord. 'Fascinating, isn't it? How the village is still so similar! Army hardly did any damage while they were here.' He tapped his nose. 'People have got their own reasons as to why, of course.'

'Really?' said Carrie.

'Oh yes. Very much so. Tony Williams.' The barman was leaning over, stretching out his thick hand towards her. 'Should have said, sorry. Very rude of me. Welcome to the Rose and Thorn.'

'Oh, not to worry,' said Carrie, feeling the strong fingers gripping hers. They were country hands, definitely, with hard patches that felt rough against her own soft skin. 'I'm Carrie, Carrie Armstrong, and this is my husband, Mark. We've just moved into Oak Cottage. Up the road. I feel like I should be wearing a name badge with all that on.'

The cash register pinged and the drawer shot open, pliant under Mark's touch. 'There you go,' he said, triumphant. 'You'll need to mark the various buttons for your different beers and what have you, but that's basically it.'

Tony eyed it suspiciously. 'If you say so.'

'I'm surprised Paul Jenkins let you have it at all,' said Carrie before she could stop herself. 'Didn't he try to get you a heritage cash register? In pounds, shillings and pence?'

A naughty smile nudged the corners of Tony's mouth. 'Have you been having some official advice on your decorating too?'

'Haven't we just.' Mark rolled his eyes. 'It's been like having a second mother-in-law. I thought we were going to be living in the house, not curating it.'

'Oh, Paul Jenkins hasn't been that bad.' Carrie elbowed him in the ribs. The last thing she wanted was to be marked out as trouble-makers. Word got round in pubs. 'I've been worse, if you must know, wanting to get it right. And now we can see how much effort's gone into making the village so lovely . . .'

Tony beamed. 'I can't disagree with you there, love. Anyway, can I offer you good people a drink?'

'That would be most hospitable of you.' Mark peered over the bar at the empty shelves. 'What have you got?'

'Ah,' said Tony ruefully. 'What have I got? Well, when that delivery from the brewery arrives, there'll be two local ales, Theakston's, Stella Artois, a good selection of wines and all the mixers.'

'And until then?'

'Orange juice.'

'Oh.' Carrie turned to Mark. 'Well, that would be nice, wouldn't it? Mark?'

Mark winked at Tony. 'Listen, I've got a bottle of something at home – I'm sure we can come to some arrangement, can't we?' He clapped Carrie on the back and made to leave. 'If you stay here and tell my wife some village gossip, I won't be a moment.'

The door banged behind him and Carrie suddenly felt very self-conscious. 'Yes, well, we've had problems with deliveries too,' she explained. 'Our furniture's somewhere between here and London. Plus . . .' She pulled a face. 'I haven't told Mark that the water's not running properly.'

'I reckon there's some kind of Bermuda Triangle round here,' agreed Tony. 'Lots of folk seem to have trouble finding St Dee, seeing as how there's only that one road in. Judith and myself, we've only come from Devizes. We had our own place on the outskirts, the Dolphin, a bit bigger than the Rose and Thorn. We were thinking of retiring, as a matter of fact, but then this came up, out of the blue.

Judith's great-aunt, it belonged to – the only thing Judith's ever had off her! Apart from some of them pictures you see on the wall. Anyway, we've been coming over every few days or so since we decided to move, just pottering about, getting the place ready.'

'It looks perfect,' said Carrie. 'Just how I imagined a country pub should be. But nice and clean too!'

'Well, that's the thing, isn't it? Getting the balance right.' Tony looked pleased, as he polished a wine glass and hung it on the rack above the bar.

'The balance?'

'Well, no point making this place some manner of heritage park, just so the likes of Paul Jenkins can show it off as a model of restoration, is there? Folk have to live here.'

'It's really important to rebuild a community,' agreed Carrie. 'I've never lived in a village before, but I really want to get properly involved.'

Tony's eyebrows lifted. 'Now, I'll be honest with you, Carrie. I had you two down as weekenders. Running back and forth to London all the time.'

'Certainly not!' Carrie pretended to look aggrieved. 'I'll be working from home – I'm an artist.'

'Are you now?' He picked up another glass. 'And what does your young man do?'

'He works with computers.' She shrugged. 'Don't ask me what, though. It's all a mystery to me. Have you just opened today?'

'Not exactly. We've had the doors open, so folk can pop in, meet each other. One or two been in today, not many. Some sightseers too.' He looked up from his polishing and gave her a knowing wink. 'It's a popular place for those conspiracy-theory people.'

'Ooh, tell me about these conspiracy theories,' said Carrie. 'Paul Jenkins let slip that there were some, but he was a bit *too* quick to say they were all rubbish . . .'

'Oh well, there's been stories for years about what the Army really wanted St Dee for. Why nothing got knocked down, like.' Tony gave her a meaningful nod. 'I've heard they tested some poisonous gas here as killed all the soldiers involved. Whole platoon of Americans, all buried in the wood, so no one could do tests on 'em. Blamed it on the Normandy Landings. That's what I reckon, anyway – happened elsewhere, you know. Some people think it was some to-do with the manor house – in that picture there.' He nodded towards the photograph of the staff on the lawn. 'Goebbels or Goering or someone being kept prisoner, or it being some kind of nuclear bunker for the Cabinet. Then it was knocked down, just after the war ended, so no one would know what they'd been up to after. Lots of stories, love. I daresay there'll be more before the week's out.'

'Really?' asked Carrie, leaning forward curiously. 'And are any of them true, do you think?'

He shook his head, then smiled. 'Who's to know, eh?'

Before Carrie could get him to go on, Mark reappeared with an Oddbins bag. 'Look what I found in the car!' he said.

Carrie's heart sank, thinking of their bottle of champagne and the plans she'd had for it, but instead Mark brought out a couple of bottles of Absolut vodka, still wrapped in their rough off-licence tissue paper.

'You packed vodka but not a spare towel?' she demanded before she could stop herself.

'Just as well, as it turns out.' Mark handed the bottle over the counter. 'We'll have two vodka and oranges, please, my good man, and have one yourself.' He turned to Carrie. 'That's how you address a country landlord, by the way.'

'Very kind. Now, what do I owe you for that practicality?' Tony pinged the till open and handed Mark a twenty-pound note, which he waved away.

'Put it towards fostering some atmosphere,' he said. 'By the way, is there some kind of official welcome party? A get-to-know-you evening or anything? I'd have thought Paul Jenkins might have organised a tour of everyone's houses, so we can admire the heritage thatching.'

'Mark!' said Carrie warningly. She glanced at Tony, then back at Mark.

But Tony only scratched his chin. 'Not that I've heard of, although it would be a sensible idea, wouldn't it?'

'For sure. I mean, it could be years before you met people otherwise. And most of the houses should be occupied in a few weeks – Paul Jenkins would know.'

'Mmm.' Tony finished his polishing and added the final glass to the rack, thoughtfully.

'A pub quiz?' suggested Mark. 'Something to get people talking to one another? I'd be on for that.' He knocked back half his drink with relish. 'Carrie? Wouldn't you?'

'Well, yes,' she said. Much as she wanted to get to know everyone, the idea of a first-day-of-school get-together made her skin crawl. She'd spent ten years of her life doing that fake 'you tell me something about you, and I'll tell you something about me' stuff with different people every eighteen months, and it had never got any easier.

Mark, of course, had no problem talking to people he didn't know. When they'd spent their long honeymoon travelling together, he'd walk into shops or accost policemen just so he could use the new words he'd picked up.

As though he could sense her momentary quiver, Mark put his arm around her shoulders and squeezed. 'Carrie's really looking forward to joining the local community. She's been watching *Emmerdale* specially,' he explained.

Tony roared with laughter. 'I hope we'll have nothing of that nature going on here!'

While Mark probed Tony for more on the conspiracy theories, Carrie slid off her bar stool and returned to the faded images of the village. It was fascinating to spot the houses outside with these black-and-white people standing in front of them so possessively. Either nothing had really changed, or the attention to detail in the restoration had been unbelievable.

As she was searching the groups for Lily and Jack, the pub door opened, letting a blast of cold outside air into the warm room, and she spun round.

'Looking for Mark Armstrong!'

Carrie saw with relief that it was Ian, the chief removal man. He looked very road-weary and eyed up the pumps with visible longing.

'There you are! Where'd you get to?' Mark asked. 'We thought you'd been abducted by aliens!'

'Funny you should say that, mate,' he replied. 'We had real trouble finding this place – sat nav sent us all round the houses. Started to think St Dee didn't exist at one point. We tried to phone,' he added, 'but you never picked up.'

'No, the reception's very bad in the valley,' agreed Tony. 'We've found that. Very on and off. Can I get you chaps a drink?'

'Drinks later,' said Carrie, quickly. 'On us. OK? But let's get everything in first.'

Reluctantly, Ian held the door open as Mark leaped off his bar stool. 'Have you got the list I left?' he said. 'Because we need things to go inside in a certain order, right? There's a lot of electrical stuff . . .'

Carrie started to feel better, her usual optimism warming her edges. With their stuff around them, the cottage would feel different. More like their own home.

'We'll see you later,' promised Carrie.

'Not too much later, I hope,' said Tony, and winked.

Chapter Four

Oak Cottage absorbed Carrie and Mark so completely that they barely noticed the first days turn into weeks: days spent unpacking, afternoons spent tackling the garden, evenings in the pub, slowly getting to know people, and nights sleeping soundly in the brass bed beneath the oak beams. By their first weekend, it seemed entirely normal to climb the stairs to bed. By the end of the second week, Carrie automatically listened out for the cockerels in the morning and woke before the alarm. Mark still slept through it all.

Even when the final box was unpacked, Carrie was surprised by how little they actually owned, once it was spread out over the parlour, and the kitchen, the bedrooms, and the separate studies they now enjoyed. In London, she'd been obsessed with clearing space and minimising, but the empty shelves and bare walls in this family house only made her feel things were missing.

What felt most conspicuous by its absence, to her, were family pictures. She put up her own family snaps, and their lovely black-and-white wedding pictures, but Mark had resisted her attempts to transfer his own family photos from the shoebox to a proper frame.

Family was all anyone seemed to talk about in the village shop – who they'd inherited from, what they'd done – but Mark steadfastly refused to pick up on her hints about doing some family research while it was still such a hot topic. He didn't even get excited when she managed to establish that it *was* Lily hugging her friends in the corner of the pub's May Day photograph; after peering closely, she worked out that the dress was the same as the one she wore in the school photograph the same year – a faint sprig pattern, obviously her best dress, though she'd almost grown out of it.

'Carrie, all this digging up the past – don't you think it's kind of unhealthy?' he replied when she casually mentioned joining the St Dee Historical Group. 'What are they going to do? Sit round and discuss conspiracy theories as to why everyone was kicked out? Or is it just a stealthy way of finding out who's got what and what it's worth?'

'Mark, you are such a cynic,' protested Carrie, though secretly, from the conversations she'd already had in the village, she suspected he had a point. 'Of course not. I'm just trying to get out and meet people. Anyway, I just think it's interesting to get a picture of how things were. Before everyone moved away.' She paused and shot a sly look at him.

They were in the garden, turning over some of the beds while the weather was mild. To the surprise of them both, messing about in the garden together had turned out to be one of the best things about their new house, and they'd spent some of the most contented hours of their marriage so far just digging and planting, listening to the radio, flicking soil at each other, then sharing a deep, hot bath to wash it all off.

It was quite a large garden, and Paul Jenkins' workmen had made some rudimentary efforts to get it back under control before the new residents moved in, but there was still a lot to do. Carrie's mother had sent her a long letter about what they should plant and when, but as far as Carrie could see, there was some way to go before it could even be called a garden. Still, the apple trees looked as if they might come back to life with some ruthless pruning and there was a good view of the chalk horse.

And it wasn't in as overgrown a state as Rose Cottage next door, which was still unoccupied, and was the cause of much pub speculation.

Carrie leaned on her spade and rubbed her hands together. 'I'm going to put some pictures up this afternoon,' she said casually. 'Do you have any photos you'd like me to frame?'

'Not really,' said Mark, turning over a rock.

She bit her lip. 'What about that lovely picture of Lily and Jack on their wedding day? I'd really like to have a photo of them somewhere, as a sort of thank you. For letting us live here. Don't you think?'

'Whoah there, Nelly,' said Mark, straightening up. 'You're spooking me out now. Stop with the offerings to the dead!'

'Why not? I was going to put it with our wedding pictures.' Carrie kept her face innocent. 'You know we still have a box of photo frames from the wedding list? We should use them. For happy pictures. And since it's their house . . .'

'It's *our* house.' Mark stuck his spade in the ground and advanced on her. 'I don't really care about who lived here before, Carrie,' he said, wrapping his arms around her. 'I only care about being here now with you.'

'But you can't get away from the fact that we're . . .'

Mark silenced her by kissing her cold nose. 'I can get away from the fact quite easily. I don't want to live in the past. Meeting you meant starting a whole clean page, and that's fine with me.'

He tightened his grip and turned his head to kiss her properly. Carrie melted into his arms gladly.

But even as he kissed her, and her arms were winding around his neck, Carrie was already thinking of the old-fashioned silver frame she was going to mount Lily and Jack's picture in, even if it meant keeping it in her own study, to let some spirit of the house know she hadn't forgotten.

*

Before they moved, Carrie had wondered how urban Mark was going to deal with living far away from all-night supermarkets and late-opening bars. But his enthusiastic adjustment to country life amazed her. For a while he got so into digging the garden and hanging out in the pub while she worked, chatting with Tony the landlord, that she started to worry that he'd actually want to start some kind of organic smallholding. She wasn't complaining: the nervous tension that had hung around Mark's shoulders for the last few months in London had evaporated, like the city greyness in their skin, and he was far more like the easy, funny man she'd waited thirty-three tantalising emails to meet.

'You look happy,' she said one morning, catching him setting up a new, improved cabling system for his study. Coloured cables and plugs and converters littered the small room, already piled with boxes of disks. Her heart lifted, because this sort of cabling meant he intended to stay.

'Well, that's because I *am* happy. You look pretty cheery yourself,' he replied, flicking a polystyrene packing bead at her.

'What reason have I got not to be?' she demanded. It was as if a dam had burst in her creative mind, and Morris danced across the keyboard with new life. She began to wonder how long she could have carried on had they not moved when they did; it was so very different, and yet so simple.

'I've got a beautiful house, a new book deal, an Aga . . .' As she spoke she moved silently across the room to where he was bent over his hard drives and picked up a whole handful of packing beads. 'A live-in gardener – what more could a woman ask for?' she added, shoving the beads down the back of his T-shirt.

Mark squirmed and roared in pretend outrage, grabbing her around the waist and wrestling her to the floor, and Carrie didn't mind when he filled her whole shirt with squeaking polystyrene.

Contrary to what she read in magazines, Carrie found she and Mark never really had Big Conversations; difficult topics just seemed to resolve themselves, but usually through some higher power rather than through mature discussion. Just as their housing problem had been solved by the solicitor's letter arriving.

But their money was dwindling, and no divine intervention had come. The same morning that Carrie steeled herself to start dropping hints about needing some help with the bills, Mark got up early, brought her tea in bed (not usually a good sign) and informed her that he was going into Devizes to set up an office computer system.

'Well done!' said Carrie, sipping her tea. 'How did you get the gig?'

'Someone in the pub mentioned it.' Mark pulled a jumper over his T-shirt. He dressed in layers, like an onion. Out in the middle of nowhere, the mornings were still colder than Carrie had ever known. 'Not that exciting, but it's a start, you know. Cash.'

'It's brilliant.' Carrie smiled and hugged her knees through the white duvet. Wasn't this the point of living in a village? People helping each other out? 'Who was it?'

'Who was what?'

'Who told you about it?' said Carrie. She sipped her tea. 'Was it a man or a woman? Was it Sandra, you know, from the shop? Blonde hair? I think she came from Devizes, didn't she? Or was it that youngish bloke we were chatting with the other night? The one with the dog that had to be put down?'

'Umm . . .' Mark thought, then shook his head. 'No, it's gone. It was a mate of a mate, anyway. You're much better at names than I am, Mrs Village Gossip.'

Which was true. Mark could talk to anyone, anywhere, about anything, but rarely concentrated on important details like names.

'I know you. Watching out of that studio window all day.' He winked, playfully. 'I bet you've got a notebook, haven't you?'

'Excuse me! Less of the gossip,' objected Carrie. 'I'm not nosy . . . I'm just a trained observer of detail.'

Mark sat down on the bed and removed her cup of tea carefully, placing it on the bedside table next to the photo of her parents and a book about wartime England.

'If you're not nosy,' he said, nuzzling into her neck, 'why have you already practically compiled a dossier on everyone in the village? Eh?'

Carrie squirmed and protested at his tickling fingers.

'You have!' Mark sat up. 'I've seen you, hanging around the village shop, peering into people's baskets. Asking questions about when the buses run into Deeting Magna.'

'That's so untrue,' said Carrie from beneath the duvet, half-hoping he'd carry on. But Mark was pulling on his socks and looking for his trainers. 'I just like to get inspiration for my work. Quirks, local colour. Besides, I don't want it to look like we're not interested in getting to know people. If we don't make friends at the beginning we'll get a reputation for being stand-offish.'

'And that bothers you?' He gave her a searching look. 'My company not enough for you, eh?'

Carrie threw a pillow at him. 'Don't be so stupid! No, it's just that you can drive and I can't. Anyway, this is my office, so I *need* to get to know people I can talk to when I can't face working any more.'

'Well, I have to tell you, it's starting to freak me out, Carrie,' said Mark, seriously. 'If everyone else in this place is as well-informed about us as you are about them . . .' He let his voice deepen into a movie-trailer growl. 'Just how long will it be before they discover a terrible secret about one of the villagers that means you have to *pay* the *ultimate price*?'

For a second, Carrie felt a quick panic, then realised he was joking. Keeping her face straight, she said, 'If you mean the fact that Sandra from the shop doesn't make her own homemade marmalade, I already know.'

Mark made his mouth into an 'o' of shock. 'And what about ours?'

'We don't have any terrible secrets!' she laughed, then paused. 'Do we?'

Mark jiggled his eyebrows and Carrie pushed away the thought that there was quite a lot about Mark that she had chosen not to know.

'I'll let you know what the rest of the village tells me,' she informed him. 'Now go and earn some money.'

'I'll be back tonight,' he said, dropping a kiss on her head. 'Have a productive day with Morris.'

'Yeah, yeah.'

She listened to Mark clatter down the stairs, which were still uncarpeted, and slam their front door behind him. Carrie let her eyes roam over the thick beam that ran the length of their room while her ears pricked for the sound of his footsteps on the new gravel path, then the metallic bleep of the car opening. Then the familiar roar of the engine, revved too hard, then the scrunch of wheels on mud and earth as he three-point-turned in the lane, then the silence as the sounds died away again.

Until there was only birdsong, and an aeroplane on the other side of the valley.

Carrie stretched out her toes in the warm bedlinen and revelled in the fact that she had the entire house all to herself.

In accordance with her newly felt-tipped work schedule, Carrie fully intended to sketch Morris's final pages, but found herself gazing out of the window, drawing the village instead, as the bright red post van came and went, then the delivery van arrived at the shop, and the sun nudged the shadow around the maypole like a sundial.

She didn't sketch the people she saw walking around, though she mentally noted them, and the little idiosyncrasies that fixed them in her mind – a wiggle here, a roaming eye there. It was the houses that were more interesting to her, each with their own emerging personality: the terraced cottages huddled together gossiping, the blowsily flower-bedecked pub, the solid church hanging back from the rest, with its modest vicarage curtseying in the grounds.

When it started to get dark, she carried on sketching from memory and was startled to see the sweep of headlights as Mark's car roared up the lane at five thirty, and realised she'd worked all day, almost without noticing.

Hurriedly, she ran down the stairs and put the kettle on the Aga for some tea. Like virtually everyone else in the village, Carrie had fallen for the romance of a non-electric kettle.

'Hi, honey!' she said, winding her arms around his neck as soon as he walked through the door. Until then she hadn't realised how strange it had been, not having him around. 'I missed my gardener.'

'And the gardener missed you.' Mark kissed her back, then started looking through the post. 'What's for supper?' He paused. 'Have you seen this?'

Carrie opened the fridge door and frowned at the random contents within. Eggs, a few rashers of bacon. All local, though, according to Sandra at the shop. 'Seen what?'

'This!' He slipped it under her nose. 'Pub quiz! My idea!'

'Oh, yeah. When is it? Friday night?' She took the eggs out of the fridge. 'We're going, aren't we? Support the village night life?'

'Yeah.' Mark nodded, then ran his hand through his hair. 'Um, actually, while it's in my head, there's a chance I might have to go back to London tomorrow. For a meeting – about doing freelance work out here, actually, with a guy from my old consultancy who's setting up on his own, doing regional stuff,' he expanded quickly, before Carrie had a chance to ask.

'Really? Oh, that's wonderful, honey. Well done.' She got up and hugged him. Now he'd got his momentum going again, there would be no stopping him. 'I guess I can spare you for one day, in that case.'

Mark shuffled slightly beneath her embrace. Carrie had new little muscles from extensive weeding and her hugs were even more intense. 'Hey, it's just a meeting.'

'Every meeting counts.' Carrie held him at arm's length and smiled. 'Anyway, you can get some stuff for me from town.'

'Like what?'

'Oh, I have a list,' said Carrie serenely.

Friday night came round quickly. When Carrie pushed open the door of the Rose and Thorn, she had an odd sense of how it must have looked when the village was bustling: for the first time it was full, with the tables crowded, all the stools occupied, and a queue at the bar. It was even starting to smell more like a pub.

They hovered by the door, scanning the room for familiar faces; there seemed to have been a fresh consignment of retired couples. Carrie guessed that there must have been a local auction recently because a new set of horse brasses and three copper bedpans were now hanging above the bar.

'Blimey,' said Mark. 'It's like the *Antiques Roadshow* in here. In so many ways.' He was in a noticeably cheerful mood since his trip to London, and Carrie had to admit that, much as she was getting into the village way of life, she'd enjoyed the pile of magazines and Japanese noodles that Mark brought back for her. She tried not to think about the end-of-season sales that would now be on all over London.

Before Carrie could warn Mark to lower his voice, she felt herself being stared at with some intensity and unconsciously turned to the source of the attention.

'Hello, hello! You must be Mark and Carrie Armstrong.' The tall, thin woman in an olive-green polo-neck spared them only a brief grimace of welcome over her glasses before ticking them off a list. 'Jolly good. Now then, I'm Barbara Purves from Holly House, down by the war memorial. Do you know it? The big house with the original weathervane and the freshwater well? Lovely. Now, can I stick this on you, so we all know where we are?'

Her high, Scottish voice was as brisk as her actions, and as she spoke she pulled two sticky-backed, star-shaped name badges out of her folder and primed them for action.

'Lovely!' Carrie stumbled a little under the force of the application. 'Now all you need is a quiz sheet . . . and a Biro, which I'll need you to initial for – I'm sorry, but you know how people make off with . . . You've got one? Oh, well done you, Mark! Clearly a man of action! Now, the quiz starts at eight, and we'd like you to get into teams of four minimum, so you've plenty of time to mingle and find some new friends! Pool your knowledge!' She steered them firmly into the bar to make way for new arrivals behind them.

'Hello!' Carrie heard her bellow. 'Is it Don and Tina Somerville?'

'Mingle?' Mark muttered, as they inched a path through toward the bar. 'There's no room in here for mingling.'

'Listen, I'm more bothered about how she knows who we are. I've never seen her before. What else has she got on that list?' Carrie waved at Tony behind the bar. 'What'll you have?' she asked. 'I'll get them in while you find somewhere to sit.'

'A pint of Flower's. Hey, I can see a seat by the fireplace.'

'Well, get it then.' Carrie felt in her pocket for some cash and edged her elbow onto the counter.

'Now then, Carrie,' said Tony, bypassing a couple of male customers with a warm smile of preferential treatment. 'What can I get you?'

'Pint of Flower's and a glass of red wine, please, Tony.'

Judith appeared from the snug and shot Tony an icy glance.

'Busy in here tonight,' said Carrie, making yet another abortive effort to engage Judith in chat. Unlike Tony, Judith wasn't a publican straight from central casting, jewellery aside. Tonight, Judith was bedecked in no fewer than four gold necklaces and from the chin down, she looked every inch the landlady. Her face, on the other hand, looked as if it would rather be almost anywhere else. On a cruise, possibly, or even just in front of *EastEnders*, watching the regulars at the Queen Vic instead of having to attend to the more mundane customers at the Rose and Thorn.

'It is indeed,' sniffed Judith. 'Although it would have been nice to have been consulted on the matter with a little more notice. I myself have no objection to the Rose and Thorn being used as a public meeting place, but it would have been courteous to have informed us in time to increase our brewery order accordingly.' She grabbed two bottles of wine and retreated into the snug.

Carrie raised her eyebrows.

'Paul Jenkins,' muttered Tony. 'Seems to have arranged it all with the Purveses. Didn't mention it to us, just waltzed in and gave us some money to put behind the bar for after the quiz.'

'Really?' said Carrie. 'That was good of him. How much?'

'A hundred quid.'

'Oh.' Carrie did some quick calculations, and came up with about forty pints. Maybe Paul had been counting on everyone drinking tomato juice.

'Don't worry, love,' said Tony, dropping her change into her hand coin by coin until it made up ten pounds, 'I'll give you a sign when I'm about to start serving the free drink so your young man can get himself to the bar.'

Carrie scanned the room for Mark and saw that he'd managed to squeeze onto a table with a young couple they'd bumped into briefly in the pub earlier in the week. Mark was already deep in conversation and from the way the woman's eyes were darting around the room, lingering on certain people, then darting back, it was pretty obvious that between them they were trying to put names to faces. It was all most people did, and had almost stopped being rude.

Feeling you had to get to know everyone immediately was just one more thing about St Dee that was slightly off-key, thought Carrie. Even more so, since everyone was trying so hard to pretend it was normal to act as if they were all playing a non-stop round of party icebreakers.

'Hi!' beamed the blonde woman. Carrie racked her brain to remember what she was called: she'd seen that cheeky grin and inquisitive expression all over the village, but since everyone else seemed to know her, she'd been too shy to ask her name.

'Hello,' she said, putting the drinks down on the table. 'Don't tell me – you live in one of the terraced houses on the way in?'

The woman rolled her eyes and grinned. 'No secrets in this place, are there?' She turned enough to let Carrie see that her name badge read 'Lucy', which jogged her memory helpfully, albeit slightly too late to appear the perfect neighbour.

Lucy; cleaner; married to Chris; no kids; house belonged to Lucy's grandmother 'who was married to the vicar – still alive, more or less – and she knew everyone!' – much like Lucy.

'I feel like I'm on *Mr and Mrs* wearing this thing,' Chris complained, flicking at the yellow star stuck to his shirt pocket.

'You think it's bad now – they're going to put all the name badges in a big hat at the end of the evening . . .' Mark trailed off lasciviously and he winked.

'Mark!' said Carrie.

Lucy giggled. 'I can see you're going to be dreadful. Hello, Carrie,' she said, extending her hand. 'Lucy Ross. This is Chris, who's the specialist thatcher and restoration expert for the village. And my husband, for my sins.'

Carrie smiled. Lucy rattled out the information easily, as if she did it all the time.

'Pleased to meet you,' said Chris. He spoke in a polite but measured way, as if he was ekeing out what little energy he had left at the end of the week. His nose and forehead were reddened from working out in the recent sun and he had the spare, ascetic look of a monk.

'Did you thatch our cottage?' asked Carrie, remembering the thick file of restoration details Paul Jenkins had presented them with. 'I didn't think there was anyone left who did that kind of thing.'

'Ooh, there are quite a few, aren't there, Chris?' said Lucy. 'Still lots of demand round here, specially for experienced craftsmen. And Chris comes from a long line of thatchers – he's very good, aren't you, babe? Proper restoration qualifications and everything. He hasn't had a day off in months, getting this place fitted up. Course he's in charge of the whole lot, but he likes to get in there himself still. Got a team working for him, but when you need to be on top of everything . . .'

Chris rolled his eyes in a long-suffering way and took a long pull on his pint.

'So, are you all settled in now then?' asked Carrie.

'Oooh, yes. Finally! We were living just down the road, anyway, so we've been popping in and out for a while, what with Chris working on the site and all that. How long's it been now, babe? About six months, on and off? Total coincidence, when you think about it, Chris being a restoration specialist and my granny being one of the villagers. Mind, I always knew about this place, because Granny, she was never happy about being kicked out, you know. There's more to it than meets the eye, if you ask me, not that you'll get any change out of Paul Jenkins when it comes to official secrets, if you know what I mean,' she finished up, taking a sip of her drink.

Carrie tried not to gape at Lucy. She didn't seem to have drawn breath once.

'Speak of the devil,' said Mark.

Paul Jenkins was shimmying through the crush with no apparent effort, blending in nicely in his chinos and pale blue shirt. His off-duty clothes were as carefully innocuous as his dark suits.

'Has he just arrived?' asked Mark. 'I didn't see him come in. I've been meaning to find him to ask whether they've managed to get this broadband problem sorted yet. This must be about the only place in the country that can't get it.'

Lucy and Chris exchanged significant looks.

'What?' said Carrie, curious at their reaction.

'Broadband,' sniffed Lucy. 'Well, there hangs a tale.'

'Now, Lucy,' warned Chris.

'I'm just saying,' she replied. 'Just making an observation that it seems very *strange*, in the same way that it seems very *strange* that Mrs Farrer's dogs won't go in certain parts of their garden at night and . . .'

'Give it a rest, Lucy,' said Chris, wearily. 'If this place was as weird as people wanted to make out, we'd all be running round in straitjackets.' He looked at Carrie. 'She thinks Paul's just here to stamp out conspiracy theories, but I know for a fact that . . .'

'UFOs!' Lucy interrupted. 'That's the latest . . .'

'Enough!'

Carrie looked from one to the other, even more curious, but

before she could ask, a high-pitched whistle and a series of short bangs heralded the start of the quiz.

'Here you go,' said a disembodied Scottish male voice, just off microphone. 'If you'd like to introduce me and Barbara . . .

'No, no, I don't need that thing. Good evening, one and all, and on behalf of Judith and myself, a warm welcome to the Rose and Thorn.' Tony's warm baritone voice boomed easily through the pub. 'It's great to see so many of—'

Then his voice vanished, to be replaced by another muted discussion.

Mark raised his eyebrows laconically.

Carrie wished she could see what was going on, but didn't like to appear nosy.

Lucy had no such qualms. 'I wish we'd sat where we could see the bar,' she said, craning her neck to see what was going on. 'Is it that Barbara Purves causing trouble? She's a right bossy cow, if you ask me. Only been here five minutes and she's trying to run everything. And she's not even local! Mind you, I'm surprised Paul Jenkins is letting her take over. Chris, why don't you go and get some drinks in and see what's happening.'

The PA system whined again, clunked, clicked, then screeched.

'Good evening, everyone, and welcome to this evening of enter-tainment, and hopefully merriment.' The smooth, inoffensive tones belonged to Paul Jenkins.

'I might have guessed!' said Lucy, triumphantly. 'Didn't I tell you? No show without fecking Punch!'

'I'm sure you'll join me in thanking Ron and Barbara for organising this get-to-know-you evening on behalf of the village management committee . . .'

'The *what*?' muttered Mark.

'. . . who have generously provided a prize for the winning team, and a free drink at the end of the evening.'

Polite applause.

'Of course, while this evening is intended to be light-hearted, it does have a very serious purpose.' Paul's voice dropped into a Tony Blair-like note of pastoral concern. 'Over the last year, the restoration committee have endeavoured to restore the houses and buildings of St Dee to their former glory, but now our practical job's complete and we're placing the future life of the village very much in your hands. St Dee is a lovely place but it can only thrive if you, the residents, build a new community – if you make these houses into homes, if you like.'

'Is he reading this off a card?' hissed Lucy to Carrie. 'I can't see from here.'

'It certainly sounds like it.'

'Is the restoration committee the same as the village management committee?' whispered Mark.

'Sub-committee,' said Chris without moving his lips.

Paul Jenkins was still talking, smoothly and comfortingly. 'There'll be a more formal meeting in the next week to discuss the formation of various community groups, such as a neighbourhood watch, village council and so on, and to give you an opportunity to meet with the designated local police personnel, but notices about that will be posted in good time, so I hope the maximum number of you will be able to attend.'

Lucy looked at her watch and coughed.

'So without further ado, let me hand you back to our hosts for the evening. Barbara? Ron?'

There was a flurry of static. 'Has everyone got their pens and paper ready?' boomed Ron's voice.

Lucy rolled her eyes. 'Yeah, yeah, yeah.'

'Shh,' said Mark. 'We can win this. Carrie's emptied our local quiz machine twice. She knows all the British *and* French monarchs in order.'

Carrie gave him a warning look, not wanting them to come across as the stereotypical competitive London couple, but by half an hour into the quiz, it was clear that Mark's competitive spirit was matched only by Lucy's determination not to lose to people she considered less worthy.

'We are so not coming after the Hodgsons,' she hissed at one point. 'First thing they did? Got Sky out to put a dish on the house! Would you believe it? Course, Paul Jenkins knocked *that* on the head . . .'

'Too right,' Mark hissed back.

Carrie felt exhausted just listening to them, and let her attention wander to the fresh wreaths of hops that had been put up around the beams. She wondered where they'd been picked.

'And now for the local history round,' announced Ron Purves.

There was a chorus of groans.

'Not fair!' shouted someone near the bar. 'Local advantage!' The voice sounded very Chiswick to Carrie, and for the first time, she was conscious of the division between the newcomers who'd come from away and those who had just moved up the road, back to what was rightfully theirs.

'Bloody Londoners,' muttered Chris savagely, then looked up at Mark and Carrie with embarrassment. 'Sorry. Didn't mean you.'

'Um, we're not really Londoners,' said Carrie, awkwardly. 'I mean, Mark's from Northampton and my mother's American and . . .'

'Take no notice,' said Lucy, patting her hand. 'I should have spotted that little bit of accent, shouldn't I?'

'Oh, I haven't lived there since I was a little girl,' said Carrie. 'It's my mother who—'

'Shh!' said Mark, then added, 'Tell her later,' more kindly.

'Which religious order inhabited the medieval monastery of St Dee?'

Chris stared at Lucy with a blank expression. His pen hovered over the quiz sheet. 'Didn't even know there was a monastery round here.'

He looked up at Carrie, who shook her head.

'Don't think anyone else in here knows, by the sound of it,' said Carrie.

'Put Franciscans,' said Mark.

'It's the only one he's heard of,' Carrie explained.

'Wait.' Lucy's brow was furrowed and she ground her thumbs into her temples as if she could wring the facts out. 'No, hang on, listen, I do bloody know this,' she said. 'We did this at school. It's just inside where the exclusion fence used to run, just a load of old stones. Oh feck, what was it? There was a big scandal.'

The background noise of disgruntled grumbling swelled.

'They were Gilbertians,' said Lucy at last. Her voice dropped to a whisper, in case anyone at the next table was eavesdropping. 'There was some kind of fight out there one night, and the monastery got destroyed. Don't ask me when, but they found headless corpses. Put that,' she added, stabbing at the paper with a stubby finger. 'We might get some extra points.'

'Wow,' said Carrie. 'I had no idea about that. Who would have thought it?'

'Not just a pretty face, me,' said Lucy. 'Am I, Chris?'

'No, love.' Chris pulled at his pint.

'Why is Paul Jenkins looking so narked?' asked Mark. 'Didn't he get all his public information announcement in?'

Carrie craned her neck round to see him. He was clicking a ballpoint pen in and out, and glaring in Ron and Barbara's direction. 'Oh yeah,' she said. 'He is looking a bit perturbed, isn't he?'

'Probably worried about the non-heritage Belgian lager,' said Chris.

'Question the second, in this our local knowledge round,' boomed Ron Purves' voice, 'when was St Dee originally evacuated?'

'1941,' said Carrie and Mark, simultaneously.

'Someone's been doing their homework.' Lucy nodded approvingly, then added, 'That's right, by the way, you can fill that in.'

'And, for an additional bonus point,' continued Ron, 'what was the manor house used for during the Second World War?'

Carrie looked blankly at Lucy and Chris. 'Do you know that?'

Mark grabbed the answer paper and scribbled furiously.

'What?' demanded Carrie. 'What?'

Lucy tipped her head to one side and read upside down what he'd written. 'Ooh, no! Really? I haven't heard that one before.'

Carrie leaned on Mark's shoulder and struggled to make out his scrawl.

'Don't read it aloud,' he warned. 'I bet no one else knows this.'

Mark's handwriting was spidery and randomly capitalised, befitting a man who assumed all non-spoken language came with an automatic spellchecker. 'Manor House was Rumored to have been used as a Secret Headquarters for British and American Intelligence Officers during The War.'

'How did you know that?' demanded Carrie.

'Internet,' said Mark. 'You'd be surprised what comes up when you Google for St Dee.'

'Is it true?' Carrie asked Lucy. 'I heard about the rumours that there were German prisoners held there.'

Lucy raised her eyebrows. 'They say a lot of things about the manor during the war. The *cellars*, especially. Where d'you want me to start?'

'Look at Paul.' Chris nodded towards the bar, where Paul Jenkins was in urgent conference with a cowed Ron and a defensive Barbara. Much of the conversation seemed to be taking place through clenched teeth, although Paul's face was as bland as ever.

Ron picked up the microphone and coughed, sending a quick blast of amplified phlegm around the pub.

'Pipe smoker,' observed Lucy, with a significant nod.

'I've been asked to stress, in relation to Question two B, that this is merely what was rumoured at the time, not necessarily an established fact.' Another phlegmy cough.

An unseen Barbara grabbed the microphone from him and added in her precise manner, 'But the question stands, as it's part of St Dee's rich and varied history.'

'Have they moved back in?' Carrie asked Lucy.

'Who?'

'Whoever was at the manor house. Their descendants, I mean.'

Lucy looked conspiratorial. 'Well. Yes, and no. I mean, they'd have a job moving back into the actual manor house, since it was knocked down years back, but the posh family who used to live there, the Maxwells . . .'

'Shhh,' said Mark, raising a warning finger.

'I'll tell you later,' said Lucy, returning her attention to the competition.

'Question three,' continued Ron, sounding a bit defiant, 'if that's all right with Mr Jenkins – how old is the white horse of St Dee? To the nearest twenty years. Bonus point for the closest estimate.'

'Come on, honey,' Carrie said to Mark, 'this is your specialist subject, isn't it?'

'Ooh, I didn't have you down as one of them archaeology experts. You're a man of hidden depths, I can see, Mark,' said Lucy with a flirty look.

'Most of them beginning with www and ending in com,' said Carrie.

Mark ignored them both. 'I think it's a very early example,' he said with as much dignity as he could muster in a *Magic Roundabout* T-shirt. 'It's probably a pagan fertility symbol. I would put it at about 850 AD.'

Chris drained his pint and set the glass down carefully on the brand new beer mat. 'Well, I don't know about that, mate. Most people round here think it's one of those Victorian follies. 1850 maybe.'

'Carrie, Tony's winking at you,' announced Lucy. 'I think you've scored there, love.'

Carrie looked over to the bar, where Tony was contorting his round face into what he obviously intended to be a discreet wink. In fact he appeared to be having an attack of Bell's palsy.

She winked back exaggeratedly, smudging her mascara in the process, then said, 'No, it just means that the free drinks are about to start. He said he'd give us the nod. What do you want?'

'Free drinks?' said Lucy. 'Oooh, I'll have a vodka and Red Bull, in that case.'

'Mark?'

'Pint of Flower's, please.'

'Chris?'

Chris unfolded himself from the small stool and stood up with a stifled groan. He stretched his arms behind his back until his joints cracked and the buttons on his blue checked shirt pulled at their buttonholes.

Carrie winced. 'Have you thought of taking up yoga?'

He grinned ruefully. 'I'll come with you to the bar. I could do with the stretch. And to be honest, you might as well settle yourself in for a long night. My Lucy won't be leaving till she's won.' He corrected himself. 'Or until she's found out what it was that they had hidden in the manor house. Or even what everyone else thinks they had.'

'I had no idea this evening would be so educational,' said Carrie, as they inched their way through the packed tables.

Chris tapped his nose. 'It's all in what they *don't* tell you, Lucy reckons.'

'Not you as well,' said Carrie. 'And how much of that do you reckon there is?'

His face cracked, unable to maintain the serious expression. 'Ah, who knows? Nothing probably. Got to have something to talk about in the pub, haven't you, though?'

'Just so long as it's not me, I don't mind,' said Carrie, leaning on the bar.

With headless monks, Nazis, Churchill and gassed GIs much further up the list, she guessed it would be a good while before the village gossip got round to her and Mark.

Chapter Five

After several pints and a lot of 'just another half', Carrie and Mark had stumbled home from their first-ever lock-in, conducted once Paul Jenkins' Land Rover had safely driven away from the village.

'I don't mind that we didn't win,' Mark had insisted, tipsily, stumbling a little as they turned out of the lamplight and up the dark path to the cottage, 'it was worth it for the crack.' Carrie had had to agree, and they'd chased each other up the stairs to bed, giggling like teenagers.

Now Carrie didn't know what had woken her from her light sleep: the heavy sound of rain drumming on the roof, or the child crying.

Woozily, she checked the clock by the bed – 3.15 AM. She could hear them both. Hard, heavy raindrops battering and pouring down the gutters outside the window, and right out on the edges of her hearing, a metallic little sob. A child caught between a nightmare and the dark. And it sounded as if it was coming from next door, but not through the brick walls. Her ears strained to place the sound: from next door's garden?

There still wasn't anyone living next door.

Carrie's sleep-heavy arms and legs remained frozen as she struggled to wake up her brain. Had the sobs bled over from a dream, or could she really hear something? She blinked her eyes open, but her lids were sticky, and it was so dark that she could barely see the outlines of the room. Outside, the rain was moving tiny draughts of air through the gaps in the window frames.

Carrie pushed against Mark's body. He slept in a tight knot of bony limbs, his face twisted up in a furious dream.

'Mark,' she whispered, 'can you hear that?'

She whispered more to reassure herself than to disturb him, wanting to hear a real voice so she'd know she wasn't dreaming. Mark slept heavily, falling asleep almost at once, waking up ready to go. Not even nightly police sirens had woken him in London. He didn't respond now.

Again. She heard the child's cry again: a high-pitched protest – of fear? Of pain? Something inside her twisted in response and suddenly she wanted Mark to be awake to tell her she was imagining it all.

'Mark?' Carrie pushed him and carried on pushing him till he stirred.

'What?' he grunted, without opening his eyes.

'A baby.' Life returned to her arms and legs, and swung her feet out of bed, searching on the floor for her slippers. 'I can hear a child crying.'

Mark groaned, muttered something unintelligible, then without opening his eyes said, 'Carrie, you're dreaming.'

'Mark! There *is*. Can't you hear it?' she whispered, straining her ears for the thin note of misery, lifting and falling plaintively. It tugged at her stomach. 'I can definitely hear something.'

Mark cursed, threw his side of the duvet off and rolled over to face her. He looked crumpled. 'Carrie, I promise you, there's nothing there. It's probably a sheep or something. We're in the middle of the countryside. Don't foxes make noises like kids crying?'

'I heard it,' she said obstinately.

She had heard children cry in the night often in London. Either in their block of flats, or, in the summer, when the windows were open in the heat and the sounds carried on the sticky city air, in the estate opposite. It was a noise that seemed to go right through her, upsetting her in a primeval, unnerving way. It made her arms ache to comfort away the distress, and she hated the fact that she couldn't articulate the feeling to Mark without sounding chronically broody.

Mark sighed, rolled over to the other side, and switched on his bedside light.

They both blinked, startled. Outside the rain drummed on the roof, and far away, very faintly, a sheep bleated, making them both jump. In the light, Carrie automatically began to doubt her own hearing. Suddenly, she felt stupid, and sank back down on the bed. 'I'm sure I heard something.'

Mark rubbed his eyes, then pulled his hands down over his stubble, dragging his face into a hangdog frown. He squinted at her patiently while they listened together.

The rain drummed in the trees, pattering directly over their heads on to the tiles, trickling now down the drains and pummelling the ground. The house itself made faint ticking noises as the wood contracted with the new central heating. Otherwise, nothing.

Carrie strained her ears, but the sound had stopped. Mark put his arms round her, pulling her between his legs, and shut his eyes again, preparing for sleep as he cuddled her. 'Honey, there's nothing . . .'

'Mark . . .'

He opened one eye, leaving the other one screwed up tight. 'Look, what if it was a baby? It's quiet round here. There are one or two people who have kids.'

'No, they don't!' she protested, unable to let such an obvious nonsense pass. If he was going to reassure her, Carrie wanted proper reassurance. 'We're just about the only ones here under forty.'

'Someone with visitors? Come on, Carrie. You were dreaming. I mean, it's not the first time you've . . .' His voice trailed off as she glared at him. Weariness swamped his face and he closed the other eye.

'I wasn't imagining it,' said Carrie. She wriggled out of his embrace and rolled over, tucking the duvet round her. Then, fuelled by annoyance and a desire to prove she wasn't being irrational, she got up again and went over to the window, not knowing quite what she expected to see. 'There was something. I definitely heard something, and it was near. It was next door.'

Mark grunted. She ignored him.

Carefully, Carrie unlatched the window and pushed it out, hooking the cast-iron catch in place. The breeze felt cool on her damp skin, and she breathed in a lungful of rain-refreshed air, feeling it sweep down her throat, into her chest.

The jangling of her nerves was giving way to a new dullness that she couldn't put her finger on. It's just the middle of the night, she told herself. Nothing makes sense in the middle of the night.

Mark turned off the bedside light. 'Carrie, why on earth would a child be wandering around outside? It was just a bad dream. Just . . . come back to bed.'

Carrie leaned her forehead against the window frame, and let her eyes sink shut. She didn't know what to say to Mark. He thought she was having her nightmares again: the ones where she was in charge of a baby, in a supermarket, who vanished as her back turned. In her dream, she raced down the aisles, searching in vain for the child – and to make it worse, the child wasn't even hers.

She hadn't dreamed that little voice.

'Come back to bed, Carrie.'

She turned round and could just about make out Mark's arm, thrown out in invitation. He had lean, strong arms, not too muscly but able to tighten around her waist hard enough to take her breath away.

The dullness spread down from her head into her stomach, and she knew the little knot of poison it was leaking from, even if she was doing her best to ignore it during the day. These weren't the sleepless nights she'd imagined she'd be having, not at this stage in her life.

And time was ticking away, with every egg that slipped, wasted, ignored, postponed, from her body each month.

Slowly, she walked back and slid under the sheet. Mark curled himself around her, holding her closely. She could feel him falling asleep even as he hugged her.

They couldn't dance around this conversation for ever. She didn't have for ever.

The bed springs creaked as she shifted against him.

'Can you imagine what our baby would look like?' asked Carrie dreamily. She could see their baby, their child, right in front of her eyes now. It would have her freckles, Mark's crooked smile, his easy way with people. She could imagine painting little pictures with her on that big kitchen table, watching proudly over the little blonde head bent in concentration. Soft, downy hair that caught the light like a halo.

'No, not really.'

Carrie felt his arms twitch. A cold sensation spread along her spine as a breeze found its way through the curtain.

'Can't you?' she asked. 'Why not?' She tried to keep her voice light. The wrong tone, the faintest trace of criticism made Mark close up like a lift door, while his brain and attention moved straight up and away.

'I just can't. I like things the way they are. You and me.'

'But we're happy, aren't we?' Carrie wished her voice didn't sound so panicked.

There was an ominous pause. 'Of course we're happy.' Mark sounded more awake. 'That's why I don't want to spoil things.'

'How could a baby *spoil* things, Mark?'

He sighed, and it sounded like a child's sigh. 'I don't want to be a dad yet. I'm not ready for that responsibility.'

'Is it about money? Because you know I've got a contract now, and we can always save more than . . .'

'It's not just about money, Carrie.'

'Then what?'

Carrie felt Mark's warm breath on her neck again. She waited, making him speak first.

'I just . . . I just don't want to move up to that rung of adulthood yet,' he said eventually. 'I don't feel ready to be a dad. I don't know if I've finished being young yet. Being with you. Enjoying what we have together. It's a big deal. Come on, Carrie, it's late. I don't want to talk about this now.'

It is late, thought Carrie, and it's getting later every day, but she bit her tongue.

'I don't think anyone ever feels ready,' she said. 'And it's not like we're eighteen and just married. Mark, I'm thirty-four. You're thirty-six. Not that it's the same for men, but you know . . .'

Mark went silent. He didn't like being reminded about his age. Carrie felt an obstinate determination to carry on – it wasn't like she could leave the conversation here anyway now. It would come between them for the rest of the night, like a bolster in the bed.

'We do need to talk about this,' she said, unnecessarily.

'We do. Yes. But not now.'

Then *when*, Carrie wanted to say. *When?* But, again, she didn't.

Soon, she would have to say it, though. She knew that. For her it was days, weeks, months left. Not years.

A long silence filled up the air between them, while they listened to the rain outside.

'You know what I like best about this place?' said Mark, unexpectedly.

'What?'

'It gets so dark.'

They lay without speaking, curled round one another. Their duvet was a winter-weight one, bought to counteract the coldness of the stone house, but Carrie's natural body heat in bed, so much warmer than Mark's, acted as a hot water bottle, pushing them apart in the night as Mark searched for cooler spots away from her. A faint breeze moved the net curtains around the bed where Carrie had left the window ajar, but the room was velvet black and as silent as if a blanket had been tucked over the whole house.

Carrie twisted her head round to see Mark's face. She could just make out his long lashes, his pointed nose. 'You like that?'

'Yes. I do.' He pressed his nose into the curve of her neck. 'It's nice. It rests my eyes.'

'You get sore eyes?'

'I do, yes. They get tired.'

She touched his closed eyelids with her lips. 'Poor Mark.'

'Poor Mark, indeed.'

'I love you.'

'I love you too, Carrie. Now go to sleep.'

Carrie snuggled down, pretending to sleep, but it wouldn't come, even when she could hear Mark's deep breaths broaden into slumbering snuffles.

She lay awake and tried to picture their baby. When she did picture it, she was cradling it in her arms. It wasn't crying. It was smiling up at her.

Chapter Six

Since the pub quiz, Lucy Ross had taken to calling in most mornings for a cup of coffee around eleven. From her studio window, Carrie could see Lucy's sturdy figure stomping down the road, regular as clockwork on her rounds of the village. Like the distant church bells striking the hour, and the small blue milk van, she found something comforting in Lucy's routine, and was flattered to be part of it. Lucy didn't stay too long, as she seemed to have built up a full roster of cleaning duties for most of the village, and usually brought her own Hobnobs with her, in her bulging red rucksack full of Mr Sheen and dusters, staying long enough to refresh herself, share and glean some gossip, then depart.

If Mark was 'working from home', he'd slip into his study or go digging in the garden. 'So as not to impede the flow of gossip,' he explained. Not that anything short of a sock stuffed in the mouth would have stopped Lucy.

'Sure you don't want me to sign you up for the weekly wash?' asked Lucy, dunking her first biscuit. 'I've got a space or two left midweek. And you always seem to be ironing.'

'No,' said Carrie. The lavender-scented linen press hadn't become a reality yet, but there definitely wasn't enough spare money around for her to become leisured. 'No, really, I don't mind ironing and most of Mark's clothes are designed to look creased.'

'Still, bear it in mind,' said Lucy, amiably. 'I'd do you a discount. Sixty shirts I did last night watching *Midsomer Murders*. Thank God for that bloody laundry room,' she confided. 'It's the size of our old flat. I could be doing laundry for the whole village if I wanted.'

'Sixty shirts! I mean, I find ironing quite soothing, but . . . sixty?'

'You just need a system. My mum had me doing them since I was ten. Still no one next door?' Lucy nodded her head in the rough direction of Rose Cottage.

'No, I don't think so.' Carrie didn't tell Lucy she'd slipped into the garden several times since her sleepless night, to check for signs of any children playing around there. But the doors were locked, the house was empty, and the long grasses weren't trampled down by any intruders. When she'd woken again the next night, Carrie had told herself it must have been foxes, took two Nytol, shut her eyes and refused to think about it further.

Lucy gave her an inquisitive look. 'Don't think so?'

Carrie corrected herself. 'I mean, no – there's no news. I tried to worm something out of Paul Jenkins when he collared me about parking permits, but he was very tight-lipped. Said the new owner was still arranging their onward move, whatever that means.'

Lucy snorted, and thumbed another biscuit out of the pack. 'Tight-arsed, more like. Sometimes wonder about that one. Who's watching the neighbourhood watch, if you know what I mean.'

Carrie was confused. 'Sorry?'

'Well.' Lucy rolled her eyes. 'You have to wonder, don't you? First all that business about having the right kind of wallpaper, and then the right kind of television aerial, and the right fecking kind of heritage bog roll.' She polished off another biscuit. 'He knows everything about everyone's houses. And everyone in them.'

'You had the security-light lecture too, did you?'

'I did indeed.' Lucy tossed her head. 'Don't know why he was telling *me*. Chris is in charge of the building! I mean, I can't complain, can I, because it keeps our Chris busy night and day, but you've got to wonder, haven't you, with the Ministry of Defence over the hill.' Her eyebrows raised meaningfully.

'I don't follow,' said Carrie.

'Well . . . Why is he still hanging around? He could quite easily leave Chris to get on with it. But no, here he still is . . .'

'You think Paul's keeping an eye on the village because . . .' Carrie faltered, unable to think of a reason. Paul Jenkins, government mole? It was impossible to equate Paul Jenkins with anything more thrilling than tax returns. But she didn't want to offend Lucy by saying so. If anyone was keeping an eye on the village, it was her and Chris. Between roofing and cleaning, they knew the domestic arrangements of virtually everyone in St Dee, even down to their preferred underwear.

'You think there might be . . . I don't know, unexploded bombs or something? Things they don't want to tell us about but don't want us to stumble over at the same time?'

Lucy shrugged. 'I don't know,' she admitted. 'But,' she added brightly, 'isn't that always the way with these conspiracies? You can't even guess what's going on because it's so top secret. Plenty of scope there. I can't believe my granny and her lot never asked. It'd be the first thing I'd want to know – why are you bastards moving me out? Still, different generation, wasn't it? I ask her and she just says, "Eeh, but there was a war on, love!"'

Carrie smiled and poured herself some more tea. 'Lucy, the most dangerous thing going on in St Dee are those hotpots Judith's doing now in the pub. Even Tony won't eat them, he says. Do you know how long they've been married? Forty-two years, apparently. If that's not love, I don't know what is.'

'Don't talk to me about those two. Hope for us yet, if Judith's fancy knickers are anything to go by,' said Lucy. Her lips pursed. 'Anyhoo. Change the subject. How's Mark?'

'Oh, he's OK, thanks. He's in London today, actually, at a meeting.' Another meeting. Mark's 'working from home' time was getting less and less every week. Although Carrie knew it was impossible for him to work from home full-time, and even more impossible for them not to get on each other's nerves even if he could, sometimes the cottage felt quite big and empty without him. Occasionally she found herself walking up to the shop for a packet of biscuits just to get away from the strange silence that stole up on her like a cloud, filling the room around her until she almost felt the house itself was peering over her shoulder.

Lucy pulled a face. 'Missing it, is he? Big city life?'

'Oh no, no. No,' said Carrie quickly. 'He's setting up some contacts so he can work freelance round here. That's the plan. Part of moving out here was because we just weren't getting to spend any time together.'

'Ah, that's sweet,' cooed Lucy.

Carrie smiled. 'It's like being newly-weds all over again. I'm making him a casserole tonight for when he gets in. Learning how to use the Aga, doing up the house . . .' Now she said it aloud, she realised how corny it sounded. 'Like a high-school domestic-science manual, aren't I?'

'No, it's lovely. Pitter-patter of tiny feet next, is it?'

'Um, hopefully,' said Carrie, her smile freezing a little.

'How long you two been married then?'

'Three years in April.'

'Get away! Is that all? No wonder you don't want kids yet. Still in the honeymoon period, eh? Me and Chris, we'll have been together sixteen years in August, married ten.' She beamed. Lucy didn't look as if the honeymoon had yet worn off for her and Chris. 'Childhood sweethearts we were. Just like my mum and dad, and my granny and grandad.'

'We do want to have children at some point.' Carrie wasn't sure why she felt she had to say so, but she did. 'Some point soon.'

'Well, it's a lovely family house.' Lucy looked round her, and Carrie was pleased she'd dusted. The details of her décor would be spread around the village like pollen on a bee, garnished, probably, with her fertility plans.

Lucy's attention abruptly sprang back from Carrie's antique laundry airer. 'Oooh,' she said. 'While I remember, you're going to come to the neighbourhood watch meeting tonight, aren't you?'

'Um, I hadn't decided yet,' admitted Carrie, guiltily. The leaflet she'd taken at the pub now had Judith sketched on the back in goose form and was pinned to her easel. Carrie realised it was much easier to remember names once she'd let her pen decide what kind of animal each villager was.

'Oh, go on. It's not going to take very long.' Lucy looked appealing. 'Me and Chris are going.'

'You're going to be on the neighbourhood watch?'

'Well . . . I thought I ought to. My gran always used to organise stuff like that, being the vicar's wife, said it was what brought a village together – united against a common enemy. Plus, I can't stand the thought of that Barbara Purves running the place and it's the best way to know what's going on,' she added, more realistically.

The phone rang, sounding long peals in the hall where Carrie had installed an old reconditioned model, and digital trills up in the studio where period appearances weren't so important.

'Sorry,' said Carrie. 'It's probably my agent – she said she'd phone this morning. I'm meant to be giving her some final artwork this week.'

'Well, I'll let you get on.' Lucy gathered her stuff together and pulled her thick curls back into a high bunch. With her plump brown arms above her head and her jumble of butterscotch and toffee highlights streaking her hair, Lucy reminded Carrie of a large tabby cat. Sleek, and perfectly at ease with herself.

All the same, Carrie was glad she was on the right side of that tongue.

'Let me know if you hear anything about next door moving in,' Lucy added, with a nod towards Rose Cottage. 'You get the phone. I'll see you there tonight. Half seven.'

'I'll try to make it,' promised Carrie as Lucy let herself out of the front door. She waved goodbye and picked up the receiver. The cream Bakelite felt pleasantly cool and solid against her cheekbone.

All the better to pretend to be the model housewife with.

Actually, she hoped it wasn't Gina. Technically, she was within sight of the finishing line with the Morris book, but things had slowed down dramatically since she'd started playing around with a new book idea that had begun to take shape in her imagination – the gradual reawakening of St Dee after the people had gone, as the wild animals from the forests and hedgerows around the valley had crept into the abandoned houses and taken over their way of life, unobserved by any human eye.

It made good use of her sketching too: a couple of afternoons she'd sat in the corner of the pub, making detailed studies of the polished wooden bar, where Judith, the honking, preening goose, served pints to thirsty worker ducks. And now she could add Lucy the tabby cat, slinking around the deserted village, on the prowl for gossip . . .

'Hey.' It was Mark.

Carrie's attention snapped back at once. 'Hi, honey!' she said.

'How's the mouse?'

Carrie twisted the cord around her fingers. 'Coming along,' she lied. 'How's London?'

'Same as it was when we left it.' A police car went past, sirens blaring, and Mark had to shout above what sounded like the evangelist preacher man at Victoria station.

'Do you know what time you'll be back?' she asked. 'I just thought I'd make a big casserole now I've finally worked out how to use that Aga. I really feel like winter food! You know,' she added, turning to the wall and dropping her voice seductively, 'I don't mind you going away for the day, because it means I can look forward to you coming home again!'

There was a slight pause at the other end. 'Um, well, actually, I don't know when I'll be leaving yet,' said Mark. 'A couple of things have come up since I got here . . .' The line broke up, or something got in the way, Carrie couldn't tell. Mark suddenly seemed very far away. His voice sounded weird, more London. More tense.

She stared out of the window, deflated. 'Really?'

'Well, now I'm here it seems stupid not to see as many people as I can. And I got a call from Sean – my old boss? – about meeting up for a drink after work, and you know how many people he knows. Be rude not to. Carrie? Carrie, are you still there?'

There was a pause, in which she could hear the birds singing outside in the fruit trees.

'I'm still here,' she said.

It was hard to imagine being in the middle of all that noise and bustle, somehow. She turned to the window and spotted Lucy's tortoiseshell head bobbing along over the top of the wild hedge. Her imagination turned to Chris. What would he be? An owl? The owl and the pussycat? Something more ascetic-looking?

'So I'll be back late,' Mark was saying. 'Don't bother making me any supper – I'll get my own in town.'

You can't be jealous of a city, she told herself. Don't be ridiculous. 'Listen. It's a casserole, hon,' she said. 'It's meant to keep for hours. That's what Agas are for, drying out food for husbands getting in late from the fields.'

'I don't want you to go to any bother . . .'

'It's not. Honestly.' She shook herself. 'Listen, Mark, I nearly forgot,' she said quickly before he hung up, 'I said we'd go along to the neighbourhood watch meeting tonight. You remember? We talked about it in the pub. You thought you might volunteer. Are you going to get back in time, or shall I just see you at the pub? Lucy says it's at seven thirty.'

'Oh, yeah.' She knew he was pretending. It hadn't even registered on the jumbled pinboard that was his brain. 'I probably won't be back in time for that, sorry. Can't you just go and tell me what happens later?'

'Well, I'd rather you came with me.' Outside, Lucy was waving to the postman, then engaging him in an animated conversation, involving much waving and pointing. At one point she grabbed him by the arm, but the postman didn't seem to mind. He was laughing too. Lucy was like that. She seemed to spread good humour, like measles. Carrie wished she had that sort of ease around people.

'Carrie, I'll come with you next time, sweetheart. Go without me, you'll be fine! Tell me what happens when I get back.'

I don't want to go on my own, thought Carrie, and had an unexpected panic that this is what it would be like from now on – her in the village, Mark in London.

'I think it's the sort of thing we ought to do together,' she heard herself say.

Mark laughed. 'What? Like the Purveses? In matching cardies?'

'No.' She tried to laugh too, but couldn't. 'I don't want them to think we're part-time Londoners. We've got to make an effort to settle in now, because before you know it, people'll have made up their minds, and it's impossible to do anything about it after that.' She pulled a face. 'I know. I've been new in enough places. And I really want us to fit in here, Mark.'

Mark's tone changed, as another police car zoomed past. 'Oh, come on. I went to the pub quiz, didn't I?'

'Well, yeah, but . . .'

'Don't be like that.'

'Like what?'

Stop it, Carrie, she warned herself. This is how petty arguments start.

'Huffy. You sound like that huffy woman from the pub. What's she called? Brenda?'

'Judith. Keep up at the back. These people are our new friends.' She was only half-joking too.

Mark chuckled. 'Yeah, Judith, right. Look, what can I bring you back from the big city?'

Sushi. Belgian pralines. Paints. Pristine paintbrushes. Soft bagels from Brick Lane. Paper rolls of flowers from New Covent Garden

Market. Fresh spices – crimson, scarlet, ochre, gold – from Brick Lane.

You to be here when you say you will.

Carrie swallowed and made her voice level so he wouldn't hear any of that.

'A mouse cage,' she said.

'A what?'

'A cage. For a mouse. From the cellar. I need a proper mouse to draw. I think that's where I'm going wrong with Morris, why it's not working. I need to catch a mouse too, so if you could get one of those humane mousetraps that would be good.'

'Why don't you just go down there and get one?'

Carrie paused. 'Because the cellar gives me the creeps. And so does the idea of catching a mouse,' she admitted. 'OK, OK, go on, laugh.'

There was a definite giggle on the end of the phone, then Mark sounded amused. 'OK. If that's what you want.'

'I'm pretty easy to please, Mark,' said Carrie, and wished she could make her voice as light and ironic as his.

'That's what husbands are for,' said Mark, 'rescuing their wives from mice. See you later, sweetheart.' And he hung up.

Carrie put down the phone, and tried not to be annoyed that Mark was already leaving the boring stuff up to her.

It's not boring, she told herself, collecting the used coffee mugs from the pine table. It'll be fascinating.

She put the mugs in the stone sink and ran the hot tap, but then something caught her ear – a clicking noise. Carrie jerked her head up to see where it was coming from. Somewhere in the kitchen . . .

Her gaze roamed around the dark Welsh dresser of china, the rocking chair in the corner, the Aga – no, nothing was caught or moving – the pine table with the post still on it, her coat hanging up by the door, the clock . . .

Carrie took a step nearer. The clock – an old farmhouse one she'd bought in an auction – wasn't ticking properly. It was ticking as though something was caught inside. And the hands had stopped at – Carrie frowned – half past two. She checked her watch. It was only ten to twelve. How had that happened? It had been telling the right time when Mark had left.

Carefully she opened the glass face and stopped the little pendulum inside. As soon as she did, the clicking stopped. The kitchen suddenly felt very still. Carrie realised she was holding her breath, but she wound the hands round to the right time, set the pendulum ticking again and carefully closed the face.

Paul Jenkins had admired that clock. 'Very period,' he'd said approvingly. It looked right in the kitchen, along with the rocking chair and the simple plates. Not a TV-set kitchen, but one that Lily herself might recognise.

Suddenly Carrie was filled with the irrational sensation that if she turned round she'd see the rocking chair rocking.

The thought almost made her laugh out of nerves. 'Not enough fresh air,' she said aloud, then let herself out of the back door. She strode down the garden, past her half-dug flowerbeds, and onto the path that led up the hill towards the chalk horse, relishing the burning sensation in her calves and thighs as she pushed herself harder. Her breath came quicker and rougher in her throat and she used the rhythm of her own heartbeat to force herself on. It was a while since she'd felt her muscles protest – since she'd sacrificed her gym membership renewal for a council tax bill, in fact.

At the top of the hill, Carrie sank down on to the grass and lay on her back as she'd done on holiday as a child, while her pulse slowed and her anger seeped out of her and into the ground. It was chilly still, but the wintry sun was bright and it warmed her face. Carrie let her eyes close, and blue and yellow light danced across her lids, in rhythm with the blood banging in her ears. When she felt calmer, she opened them again and saw the fraying clouds drifting slowly across the china-blue sky like sailing boats, and she felt her body sinking gratefully into the earth with a sense of total surrender she'd never achieved at yoga.

Across the valley, the church bells in Deeting Magna struck twelve and she counted each chime. For how many hundreds of years had they made that exact noise at that exact time? There was something comforting about that thought, but also kind of unsettling: it made absolutely no difference that she was there to hear it.

Carrie sat up and looked down the valley at St Dee, at her new house and its identical twin, and wondered if Lily had climbed up here much. Had she climbed up here with her schoolfriends? Or with serious, tweedy Jack? Had she brought her baby up here, Mark's father, to lie on the grass for a moment's peace and quiet? Or had there been no peace and quiet? Was that what had turned her so sour, like a pail of thick cream gone off – the baby?

I don't know, she thought, with a heavy pang of regret. And I won't ever know. I *can't* know now.

Is that why I'm feeling so frustrated with Mark? she wondered. Because living in the house hasn't suddenly opened a treasure trove of family secrets? Did I imagine it would?

Carrie rolled the thought around in her mind, trying to catch her instinctive responses, the true ones, before her eagerness to please adapted them. Yes, she acknowledged. I wanted to be the one to present Mark with his lost family. And in the end, it's just a house, with us in it.

She sat up. Was that a bad thing or not?

Her first response slipped away from her before she had time to catch it and see.

Since she'd more or less hit her lunch break, Carrie walked back down the hill and around the green to the village shop to pick up some more milk and bread. Before she walked down the path, she could tell by the warm, yeasty smell that they'd just taken out the batch of par-baked French loaves, which apparently sold out within half an hour of being on the shelves. The modern version of the bakery Lucy informed her had been three doors down from the pub – a floury photograph of which hung in the ladies' loo of the Rose and Thorn.

She bought a baguette and a tin of tuna and read the notices pinned neatly on the board by the door. Lucy's laundry and cleaning services took pride of place, but others were jostling for space beneath: excess furniture for sale, red-felt-tipped reminders about signing up for the neighbourhood watch meeting that evening, someone wanting a car share for the school run into Deeting Magna.

Oh good, she thought, with some relief. I'm not going mad – there are some kids here, after all.

Mark was missing out, she thought. He was never going to settle in if he didn't start taking a real interest in his neighbours. Well, a more proactive interest than just gossiping about them when they were in the pub.

'You'll be signing up for that, will you, Carrie?' asked Sandra meaningfully when she took her items to the till. 'Neighbourhood watch. We need some big strong men like your husband on board.'

'Er, well . . .'

Sandra was looking at her expectantly. She was a few years older than Carrie, highlighted and lowlighted, with a 'Mum' pendant hanging over the crewneck of her T-shirt. If local knowledge was power, Sandra was clearly up there competing with Lucy for prime position.

'I don't think Mark would be much use.' Carrie tried a smile. 'He's had his phone stolen eight times in London and he's hopeless when it comes to confrontation. He just hands it over.'

'Really? Eight times? I'd have thought with those fancy trainers he'd be able to run fast enough to catch Linford Christie.'

Carrie's smile faltered for a second. How much Sandra did know about her and Mark in comparison to what she knew about her? When had they noticed Mark's trainers? When they were discussing what a big, strong man he was? And what did she mean by 'they'?

'Are you going to join?' Sandra enquired.

Carrie tried to read Sandra's face but it wasn't giving much away. She'd met hundreds of girls like her at the diplomatic schools where she'd had her nomadic education. They'd all been true children of diplomats – no overtures of friendship until they knew what you had to offer. 'The neighbourhood watch?'

'Well, yes.'

'I guess so,' she heard herself saying. 'I'm going to the meeting tonight.'

Sandra seemed to melt visibly at that. 'Good. We had you down as one of them townie couples who'd be here for weekends and away the rest of the time.'

'Oh no,' Carrie assured her, conscious that everyone seemed to have her and Mark down as fair-weather residents. 'No, I work from home, I'm an artist. In fact, I do a fair bit of neighbourhood watching already, you know, from my studio? I can see right over the fields one way, and almost to the village green.'

Oh God, why did I say that, Carrie thought in despair. I sound like a real nosy old biddy.

'You can?' Sandra's hands paused on the till. 'Ooh, that's interesting. Because you're a bit away from the main village out there, aren't you? Still, maybe you can tell us about your new neighbour.'

Carrie sensed at once that perhaps she'd gone too far. And, anyway – 'us'? 'My new neighbour?'

'Yes, the writer bloke.'

'He's moved in?'

'You didn't know?' Sandra affected massive surprise. 'No, you've got some egghead moving in next to you. Any time now, apparently. From somewhere up north. Did no one tell you?'

Carrie didn't ask how Sandra knew, or who was on this information-distributing power panel. If Lucy didn't know, she couldn't believe it was common knowledge. Instead, Carrie just said, 'Well, I've been pretty busy recently,' and tried not to let her curiosity show on her face.

She'd got used to them having that lane to themselves. It was almost like a private drive, set off from the rest of the village. How thin would the walls be? How much of their lives would they be forced to overhear?

How much of *their own* lives, more to the point, would be overheard?

'Anyway, I'll put you down for the neighbourhood watch, shall I?' Sandra retrieved a notebook from beneath the counter. 'Carrie Armstrong, Oak Cottage. Very good.' Sandra clicked her Biro. 'Look forward to seeing you tonight. See what you can do about persuading that nice strong husband of yours.'

Carrie assumed she must have looked askance, because Sandra leaned forward and added, 'He *is* your husband, isn't he? Don't want to assume anything – I know you do things differently in London.'

'No,' she said firmly. 'He is definitely my husband.'

Sandra made a face that clearly said, 'Lucky you', and Carrie smiled.

I am lucky, she told herself. Don't you forget it.

Chapter Seven

Carrie wasn't entirely sure what to expect from the neighbourhood watch meeting. There was something faintly worrying about the fact that the locals already felt the need to take up arms against crime in a village when they'd barely had time to move in, let alone get lax about allowing youths to burgle their sheds. It certainly didn't fit in with her vision of peaceful rural life.

Besides, what youths? thought Carrie as she picked her way self-consciously across the green towards the pub, wrapped up against the cold in her duffle coat. If anything, the new inhabitants of St Dee were more at risk from silver-haired con-men diddling them out of pension money for non-existent cruises than from the sort of ugly urban crime wave she'd learned to ignore in London.

Next door to the post office, in the gentle yellow glow of a reproduction gas-light lamp post, a middle-aged couple were unpacking a large supermarket shop from the boot of their Rover. They watched her walking around the green, but not in an unfriendly way. Carrie raised her hand in greeting. They smiled and waved back.

'Good evening!' they called.

'Good evening!' replied Carrie.

A pleasant warm feeling washed over her, dispelling any misgivings she had about the meeting. This was what English village life was meant to be like, hailing your neighbours and making them feel like you were interested, but not interfering. Mark just didn't realise you had to work at fitting in, even if it was only by being there.

She hesitated shyly at the door of the pub, overcome for a moment with nerves at going in without Mark's easy banter by her side, then took a deep breath and pushed it open.

Inside, an overriding smell of Pledge indicated that Lucy had given the place a thorough going-over before the meeting. A big-band CD was playing in the background – Tony was into his big bands – giving the place a curiously nostalgic feel. It wasn't busy, maybe seven or eight drinkers in, and the neighbourhood watchers were easy to spot, sitting around a table in the small snug, with pads and pens in front of them, and an overflowing bowl of assorted nuts in the middle and a collection of empty glasses.

They looked up expectantly when she came in, and Lucy Ross waved her over before anyone else could. Carrie felt an unfamiliar glow of belonging as a middle-aged couple she hadn't seen before gave her a nervous once-over.

There was also Sandra from the shop, Chris Ross, looking exhausted as usual, a grey-haired couple she hadn't met, another older woman on her own, and Barbara and Ron Purves, the pub-quiz organisers. Next to them was a young-ish man in a navy fleece, who seemed distinctly uncomfortable. He had off-duty policeman written all over him, underlined by the official folder of documents he was leafing through, seemingly for protection from the accusing stares around the table.

'Carrie!' cried Lucy before Sandra could open her mouth. 'Do you want a drink? Let me get it.' And she stood up and edged her way past the Purveses and hustled Carrie to the bar.

The conversation restarted at once behind them, carrying through the empty pub, easily cutting through the faint sounds of 'Moonlight

Serenade'. 'So you're saying that these window locks are not one hundred per cent safe?' demanded Barbara Purves.

'Well, nothing in this life is ever *one hundred* per cent safe,' replied the policeman wearily.

'Dear God,' said Lucy once they were safely out of earshot. 'Am I glad to see you. Hello, Tony. A vodka Red Bull for me and . . . what'll you have, Carrie?'

'A, um, orange juice.'

Lucy rolled her eyes. 'You'll need more than that, let me tell you. Stick a shot of vodka in there for her, will you, Tony? Cheers.'

Carrie thought about protesting that she rarely drank in the evenings, but then decided Lucy was right: Dutch courage was probably needed. She was embarrassed to admit it, even to herself, but working alone all day, relying on the occasional phone call, or, back in London, email, had left her quite nervous about talking to people she didn't know. Especially a group like this lot, who remembered everything.

'Have you been here long?' she asked, as Lucy paid from a thick roll of notes.

'Long enough. There's a right power struggle going on between that Sandra from the shop and Barbara. Sandra's losing. You wouldn't believe how bossy some folk are. We've been here about half an hour. We're waiting for Paul Jenkins to shimmer in. If he doesn't get a move on, PC Plod'll have to leave.'

'The light was still on in the site office,' Carrie ventured. 'I'd have thought he'd have had plenty to say about keeping security in line with rural heritage principles. Laying authentic mantraps, and installing stocks, ducking stools for bad wives, that sort of thing.'

Lucy snorted with laughter, and Carrie felt ridiculously pleased.

'Suggest it to him when he comes,' she said, nudging Carrie back to the table. 'I could give you a list of candidates right now, starting with that old trout Barbara. God almighty. If we've heard about the council refusing her permission to build her fecking conservatory once . . .'

Her expression sweetened up as they approached the table. 'Does everyone know Carrie? Carrie Armstrong?'

Sandra nodded, as did Barbara and Ron Purves, but the older couple shook their heads.

'Ted and Maria Barrow,' said the man, holding out a hand. 'Four, Church Lane. With the roses.'

Carrie shook it, then his wife's. 'Hello, I live in Oak Cottage,' she said, and they both made 'ooh, lovely' faces in response.

Carrie looked over to the lady on her own. She flashed a brief, wry smile that indicated that she felt just as awkward as Carrie did.

'I'm Kathleen Maxwell.' She held out her hand formally, and at an ambiguous angle that suggested that she was as used to having it kissed as shaken. Carrie shook it. 'I grew up in the manor.'

Kathleen had cool, soft skin and two beautiful emerald rings on her right hand. She spoke in a low, melodious way, as if she'd spent her career being listened to without needing to raise her voice once. A solicitor, maybe, or a doctor, Carrie guessed. Something respectable. Well, if she'd come from the famous manor family, then she had to be well-to-do.

The manor that had been knocked down, of course, secrets and all. How sad, Carrie thought, to be the only one who could come back, and yet without a house to come back to.

'Lovely to meet you,' she said, and was about to ask where she was living now, but Kathleen Maxwell had already turned expectantly to the policeman. Out of the corner of her eye, she caught Sandra pulling a lemon face at Lucy, who returned it.

'Is this everyone?' asked the policeman anxiously when they squeezed themselves back into the snug. 'Because I really have to go quite soon.'

'This is the core volunteer group, yes,' said Ron Purves, firmly. 'We'll just have to start without Paul.'

'Well, then.' The policeman coughed. 'For those that don't know me, I'm Sergeant Andy Wilson, and it's great that St Dee wants to start a neighbourhood watch scheme . . .'

'Just as well, I'd say, given we're not to have our own police officer,' snapped Barbara Purves.

'We're a very stretched rural force,' said Andy Wilson, with the air of a man who had made the point at least once already. 'And with the limited numbers of villagers you have here in St Dee, I don't really feel that you're going to be . . .'

'How long would it take a police car to reach us?' she demanded. 'Or a fire engine? There's just that one single-track road through this place, and if we were flooded, or if there were some tragedy . . .'

'Now then, Barbara, there's no need to be the voice of doom,' said Ron, patting her hand. 'I'm sure if we all keep an eye out for one another, it should be fine.'

'That's what they said in Soham,' she replied darkly.

Lucy leaned towards Carrie on the pretext of getting something out of her bag and murmured, 'Ducking stool,' under her breath.

'It's happened before in this valley,' Barbara went on, undeterred. 'I've read about floodings in the past. I read that the water table is unusually high . . .'

'We can certainly talk about emergency first responder training, if you like. But our crime rates are really very low,' said Andy Wilson. 'Honestly. We're quite a peaceful area.'

Barbara didn't look convinced. 'That's not what I've heard.'

He glanced appealingly at Lucy. 'I'm sure people who've moved from other local towns will back me up here.'

'I've heard of worse places,' agreed Lucy, reluctantly. 'Mind, it's sometimes the quiet types you have to worry about, isn't it?'

'I know lots of you will have come in from towns,' Sergeant Wilson went on, more determinedly, 'but you'll probably find that being a little . . . isolated will act as a deterrent to criminals. You'll know who's coming in and out of the village . . .'

'And anyone who wants to nick stuff will have to make a special journey in,' Sandra finished for him. 'We're an out-of-town burgling centre.'

'Yes,' he said, wrestling down a grin. 'Exactly that. Thanks.'

Carrie looked from Lucy to Sandra to the policeman to Barbara Purves and felt a tremor of trepidation. 'But if there was a blizzard,' she began, 'or a flood or something . . .'

'We'd check the weather forecast and stock up,' said Lucy.

Barbara Purves, too, was looking less than convinced. 'I already have,' she said.

'Let me give you some leaflets, anyway,' said Andy Wilson, with a discreet glance at his watch. 'You need to discuss your charter and decide who's going to be in charge of what . . .'

Sandra, Lucy and Barbara immediately opened their mouths at the same time to volunteer, and when Carrie looked away to stop herself smiling, she caught Kathleen Maxwell's eye.

Kathleen raised one wry eyebrow, which was enough.

When the policeman left after forty-five minutes of intense discussion about rotas and window locks, Chris went to the bar for more drinks, dragging Lucy with him. Sandra turned to Barbara Purves and demanded to know where she'd got her new kitchen from and if she'd had any trouble with her oil central heating.

The elderly couple began a whispered conversation that was obviously meant for their ears only.

Carrie felt awkwardness settle on her again. She wasn't that great at small talk at the best of times – Mark tended to do most of the talking – but while she was as curious as anyone else about her new neighbours, she had a morbid fear of coming across as nosy.

But as she squirmed, trying desperately to come up with some non-nosy question about thatching, Kathleen Maxwell turned to her with a garden-party smile.

'Are you settled in now?' she asked. 'Um, is it Carrie? My memory isn't what it was. All these introductions all the time.'

'Yes, Carrie. I'm worse,' she said, relieved to be rescued. 'I don't know how Lucy does it. She knows everyone.'

'Oh, but she sees the inside of their houses, and it's much easier to remember who's who when you're thinking of them and their life-size jade hearth dogs.' Kathleen smiled knowingly, and Carrie wasn't quite sure how she was meant to respond. 'Still, it's a necessary evil, isn't it? Getting to know everyone. It reminds me of those first days of term at boarding school. Everyone being extraordinarily nice, until they've worked out what the pecking order is. Then we can all go back to being ourselves.'

She said all this, Carrie noted, with the air of someone already pretty confident of where her place in that pecking order would be.

'You know, that's just what I was feeling,' she said. 'My father was in the diplomatic service and I had to start over so many times, in so many schools, all over the place. Still, I suppose it's the same for everyone, all beginning afresh in a new place.'

'Well, not quite.' Kathleen sipped her drink. 'I'm afraid I've got a bit of a head start on you, in that respect. I'm one of the originals. I was born here. And of course, I am a Maxwell,' she added, as if that would explain everything. 'Our family lived here for centuries. I was only a young girl, of course, when the village was evacuated, but I still have a few vivid memories of the place.' She smiled sadly. 'In many ways, they've managed to restore it so well that I've looked out of my window a few times and given myself quite a jolt.'

'How fascinating!' Carrie was now conscious of sounding 'extraordinarily nice'. 'I mean that,' she added, awkwardly. 'It must be rather different for you, than for the rest of us.'

Kathleen tipped her head graciously. 'I suppose it must be. I believe I'm the only surviving villager who's taken up residence.'

'Really?' A little flame of excitement flickered in Carrie's stomach. Kathleen would remember Lily and Jack – but she shied away from coming straight out and probing for information. 'So what memories do you have of the village as it was?' she asked instead.

'Oh . . . goodness. I can remember the harvest festival the year before we left, and I have a strong recollection of the heavy horses the farmers kept for ploughing, and being allowed to ride on their backs as a very special treat. Red ribbons in their manes, chalk on their feathers – massive creatures, but so gentle.' She smiled wistfully.

'I can remember the blacksmith shoeing my pony in the forge, and the horse-and-cart man next door. And we had a May Day celebration every year, with a May Queen and a Jack-of-the-Green, and my parents would hold a huge house party at the manor, with all sorts of friends coming up from London for dancing and shooting and that type of thing. In many ways, it was still quite an old-fashioned place, even just before the war. We were so isolated, you see. Kept to ourselves.'

It wasn't really any less isolated now, thought Carrie, not really. 'St Dee is already how I imagined an English village would be,' she said. 'It's just so beautiful, and peaceful. I used to love reading about villages like this when I was growing up – we travelled a lot,' she explained. 'My dad always promised he'd try to get posted back to England, but he never did. And this is just the picturebook village idyll,' she added, wistfully. 'Protected from all the nastiness of the outside world.'

'Quite right,' beamed Miss Maxwell. 'And I've been longing to come back all my life.'

Before Carrie could ask anything else, Lucy's hand suddenly clapped her on her shoulder. 'Got you another vodka orange,' she said. 'And a bitter lemon for you, Miss Maxwell, is that right?'

'How kind of you,' said Miss Maxwell, with a social smile. 'And how clever to remember. You must have some kind of notebook with all our details in.'

'I do not!' Lucy protested.

Carrie caught Miss Maxwell's mischievous wink, and felt a moment's guilt for betraying her friend by enjoying it.

'Nah, all up there,' said Chris, tapping Lucy's freckly forehead with a stubby finger. 'Lots of room for it.'

Lucy swatted his hand away with pretend annoyance, and Chris caught her fingers, twisting them playfully up to his mouth, where he kissed them as she tried to wriggle away.

'Of course. I was joking,' said Miss Maxwell, smoothly. She turned back to Carrie, as if anxious to continue a conversation Lucy had interrupted. 'Did I hear Lucy say you're living up by the haunted house?'

Carrie's eyes widened. 'Excuse me?'

'Rose Cottage? We used to call it the haunted house. Oh my dear, don't look so horrified!' Kathleen put a hand on Carrie's arm. 'It was just one of those silly village ghost stories!'

'We live next door,' Carrie stammered. 'In Oak Cottage. There's no one . . .'

'What's that?' demanded Barbara Purves, abandoning her conservatory woes in midstream and swivelling her head – very like a heron, Carrie noted automatically. 'Rose Cottage? Haunted?'

Kathleen Maxwell now had the attention of the whole snug. It didn't seem to bother her. 'Oh, heavens above, I wouldn't like to put it down as gospel in the village guide,' she laughed. 'But there were always lots of stories in the village about that well next door, and children falling down it. I imagine it was just a cautionary tale to stop us poking our noses in, but it certainly worked. My sisters and I were simply petrified of it.'

'What was the story?' demanded Lucy.

Miss Maxwell looked amused. 'Really?'

'Yes,' insisted Lucy. 'If there's some kind of spooky goings-on, we ought to know. Carrie definitely ought to know.'

Carrie managed a nod, though her skin had gone goose-pimply. Just as she'd got herself convinced that it was foxes or someone else's kids, too.

It still probably is, she told herself, firmly.

Miss Maxwell took another sip of her bitter lemon and cleared her throat. 'Oh, well, there was some village gossip about the well in the garden. That it was an ancient one, full of bad luck, and that in medieval times the monks had put some miscreant down the well as a punishment, and they'd died down there. We were always being told as children that if we went too near the edge, a skeletal arm would reach up and drag us down. You know what people say to children to scare them into behaving! But the story that we always used to tell

was that two children did fall in, around the turn of the century –
before I was born, I might add!'

Barbara Purves made a sycophantic demurring noise.

'Really?' asked Carrie in a small voice.

Kathleen shot her a quick glance and went on, 'Well, as I
understood it, they were brother and sister. They went off to play on
their own while the adults were celebrating the May Day festival on
the green, and the little girl fell in, looking for the mysterious hand.
Then the brother fell in after her, trying to help her out. She broke her
neck straight away, poor little thing, and the brother was very badly
hurt – the doctor was delivering a baby in Deeting, and couldn't get
back in time. Terribly sad. At Halloween we used to scare each other
silly, trying to listen out for them crying in the night to be rescued!'

The goose pimples ran up Carrie's arm and along her neck, and
she shuddered.

Sandra shuddered too. 'Ooh, I'll be having nightmares now.'

'It's a picturesque story,' said Barbara Purves, smiling at Miss
Maxwell, then turning her focus sharply back to the agenda. 'But if
there are wells extant in the gardens then that's another issue we
should add to the neighbourhood watch remit. We don't want our
dogs getting stuck down there.' She sniffed. 'Not if it's going to take
three hours to get a fire engine out to an emergency like that.'

'And did *you* ever hear the cries?' asked Carrie.

Miss Maxwell shook her head. 'No, no. But my sister claimed she
did. But then she always was rather melodramatic!'

'Why?' demanded Lucy, shrewdly turning to Carrie. 'Have you
heard something?'

Now all the eyes were on her, and for a second, she contemplated
telling them she had, rocketing herself to the top of the village must-
talk-to list.

'No,' she said. 'No, I don't think so.'

'You don't *think* so?' cried Lucy. 'You mean you *have* heard
something?'

'It's all children's stories,' said Kathleen Maxwell firmly. 'Just to stop us tampering with things we shouldn't. Besides, isn't someone moving in there soon?'

Barbara nodded. 'Oh yes. I've heard that.'

'In the next few days,' offered Sandra. 'He's a writer.'

'From Newcastle,' finished Lucy triumphantly.

'Lucy!' snapped Chris.

'Oh, come on,' she sighed. 'There have to be some perks to you working with Paul.'

'Well, then, he won't want to arrive to a village buzzing with silly rumours about his house, will he?'

'Speak of the devil,' said Carrie, as Paul strode into the bar, clutching his leather portfolio case, his eyes taking in everything, including Tony's discreet new loudspeakers, partially concealed behind bunches of hops.

'Have I missed anything?' he asked.

'No,' chorused Lucy and Sandra, and Carrie got a sudden sense of the community closing around information and keeping it for themselves. And she was in on it.

It was a curiously satisfying feeling.

'Sure you won't stay for another?' wheedled Lucy, as Carrie finally got up to leave.

'Lucy, you can pour vodka and orange down my neck all you like,' protested Carrie, laughing, 'but there's nothing I can tell you, about either the ghosts in the well or the man in the house!' She zipped up her jacket. 'Besides, I have a husband to feed.'

Lucy turned to Chris. 'Well, huh. No point staying here, is there?'

Chris looked relieved. 'Let's make a move, Luce. I've got work in the morning.'

'Do you want us to walk you back?' asked Lucy, as the three of them left the pub, flinching slightly in the cold night air. 'That's a creepy old lane you live down.'

'God, no, I'll be fine. Has Barbara Purves and her one-woman out-of-town-crime-wave fears started to get to you?'

'Eff off,' said Lucy, nudging her playfully. 'I thought Mark was meant to be coming along tonight. Didn't he get back in time from . . . wherever he was working?'

Carrie spotted the disguised nosiness and tried to brush it off lightly, even though now Lucy mentioned it, she was freshly annoyed. 'No. He texted me again to say he'd be too late. London's like that – you can't really say how long it takes to get home.'

'London? What's he want to be going back there for?' asked Chris.

'You tell me,' Carrie said with a shrug. When Lucy seemed concerned, she added, 'Business, actually. Someone he used to work with needs an IT specialist for a start-up company.'

'I see.' Lucy gave her an inscrutable look.

Why am I so worried about what Lucy thinks? Carrie wondered. It's perfectly normal for Mark to be commuting. Half the village probably are, one way or another.

'No, no, it's fair enough,' said Chris, slinging an arm round his wife's shoulder. 'Not up to us to judge. Man has to find work where he can.'

'Can't he work from home, though?' demanded Lucy. 'He wants to get onto Paul Jenkins again, find out why they still haven't got that, what do you call it, broadband sorted out . . .'

'That's enough, Luce,' said Chris abruptly. 'I need my supper.'

Lucy glared at him but didn't add anything. 'You're sure you don't want walking up the lane?'

Carrie shook her head. 'I'll be fine. I've got my little torch.'

'Rather you than me. All those trees – ugh!' She shuddered. 'Well, then. Night, love,' Lucy said, touching Carrie's arm in farewell.

Carrie secretly liked the way no one here seemed to go in for goodbye kisses; it was a feature of her London life that made her uncomfortable. Jealous of her own space, she hated the feeling of invasion, and the awkwardness that bloomed between her and the well-meaning social kisser when her discomfort showed.

'Night.' She raised her hand in a goodbye to Chris, who smiled briefly before steering Lucy down the other side of the green, towards their cottage.

It had gone nine, but the night was clear, showing bright pinpricks of stars in the velvety dark sky, and as Carrie walked slowly back up the track, using her torch to guide her the last unlit metres, her nose was filled with the sharp, fresh scent of the hedgerows and the coldness of the air.

It was the quiet that was so unnerving, she thought, listening to the sound of her own trainers scrunching on the loose pebbles as she passed the stile that led up to the dark and forbidding woods. Unnerving and soothing at the same time. Any movements would be easy to make out, but her ears swivelled like a cat's whenever an owl hooted or a twig snapped.

Carrie realised she was partially listening out for the eerie faint sobbing, despite the fact that hearing anything would have made her stop breathing with panic. It was hard to stop herself listening as she fell asleep each night, extending the strange time she spent in half-sleep when her roving imagination could have turned any barn owl into a child trapped in a slimy prison.

A sudden gust of wind shook the hawthorn bushes down the lane, as though a giant hand had trailed casually past her. Her heart jumped in her chest and she increased her pace, suddenly needing to be in her own warm house.

Carrie made a conscious effort not to look for Mark's car until she was right outside the house. If he was already back, that would be great. If he wasn't, she wouldn't make a fuss.

If he wasn't, she would switch on the radio and possibly the television too, and not even think about the well in next-door's garden. Or all the children in the village who'd grown up having nightmares about it.

As she hurried towards her gate, Carrie's eyes were drawn to the dark façade of Rose Cottage, even as she willed herself not to look for fear of what she might see. Only the moon was reflected in the windows, moving slowly as the clouds parted and shifted around it, but the effect was sinister. The lights were on in her own house, meaning Mark was back, but Rose Cottage's blank windows seemed dead in comparison. Inside it would be full of dust settling on the new floorboards, she thought with a shudder, and fresh cobwebs stretching again over the beams. Were there any spirits waiting to be let back into Rose Cottage? Or had they already slipped back in to inspect their old house brought back to life, their ghostly hands sliding up the banisters, drifting soundlessly along the landing, only a thin wall away from her own?

While her eyes were trained on the windows, something in her peripheral vision moved and Carrie let out a muffled yelp of fear. Her hands went to her mouth of their own accord and she could feel the blood banging in her neck.

The rustling continued, surging nearer and nearer through the garden towards the path, and she was about to scream when she saw two shining eyes emerge from the thick hedge.

It was an old fox, with white flecks dappling its muzzle, but in the bleaching moonlight, its red coat seemed grey, like one of the old photographs in the pub. The Deeting Hunt, stiff-backed riders, scruffy foot hunters, bloodied hounds, gathering in front of the pub at the end of the day.

Carrie and the black-and-white fox stared at each other for several seconds that hung in the air for an eternity, then it streaked away down the path, slipping soundlessly through the hedge, up the path to its forest den.

Carrie quickened her pace up the path, her heart racing.

'Hi, honey!' she called as she pushed open the front door. Mark was watching television and drinking beer straight from the bottle, his feet up on the old trunk she was using as a coffee table. Several crisp packets and an empty cereal bowl suggested that he'd been there a while, but she barely registered annoyance in her relief to be back inside.

'Well, hello! So, where've you been?' he asked, throwing out his arm in invitation for her to sink into the sofa next to him.

Carrie wriggled in next to him. 'Neighbourhood watch meeting. In the pub. Remember?'

'Sorry.' Mark didn't look that sorry. 'By the time I got in and had a beer, and put my feet up . . . Anyway, what did you discuss? Who's going to patrol the place with torches? Who's going to be in charge of the newsletter? Who'll decide who goes in the stocks?'

'We're still debating between stocks and a ducking stool, since you ask. Sandra's putting a voting form up in the shop. Text DUCK for the stool, and STOCK for the stocks.'

'I can't *stand* things like that,' said Mark. 'All that judging and nosing.'

'Mark, we live in a village now,' said Carrie. 'One day in London and suddenly you're Mr Clerkenwell again!' Only a few weeks ago, he'd been digging over their borders and talking about planting rose bushes like a real country gardener. 'I want to be part of it. It means looking out for each other. Joining in. I mean, I know you've got a short attention span and all, but we have to make the effort.'

'Carrie, give me a break – neighbourhood watch is just an excuse for nosiness. No, don't tell me, I bet I can guess who was there – Lucy Ross, and that odd couple from the pub quiz, the Purveses? And that blonde woman from the shop, the one who looked at me like she expected me to ask for ciabatta and hummus when I went in for some milk? Yeah? Am I right?'

'Well, yes, they were there,' Carrie admitted, 'but there were a couple of other . . .'

'See?' Mark looked pleased with himself. 'Now do you want to be labelled a nosy parker as well, hmm?'

'Don't be so chippy!' Carrie tried not to let her irritation show through. 'What's the point of coming here to be part of a community if we're going to stand on the outside laughing at them?'

'I didn't think we *did* come here to be "part of a community".' Mark's voice was amused, but slightly distant. 'I thought we came here to live in a free house while you finished off your book and we decided what we were going to do next. How is my friend Morris coming on, by the way?' he asked, taking another Pringle from the tube between his knees. 'Haven't you nearly finished now?'

Carrie felt the chilly finger of guilt slide down her back. Mark was so good at distraction techniques to divert rows. The book. It was scary how quickly that initial burst of activity had slowed down in favour of nosing about the village. The book, like London, suddenly seemed part of another life.

'It's coming on,' she said. 'It isn't just a case of sitting up there and banging it out, you know. I need . . . time. To think about . . . context.'

'You need to get it in by the end of the month,' said Mark. 'Or else we're in serious trouble with the car payments, free house or not. Here, let me pour you a glass of wine.' He got up and started searching for the corkscrew. 'I got some of that Chablis you like – picked up a couple of cases from Majestic on my way back. Is this about me going back to London for the day?'

He turned, wine bottle in one hand, wine glasses in the other, and Carrie was startled by how different Mark looked in his work clothes, after getting used to his scruffy gardening jeans and jumpers. One day in London seemed to have freshened him up; his face was bright, and his hair, she noticed now, had been cut into newer, sharper spikes.

He looked revitalised. Fresh. And she felt dull in comparison.

'Because you seem to be in a really weird mood tonight,' he went on.

'I am not! No, no, it's not. Of course not,' she stammered. 'You're the one who's being weird.'

'So we're both being weird – fair enough.' He turned back to the counter and poured the wine. 'Listen, it's not that I don't want to be here,' he said, filling her glass. 'But I might have to go back to London more regularly, if this project gets off the ground. It takes a little while to wind down, change pace, you know? Don't you think I'd rather be here, spending time with you?'

He didn't seem that unhappy. In fact, Carrie thought she could detect a note of jubilation in his voice.

'I thought you'd be glad of the peace and quiet,' Mark went on, taking her silence as mute opposition. 'You were always saying how

I disturbed your train of thought. Well, now you've got all day to yourself. Plus, I get to come back to you at the end of the day! Everyone's a winner! Here you go.' He handed her the wine. 'Cheers!'

'And you can't do it from home?' she said. 'You still can't work online?'

Mark shook his head. 'No, honey, I told you. Not until they get broadband rolled out this far. Something to do with the Army on the plain, I guess.'

Carrie took a sip of her wine and turned to look out of the window. The stars were still sharp in the sky, and the moon reflected off the broad white back of the chalk horse.

It should have been a romantic evening for walking up the hill to the chalk horse, she thought. We should be running through the overgrown grass in our orchard, or smelling the night-scented stock at the end of the garden. Enjoying this place the same way Lily and Jack would have done. We ought to be looking for the simple things that would make our lives touch theirs.

Like putting a new baby in the old nursery.

Carrie paused. That part of the story still didn't fit properly in her mind. Such a young girl falling pregnant – and to a man supposed to be in a position of responsibility. Hadn't there been disapproval, a scandal as there would be now? Or were things different then? What if it *had* been a love-match? Carrie weighed it up. How could anyone ever tell now?

She took another sip of her wine, thoughtfully.

'You've gone very quiet,' said Mark. 'What are you thinking about?'

'Lily,' she said. 'Do you think she was happy here?'

Mark pretended to consult a crystal ball. 'Yes. Apart from in May 1940, when she left her red bloomers in the whites wash, and then again for most of 1941, when she was evicted.'

Carrie didn't let herself be put off by his flippant tone. Just because it didn't interest him, didn't mean that she couldn't be curious. If they had kids of their own, then Lily's genes and traits would run in their veins.

She gazed out of the deep-set windows, into the silky darkness outside. For every unanswerable question that popped into her mind, another two came trailing on behind it, like streamers. What had home births been like then? Which room *had* Lily chosen for the nursery? Had Mark's father been born here, in the bedroom upstairs? How soon would it be before she could decorate a room herself? She already knew the murals she wanted to paint on the white walls of the spare room: dancing mice and a maypole like the one on the green . . .

'Anything for supper?' Mark was rooting through the fridge.

'The casserole,' said Carrie automatically. 'It's in the Aga, keeping warm.'

'Lovely,' said Mark, rubbing his hands. 'Carrie, you are the perfect wife.'

Carrie went up to bed early, and lay in the deep roll-top bath for half an hour still thinking about Lily.

This had been one of the few houses in the village to have a bath. Carrie's imagination lingered on that idea. What privacy would Lily have had? How often would she have had time to wallow in warm water the way Carrie did? Would Jack have bathed in front of her, the way Mark often slipped into the shower with her? The photograph was so formal, she couldn't imagine buttoned-up Jack unbending sufficiently to scrub his young wife's back.

But then if she was a pregnant seventeen-year-old bride, he must have been unbuttoned at some point.

Where, she wondered? At the school? In the woods? In the hayricks?

Carrie sighed, frustrated, swishing her fingers through the bubbles. If only there were old love letters she could read, or a diary to fill in the blanks. She wanted to know more than the nervous couple in Mark's photograph were letting show. If they'd wanted to keep their secrets from their family, they'd succeeded, and the only person who could really tell her any faded shreds of gossip was Kathleen Maxwell.

I'll go to see her, decided Carrie. It's what you do in the countryside, isn't it? Call on your neighbours and chat over a cup of tea?

She got out of the bath, her skin steaming in the cold bathroom, and wrapped herself in a thick towel. Downstairs, Mark was playing some driving game on his Playstation and she could hear the keening noise of high-speed braking. As she dried herself off, one ear was cocked for other, more human keening noises coming from next door, but there was nothing, other than the rustling of wind through the hedges.

Three times she'd heard something now, but nothing for three days.

Carrie stood in front of the large bathroom mirror and pulled her hair back off her face. She leaned nearer to the mirror and examined her face. There was an angry red stress spot beginning on her chin. Carrie didn't often get real spots, but no matter how hard she tried to swallow stress away, it emerged on her milk-pale skin.

Carefully she scooped a pea-sized blob of cleanser out of the jar, and massaged it between her palms until it warmed and liquefied, slipping and releasing herby oils into her hands.

How can it be that the house is so exactly as I'd imagined it, exactly as I'd hoped for, and yet I still feel there's something missing? she wondered, stroking her face with rhythmic, massaging movements.

It's not the house.

It's the life you thought would come with it.

Carrie started at the clarity of this thought, which just seemed to pop into her head, as if someone had dropped it in.

But it was true; the house itself was perfect. It had fulfilled its brief. Now it was her and Mark who weren't falling into line.

Mark can't keep living his single-bloke life out here, she thought, automatically picking up her packet of contraceptive pills and squeezing out the next one. We've moved on, haven't we? On to the next phase of our lives.

For a second she looked at the tiny dot of orange on her fingertip, holding a million possibilities in one tiny pill. More momentous than any of the drugs she hadn't taken in her desperately conforming youth.

How many more months did she have left to put off making a decision? And the decision that didn't automatically lead to what she wanted anyway. The chances, Carrie knew, were dropping every month, as her odds of having a baby rose dramatically, like an ageing horse in the Grand National. Mark 'didn't want to talk about it yet', but soon there'd be more to talk about than just leaving things up to nature.

Was it greedy to want more than the funny, sexy, loving man she already had? Was it wilfully stupid to risk losing him – for the sake of some strange urge?

She stared at the pill on her finger, thinking about the times she'd panicked in her twenties about bouts of sickness or antibiotics sabotaging her life in a sideways trip. It didn't take much to throw hormones into confusion. One 'missed' pill might be enough – not such a huge transgression.

Should I?

Shouldn't I?

Carrie held her breath, teetering on the edge of a different life.

Surely it was the *idea*, the *decision*, that Mark found hard. Not the reality.

But it would be irresponsible. Babies had to be a joint decision, a blessing, not used as emotional handcuffs.

Carrie put her fingertip to her lips and swallowed the pill.

Half an hour later, Mark came to bed, and curled himself around her already warm body, tucking his nose into her soft neck.

'Not asleep yet?' he murmured.

'I was dozing.' Even though she didn't want to hear anything, her ears couldn't help pricking at the slightest rustle in the trees outside. There had been little yelps and her skin had crawled, but nothing that sounded human. Nothing yet.

Mark shifted next to her. 'Stop listening,' he said, as if he could read her mind. 'It's just the countryside. It makes these noises. You never used to get freaked out by the sirens and people fighting in London. That was *real*.'

Carrie rolled over. 'Well, *actually*, this might be real. I was talking to Miss Maxwell at the neighbourhood watch meeting – you know, from the manor house? – and she says that other people used to hear crying next door. She said her sister heard something when they were little girls, before the village was evacuated. Crying. Like I did.'

'Oh, Carrie,' said Mark, 'she's just winding you up. Giving the place some local flavour.' He nipped her ear playfully. 'What's a village without a ghost story, eh? Paul Jenkins has probably got a whole file of them he's planting.'

'No, honestly.' Carrie felt properly awake now, and she propped herself up on her elbow. 'Apparently the well next door was always supposed to be sinister in some way, then two kids fell down it one summer – a little girl broke her neck, and her brother was so badly injured that he died not long after. Miss Maxwell said people used to hear them crying for help. And I didn't know that, did I? But I still heard it coming from that particular place.'

Mark laughed. 'Carrie, that's exactly the kind of thing parents tell kids to scare them out of doing naughty things. Total bollocks. There's enough ... *theorising* going on already without you getting sucked into it.' He gave her a firm look. 'We're meant to be the cynical voice of urban reason, remember?'

She fell back on the pillow, turning herself away from him so he could curl his wiry arms and legs round her. 'OK. Maybe. She said she'd never heard it herself. But don't you *like* living in a place with ghost stories? Isn't it better than living in some soulless converted warehouse?'

'Perfectly hauntable, warehouses, I think you'll find.'

Carrie thought of the stiff photograph of Miss Maxwell's former staff, arranged on the lawn in front of the rusty-ivy-covered façade. The house was gone. They were gone. And yet their presence still lingered in the village. 'I thought I'd pop round and have a proper chat. It must be really weird for her, coming back. I wonder if she remembers much about Jack and Lily? It would be so fascinating to talk to her about them.'

Behind her, she felt Mark's body tense and he didn't reply at once. The wind picked up outside, rustling stealthily through the hedgerows.

'Mark?' Carrie didn't look round. 'You wouldn't mind?'

'Would it stop you if I did?'

'Well, of course, it would. But . . .'

Mark let out a long breath against the back of her neck. 'I don't like ghosts. They don't exist. I only believe in things I can see.' He tightened his arms around her. 'And that's you and me. OK?'

'OK,' said Carrie. 'OK.'

As Mark started to fall asleep, she listened to his breathing deepen and felt his body turn heavy and slump against hers. The house ticked and sighed, as if in its own sleep, and gradually Carrie herself slipped into a fitful unconsciousness.

Chapter Eight

Though she'd tried to ignore it for as long as she could, Carrie had forced herself to come to a worrying conclusion, in so far as her relationship with Morris was concerned: she was freaked out by real mice.

In response to her noble intentions to get a proper life model for Morris, Mark had somehow acquired an elaborate cage that looked like a mad Victorian birdcage: the white-painted iron bars had finials and looped details, and it came equipped with a mouse wheel, and the right sort of bedding and everything. It had been staring her in the face for days, majestically uninhabited, reminding her that the next step was to get down to the chilly cellar and find a volunteer.

Carrie put off the dreaded moment of checking the humane mousetrap for as long as she could. In any case, the more she settled into the daily routines of St Dee, the more she wanted to draw her other book, in which the animals moved around the village, settling in just as the humans were doing now, with exactly the same expressions of curiosity and excitement on their beady-eyed faces.

She felt a strange reluctance to open her Morris sketches, much less start poking around the dark and musty corners of the cellar.

'Are you ever going to use that cage?' Mark demanded one morning over breakfast. He now took clear-tasting tea and crispy Aga toast for granted with a speed that Carrie found astonishing. Free-range eggs, local bacon, fresh milk – he consumed it all as casually as he used to swill back his espresso.

She looked defensive and stopped doodling on her sketchbook. 'Yes. I just need a mouse.'

'Well, I put the trap down in the cellar last week. You should have at least one by now.' Mark made little clawing gestures with his hands. 'Maybe more than one, squashed in the box, desperate to get out.' He wriggled his nose, showing his small white teeth, and Carrie shuddered.

'Was there nothing there when you put the washer on?' she asked squeamishly, topping up her tea.

Mark's sole contribution to household chores was to load and unload the washing machine, giving Carrie an excellent reason to avoid the cellar as much as possible.

'Nope. You want me to go down there for you?'

She nodded.

'And I thought you were meant to be the country girl these days.' He folded his over-buttered toast in two and squashed it in his mouth, pushing his chair away from the table at the same time. 'I'll have a look. You go and get the cage, I'll go and get you a model, then I really have to make a move. What's that?'

He peered over her shoulder at her sketchbook, open at a picture of a tabby cat chatting flirtatiously with a jolly pig in a navy blazer.

'Oh, just . . . doodles.'

'You never stop, do you?' Mark looked closer and giggled. 'Is that Lucy?' he asked. 'Talking to Tony from the pub?'

Carrie nodded, and felt her mouth twitch into a smile. Mark was turning the pages, trying to see what else she'd done, smiling each time in recognition.

'You know, that's absolutely perfect,' he said. 'God, you're clever. You've got Tony's eyes just right.' He dropped a kiss on her head. 'Have you drawn me yet? Or don't I want to see it?'

Carrie hadn't drawn Mark. She hadn't drawn either of them, and suddenly she wasn't sure what animals they'd even be.

'This a new book?' he asked.

'It's nothing, really,' she said, modestly.

'It's definitely not nothing,' he replied. 'But I wouldn't let Lucy see it, if I were you.'

'Where are you going today?' Carrie tried to keep her voice casual, but she'd seen the laptop bag appear by the door, and realised with a pang of disappointment that her plans for a day's companionable gardening weren't going to happen. Again.

'Swindon. Firm of accountants need their software spring-cleaning. Mate of Sean's put me onto it. What about you? Work? Or more gossiping over the garden fence with the Mothers' Union of Ghost Hunters?'

'Don't be mean.' Carrie flashed him a look from under her eyelashes. 'If you're going to mock, I won't tell you about the man who's moving in next door. He's a writer.'

'You'd better warn him about his ghosts,' said Mark, swilling down his toast with the remaining tea. 'Now,' he scrabbled with his fingers, 'Morris!'

Carrie waved at the door until Mark's car vanished beyond the end of the high hedges. Discreetly, in case anyone was watching, she peered over the fence into Rose Cottage, but there was still no sign of any new neighbours.

It would be nice to have someone working next door, Carrie thought, especially if Mark was going to be out most days. She couldn't keep popping to the village shop every time she needed a break, to hear someone else's voice and to get away from the silence of the house.

She made herself a cup of peppermint tea and climbed the stairs to her studio, her bare feet making little noise on the treads. The warmth of the central heating spread through the wooden floor-boards, and she felt sorry for Lily, thinking how cold it must have been out here in the middle of winter, with no warm bath and only a stone hot water bottle for her bed.

She'd have had Jack to keep her warm, though, Carrie thought, trying to picture them in bed together. Since her imagination was all she had to go on, she worked it as hard as she could. The framed photographs of Lily and Jack were kept in her study where Mark wouldn't notice, their shapes now completely familiar to her eye, but with only those stiff images to go on, it was hard to imagine Jack without his teaching jacket on, much less naked.

Carrie paused on the landing, one hand on the glossily var-nished banister. Sometimes, as she climbed the stairs, she glanced quickly into their bedroom, in the hope that a shadow might be left in the air, the shape of Lily leaning over to tuck in the sheets as she made the bed. It felt, in the morning stillness of the house, as if the two of them were going about their daily routines in the same house, one overlaid on the other. The odd draught or unexpected creak seemed to Carrie like Lily trying to make her own presence felt across the expanse of time that separated them, but the more she looked, the more empty the rooms seemed.

There was nothing in there now. Just a broad band of brisk sunshine falling on the cloud-like whiteness of their duvet.

Carrie wished there was some way Lily could speak to her, then immediately wished it away again, unsure how she'd cope if she did.

Mark had borne the cage upstairs triumphantly, and Carrie could tell from the scuttling therein that he'd found a model. When she peered through the fancy bars now, she could see it was asleep, half-buried under a pile of straw with its long hairless tail snaking out.

'Wake up, Morris,' said Carrie, masking her revulsion with an unconvincing display of matiness. She was slightly revolted at her own squeamishness itself. 'Showtime.'

Morris stirred at the sound of her voice and scuttled cravenly further beneath the bedding.

I need to look at it more closely to get a better idea, she thought. I need to pick him up.

Her flesh crawled at the idea.

Don't be so silly, she told herself. The sooner you get this done, the sooner you can let it go.

Tempted by the food, the mouse emerged and began to nibble at the oats. Carrie tried to see it as Morris the tiny computer whizz. It was no use. The tiny sharp teeth and weirdly pink nose still looked horribly real. And not a pretty shell-pink, either. Fleshy pink. The pink of tender, inner skin. Too naked. Too vulnerable. The blood so close to the surface.

Before she could think herself out of it, Carrie reached into the cage, picked up the mouse by its tail and dropped it into the wheel, where it began spinning angrily, tiny claws clicking on the plastic. The idea of all the specks of dust and dirt and germs and filth that would be clinging to its fur made her bile rise.

She shook her hands in the air, all the nerves jangling down into the tips of her fingers, as if any germs would fly off.

How easy it would be to tip the mouse into the garden, buy a book about mice and draw Morris from there . . .

'No,' she said aloud. 'No, you're going to do this.'

Her hands trembled as she scrubbed them over and over again with a wet wipe from the packet she kept by her easel.

It was just a case of adjusting. Of seeing things more objectively.

The mouse stopped spinning in the wheel and twitched its nose at her.

Carrie stared back at it, fascinated and horrified at the same time. There were hundreds of these things, running around in the cellar, in the basements of all the houses in the village, in their attics, in the fields, in the gardens. Hundreds. Thousands. And how many more had there been before, when the place had gone wild? How many mouse families had lived in this house, popping out litters of tiny mice every few months?

Carrie began to sketch, though her skin didn't stop crawling.

At eleven o'clock, Carrie heard Lucy's voice in the lane in front of the house, and looked out of the window to see what was happening.

Lucy, dressed for warmer-weather cleaning in a tight vest top and velour sweatpants that somehow made her look like Jennifer Lopez, was standing with her hands on her hips, talking in an animated fashion to Barbara Purves. Barbara was clutching a clipboard protectively to her chest and a large peaked cap shielded her face from view, but Carrie could guess from the body language alone what sort of expression she was sporting.

They were talking so loud Carrie could make out fragments of speech through the open window.

'. . . ask Carrie! She was there . . .'

'. . . she in now? Maybe we should ask her . . .'

'. . . assume you know exactly what should be done just because . . .'

'. . . fair-minded . . . opinion . . .'

Carrie hurriedly leaned back, on the off-chance that one of them might look up and spot her.

Despite, or maybe because of, her feelings towards her model, she had sketched feverishly all morning, covering large sheets of paper with families of dancing, scampering mice, carrying their worldly belongings in tied-up handkerchiefs and moving into Oak Cottage with glee, sliding around the abandoned plates like mini ice-rinks, and chasing each other up the banisters.

They weren't the right sketches for her Morris book, however, as a faint reproachful voice in her head pointed out.

Even though it was Lucy's usual time for dropping in, and a valid time for a break, the last thing Carrie fancied now was to be drawn into some agenda-constructing argument between Lucy and Barbara.

On the other hand, it would be really rude to pretend to be out when Lucy rang the doorbell. Lucy wasn't averse to trying the front and back doors to check.

Best to be out for real, she decided.

Carefully, Carrie withdrew from the window. This was a good time to have a closer look at the chalk horse. Grabbing her sketchbook, she slipped quietly down the stairs and out of the back door, locking it behind her.

It was a good, chest-burning walk up the hill, but the view over the village was worth it. Carrie had thought, originally, that she'd make herself walk up to the top once a day, as a country substitute for her miles on the treadmill in London, but she and Mark had only climbed up to the chalk horse once since they'd been here.

And how long ago was that now? She calculated, powering up the hill. A month? Four weeks on Wednesday? It felt like she'd been in St Dee for ever.

As she climbed higher, the outline of the horse spread into great areas of white chalk, losing its definition until the only sign that it was meant to be an animal came from the glittering eye, composed of upended bottles, greeny-yellow with age, and packed too tight to prise out. Winded, Carrie sank down nearby, and stretched out on the grass.

The horse lay close to a thick wood of dark trees. Carrie hadn't been close enough to it to find out what sort they were, and she didn't want to. It looked like the sort of forest you could get lost in. While she liked taming the wildness of her own little garden, and planting new things, there was something odd about the sheer density of the trees, even now when nearly everything else was bare of leaves, something that reminded her of a Grimm's fairy-tale forest: spiked branches that would pluck at your clothes, and roots that would reach out to trip you. From a distance, the horse seemed to be galloping out of them, at very high speed.

She took out her sketchbook from her bag and began to draw, but after a while, as usual, her attention wandered back to Lily. Without thinking, she began to draw her in class, in her long pinafore, reading to the smaller children. Carrie didn't like to think of the sad, dried-up Lily. It was nicer to think of her before she was uprooted, when the village was still as blooming as she was.

The school hall where Jack had taught was visible from the hill. Carrie had walked round it a couple of times, touching the rough brickwork in a vain attempt to pick up faint vibrations of something, but she hadn't liked to peer into the windows, as it was now inhabited by two somewhat unfriendly couples. The large, high-ceilinged space had been converted into two self-contained apartments; according to Paul Jenkins, the architects had agonised over how to position the new floor that split the long windows, and had tried to keep the small fireplaces and the panels where bored pupils had carved their initials.

The direct sun was warmer than Carrie had anticipated and she felt her eyelids begin to droop. Quite often she woke up tired, as if she hadn't slept properly.

She put down her pencils and rubbed her eyes. I'll have a quick nap, she thought, covering her face with her arm. Five minutes, then I'll get back for lunch . . .

The church bells in Deeting Magna striking one o'clock woke her, and with a start, Carrie sat up, blinking and disorientated.

Fragments of some strong sensation still flickered around the edges of her consciousness – had she been dreaming about the wood? Being in the wood?

She looked over and shivered instinctively at the unmoving trees. It was enough to give anyone the creeps. Pulling herself to her feet, Carrie stuffed everything back in her bag and made her way more quickly than normal back down the hill to her house.

There was only a rickety fence separating the gardens of Rose Cottage and Oak Cottage, and out of habit, she glanced over it to see if there was any sign of life next door.

To Carrie's surprise, there was.

She blinked at the unexpected vision presented to her: two small children were sitting silently on the wrought-iron bench, a girl of about five or six and a little boy, perhaps a year or two younger, both slightly built and milky-pale. So pale that the sun seemed to wash straight through them, turning their fine, coppery hair into a glowing halo of curls around their heads. A huge ginger cat sat on guard next to them, by contrast, as solid as an old fairing pottery figure with round yellow eyes that looked straight at her.

Carrie's skin tingled with goosebumps. Were these the ghostly children she'd heard crying in the night?

They were engrossed in some game they were playing between them on the bench, their foreheads almost touching in concentration, but either they were whispering or not talking at all, because Carrie couldn't hear a sound, even though her ears were straining to catch some indication, any indication, that they were human flesh.

Her eyes skated feverishly over the scene, searching for something real, something reassuringly modern. The little girl was wearing a pale green sundress, and the boy was in shorts and some kind of cotton top, but she couldn't tell whether they were real old-fashioned clothes, or just the new middle-class versions, for parents who wanted their kids to look like kids.

They're just Boden, she told herself, those posh Boden summer clothes; but the children were so quiet, and so other-worldly, that cold shivers were tickling the back of her neck.

Then, to her horror, the little boy seemed to catch sight of her.

Carrie stopped breathing, as he lifted his eyes from the game, and fixed them on hers. They were pale blue, and so bright she could distinguish their colour even at a distance. He nudged his sister, who looked first at him, then at Carrie. Her eyes were blue, too, but her expression was more wary and guarded.

Neither spoke.

Carrie swallowed, her throat suddenly parched dry.

'Hello,' said the little boy, and his voice broke through the atmosphere.

Carrie's pent-up breath rushed out in a gust.

His sister nudged him hard, and glared, then whispered something crossly in his ear.

'Hello,' said Carrie, and smiled in what she hoped was a reassuring way. 'My name's Carrie. I'm your next-door neighbour.' She pointed to her own house. 'What are your names?' she asked when they didn't reply.

There was a pause in which they looked at each other, their eyes communicating silent concerns about whether or not to talk to strangers, then at last the girl said, 'I'm Betsy. And he's Ivor.'

Her voice was quiet, but confident for a little girl. Carrie couldn't place the accent: the words were beautifully articulated, with the lightest trace of an accent behind them. It wasn't all-purpose southern, like Mark's, but neither was it the up-and-down northern accent she knew from soap operas. Carrie's experience of English accents was restricted to the bland received pronunciation of the nomadic diplomatic kids – everyone she'd known in London had seemed to go to great pains to hide any traces of where they'd come from.

Carrie tried a reassuring smile, but got nothing in response. 'Did you come here this morning?' she asked. 'I didn't hear you arrive.'

No reply. Betsy's lower lip jutted as she struggled between talking to a stranger and ignoring a grown-up.

Oh dear, thought Carrie. Is this not how you're meant to talk to kids? 'Have you been here long?' she tried. 'Would you like to come in for a cup of tea and a biscuit? With your mummy, of course.'

Ivor's face crumpled and he hid it in Betsy's shoulder. She put a brave arm around him and glared at Carrie. 'We don't have a mummy any more,' she said. 'And we don't take food from strangers.'

Carrie flinched in embarrassment. 'Oh, my goodness. I'm so sorry. I, um . . .'

'Ivor! Betsy! Where've you got to?' A very real man's voice yelled through from the kitchen, and this time Carrie knew where the accent was from: it was north-eastern, a dark, undulating Geordie. 'Did I not tell you to stay put and not wander off?'

'Da!' yelled Ivor, and scrambled off the bench and ran inside.

Betsy gave Carrie a long, searching look, then slid off the bench and followed him. Her shoes made no sound on the stone path.

Carrie remained frozen to the spot. Again, this wasn't how it was meant to go. In her ideal village fantasy life, she was meant to fling open the doors of neighbourly hospitality and have the whole new family eating homemade shortbread around her kitchen table before the first crate was unpacked. Instead of that, she'd managed to upset the kids, who were probably in tears with their father right now, telling him about the nosy woman next door.

Oh, God.

Much as Carrie wanted to slink away, she knew she had to meet the father now, and see if she could make social amends somehow. And so she walked self-consciously to the end of her garden, out through the gate, and hauled up the rusty latch on the gate of Oak Cottage.

How was I meant to know? she thought, picking her way down the overgrown path.

As she passed the bench she saw what the kids had been looking at. A fawn-skinned mouse. Its eyes were closed peacefully, but Carrie could tell it was definitely dead.

It was very similar to the one she'd just been sketching. She felt a shiver of revulsion crawl over her skin, but then told herself to get over this squeamishness.

The back door had been left ajar and she could hear a conversation rising and falling into the kitchen. Carrie hovered by the bench, ears straining to pick up the words from the torrent of childish complaint.

'No, you were quite right,' the man's voice was saying. He didn't sound cross, but the way he spoke was quite abrupt, which only increased Carrie's shyness. 'I did say you shouldn't talk to people you don't know. But sometimes it's nice to be friendly, Betsy.'

'But what if the cakes were poisoned?' demanded the girl's voice, quick and persistent like a miniature barrister. 'What if she offered us poisoned cakes and we didn't know they were poisoned?'

'Then you'd have to say you were on a diet and didn't eat cakes, wouldn't you?' he replied. 'Now then, the delivery men will be here soon with our things, and we'll be able to unpack. Ivor? Are you hungry?'

'She looked nice,' said the little boy. 'She was very pretty.'

'Shut up, Ivor.'

'Betsy!'

There was a slam, and this time Carrie could quite clearly make out the sound of small shoes running angrily on wooden floorboards.

She swallowed and walked the remaining few feet up the path to the back door.

'Hello?' she called, as she knocked, to make sure no one could accuse her of barging in.

Does this look friendly, or over-friendly, she agonised, shifting from foot to foot. Does this look as if I did scare the children and I'm trying to cover up?

Too late.

A man appeared at the door, and his bulk seemed to fill the narrow space.

Carrie took an unconscious step back.

'Philip Gladstone,' he said, extending a hand. 'You must be the witch from next door.'

Carrie shook his hand, which engulfed hers. Even though she knew logically that the cottages were built for much smaller times, Philip Gladstone still seemed like a giant: well over six feet, and broad-shouldered, with collar-length dark hair curling round his ears, and a beard of various silver-greys, which made him look older than he was. On closer inspection, she guessed he was in his early forties, late thirties, maybe, with unlined skin, smooth between the curls of hair. He looked like a rock star or a warlock, not quite of this world, despite the thick jumper.

She wondered how he'd managed to move in while she was only up the hill, dozing undisturbed. There'd been no sound of a van, and yet she could hear removal men tramping up and down the front garden now. The valley really did seem to swallow some sounds and amplify others, like the dull booms from the firing range that sometimes seemed startlingly close.

'Carrie Armstrong,' she said. 'I don't do poisoned cake. Well, as far as I know. Sorry, I couldn't help overhearing.'

A wry smile spread across Philip's face, showing white teeth behind the curling beard. 'I'm sure you don't. My children are well-schooled in fairy-tale lore, I'm afraid. Next-door neighbours, wells in the garden, new village, you see. They like to leap to their own conclusions.'

'Don't we all?' Carrie tried a wry smile.

'Well, they're usually more entertaining that the ones I leap to.'

Despite his intimidating size, there was some mischief about Philip Gladstone that Carrie picked up at once: while his face remained solemn, his dark brown eyes glittered with amusement and the well-shaped mouth beneath the beard turned up at the corners, as if to underwrite his joking with a sort of dry self-awareness. The cable-knit lines of his jumper stretched across his barrel chest, above a pair of well-worn, honey-coloured cords. A gentle bear. And yet at the same time, Carrie also had an instinct that this was a playfulness that could blow up into fearsome in an instant, then back to playful in a bewildering sweep.

'But of course witches don't always come with hooked noses and warts, eh?' he added, lifting a dark eyebrow. For a moment, Carrie couldn't quite tell whether he was drawing her into his house, or warning her off.

She realised it was an odd sort of compliment. 'Well, they were quite right not to accept food from a stranger,' she said. 'But the offer of a cup of tea still stands. I know it took us about nine tea breaks before we got the boxes unpacked.'

'Ah, listen, I'm forgetting my manners,' said Philip, hitting his head with his paw-like hand. 'This isn't very neighbourly. Can I invite *you* in for a cup of tea?'

Carrie looked over his shoulder to the kitchen, which was piled up with boxes and carrier bags. There wasn't a kettle in sight. The huge marmalade cat glared angrily from the kitchen table: the source, she guessed, of the dead mouse.

'It might be easier if you came over to our house,' she said. 'But, I guess, the kids . . .' She trailed off as Ivor appeared from behind his father's leg.

He stared up at Carrie with wide blue eyes.

'Hello again,' said Carrie, smiling in what she hoped was a nice way.

Ivor mumbled something and hid his head in the fabric of Philip's trousers.

Philip gently unpeeled his son's fingers. 'Now, Ivor, you've to be a big brave lad, and stop doing that now, d'you hear?' He picked the little boy up, as easily as if he were a small cat. 'That's kind of you, but I'd rather not leave madam while she's in a mood upstairs. Things get broken. So I'll have to decline.'

'Would you like me to bring a pot of tea to you then?' said Carrie. 'And some biscuits?'

Ivor's face lit up. 'Biscuits!'

'They're from a packet,' Carrie added, making her face serious. 'No poison.'

'She might just be saying that.' Philip held Ivor at arm's length and gave him a grave look. Ivor's face immediately mirrored his father's. He was a beautiful, solemn-faced little boy. 'How do we know she's telling the truth, eh? What do you think?'

'Biscuits,' said Ivor. 'Biscuits, please.'

'Oh dear,' said Philip Gladstone, putting him down. 'What a pushover. But I wouldn't say no, if you really don't mind?'

'Not at all. I was about to have a break anyway. Do you have cups?'

Philip cast a despairing hand around the room. 'I do. But I couldn't tell you where.'

'Give me one minute,' said Carrie, holding up a finger, and felt positively neighbourly.

*

Underneath the stacks and stacks of boxes, Philip Gladstone had a pine table just like Carrie's, and Lucy's, and Sandra's. Perhaps Paul Jenkins was wholesaling them, thought Carrie, as she moved a cardboard box marked 'Abbey Notes' to make room for her tea tray, piled up with her best cups, her teapot and a packet of chocolate digestives.

Her eye was drawn to the teetering towers of books stacked up against the wall: dictionaries, English and foreign language, thick reference volumes, Bibles, what looked like tall art monographs . . .

'Not the half of it,' said Philip, seeing her looking round. 'This is just my work stuff. The rest of our worldly goods are somewhere en route – I hope. I thought it best to get the kids here on their own first and worry about the sideboards later.'

'We had problems too. Everyone did,' said Carrie, pouring the tea. 'Sat navs go funny, people get lost, mobile signals are erratic. It's all part of the village mystery.' She looked up to make sure he could tell she was joking. Sort of.

'Am I the last one to the party, then?' Philip asked, shifting a box so he could see her on the other side of the table. 'I see most of the houses have cars outside.'

'Just about. We've been here about a month now, and most people arrived at the same time as we did.' She passed him a mug, and pushed the sugar and milk toward him. 'But it feels like I've been here for ever. It's amazing how the village sort of draws you in.'

'It's like that, is it? How many people are there?'

Carrie shrugged. 'I don't really know – a hundred? About forty houses?'

'And everyone knows each other?' He said it with a mixture of fascination and dread. 'You'd better fill me in quickly.'

So Carrie did.

It felt nice to be the one explaining St Dee's curious set-up for a change, instead of feeling like the new girl, supervised by Lucy and Barbara. And Philip Gladstone had the sort of interested manner that coaxed the chattiness out of Carrie. As she rambled on about the evacuation, and the neighbourhood watch meeting, and the little village shop, and the cliques in the pub, and the various conspiracies that had been debated and dismissed, she surprised herself by how warm she felt about St Dee and its oddities.

'So you work from home because you're an artist?' asked Philip. 'What sort of art do you do?'

Carrie fiddled with her cup. Talking about her work always made her feel self-conscious. 'Um, that makes it sound more grand than it really is,' she admitted. 'I didn't go to art school or anything. I mean, my degree's in English literature – I just sort of stumbled into the children's book thing.'

'Really?' Philip sipped his tea. 'It doesn't seem to be a career you stumble into.'

'Oh, it was. I mean, I've always enjoyed painting, but my parents weren't keen on me going to art college when I could do a degree instead, so you know . . .' Carrie pulled a face. 'I used to do some freelance illustration work for magazines – watercolours of food, that sort of thing – but I had to temp at the same time to pay the bills. Then Mark, my husband, showed some sketches I'd done to one of his friends who worked in children's publishing and pretended I was thinking of making them into a book. Without telling me, of course – I think I'd probably have stopped him if I'd known!'

That sounds really negative, thought Carrie, hearing the words as if for the first time. She was so used to underplaying it, for fear people would think her pretentious or call her on how easy it had been.

Philip didn't seem to think it was anything out of the ordinary though. He looked over the rim of his mug, his thick brows lifted in question. 'You didn't really *want* to be a writer?'

'Well, yes,' she amended, 'yes, I did. I just never thought I could. So really, I'm glad Mark kicked me into gear. He's always had more confidence in my work than I do. Mark's a much more proactive sort of person altogether, much more . . .' She searched for the right word, one that wouldn't make him sound pushy. 'Much more ambitious than me.'

That's what he was: more sure that things would work out of their own accord, without the plans and confirmations she needed.

'Well, yes, sometimes it's easier to have confidence in someone else. Go on,' said Philip, encouragingly. 'So he showed these drawings to a publisher . . . ?'

'And the editor called me in, and we talked about children's books, and what else I was thinking of writing, like I knew what I was doing . . .' She pulled a self-deprecating face, then corrected herself. 'And, er, suddenly I had a deal, and an agent. And now Morris Mouse – which is the series of books I write – he's doing well enough for me to work from home. Well, as long as I don't develop an addiction to oysters and champagne.'

'Well done, you,' said Philip. 'Sounds like a dream come true.'

'Thanks. I mean, I'm really lucky. When you think of the number of people trying to get their work published . . .' Carrie cupped her hands around her mug, surprised by how easy it was to talk to Philip. Any moment now she was going to tell him she was constantly panicking that they'd unmask her as a charlatan and ask for their advance back. There was something about his manner that was deceptively easy. 'I am a very lucky woman, all told.'

'Ah, luck's a curiously specific thing. May I help myself to your biscuits?' He gestured to the biscuits and thumbed three out of the top. 'Cheers. But, listen,' he dropped his voice and looked conspiratorial, 'I know it's a bit controversial, but don't you find working from home a mixed blessing? Or are you very disciplined about distractions?'

Carrie nodded, a little surprised to be asked. She'd never really admitted to anyone else that working from home wasn't quite the idyll it appeared. 'No, I have the attention span of a small child. Especially here, in this house. I spend more time thinking about the couple who lived here before me, Mark's grandparents, wondering what their routines were, how they talked to each other, what their marriage was like . . .' She stopped herself. That hadn't been what he'd asked, but the glinting eyes seemed to be teasing information out of her like spun wool. She pulled herself together and gave the stock answer she always gave at parties. 'Most people say, "You lucky thing, being able to work from home!" but they don't know the half of it.' She looked over the table at him. 'How do *you* find the lure of the housework?'

'Oh, not as bad as the lure of the fridge.' He raised his silvery eyebrows in shared sympathy. 'As you can see. I'm not at home all the time – I lecture, at Durham University. I also write books. But not as much fun as yours, I'd bet. I'm on sabbatical for a year, to finish one now, so what with one thing and another . . .' Philip paused and shrugged, as if he'd said too much. 'Well, I've been working at home more than ever. You think you're going to get some peace and quiet, but you don't, do you?' As he spoke there was a dull crash from upstairs, followed by a piercing howl of protest.

'Daaaaaaaaad!'

He smiled wryly, as Carrie flinched. 'Don't worry,' he said. 'That's an attention howl. I'll let you know if it escalates to a serious one.'

Carrie tried not to notice how sensitive her ears now were to children's cries, and how oddly familiar the sound was to her. This wasn't really the time to mention the story about the well outside. But then when was?

She poured herself more tea. 'And now you're writing the book in St Dee? Don't you need to be near the university? For research?'

'Well, actually, no – the book is sort of about St Dee.' He raised a hand as Carrie's eyes lifted curiously to his. 'Don't panic, it's not some kind of exposé. I lecture in English paganism and its relationship to early Christianity, and St Dee features quite prominently in early records about that. The heart of the book,' he added, 'if you can bear a little boring detail, is the mysterious sacking of the abbey here.'

'It was sacked?' Carrie thought of Lucy's sudden volunteering of information in the pub quiz. So it was true – the fire, the demolition, the rumours.

'By someone, yes – records are confused about how it actually happened. Then rebuilt, then destroyed again by Henry the Eighth.' He looked apologetic. 'You've probably heard this a million times by now, but the St Dee valley has quite a reputation for blood and guts – clashes between Christians and pagans, problems with the Romans, resistance to the Reformation . . . Really quite dark stuff. Only natural that it should end up appropriated by the Army for bomb testing.'

'Well, yes,' said Carrie. She paused, and winked. 'If that's what you *believe* it was appropriated for.'

Philip looked at her, then beamed with delight. 'Well, quite.'

'It's funny how it all works out, isn't it? Did you know about your connection to St Dee before Paul Jenkins got in touch?' Carrie ran on, conscious that she could hardly ask for private information if she didn't offer any. 'Was the evacuation a family story? Mark, my husband, didn't really know anything at all about it, just something about his grandparents being moved out during the war for security. I couldn't believe something so intriguing would just be brushed under the carpet. But then what do you know about families? They keep the juiciest stuff to themselves and bore you rigid with minutiae about someone borrowing gardening shears in 1976 and never returning them.'

She looked up at him with a 'what can you do?' smile but a shadow drifted across Philip's face, and he looked down for an instant. When he lifted his eyes again, the shadow had gone, but Carrie felt a flush of embarrassment.

'Is this what village life is like then?' he asked, with what passed for amusement – but which, Carrie realised, might be anything but. 'Working out what everyone's scandal is?'

She clutched her mug. 'Um, yes. I'm afraid it is.'

He ran a hand over his face, and it seemed to wipe away any traces of annoyance. 'Well, since you ask . . . The house belonged to my grandparents, and it's where I started to get an interest in Druids, actually,' he said. 'They moved away to Durham after the war, and I used to hear all the old stories about the shrine in the woods and the evacuation. Never paid proper attention to the detail, though – my grandad died shortly after I married, and my grandma shortly after that.' He prised off another biscuit from the top of the packet. 'So I can't tell you a lot about any old gossip, but I've got some stories about that chalk horse that'd make your hair curl.'

'Is the chalk horse part of your research?'

Philip nodded. 'Indeed it is. It's a major part of my thesis. Fertility rites, May Day celebrations, and so on. Have you been up there to see it?'

'I was up there just this morning. It's an amazing thing, seeing it for the first time driving into the valley.'

'Isn't it? Did you know that they—'

'I'd like a cup of tea too,' announced a determined voice behind Carrie's chair. 'What's she doing here?'

Carrie jumped.

'Excuse me,' said Philip, and pushed his chair away from the table, so he could swing round and give Betsy the full force of his dark-eyed glare.

Betsy merely glared back, her own blue eyes just as steely as his.

'Betsy! Don't be so rude to our guest.'

'Why?'

'Because Carrie has brought us some tea. Would you like to join us? You'll have to sit up and be nice.'

Betsy glared at Carrie. 'Don't want to.' And she spun on her heel and flounced off.

'Sorry about madam,' said Philip as the footsteps retreated down the bare wooden floorboards of the corridor. 'She's rather enjoying being the woman of the house these days. I think for the sake of her amateur dramatics she could do with some company other than her brother and her grumpy old dad.'

'Not many children round here yet, I'm afraid.' Carrie pulled a sympathetic face. 'But I think there's a playgroup in Deeting Magna? There's bound to be a notice in the village shop about it.'

'No children next door?' Philip raised an eyebrow.

'Not yet,' said Carrie, automatically. 'But it's early days.'

Another stock answer. Philip looked at her in a way that suggested he knew it was.

'Well, spend too much time near my two and you might change your mind,' he sighed. 'Look, I don't want to keep you from what you were doing.' He finished his tea and got up, and Carrie had the strong feeling she was being dismissed, albeit politely.

'It's okay,' she said. 'Maybe Betsy can join us next time?'

'Maybe,' said Philip. 'I'll be having a word with her about tea-party manners later. Do you want me to wash up the cups?' He opened some boxes. 'I think I put ours in one of these . . .'

'Oh, keep them until you're unpacked. I have lots,' said Carrie, waving them away. 'Bring them back whenever.' She paused. 'Drop in for coffee whenever you like. I warn you, people do that a lot round here. I'd go to the shop and get some biscuits in, if I were you.'

'Very neighbourly,' he said with an ironic smile playing at the corners of his mouth. 'I'll knock on the wall if I need some help.'

'You do that,' said Carrie.

He walked her to the back door, since that was the way she'd come in. As she stepped out into the overgrown garden, Carrie realised they were both looking towards the well.

She half-turned back to Philip, not sure what she should say, but as if he could read her mind, he winked and said, 'I know all about the poor little Victorian children down that well, before you ask.'

Carrie opened her mouth to tell him what she'd heard in the still night, then stopped herself.

'Funny thing, these stories they tell little kids,' he added. 'Keeps some of them right away from the danger, but just makes it even more fascinating for others.'

'Did it keep you away?' she asked, guessing the answer.

Philip shook his head. 'Not once I'd found something to hang on to while I looked. I'll drop the cups round later, OK?'

'OK,' said Carrie, and waved goodbye, suddenly glad to be back in the fresh green air of the garden.

Chapter Nine

Despite the life model now firmly established in Morris's palatial house, Carrie's book was not coming on well. She suddenly seemed less able to draw him than before she'd left London. Even Mark, who took little interest in preliminary sketches, felt obliged to comment on Morris's rigid appearance on the page.

'You live in the countryside now,' he observed, smearing Marmite on his toast with an enthusiasm that turned Carrie's stomach. She noted he was using the butter knife, but didn't say anything. 'You've got no excuse. I have to be honest with you – it looks like he's constipated. And his legs are wrong.'

'Thanks.' Carrie, like Mark, was fully dressed. She no longer ate breakfast in her pyjamas. St Dee had reset her internal clock so she woke at six thirty, twitching to begin the day, along with the noisy chickens someone was keeping.

'If you got a full night's sleep it might help,' he said, looking at her squarely over the table.

Carrie frowned. 'But I'm sleeping fine,' she lied.

She wasn't. Although she'd stopped lying awake listening for phantom crying, recently she'd started awake in the early hours in a panic, her heart still pounding from an oppressive dream she couldn't remember. Then she lay in the inky blackness of their room, listening to the ticking of the beams, and the distant shrieks of bats and owls, unable to let go of her wakefulness, but not knowing what was causing it.

'I know I'm a sound sleeper, chick, but it's hard not to notice your wife kicking you like a donkey. Even if she claims to be asleep at the time.' Mark tipped his head sympathetically. 'I worry about you when you're stressed. Something on your mind? Is it your deadline?'

'No,' said Carrie, rubbing her arm. She didn't know what it was. 'No, that's under control.'

'If there's something on your mind, tell me.' Mark's face was concerned. 'Maybe I can help? That's what I'm here for.'

'Nope, nothing to discuss.' She smiled. 'Maybe it's Lily – waking me up early to get on with scrubbing the floors.'

'Enough of that.' He stuffed an apple into his bag and slung it over his shoulder. 'Want anything from the big town?'

He meant Devizes. He'd been working there for the last few days.

'Just you to come home early,' she said. 'Now the weather's getting nicer, can't you take some time off so we can have a few days together? In the garden? I mean, it's good to get you out of the house, but I do miss you by teatime.' She looked around the kitchen, making her eyes stage-wide to hide the fact that she meant what she said. 'This house gets so big when it's just me. And I miss my sexy gardener . . .'

Mark grinned. 'I'm sure you could have half the village over for coffee if you wanted some company.' He leaned over and kissed her on the curl of her ear. His breath warmed up the skin on her neck. 'But I'll see what next week's looking like, OK? Are you going to make me something nice for supper?'

'Maybe.' Carrie lifted her face and closed her eyes so he could kiss her properly. 'That depends on how much time I spend with the rest of the village.'

Mark laughed, and left.

Upstairs, Carrie savoured a moment's delight at the early-morning sun filling the studio with fresh lemony light, a shaft of which was falling on her most recent sketches of Morris dancing on a laptop. That dissolved her satisfaction at once. They weren't right, she knew, and a childish feeling of letting her new life down increased the frustration knotting up in her stomach. She rubbed out Morris's legs and tried again a couple of times, until she couldn't remember how she'd wanted them to go in the first place, then she gave up altogether, bouncing the eraser off the wall in annoyance.

Despite the light and peace of her new studio, Carrie's attention kept wandering: to the flecked windows, and the rolling view outside; to the odd clicks and whirrs of the heating and the wooden floors; to the rustlings in the roof. The house was never silent. It seemed to want to talk to her, show her its nooks and crannies, after sixty years of standing empty in the deserted plain while life went on over the hill.

Focus, Carrie told herself. She ignored a fat wasp buzzing furiously against a window on the landing and stared at the mutant mouse on her easel with something approaching dislike.

I could always put the washing on, she thought, and pushed her chair back.

Carrie's plans for a lavender-scented laundry room had initially come up against a literal brick wall. The cellar had been bricked up when the renovation work started, and the builders had had to break into it to rewire the house. The idea of a bricked-up cellar had spooked Carrie, and in a panic she had called Paul Jenkins to check whether the police should be in attendance, as well as the heritage electrician.

'Oh, you're not the first to ring about this,' Paul Jenkins had reassured her in his too-calm monotone. 'I understand some of the, well, *less trusting* homeowners hid larger possessions that they couldn't take with them, then bricked up their cellars before they left, just to be on the safe side.'

Carrie didn't like the way he made Lily and Jack sound ignorant, and she bridled a little on their behalf.

'It's understandable,' she said. 'Considering that they were being asked to leave their house for an unspecified amount of time.'

'Quite so,' he'd replied smoothly. 'In any case, it'll be perfectly safe. The builders will go down there first and check everything out.'

'But what if there are . . . things still down there?'

A cat, maybe? Or just the lingering air, trapped for sixty years, festering away?

Paul Jenkins chuckled. 'There are no dead bodies, if that's what you're worried about!'

'I was thinking more of . . . larger possessions,' said Carrie, stiffly.

'Well, in that case, legally, they'll be your husband's, won't they?' he replied. Phones were ringing in the background – other families needing advice, wanting reassurances. 'So that's really something for you to work out. Now, does that put your mind at rest?'

'Yes, yes, it does,' said Carrie automatically. 'Thank you.'

Conversations with Paul Jenkins, Carrie realised much later, often felt more satisfying at the time than they actually were. A bit like Chinese takeaways. Now, months later, it struck her as odd that the cellar had been left locked as it was. No looting by the Army? No damage? No investigations?

After all that, it had been almost disappointing to learn from Ken, the foreman, that there was nothing down there, bar a large chest of drawers that 'the lads' had hauled upstairs to the main bedroom, and several dark chairs, covered in dust and wheezing with mites and woodworm. Mark had earmarked those for the fire and chopped them up with enthusiasm for the wood basket by the fireplace.

Tucking the basket of washing under her arm, Carrie tentatively opened the cellar door. It said something about how keen she was to escape work that she was willing to brave the cobwebby, earth-musty darkness to do a chore Mark was happy to do for her.

Even with the bright sun streaming in through the hall windows, Carrie hesitated at the door leading down the flight of wooden steps.

'There are no bodies in this cellar,' she said aloud, and immediately felt ridiculous. Who was she talking to? The house? In which case, what did she expect it to say back?

Still, she went over to the radio and turned up Radio One until cheerful music filled the room, loud enough to be heard in the cellar. Then she swung open the door and made her way awkwardly downstairs, turning her feet sideways on the narrow treads.

The workmen had swept away some dust, but had had little time for much else, and more dust was starting to build over the areas that had been disturbed. The air still smelled close and old in her nostrils, as if even the motes had hung in suspension for sixty years. It smelled of damp and age, not of laundry or apples or beer, as Carrie expected it to. Irrationally, she now knew. If she wanted it to smell of apples and laundry, she'd have to put them there herself.

The stairs were bare board and her trainers made hollow noises as she descended into the series of small rooms. The builders had fitted 100-watt bulbs, throwing hard light in three bright circles, and even in the corners of the dark brick walls there was nowhere for skeletons to lurk. Even the cobwebs seemed too thick to be real.

As she walked, Carrie kept one ear on the radio upstairs and trained the other for the scuttle of tiny feet across the brick. She realised she was holding her breath, steeling herself.

They're just *mice*, she told herself. They've been in this house longer than you have. How do you think they feel?

She opened up the washer and began sorting the clothes into piles, unbuttoning Mark's shirts and emptying his pockets.

Carrie paused, and smiled, holding a shirt that hadn't been unbuttoned at all. He'd pulled that off quickly enough.

She tugged the belt out of a pair of black jeans, with the cotton boxers still tucked inside in the rush to get undressed, enjoying the memory of a particularly energetic night in the big white bed. The famous country air, living up to its clichés.

'Mark,' she said to herself, in a chiding tone, pulling out a wad of receipts and notes from his back pocket. He'd need those for his accounts – a taxi receipt, a travelcard, a ten-pound note . . .

She tucked them into her back pocket and turned the machine on.

The smell of washing powder and the warm hum of the machine were comforting, and feeling more in charge of her nerves, Carrie tried to picture how it must have looked before the evacuation. Much the same, presumably. Who had been the last person to come down here, before it was bricked up? Lily? Were hers the last footsteps on the stairs, before the workmen came in to wake the air up again? Had she come down here one last time, for one last look before Jack starting bricking up the door?

Carrie's gaze wandered round the corners where their modern packing cases now stood, gathering fresh dust of their own. They'd had three weeks to move and still hadn't seemed to have enough time to pack up their tiny flat. She wondered if Lily had been clutched by the same panic, deciding what relics of their life were necessary and which could be jettisoned. The families in St Dee had had a month's notice – time for most of the furniture to be packed up and moved, taken to their new home. How much of Lily's old house would have fitted in her new one? Had they gone somewhere smaller, less accommodating of Welsh dressers and oak chests? Or was Lily one of the optimistic wives – did she take only the bare minimum, sure she'd be back soon enough?

Carrie wondered about the heavy oak chest, which now stood upstairs at the foot of their double bed. She'd filled it with soft spare blankets and lavender bags, packing them in layers as Lily had. Had it been too heavy to move on a horse and cart? Had anyone brought them a van? Or maybe the chest had been left as a sort of defiance, something left behind for faith; proof that she did believe the family would return. Proof to herself, to the house, to the ghosts of all her family, born and buried in this village.

Would I have left something? Carrie asked herself. All her life she'd been moved around from place to place, uprooted and repotted like a sturdy little plant. Friends, secret places, rooms, all left behind. Would I have hidden something, she wondered, if I'd lived here all my life? Surely if you have to go, you have to go.

Then she remembered her British Library Reading Room card, still in her purse, tucked in behind her Visa card.

But that was practical. I'll be going back for odd days, she argued. And I wanted to come here, I wanted to leave that life behind. Not like Lily, or any of the other people who stood here, wondering whether they'd see these walls again. I *wanted* to start afresh.

This is my home now, she thought, trailing a finger along the exposed brickwork, feeling the old cement crumble against her fingertip. My new family: just me and Mark – and our children. It'll be like waking up something we never knew, like grafting new stock onto these dormant roots. People who must have looked like him, who must have walked down these stairs a thousand times, but who I'll never meet, and yet there might be flickers of them in the faces of our own children. And we won't really know what we're looking out for.

Carrie was suddenly aware of how chilly it was away from the warm sun, and she rubbed away the goosebumps that had sprung up on her pale forearms.

She turned her attention away from herself and out into the cellar. I'm going to whitewash these walls, she thought, running her eyes into the shadowy corners and dusty shelves. I'm going to get one of those roller brushes and make everything light and fresh, then build storage units, and fill them with spring bulbs potted in terracotta planters, and boxes of dried . . . stuff, and hang sheaves of lavender from hooks in the ceiling . . .

It was so clear in her mind's eye. So clear it could almost have been there in front of her, glowing with brightening colours: the drying herbs, the shelves and boxes, the tea chests . . .

A scuttling broke her concentration and Carrie jumped, sending the scuttling in a different direction. She grabbed the big torch on top of the laundry shelf and shone the beam of light over to the perspex mousetrap – which was empty – and in doing so, noticed a hatch in the wall that she hadn't previously spotted, so dark and sooty that it blended in almost completely, half-hidden behind an empty computer case.

For a moment she stood, staring at it. Then she steeled herself, and on closer inspection, realised it must be a store of some kind. With a confidence she didn't feel, she set the torch on a packing case and tried to open the hatch. It was locked.

Carrie stepped back and thought hard. There were no useful bunches of rusty keys in the dresser – that would be too much to ask. She knew that if she moved too far from where she was to find a screwdriver, she'd find a reason not to climb back down the dark stairs. Taking a deep breath, she balled her hand into a fist and gave the whole thing an almighty thump.

Nothing.

She looked round and saw a pair of scissors hanging from a hook – scissors they'd used to cut up some boxes.

With trembling hands, she shoved one arm of the scissors into the lock and jiggled it around. To her surprise, it clicked and undid.

For a second, Carrie stared at the door. Then, trying not to think about spiders or dead rats, she held her breath, and tried to open it, prising it open with the scissors, then with her own fingertips, barely noticing her nails breaking with the effort.

Nothing leaped out, and it didn't smell too bad. Cautiously, Carrie shone the torch inside the space. What was it used for, she wondered? Then she remembered the coal hatch outside – presumably this was where it led to. She swept the torch round again, peering further in this time, and spotted something flat just behind the door. Dark motes of dust caught in the torch's beam, and a few lingering traces of coal dust caught in her throat, making her cough.

Holding the torch between her shoulder and her ear, she leaned in: it was a box. With some effort, she dragged it out, setting it down on the floor in front of her.

Carrie's heart was pounding, and she had to force herself to stop and look carefully before she disturbed anything in her excitement. It was a wooden packing box, well made, with a very faded label on the top. 'Mr & Mrs J. Armstrong, Oak Cottage, St Dee' was written in brown cursive script.

Carrie ran her hands over it, trying to pick up any traces of Lily that might still be clinging to the surface. Her skin prickled, but rationally she told herself that that was the chill in the stone cellar, not some psychic intuition. The box was secured with two screws and some string, so calmly, she made herself get up and look around for Mark's tool kit, and with a proper screwdriver, she began to undo the rusty fastenings, working as slowly as she could.

Inside the packing chest was old straw. She slid her hands into the scratchy depths until she felt the cool smoothness of a plate, and then gently, holding her breath, she lifted it out.

It was a dinner plate, plain white with a single band of red around the edge and a gold rim which shone as brightly as the day it was hidden away. There was no hallmark on the back, but it felt heavy and seemed very good quality. Carrie closed her eyes, as recommended in a sixth-sense book she'd once read, and tried to tune into the last pair of hands to have held it, sixty years ago. What had they felt? How quickly had it been buried away? What was the last meal eaten off it? Had that straw in the box been harvested from the fields outside?

Without warning, there was a bang from upstairs and her eyes sprang wide open.

Carrie held her breath, nervous ears twitching like a cat's with each click of the boiler. Was the house cross that she'd found something? Had she disturbed it?

But she heard nothing except the distant beat and thud of the radio, upstairs in the kitchen.

Then abruptly the radio stopped dead.

Carrie dropped the plate in shock. It landed, with a dull rustle, in the packing straw.

Upstairs, there was no sound, as if a heavy blanket had fallen over the whole house. Carrie could hear the sheep bleating in the distant fields, and the pounding of her own blood in her temples. She suddenly had the unsettling feeling that she was listening to the house itself, not for signs of movement upstairs.

And the cellar itself was deathly quiet, apart from the humming of the washing machine, which shifted into an angry spin cycle, rattling against the brick wall.

Carrie forced herself to think like Mark would, and not give in to the fluttering panic pushing against her ribcage. It's just a fuse. Or some alarm preset I didn't know about on the radio. Maybe someone's popped round. Get up there and sort it out.

Her feet were moving before she was aware she'd even told herself to move, but with an iron will, Carrie made herself walk slowly, and not scramble up the stairs as if something were chasing her out of the cellar. She didn't know who was watching, but she was determined not to seem afraid.

Her feet scuffed and slipped on the stairs.

'Hello?' she yelled, halfway up. 'Hello?'

There was no one in the kitchen. No one sitting at the table. No one who could have turned off the radio. No open windows to have banged in the breeze.

'Hello?' she yelled again, less certainly.

If Mark was here, he'd laugh this away, she thought fiercely.

But Mark wasn't here. And the cold tap was running in the stone sink, splashing water up onto the wooden draining board. Was it her imagination, or had she left that tap running when she went downstairs?

'Hello!' she shouted, unexpectedly close to tears.

Lucy Ross's blonde head popped round the kitchen door. 'Oh, you're there!'

Carrie clapped a hand to her chest and sank into the nearest chair. 'Christ Almighty, Lucy, you gave me a shock.'

'Did I?' Lucy looked nonplussed. 'I was passing, heard your radio and thought you must have popped out. So I switched it off for you.'

'I was in the cellar,' said Carrie. 'I was . . .' Her voice, too high, trailed away.

'Do you want a coffee?' asked Lucy, putting down her basket of cleaning products and turning off the running tap. 'You look like you've seen a ghost, my love!'

Carrie struggled to get a grip on herself. She didn't want it all round St Dee that she was, nudge, nudge, 'highly strung'.

'No, let me.' She pushed herself off the chair and went to get two coffee mugs off the dresser. 'I feel like I *have* seen a ghost, funnily enough. I just found a tea chest of crockery, hidden in the coal hatch in the cellar. It must have been there since the village was evacuated.'

'Really?' Lucy sounded surprised. 'Well, lucky you. Most people've been searching their houses for buried treasure, but I reckon either the Army would have swept the place when they moved in, or the builders would've done when they came in to do it all up.'

'Yes, I guess so.'

'Wonder why they missed a whole tea chest? Must have been well hidden, was it?'

'Well, the cellar was bricked up when they moved out. And it wasn't really obvious.' Carrie tried a smile. 'And it is next to the haunted house.'

'There is that,' said Lucy.

I wonder how I found it then, thought Carrie. It was almost like it wanted to be found.

Lucy helped herself from the packet of Hobnobs. She dunked her biscuit and looked up at Carrie. 'So,' she said, 'let's have a look at these plates then?'

'Really?'

'Yeah. Really.'

They went back down into the cellar together, and with Lucy by her side Carrie was surprised at how the atmosphere seemed lighter, warmer – when she saw the cobwebs now, she found herself getting embarrassed at her lack of cleaning dedication.

'Ooh, you could knock through all down here!' Lucy was saying, peering round the corners. 'What a great space!'

'Mark's talking about building a wine cellar,' said Carrie.

Lucy gave her an inscrutable look.

'What?' said Carrie.

'You just reminded me that we still haven't worked out a night you can both come round for a drink.'

Carrie turned red. Lucy had asked a few times now, and she hadn't been able to pin Mark down. 'Oh, tell me about it. He's working so hard I have to make appointments with him myself. I'll, er, I'll talk to him tonight, make him get his diary out. Look, can you take one side? It's heavy.'

Together, they got the box upstairs and started to unpack it on the kitchen table, removing piece after piece until there was a whole dinner service – plates, side plates, serving dishes, even a gravy boat. Privately Carrie wondered if it wasn't a bit fancy, for a school teacher and his young wife.

Lucy scrutinised the soup dish that Carrie handed over and her mouth twisted up in concentration. 'Nice,' she said.

'Do you . . . know much about antiques?' hazarded Carrie, not wanting to sound rude.

'Well, you know. I watch *Flog It*.' Lucy turned it over and examined the stamps on the back. 'You know where this is probably from, don't you?'

Carrie shook her head. 'No idea.'

'I'll bet you a tenner it's from the manor house. Is there no card in the case? My gran had a set like this – it's the standard wedding present from the manor house. They used to hand them out to their staff and favoured locals, according to her.' Lucy held the dish up to the light. 'This one's nicer than my gran's though, I'd say. Look at all the gold bands. Plus it hasn't been used.' She handed it back. 'Worth a few bob. The Maxwells must have liked your grandparents. Did they work up there?'

'Mark's grandparents,' said Carrie automatically. 'And I don't know, to tell the truth. Jack was the teacher, and I assumed Lily just helped at the school. I wonder why they didn't use it?'

'Kept it for best, probably. What's the point in eating your eggs and chips off that?'

Carrie's mind was whirring. Lily hadn't been married all that long before the village was evacuated, so maybe there hadn't even been a chance to bring it out for best. Shame she'd packed it away so carefully then never got to enjoy it. 'Kind of the Maxwells, though, wasn't it?' she said. 'Making sure they had some nice things to start their married life with.'

Lucy's lips pursed. 'Yes, well.'

'Well, what?'

'Well, they certainly got their money's worth out of the village, what with one thing or another. A few dinner services here or there isn't a lot, not when you consider.'

'How do you mean?' Carrie was curious. She'd been able to reconstruct the village in her head, going on Paul Jenkins' guidelines, and the photographs in the pub, but the shapes and shadows of the actual people who'd lived here were proving far more elusive. To find them in the brisk shape of Lucy Ross was quite odd, and for a moment she envied her the rich threads of family gossip that connected her to the old village.

'Oh, you know. Having people to skivvy for them, making sure everyone doffed their caps in the street, owning this, that and the other. I'm not saying they were any worse than other landowners round here, but . . .' Lucy's voice trailed off. 'My gran, she kept her eye on things, if you know what I mean. She knew people who worked up at the manor – knew Kathleen Maxwell's nanny even. There's a lot she's not saying. Her generation's like that, aren't they? Don't like to say much. But she certainly perked up when she knew I was moving back.'

'She didn't want to move back herself?'

'Oh, no. She's in a home now.' Lucy tapped her head. 'Not all there any more, poor love. But she sometimes has a good old ramble about *the way things were.*' Her face turned mischievous. 'I should see what she can remember, eh? Lily, right? And Jack?'

'Do that,' said Carrie, eagerly. 'I'd love to know what she remembered about Lily and Jack. Mark doesn't know much and he's . . .' She hesitated, unwilling to trade the sad facts of Mark's tough childhood for information. 'He's not so interested in family trees and all that sort of thing.'

'I'll ask her,' said Lucy. 'But don't get excited. Some days she thinks she's still living here herself, some days she's convinced she's been kidnapped by aliens.'

When there was no sign of Mark by seven, Carrie called his mobile and got no reply. She left another message at seven thirty, put some pasta on for herself at eight thirty, and when he finally rolled in at eight forty-five, Carrie bit her tongue on her objections, because he looked shattered. The spikes on his hair had gone flat and his eyes were bloodshot beneath his glasses. He only wore his glasses when his eyes were too tired to cope with contact lenses.

All this, she marvelled, just from going to Devizes?

'Can I get you a drink, hon?' she said from the kitchen sink, watching with mild horror as he threw his jacket on the stairs and shuffled into the kitchen like a zombie.

'Please.' Without looking up, Mark pulled out a chair and slumped onto it.

Carrie waited for him to say something that might explain his exhaustion, then, when nothing was forthcoming, she shook the washing-up bubbles off her hands and opened a bottle of wine.

'Are you OK?' she asked. 'Computers playing up, were they? Putting up a fight against your magic powers?'

Mark didn't open his eyes. 'I've had a long day, OK? Let's just leave it at that.'

Carrie gazed at her husband, trying to piece together what was wrong without having to ask. Maybe Devizes didn't offer the buzz that London did. Maybe the reality of a provincial daily grind had finally hit him. Maybe the people, or the computers, he was working with weren't bending to his will as easily as normal.

Then it's up to me to make this place even more relaxing and wonderful, she thought. Make Mark see it's worth sacrificing some of the old life for this new one.

Carrie put the glass of wine on the table next to him and curled herself around his lethargic form, tucking her chin into the hollow of his neck. He smelled grimy, and tired. 'That wasn't the point of coming out here, though, was it? For you to be exhausted. Can't you work from home some days?'

Mark let out a long, cross breath. 'No. I can't. I don't know if you've noticed while you've been painting up in your studio, but there's still no broadband access out here. There's barely even telephone lines.'

Carrie pressed her tongue against the sharp edge of her teeth. She hated doing anything to upset the light, easy balance of their happiness. He could flip so quickly from charm to moodiness, like a child, and she'd got very good at massaging his moods, knowing exactly when to stop. Like now, for instance.

'I know, I'm sorry,' she said, stroking his hair down soothingly. 'I know it's hard, starting again, but it's going to be worth it, honestly. Don't you feel this house is the beginning of a new life for us?'

Mark was silent. Then he said, 'Yes. Yes, I do. And I don't want to spoil that. I don't want *anything* to spoil it.'

'You're not!' said Carrie. 'And nothing can. Don't be silly.' She straightened up. 'Look, I've got a surprise for you.'

She went over to the Aga and ladled the pasta onto the new plates, which she'd carefully washed and dried until they shone. 'There you go!' she said, putting Mark's in front of him.

He opened his eyes long enough to register the plates, then jerked awake. 'You've bought new plates.'

'No, I haven't.'

'You have.' Mark glared up at her. 'How come it's OK for you to buy new plates when apparently we don't have the money for Sky?'

'Because these aren't new plates!' she said triumphantly. 'They came free with the house!'

'You what?'

'I found them this morning, in the coal cellar,' she explained, sitting down and picking up her fork. 'They were hidden in a packing chest inside the coal cellar. Lily must have left them, in case they came back. Just think – the last time these were used for a meal was during the Second World War! Don't worry,' she added, mischievously, 'I've given them a good wash.'

Mark stared at the spaghetti in front of him. 'These were in the coal cellar?'

'You're very quick tonight,' said Carrie. 'Don't know why they didn't take them. They're lovely. A wedding present from the Maxwells at the manor, Lucy reckoned. Apparently they gave them out to favoured villagers.' She lifted her eyebrows. 'I wonder if *they* had a list?'

Carrie and Mark hadn't had a wedding list. They'd had pledges instead, on a round-the-world honeymoon. It had made sense at the time; they had all they needed, they had no elderly relations to give them towels or fish knives, and it felt weird to ask their few friends for vases, especially when their wedding had been so small and they already had two sets of everything they needed.

Only now did Carrie feel a little twinge that she didn't have more little mementos like these – not for the sake of having new cups, but just things that would remind her of the giver.

'I really feel like I'm starting to get to know Lily,' she went on. 'Isn't it funny how you can start to get a feeling for people without having ever met them? Sometimes I almost feel as if she's here with me in the kitchen, watching me wash up at her sink. And now I'm eating off her plates. I think she'd be happy to see them being used again, don't you? Something from the past coming back to life in the present?'

Mark looked at her with a funny expression twisting up his mouth.

'Oh, sorry, Mark,' she said quickly, clattering her fork down. 'I didn't mean to . . .'

'Forget it,' said Mark, and Carrie saw the fine protective shield fall over his blue eyes.

It was at moments like these, when she had no idea what was going on behind the blank expression, that Carrie realised how much she still had to learn about her husband, the man she'd promised to live with for ever. Standing with his hands in hers as they recited their vows, she'd relished the vast expanse of unexplored anecdotes and fresh, untrodden memories. It was like setting off on a journey into a lush jungle without a map, she'd thought at the time, full of confidence.

Now, though, Carrie wished she had some signposts, even if it did mean that someone had beaten down those paths before her.

Chapter Ten

As the weather got better, and blossom started to fill out St Dee's apple trees, matching the beautifully manicured village green with their light-infused intensity, Carrie found herself spending more and more time avoiding work by wandering around the village with her sketchbook.

One of her favourite places was the secluded spot where the manor house had once stood, dominating St Dee with its elegant windows and sprawling outbuildings. Now, only a pile of old bricks and some overgrown foundations marked the spot where the crenellated faux-turrets had loomed until its demolition in 1945, 'just before the end of the war', according to Paul Jenkins' helpful village notes that were gathering dust on everyone's telephone tables. Box trees and roses, gone wild and lush, outlined a garden that had once demanded three men to tend it, but when Carrie walked up the short drive to the ruins, it was hard to picture the elegant house illustrated in the notes from the few mossy half-walls that remained.

Some days she sat on the broken walls and tried to imagine what the soldiers had done when they'd come here – how they'd treated the houses, or decided which ones were going to be used. And what for? The cold stones didn't give her any clues, but they did make her realise that the Maxwells had definitely grabbed the best location in the village for their ancestral pile.

The house where Kathleen Maxwell now lived was set apart from the cluster around the village green. It looked a little left out, like a child last to be selected for a game – an effect heightened by its comparative newness. Unlike the old mid-Victorian terrace, Church Cottage was later, more Edwardian-looking, Carrie guessed, built with red-brown bricks, and pretty diamond shapes picked out between the storeys in paler brickwork. It was definitely one of the nicest houses in the village, probably the smartest after the manor at the time. Presumably Kathleen, as the returning grandee, had been given first choice of the lot.

An old-fashioned bicycle with a wicker basket on the front leaned, unlocked, against the fence. Carrie had spotted it outside the post office and the pub a few times already, and secretly, she was pleased that maybe, like her, Kathleen was a non-driver – and so even more committed to finding everything she needed within the boundaries of St Dee.

She rang the doorbell and heard it peal inside the house. The curtains in the window were new, cream sprigged with pink flowers, and some troughs of young lavender were balanced on the thick sandstone sills. There was something hopeful about their small bushy heads in the large trough, as though Kathleen was bedding them in for a long stay.

We should all be like that, thought Carrie, planting for a long stay, and for a moment, she was glad she'd made the effort and joined the neighbourhood watch, even if Mark did think it was stupid. For a start, she now knew who to ask about the plates in the cellar, and the thought of taking a real step closer to Lily gave her a little thrill.

Carrie adjusted her face into a polite smile as the door opened, and Kathleen Maxwell appeared on the step. She was wearing a heathery tweed suit, and pearls, and full, if subtle, make-up, as if she were about to receive guests.

'Hello?' she said. 'Is there something wrong, dear?'

Carrie felt slightly foolish. 'I, um, I just popped round to say hello,' she said weakly. 'Is it, er, is it a bad time?'

How come Lucy could breeze in and out of all the houses in the village, and make it look so neighbourly? Carrie shifted from foot to foot. She felt more like a cold caller.

Kathleen's face softened. 'No, not at all. Why don't you come in?' She opened the door so Carrie could step inside.

'Thank you,' said Carrie, feeling distinctly as if she should be carrying a basket of cakes.

Although Kathleen could only have been living in the village for the same few weeks as she had, Carrie was surprised by how little trace of newness there was about her house. There was no trace of the all-pervading fresh-paint smell that she couldn't quite get rid of at Oak Cottage, for a start. The glass lampshades and thick, dark rugs looked as if they'd been there for ever; the watercolour paintings and solid mahogany furniture fitted easily with the wooden floorboards and tasteful buttercream walls. There wasn't a lot of furniture, but what there was looked old, and extremely good quality – inherited, not bought. It had clearly come from a house much larger, and much more elegant than the simple cottage it now filled.

Here and there were large framed photographs of smart-looking people, some taken outside the old manor house. Carrie was tempted to stop and examine them more closely, but she felt herself being herded genteely towards the back of the house.

'Come into the kitchen,' said Kathleen, 'and I'll make a pot of tea. You do drink tea, don't you? Everyone seems to drink instant coffee these days, but I only keep it in the house for Lucy.'

'No, no, tea's great,' said Carrie, pulling out a heavy carved oak chair from the kitchen table. A large grey cat, coiled like a fur stole on the cushion, glared up at her, so she hurriedly pulled out the next one instead. 'I wouldn't expect anything else in such an English village!'

'Indeed. Now am I right in thinking you're American?' asked Kathleen.

'I'm half and half, really,' said Carrie. Lucy, presumably, had passed on that detail. There was, she knew, practically nothing Lucy couldn't win now in the course of conversation. 'My mother's from Minneapolis, and my father's originally from Manchester, though he hasn't been back in years. But,' she added, 'my grandmother was a GI bride, too. She met my grandfather on an airbase in East Anglia and he swept her off her feet. Well, that's the story, anyway.'

'I can imagine.' Kathleen lifted up the Aga lid to put the kettle on to boil. 'My old nanny was rather swept off her feet by some airman she met in Devizes one weekend. Quite literally, I understand. I think a lot of young girls were quite pleased to be flown off to the States at the end of the war. Saved a lot of explaining, if you know what I mean. Villages like these can be terribly unforgiving about slip-ups.'

'So I hear,' said Carrie.

'So should I assume that if you and your husband are living in Oak Cottage, Lily and Jack are no longer with us?' Kathleen asked. 'I'm afraid I'm not really up on what happened to everyone. My family moved to our London house after the war, and that's where I grew up.'

'Oh, they died quite a long time ago,' said Carrie. 'And so did their son, Mark's dad. Ben. Both Mark's parents were killed in a car crash when he was still at school.'

'Oh dear, how very sad.' Kathleen turned away from the Aga to look sympathetically at Carrie. 'Your poor husband.'

'I know, it is sad,' Carrie agreed. 'He really doesn't have any family left on that side at all, so it's quite odd that we've ended up here. It's like a very long-distance gift, I suppose, from Lily and Jack.'

'Indeed.' Kathleen tipped her head to one side. 'Rather strange for him, though, coming back to his roots without knowing quite what they are.' She touched the string of pearls at her neck. 'I can't imagine what it's like to have no sense of your own family. I've always felt at the end of a very, very long line. Portraits, and gravestones, and so on . . . All still up at the church, I'm pleased to see.'

Carrie nodded, feeling appropriately awed. *That's why Kathleen gets Lucy's back up*, she thought, wryly; *she knows even more about this place than Lucy.* Still, she was new enough to it all to feel rather charmed by Kathleen's regal graciousness. Every village needed a queen, she supposed. 'I guess so, yes. But interesting too, to find out about them – *I* think, anyway.'

'Quite brave of you both, in fact.' Kathleen turned back to warm the teapot. 'Quite brave to move from the big city where no one knows you, to a village where everyone will know everything you're up to, even before you do. Spies everywhere!' She made a warning face. 'Beware the women with little else to do but observe what's on your washing line!'

'Yes,' said Carrie, wryly, 'I'm finding that.'

'Well, as my mother always used to say, the busier you keep the village gossips, the more time you have to get on with whatever it is you want to get on with.' Kathleen paused. 'Then again, she never used to bother too much about what they said. What was it you said you did?'

'I write children's books,' said Carrie. Her eye was wandering around the kitchen, noting all the heavy bits of silver and elegant chinaware, transplanted from a much grander time. 'I'm meant to be working on a new book at the moment, but since I've moved here, I've sort of side-tracked myself.'

'I know. Moving can be such a distraction.'

'Well, yes, that too, but actually it's with a different book. One about the evacuation.' Carrie paused, not sure whether it would make her sound like another village spy. 'I had this wonderful picture in my head of all the mice and rabbits and, you know, the animals in the woods moving into the houses when all the people were evacuated, then living here for years, undisturbed by the humans, listening to the shell testing over the valley, living their own lives until we came back and evicted them again.'

'What a fascinating image!' said Kathleen. She pushed an old Chinese biscuit barrel over the table to Carrie. 'I can quite see that. I suppose you'd have publican mice and some religious otter and his nosy wife to run the church – and then some rather smart rabbits to have shooting parties and dances up at the manor house?'

Carrie smiled. 'I don't know enough about the village to know who would have gone where,' she admitted. 'I'm not even sure I would now! I mean, I wouldn't know where to start.' She looked up hopefully across the table, spotting a door into the village's closed past. 'Maybe you could fill me in?'

Kathleen put a hand to her chest. 'Oh, that makes me feel old! I'm a walking history book!'

'No, no,' said Carrie, scared she'd offended her. 'No, I just meant you must have known . . . I mean, obviously you were very young . . .' She blushed.

'Don't be a silly goose,' said Kathleen. 'I was a little girl when we moved out, and I barely knew a thing about anything.' She broke a biscuit in half. 'Not that anyone ever told us anything directly. When I was young the children were kept well away from the adults, and told to be seen and not heard. But you'd be surprised what a hotbed of gossip this little place was!'

'It's quite a hotbed now.'

'Much worse then. We didn't have television, for a start, so between the pub and the church . . .' Kathleen shrugged, her eyebrows hiked up sardonically. 'Not that I ever heard anything from my parents. They were much too discreet. But I used to hear things in the kitchen or from Nanny, and sometimes the girls from the village would come in and gossip, around harvest time, or when we were making garlands for the May fete.' She smiled, and then the smile hardened, and faded. 'All those traditions we used to have – all gone, you know. I bet there's no one left who'd know how to start making those garlands. And the secrets!'

'And there were lots? Of secrets?'

'Oh, there always *are* in a village this small. No one leaving, few people coming in, children growing up rather too fast . . .' Kathleen's voice trailed off, and she looked away, pressing her lips tightly together. 'Well, I didn't grow up very fast. I think now that I must have been very innocent, especially by today's standards. But the ploughmen were always turning up some old bones or other in the fields, and some girl was always running off with some farmhand.' She made chattering beaks with her hands, and for a moment, her dry expression was almost funny. 'Whisper, whisper. Gossip, gossip. We thought some of them were so important, but I suppose the really important ones we never even knew about. Just the silly little ones that gave us all something to chew over. Still, one shouldn't speak ill of the dead. Now, how do you take your tea?'

'Oh, no!' protested Carrie, her curiosity piqued by the abrupt change of subject. 'Please don't think I'm prying. I'm just very curious about what village life was like then. It's all so weird, um, *new* to me. We moved round a lot when I was growing up, with Dad being posted somewhere different every couple of years, so I've never really known what it's like to grow up in such a small community, where everyone's been here for ever. It would really help me with my book.'

She widened her eyes at the old lady, hoping her eagerness wasn't showing too much. 'I mean, if you could just tell me about the people I already know about, it would be fantastic. Do you remember much about Mark's grandparents? Lily and Jack Armstrong? Mark knows so little.'

'Lily? Oh, yes,' said Kathleen with more enthusiasm. 'Everyone knew Lilian. She was *extremely* popular. Very pretty girl, she was. Blonde hair, blue eyes. Well, I say girl – she used to mind me and my older sister sometimes, before she married Jack Armstrong. We didn't call it babysitting then. But if Nanny had a day off, Lily used to come and keep an eye on us. She always had barley sugar in her pockets, ready to pop into our mouths so that we'd be nice and quiet if anyone dropped by to check on her.' She smiled. 'A very nice girl, Lily.'

'Was that what she did? Childminding?' Carrie sipped at her tea. It was very strong. She wondered it if would be rude to take notes.

'She was going to be a teacher, I think.' Kathleen stirred the brick-brown contents of her cup with a silver spoon. 'That was why she stayed on at school as long as she did. Most of the village children left when they were twelve, thirteen. If they turned up at all, during lambing or harvest. She used to take the smallest ones for classes, in a separate little room around the back of the schoolhouse. And then . . .'

Kathleen paused, looked down at her spoon and placed it carefully in her saucer. It clinked discreetly. 'Well, then she got married and that was that. But she did used to look after children in the village. Whenever there was a village party, or if the women were needed in the fields, all the children would end up at Oak Cottage. Sometimes we were allowed to go along and play too. My sister Josephine and I, I mean. She used to ask us specially, so we didn't feel left out.'

Carrie smiled encouragingly. That fitted in with the idea she was building up of Lily – gentle, kind, easy with children. The sort of girl who always had barley sugar in her apron pocket, or a funny story to nip squabbling in the bud.

'We didn't feel left out, of course,' Kathleen added, with a touch of pride, 'but it was sweet of her to ask.'

'I suppose they'd both be good with children, were they?' Carrie asked. 'What with Jack being a teacher?'

Kathleen frowned a little, trying to remember. 'I wouldn't say Jack was really terribly keen on children, you know. He was a bit of a disciplinarian, I heard.' She looked up from her cup, making Carrie start at the intensity of her blue eyes. 'We didn't go to the village school, you see. That's what I mean about being left out. Josephine and I had a governess at home until we were eight, then we were sent away to school.'

'Oh,' said Carrie, feeling somewhat socially inept for not guessing that already. 'I wonder whether Jack minded Lily having the kids running around the house? If he saw them all day at school?'

'Well . . . he was quite patient. And he adored Lily, so whatever she wanted, I think he'd have allowed. She loved children.' She paused. 'How many did she have herself?'

'Just one, I think,' said Carrie. 'Mark's father. As far as I know, there were no siblings.'

'Oh,' said Kathleen. 'Oh, I thought she'd have had more. Of course, she wasn't much out of her teens herself when she got married. Jack was a good bit older than her, though. I mean, at the time, people did talk, what with Lily being . . .' Kathleen caught herself, too late.

Carrie's heart skipped. 'Lily being pregnant?' she asked. 'When they got married? I know about that.'

Kathleen looked up, her eyes more guarded. 'Well, I suppose it's not a secret, really, to anyone who could add up.' She sighed, as if she were cross with herself for indulging in the sort of gossip she'd disapproved of. 'That's what happens when the whole village knows your business. It's just common knowledge, to be passed on like the weather forecast. You can't keep anything secret, even fifty years later!'

Sixty, actually, thought Carrie. It was only now the isolation of this odd village was beginning to rise up around the edges of her conscience, like long grass, that she realised just what a predicament that must have been. How trapped Lily must have felt, not just by the village where everyone knew everything else, but by her own body and its mysterious workings. Binding her in, conspiring against her will. And Kathleen's obvious awkwardness – still! – was just a flicker of what people must have thought. And said, behind her back.

Carrie stopped herself, conscious that she was judging by her own standards.

But what if she'd *wanted* the baby, though? What if it had all gone according to plan? Who's to say what this silent girl and her silent husband had wanted?

'I think it would have been very hard to keep quiet about,' she said, trying to defuse any awkwardness Kathleen might be feeling. 'It wasn't talked about much in the family, but Mark did mention it.'

Kathleen sighed and rapped the table with her spoon. On closer inspection, Carrie realised she wasn't displaying awkwardness at all. If anything she looked faintly bemused. 'Such a shame, you know. Lily was bright, a really intelligent girl. I remember her telling me and Josephine about how she was going to go away and learn how to be a proper teacher. Looking back now, it seems such a waste.'

'But I thought there was no shame in being pregnant before marriage, not in the countryside!' Carrie protested, as gently as she could. 'Didn't that sort of thing happen all the time?'

'Well,' said Kathleen firmly, 'I don't think it wasn't quite as straightforward as some farm girl falling pregnant to her boyfriend, if you know what I mean.'

Carrie blushed, despite herself, feeling a whole village's disapproval.

Had this been a habit of Jack's? Had either of them actually *wanted* to be married to the other? And was Lily the first?

The cat slid off the chair next to her, landing on the floor silently, and slunk away into the house.

A whole new barrage of questions jostled for space in her brain, and they were even more impossible to ask, let alone answer.

Kathleen regarded her with a sympathetic gaze.

'Were they . . .' She swallowed, and tried again. 'It sounds like they were a happy couple though?'

'I'm sure they were,' said Kathleen, quickly. 'Lily was a very clever girl, very smart, and she ran rings round the lads in the village. The boys her own age, I mean. Mind, she ran rings around her parents too. She and Jack – well, they were always close. At least, that's what I understood.'

Carrie stared into her china teacup, and tried let her imagination swirl up images. The gifted girl, finding a friend in the schoolteacher, who encouraged her to aim a little higher than the farm or the manor house. Maybe encouragement turning into something more, staying after school finished to discuss books, walking up the valley to look down at the crumbling history surrounding the village, stretching out to talk on the back of that white horse . . .

The very fertile white horse. Looming over the village.

Or am I just trying to put a positive spin on all this?

She looked at Kathleen, who was pouring herself a second cup of tea with a good steady hand, using an old-fashioned silver strainer.

But if people had entrusted their children to Lily's care, even afterwards, they couldn't have disapproved so much? And what about Jack? Surely *Jack* would be the one mothers didn't want near their kids? And he'd carried on as the schoolmaster, not been run out of the village as a pervert.

Carrie wondered if she could ask these questions, and saw a reserve in Kathleen's face that clearly said 'no'. Kathleen wasn't a gossip like Lucy – it wasn't the done thing.

'I'm afraid I don't know much,' said the old lady gently. 'I was very young. And people did manage to keep some things private, even here.'

Carrie realised, dully, that she might have to resign herself to never knowing the answers, not through any concrete source. She stared into her china cup. Only by opening herself up to the stories and the ghosts and the fleeting images and sounds, letting them march through her dreams and slither through her pen as she sketched. Maybe that was what was disturbing her sleep these nights, the house trying to wake her up . . .

'Did you think you were going to come back to St Dee?' Carrie asked, changing tack. 'When you left, I mean?'

'I don't know. I didn't really think too much about it. My father went off to do some kind of government work, and my mother and I stayed with some of her family in Yorkshire for the rest of the war. Then I joined my sister at school and, well . . . We came out, lived in London, settled there. I never really thought I'd live in St Dee, after that. Things were very different after the war. I don't think any of us *realistically* expected anything could go back to the way it was. I know there were some of those protest groups, but really . . . You just have to get on with it.'

Carrie refrained from pointing out that it must have been considerably easier to get on with it when you had additional houses around the country. As she watched Kathleen stir milk into her tea, her eye stripped away the years until she saw the fine-boned child, watching from the sidelines with her pale blue eyes. She must have seen a lot, more than she could understand perhaps.

Carrie shook herself. Kathleen was speaking again. 'Plenty of folk did believe the Army would hand the land back.' She tipped her head to one side, like a bird. 'The older ones, mainly, who'd never known anywhere else. They used to come here, after the war, and hang around the perimeter fence, and protest about wanting their houses back. Not that it did them any good. The Army wasn't about to hand the village over. Rather sad, I felt.'

'You think it was better to make a clean break?'

Kathleen nodded. 'Lily and Jack, they moved right away. North-ampton, wasn't it? And they had a good fresh start. The young people too – they were glad to get out, start again in the towns. I can think of more than one family in St Dee who was pleased to wipe the slate clean, not be followed round by old gossip and stories. Whispers everywhere they went. You might say that the war did some people a good turn.'

Carrie looked out of the window, frustrated with questions. Kathleen's garden, like hers, had fruit trees, and beyond that, a view of the chalk horse on the hillside. A couple of the trees had been chopped down, revealing milky white stumps, and the rest seemed straggling and barren. Carrie suddenly imagined the roots, driving down into the earth still, even though the tree had gone. Mark was like that. The roots of his family were still here, even though they were long gone from his life. Roots curling under their house.

'In any case,' said Kathleen, 'I'm very happy to be back here, dear. I think it's wonderful to see the village come to life again, with new folk. Young folk.' She smiled. 'It's nice to remember history, but good to look ahead too.'

'Well, there'd be no history at all if people like you weren't around to pass it on,' said Carrie. 'You should write down all the old stories, before they're forgotten. Like that story about the well in Rose Cottage.'

'Oh, that.' Kathleen sighed. 'I shouldn't have mentioned about that silly ghost story the other night. I don't know what came over me.' She corrected herself. 'Well, I do. I do know. I was just a little tired of Barbara Whatsit and her ridiculous husband going on and on about the village as if it was their own place, and no one had ever lived here but them.' She pulled a face. 'Isn't that a terrible thing to admit?'

'Not at all,' said Carrie. 'I feel like that sometimes. I mean, I have absolutely no connection to this place at all, but sometimes, when I'm walking around the house, or in the garden, I wonder to myself if they mind . . . If they *mind* us coming into their village after all these years and making new plans.' She turned her lips under her teeth like a child. 'Does that sound stupid?'

It did sound stupid, she told herself. You're confusing your little story about the rats and mice with real people. And who do you mean by *they* anyway?

'No, not at all.' Kathleen refilled Carrie's cup. 'I quite see what you mean. It's even more strange for me, seeing all these young folk coming out of houses where I used to remember old ladies knitting on the front step. I often wonder if the *houses* mind, let alone the ghosts.'

'Ghosts?' said Carrie.

'Well, there are ghosts everywhere, dear,' replied Kathleen. 'Don't you think? When you look into the snug in the pub, or see that war memorial on the green?'

Carrie thought of Mark, and his passionate refusal to believe in them. He was very good at ignoring things he didn't want to deal with, until, in his mind at least, they ceased to exist: his past, her past, their overdraft limit, her ticking biological clock . . . But then he made the present such a distracting place to be, that she could only have thoughts like that when she was alone. And then she could see the ghosts in their relationship clearly enough, the years neither spoke about, the relationships left uncharted and formless next to work anecdotes they were happy enough to share.

'Yes,' she said. 'You're right.'

As Carrie was leaving, she passed a Welsh dresser, stacked with pearly white porcelain, and suddenly reminded herself of her original reason for dropping in.

'Oh, I hope you don't mind me asking,' she said, 'but I found a crate full of china, hidden in our coal cellar, and, um, someone suggested that it might have been a wedding present from the manor house? Could I bring a piece round some time and let you have a look?'

Kathleen paused, her hand on her pearls again. She smiled, and the effect reminded Carrie of the Queen's Speech. Much as she warmed to some faint mischief in Kathleen, Carrie was still rather intimidated by her lofty demeanour. 'I daresay it would be. White, was it, with a gold band? My mother used to give a dinner service to any of her staff who got married, or to the more professional people in the village. She liked Jack. He played the piano beautifully, so he often came up to the manor for Mother's musical evenings. My mother was a great entertainer. She took great pains over her dinner parties – she always said any old dinner tasted better when you ate it from a pretty plate, so she liked to think she was helping them along.'

'How thoughtful!' said Carrie, wondering if Lily and Jack had qualified for a better rank of china than the cook or the butler. 'Well, I'm using it now. You must come over some time and have some tea and cake off it.'

'I'd be delighted to see it in use,' replied Kathleen. 'Thank you so much for calling by.' She paused. 'I'll have a look through my boxes to see if I can find you any photographs of Lily and Jack.' She smiled conspiratorially. 'Some clues?'

'That would be really kind of you,' said Carrie. 'I would love that.'

It was only when Carrie was hurrying down the lane to her house, trying to get home before the first drops of rain turned into a heavy shower, that she realised that, beyond the logistics of her childhood, Kathleen had really told her almost nothing about her own family, or what it had been like to grow up in the manor house, overlooking all of St Dee.

She stopped, by the unweathered bench, in memory of someone's lost grandfather. In fact, the only impression she took away was of a rather lonely little girl, surrounded by exquisite cream teas, greedily nibbling up other people's gossip.

Chapter Eleven

Carrie walked home, turning the new pictures over in her mind, letting them take on colour and movement as her imagination worked them into life.

As she let herself through the squeaking ironwork gate, she spotted Betsy and Ivor on their doorstep, just out of the rain, playing quietly while their big marmalade cat stood guard over them. She waved, and Ivor waved his stubby hand at her, but Betsy affected not to notice.

The clouds settled in over the roofs of St Dee, battleship grey and ominous. Carrie spent the rest of the afternoon in her studio, drawing houses in silence, listening to the heavy raindrops battering the roof and trickling through the gutters while Morris spun, unsketched, in his cage. When the storm passed, she could hear the trees whisper and shake as the rain dripped off the leaves and the birds returned to their chirping and swooping.

Though her pen scratched automatically across the paper, Carrie's mind was full of Lily, now recast in her mind as the blonde bombshell of the village, tormenting the boys and driving them wild with her smart tongue and quick wit. That fitted in better with the image of her stretching out her long, tanned legs by the forest than the one of her looking nervous as a bride.

She drew a maypole in the middle of the rows of cottages, with schoolchildren mice dancing around it with ribbons in their paws, then stopped to chew her pen, imagining Lily, weaving with a bright blue ribbon, ducking under her schoolfriends' ribbons with a teasing smile.

Or would she be bored?

But how did that fit in with her being 'close' to the older schoolteacher?

Something wasn't quite fitting together.

Carrie tore the sheet off the sketchpad firmly. 'Draw Morris,' she said aloud. 'He pays the bills.'

Mark was right, she thought. They had to keep part of their brains outside St Dee's womb-like world, or else they'd be completely swallowed up by the slow-moving valley life.

She would, Carrie corrected herself. He wouldn't.

When the church bells across the valley struck five, Carrie stopped working, pleased with how much she'd done – more than she'd have done in a week in London – and wandered downstairs to make herself some tea.

She went through the motions of peeling some potatoes for supper, but what she really wanted to do was go through Mark's box of photographs again, just to see what echoes of Lily and Jack there were in Mark's father. He was so protective about that box, though, that she felt uncomfortable looking without his permission.

Carrie didn't really know why Mark was so secretive about it. It wasn't like he had any skeletons in his closet – and if he did, surely he'd keep the evidence separately? She hesitated over the last potato, and resolved not to look without asking first. No. It would be too much like reading his diaries while he was out of the house.

She put the lid on the pan, threw herself onto the sofa, turned on the news, and struggled with her curiosity and her sense of duty.

Of course if he was here, I could ask him, she thought, picking crossly at the tassles on her cushion. She looked at her watch.

It was a quarter to six. Why wasn't he home yet? Swindon wasn't that far, and Mark usually only worked after five if they had a gun to his head.

Carrie stared at her silent mobile. When they lived in London, Mark had called her two, three times a day, just to find out what she was doing, or tell her about something he'd seen on the Internet. Then, it had been cute, bordering on the disruptive. Now, of course, she missed it.

Would calling him now sound too much like checking up on him?

It would be fine, she decided. It would be wifely and caring.

She speed-dialled his number but it went straight onto voicemail.

She bit her lip, waiting a few moments, then tried again. Still voicemail.

'Hello, it's Mark. This phone's at the bottom of a big bag. Leave a message while I find it.'

Carrie sucked her teeth. Why wasn't he answering? Then again, reception was pretty poor around St Dee. He could just as easily be over the valley, already nearing the turn-off, as miles away.

She waited for the tone, letting her gaze wander around the room. The big candles in the hurricane lamps bridged the gap between dusk and night-time with a gentle glow, reflected in the mirror over the fireplace.

God, she thought, inspecting her reflection more closely, I'm getting older. Even the soft lighting revealed a furrow in her forehead that hadn't been there last birthday. The shadows shifted slightly, and a sudden superstitious panic about seeing something in the mirror over her shoulder overcame her. Carrie dropped her gaze back to her phone.

He's probably driving, she thought. And you wouldn't want him texting and driving, would you?

Outside, the first heavy drops of a fresh raincloud started to beat against the windows, and she remembered Barbara's concerns about – what was it? The high water table? How easily the village could be cut off in a flood?

Carrie ignored the voice in her head asking what she'd do if she heard something moving around in the cellar. Who she'd call. How long it would take Mark to get back. What she would do, out here, on her own, while she waited.

She took a deep breath and told herself not to be so irrational. There was Philip next door now, for a start. What was the point in getting stressed out, and being all tense when Mark did get in? He'd looked so shattered the other night – maybe finding new work wasn't as easy as he was making out.

Carrie stretched out a hand to turn on the radio for some company, then slowly pulled it back. No, she thought, I should use this time to listen to the house. There's nothing here except memories, after all. OK, maybe a few mice in the cellar and spiders in the attic, but I don't have to go there.

Taking long, slow breaths, she let her eyes travel slowly around the kitchen, running her gaze over the old plate-drying rack, the heavy wooden cupboards, the china service now arranged along the dresser.

It was starting to look just right at last, especially in the candlelight. All the nights she'd spent poring over old books and Internet sites to find period details were worth it; it felt as if she'd brought the house back to life, rather than merely filling it with her and Mark's new stuff. But in the deepening twilight, the lines between pastiche and the past seemed to blur, and it was easier to imagine the shadows of Lily and Jack gliding around their old routines, as if the intervening years had never passed. The thought only stirred up her twitchiness, and she laid a hand on her stomach to smooth down the butterflies of tension that had suddenly fluttered up into her chest.

What was that odd feeling? Where was it coming from?

I don't feel alone, she thought, running her eyes around the room, avoiding the mirror above the fireplace. I'm on my own, and yet I don't feel alone here.

If you were really happy somewhere, she thought, you'd want to stay, wouldn't you? You'd leave a part of yourself behind, every time you cast your mind back and remembered your orchard, or the best times in the bed upstairs. Or on the hill outside.

A sudden clattering at the window, something hard and sharp scuttering at the glass so fiercely it sounded on the verge of shattering, made Carrie's heart leap into her throat.

She spun, terrified, grabbing at the table for support, to see what it was.

A huge black crow had flown into the new long window, mistaking the glass for air in the fading light. It hung in the air for a second, glittering black eyes trained on her, yellow claws outstretched and scrabbling, black beak jabbing furiously at the glass, then it was gone, leaving only a faint trail of mud on the pane.

Carrie sank into a spindle-backed chair, her heart hammering against her chest, and balled her hands into fists.

This is the *countryside*, she told herself, fiercely. There are animals all over the place. Mice in the cellar, crows in the trees, spiders, flies, ticks … How long have the birds been flying through broken windows in this village, before we came along and shut them out again with new glass? How angry must they be?

I should make a note of that for the book, she thought, automatically, but her panic-filled limbs felt too heavy to move. Instead, her eyes skated round the room, darting nervously from object to object as her peripheral vision played tricks on her.

Her ears pricked as a car pulled up at the other end of the lane, but it wasn't theirs, she could tell. The engine stopped, a gate squeaked, and then there was silence again, broken only by the faint birdsong in the trees outside and the sporadic clicking of the wooden floorboards as they contracted and shifted in the chilly night air.

It's the house, she thought. More than anything, it felt as if the house itself was keeping her company with these little creaks and coughs, stretching in the heat of the day, shivering as the night fell, echoing.

Carrie shook herself. That was the worst thing about being

creative during the day; it was impossible to switch your imagination off at night. She leaped to her feet and turned the main lights and the television back on, letting the grating noise of the adverts cut right through the atmosphere, bringing the house back into the twenty-first century.

Why didn't I just leave a message? she wondered, confidence restored by the familiar theme tunes. I'll leave a message now, let him know not to rush back.

She dialled Mark's number, heard it ring twice, then it diverted onto voicemail.

'Hi, honey, it's me,' she said. 'Just wondering what time you'll be back. Give me a ring when you're near, so I can put the supper on.'

She hung up, and leaned on the back of the rocking chair. The important thing was not to sound like a nagging wife.

Well, if he wasn't going to be back, she might as well find those photographs herself.

In the beginning, Carrie had suggested that she and Mark sit down and put his photos in an album as she had with hers. Any happy snaps from their life together were carefully archived – by her – in the huge leather album her agent had given them as a wedding present. Photo corners, tracing-paper sheets, neat captions – the lot. Mark had teased her about her meticulous efforts, and she'd told him she was trying to pin down something of their lives to pass on to kids who might not believe that their parents ever had fun.

'We'll *always* have fun,' he'd protested, a little too cheerfully. He didn't, however, give her the correct answer, which was that children would only make their lives even happier.

She didn't push it, because Mark's family pictures told the whole sad story of his childhood: one small envelope of black-and-white snaps, and a huge stack of cheap colour prints of his numerous holidays.

His *travelling*, Carrie corrected herself. Mark rolled his eyes if she ever referred to them as holidays. He was a *traveller*.

I'll only look in the box if it's on clear display, she bargained with herself. And I'll only look for pictures of Lily.

She got up from the rocking chair and went through to Mark's study, her stockinged feet padding softly on the wooden floor. There were two pots of hyacinths on his windowsill and the fragrance had filled the room while the door was closed. Beneath that the room had a faint smell of Mark himself. Carrie paused, closed her eyes and drew in a deep breath of cool air.

Mark's study was gloomy compared to the well-lit kitchen. Only one large window faced onto the garden, and it was partially obscured by the overgrown tree. The little fireplace and old built-in bookshelves made her imagine Jack had had it as his study.

Carrie hesitated on the threshold, and she was suddenly unable to stop the flood of vivid pictures tumbling into her imagination: Jack the schoolmaster, working at his desk, marking books, screwing up his face in concentration while Lily's babysitting charges made a racket in the kitchen next door.

He'd have had his desk *here*, she thought as the images jumbled into her mind, up against the wall, opposite the fireplace. A big desk, oak or mahogany, with drawers and ink stains, with blotters and books in neat piles. There would always be a fire going in here, even in the summer – Lily would make it every morning. He would keep his gown hanging on the hook on the back of the door, and he'd keep the key in the lock on his side. To shut himself away if he had to.

Carrie blinked, startled by her own certainty, and looked at the door beneath her hands. It was an old one; the builders hadn't replaced them all. Slowly she pushed the door around: there was a very old hook, rusting around the old screws, but still fixed firmly in the solid wood. The hairs on the back of her hands tingled.

Oh, good guess, she thought, battling to keep her breathing regular. Most doors have hooks on the back. You're letting your imagination run away with you.

To prove something to herself, she stepped over the threshold of the room and looked purposefully along the bookshelves lining one wall. Mark had stacked his computer-language manuals next to his huge collection of dog-eared *Rough Guides*, propping them up with the occasional heavy Asian artefact, lugged back through Customs.

No wonder he was finding it hard to settle down in St Dee, she thought, running her eyes over the brightly coloured spines. Thailand, South-East Asia, Australia, India, New Zealand. He'd seen so many different places and things, always searching for something new, something more exotic, whereas her own travels had only made her long for the reassuring smallness of a village life.

Carrie ran her eyes up and down the box files on the lowest shelf. The trainer box was there, under his box file of receipts for his tax return. Carefully, she slid it out. The lid was starting to tear at the corners, stretched by the stack of photos inside.

She reminded herself that she wasn't snooping. They were married, weren't they? It wasn't as though he was even interested in his family. And how else was she ever going to learn about his past? Maybe it was just the process of talking it all through *with* her that Mark shied away from . . .

That isn't true, warned a voice in her head, but she pushed it to one side.

She searched through the packets of modern photographs for the small brown envelope that she knew contained his few family snaps. It didn't take long to find – only two packets down from the top.

Carrie slid out the contents carefully. Here were Mark's mother and father, Pauline and Ben, at a party in the Seventies: Mark got his dark, heavily lashed eyes from his mother, and his lanky build from his dad. In fact, if it wasn't for the bushy sideburns, it could almost be Mark leaning against the doorframe in the patched flares and T-shirt.

She examined the photograph with a critical eye. Lily's long legs? A hint of a cheeky grin – that looked the same. But what about temperament? Was Mark's jokiness passed down from Lily and Jack? Or his restless nature? Could you know, on the basis of one or two pictures?

There were a few more; some formal, awkward wedding pictures, taken in a very beige registrar's office. Pauline's thick curls tumbled beneath her floppy-brimmed hat, and with her lacy cravat and short skirt, she looked incongruously like Charles the Second. Ben was equally well-covered in a three-piece suit and copious facial hair. She could see Mark's impatience in both their faces. A couple of flared, frizzed friends stood behind them, next to one old lady in a hat that looked like a giant Quality Street toffee – Lily.

No sign there of the golden-haired May Queen. She looked smaller and sharper, like a dried-up apple, and while everyone else was raising glasses and toasting the happy couple in advocaat, Lily was staring blankly into space, lost in thought. She seemed to have forgotten how to be happy.

Next to her was Jack, still wearing a brushy moustache and standing up very straight. He hadn't embraced the Seventies fashions. He didn't look the sort to embrace anything.

Carrie turned over the photo and saw that someone, presumably Mark's mother, had written, 'Birmingham Registrar's Office, May 18, 1971'. Was Ben born here in St Dee then, wondered Carrie, realising she didn't even know Mark's parents' birthdays. Was he a baby when they left the house? Had he run around the kitchen with the other kids?

If he had, he'd have to be nearly thirty when he got married. Was he? She squinted at the picture. It was so hard to tell how old anyone was in the Seventies. Everyone looked like children wearing their parents' clothes.

There was just one photograph of Mark with his mother: Pauline was cuddling him tightly outside a solid Victorian church porch; Mark was wrapped in a christening robe, barely visible beneath the frothy lace, while Pauline struggled with a high wind, a handbag the size of a breadbin, and another huge hat. Her expression was somewhat inscrutable, probably due to the complex juggling act she was carrying out, but on balance she looked pretty happy.

Poor Mark, thought Carrie, feeling a tug of pity for her husband.

If this were my picture, I'd have it in a frame somewhere, not shoved in a shoebox.

She hesitated over a snap of Pauline sitting on the bonnet of a red MG sports car, one foot still tentatively in contact with the ground, the other wrapped self-consciously around it. Carrie knew that pose – it was one where you were trying to put as little weight on the bodywork as possible for fear of dents.

Had that been the car they'd crashed in? The MG? All Carrie knew was that Pauline had been driving, it had been a wet morning, and they were on their way to collect Mark from football. He'd told her this once, lying in bed the day before he proposed, and he'd never spoken about it again.

When your parents could just vanish while you were enjoying yourself, playing football with your mates, no wonder scraps of photographs didn't mean much to you.

It was stories like that that put her off learning to drive. So easy to be hurtling along one minute listening to the radio and laughing, then suddenly to feel the car slide on ice, or skid on a dry spot, and have no control over this toy that was about to trap you in twisted metal and fire and . . .

She cocked her head, convinced she'd heard a squeal of brakes. Was it just the television? Carrie listened for a moment, then shook herself, horrified at her own over-fertile imagination. It was about the right time for *The Bill*, or some other police drama.

Being alone was really starting to get to her.

Carrie lifted up a handful of loose travelling pictures to start repacking the box, and though she'd promised herself she wouldn't look, she couldn't help flipping through them. Photos like these always made Carrie feel a bit strange: it reminded her how many other people had known Mark, had chatted with him, shared experiences with him, before she'd even known him. He was like an iceberg – she knew the visible, present part of Mark like the back of her hand, but his past was almost completely submerged in reticence.

Like this moustache. Carrie peered at Mark, perched confidently on a rickshaw, looking about twelve with a fluffy brown moustache. Why had he thought that was a good idea?

Why had they never sat and gone through these pictures together and had a laugh at it, either?

She sat back on her heels. It might just be that he thought the photos were boring, compared with the drama of actually being there. Mark seemed to have perfected the art of taking pictures at arm's length, allowing him to appear in shot at the same time as the Taj Mahal, Koh Samui beach, the Grand Canyon, various geysers in Iceland, lots of places that looked hot and uncomfortable, countless red sunsets and orange sunrises, dramatic beaches and crowded markets, one or two close-ups of huge insects.

Carrie dealt them into piles on the rug like playing cards. She preferred pictures with people in, where you could see how they were reacting to their settings. Mark hadn't travelled alone, it seemed; there were plenty of tanned girls and young men with travelling moustaches and patchy beards, all grinning up at the camera as if they knew they were having the time of their lives and that one day they'd look back and want to remember how much fun it had been.

None of them seemed to be reacting much to their settings. They were just there, sweating. And in the background, the tide came in, and the sun set, and Machu Picchu loomed.

Carrie wondered where all these young men and women were now. Merchant bankers and teachers, probably. Only Mark seemed to have found a job that allowed him to carry on 'travelling' well into his late twenties, in between contracts. When they first met, he'd just spent the best part of three months hitching across Canada.

She turned a couple of photos over to see if he had written on the back: he hadn't.

Carrie bit her lip and looked thoughtfully at the piles around her. Who had taken the full-length photos of Mark? Who had he handed the camera to? A travelling companion? A girlfriend? A policeman?

For a second, she yearned for someone to ask. Someone who could fill in some of the blanks. His mother, maybe, might confide in her about some unsuitable girl they were so glad he hadn't ended up with. Or a sister she could gossip with, invite to stay in the new guest room, someone who could tell her what Mark had been like as a child, so she might know what to expect from children of her own.

But there was no one who could throw any light into the dark corners of Mark's past, no one who could help her understand him better, or give her any clues about what had gone before.

Carrie suddenly felt an awful loneliness wash over her. Here she was, thirty-four years old, in a grown-up house, in a grown-up village, to all intents and purposes a successful, married woman, and yet all on her own, and with no idea what a married woman was supposed to be like.

To her horror, she felt panicky, hormonal tears pricking at her eyes.

'Oh, come on!' she said aloud, chafing her arms to stop the goose pimples that had broken out along her bare skin. It had turned very cold, so cold that Carrie wondered if the boiler had gone out. I should think about lighting that fire, she thought, looking at the empty iron fireplace. There should be a fire in here. In her mind's eye, she could see it flickering and burning, filling the house with the smell of old wood.

She turned her attention back to the photographs in front of her. None of the people were familiar – Mark's nomadic travelling had yielded no lasting friendships. You're just tuning into Mark's loneliness, she chided herself. He's the one who should be feeling sad. And he copes with it. Maybe that's why he doesn't like to look back. Maybe the present and the future is where he feels his life is.

Where *our* life is.

There are plenty of things he doesn't know about *your* past, she thought, flicking through another handful of pictures: Mark on a camel, Mark in a mudbath, sunset, mountain, sunset, sunset, sunrise.

Not that I'd mind telling him. If he asked.

A tiny part of her wished that Mark *would* ask. Maybe even be a little bit jealous of the time she'd had before they'd met. But he wasn't like that.

Carrie reminded herself that keeping some mystery was what kept marriages alive, especially when you came to the whole thing a bit late. That was what all the magazines said, anyway.

The photos slapped on top of each other as she dealt them into piles. Mark in an airport, a beach, another beach, a raft, a waterfall . . .

Why did he never really talk about all these places he'd seen? And how much had this constant travelling *cost?*

Carrie's brisk dealing stopped as she reached a small envelope of photos, kept apart from the rest. She tipped them out, turning the envelope over to see what was written on it: it was postmarked 12 October 1998, and was addressed to Mark in Shepherd's Bush. (Had Mark lived there? On his own?) The handwriting was obviously female, and the misalignment of the postcode suggested that whoever had written it wasn't familiar with British addresses. Carrie felt pleased with her own Miss Marple detective skills.

But her smile faded from her face as she looked at the pictures.

They were all of the same girl. Carrie enumerated her best points automatically, but she had the sort of attention-grabbing beauty that made it impossible to separate out her attractions: broad, straight-toothed smile, long tanned thighs, thick plaits of hair so white that for a moment Carrie thought it was bleached Debbie Harry-blonde. It wasn't, though. The spontaneously caught snap of her leaping naked into a pool of pellucid water revealed a long, pale body like a streak of whittled bone, the hair between her legs only slightly less golden than the streams of light feathering out around her thrown-back head.

Feeling unexpectedly dirty, Carrie covered it with the next snap, and even though in this one the girl – and she was a girl, in her late teens or early twenties – was sitting fully clothed on a rock as a crimson sun dissolved into the sea behind her, there was something about the way she was looking into the camera that gripped Carrie's stomach into a tight knot. It was an intimate, sly, 'don't photograph me now' glance, but one made sure in the knowledge that the person behind the lens had seen her many, many times before.

Quickly, she turned it over to see if there was anything on the back.

'Queensland', Mark had written. No date. No name. But Carrie didn't see that as carelessness this time. He didn't need to write the name or the date because he wasn't going to forget a look like that.

There were more pictures of this girl, but even as Carrie laid them out on the polished floorboards, she wasn't really taking in the details.

This was what Mark didn't want me to see when he wouldn't go through his photographs, she thought, as a long blade of jealousy drove into her heart. Not just for the woman, and what she might have meant to her husband, before he was even her *boyfriend*, but for the fact that Mark had kept this woman secret.

Why?

Carrie let her pent-up breath run out of her in a long stream.

She gnawed her lip. It wasn't as simple as jealousy. There were at least three dozen other packets of photos. How many more would this woman appear in? Would there be whole sets of her and Mark together?

But Mark had set those ones aside, just as he'd set aside the precious few pictures of his family. Whoever she was, she must have meant something to him. Well. *More* than something.

Carrie slid her fingers into the envelope, hunting for a letter or a card she already knew wasn't there, desperate for something to explain. There was nothing.

Clumsily, she ran through the remaining packets, letting photographs spill out as she searched for the golden hair amongst the landmarks. Here she was again, and again – and the two packets on top of the box were full of her. Her and Mark together, in that familiar arm's length 'both of us' shot. Mark on his own, looking relaxed and incredibly happy. Pictures of feet with toes intertwined in the sand. And they were above the pictures of his family, so Mark must have been looking at them quite recently.

Carrie sat back on her heels again. Her options were to ask Mark, and admit she'd been snooping, or try to put it out of her mind.

'Come on,' she said aloud. 'It was years ago. Years ago. And he's obviously not in touch with her any more, is he?'

That much was true. Their Christmas card list was pretty minimal. She and Mark had hundreds of acquaintances, not so many friends. They'd been enough for each other from the moment they'd met, letting other outside friendships dwindle and die as their lives twisted together in a self-sufficient strand.

Outside, a car honked its horn further down the lane. The complaints there'd be about that, Carrie thought automatically, then smiled ruefully at how soon St Dee's small-town preoccupations had taken over her mind. She looked down at the debris surrounding her, the fragments of Mark's life, and felt like Bluebeard's wife, horrified by what she'd found and guilty that she'd looked.

She sat on her heels, staring at the smiling, tanned Mark she hadn't known.

Then the front door slammed and Carrie jerked backwards.

'Where are you, Carrie?' Mark sounded stressed.

'In here!' she replied, frantically shuffling the photos together as best she could.

'Where?' His footsteps were coming nearer on the bare wooden floor, as the photographs slithered and spilled out of her grasp.

'In your study!' she shouted, scrambling to her feet to push the shoebox back on the shelf.

'What are you doing in here?' Mark was suddenly standing over her, his hair standing up in peaks where he'd obviously shoved his hands into it. He looked dishevelled, and not in the artful way he contrived for work. Carrie could smell sweat, and beer.

'I was looking for pictures of your grandparents,' replied Carrie, leaning against the bookshelf.

It was then that she saw a photograph lying beneath the desk. It was the girl in the shorts again. This time she was in a minuscule bikini, but the expression was just the same. Private. Intimate.

Funny. It couldn't have fallen out of the box from where she'd been looking at the pictures. Unless Mark had been looking at the pictures too.

Carrie looked up to ask who she was, then she saw the expression on Mark's face, and the first jumbled words stuck in her throat.

Mark was ashen. He looked like the audience member whose card had just been picked by the magician; the tarot reader who had just been shown the Tower, or Death; more stunned than shocked.

'Carrie,' he began, then saw what she was looking at. Carrie noticed with surprising detachment how his skin had turned another few shades paler under the stubble.

She waited, then bent down and picked up the photograph. There was another one underneath it. The same girl, but this time she was wound around Mark, who held her with a protective arm. They looked like a pair of beachbound angels: salt-matted curls, bright wide smiles and glowing skin. She was as golden as Mark was dark. In the second picture they had their hands held up to show off matching onion rings on their wedding fingers.

Carrie felt nauseous with jealousy. She'd never seen Mark's skin look anything less than pallid. She'd certainly never seen him look *matched*, like this. In adventurousness, in charisma, in sheer ebullience.

'Who's this?' she asked, lightly. 'I don't think I've met her.'

Mark rubbed his face with his whole hand. 'Listen, Carrie, we don't have time for this now . . .'

'No, come on. Who is she?'

He seemed to debate with himself, weighing up something in his head.

'Mark,' said Carrie with a forced smile, 'I'm not going to throw a fit. She's gorgeous. Is she an old girlfriend?'

'Yes, she is.' Mark sounded harried. 'Her name's Astrid. We met while I was backpacking round Australia.'

Carrie processed this information. It didn't lessen the jealousy. 'And . . . do you keep in touch?'

'It was years ago. Listen . . .' He ran his hand over his face again. 'Oh God, Carrie, something awful's happened . . .'

'What?'

Outside, she could suddenly hear the air-shredding keening of a child, and a cold sweat sprang up on her chest. 'Is that a baby crying, or am I hearing things?' she demanded.

'It's a child crying,' said Mark. 'I've run over next door's cat. I only just missed the little boy. Shit.' He sank down against the wall. 'I didn't even see him,' he said, half to himself. 'I just saw something moving in front of the car – he was across the road before . . .'

A terrible howling set up next door, as a second voice joined in, even more plaintive than the first.

Carrie stared at him, then felt a surge of adrenalin, overwhelming her own feelings. 'Don't just sit there,' she yelled. 'What have you done?' She scrambled to her feet, and made for the door as fast as she could.

Carrie flinched when she saw the pathetic scene in the kitchen of Rose Cottage.

In front of the Aga, Betsy and Ivor were crouched around a shoebox containing the muddied remains of the big ginger cat. Ivor was sobbing in painful gasps of misery, while Betsy tried to comfort him, big fat tears rolling down her pale face and splashing visibly onto the floor tiles. Philip stood making hot cocoa, looking fierce and protective at the same time.

Carrie felt beyond terrible. 'Oh God,' she breathed. This wasn't the neighbourly meeting she'd had planned for Mark.

'Quite,' snapped Philip.

'Fuck,' said Mark under his breath, and Carrie shoved him hard before Philip could turn his wrath Mark's way. He looked on the verge of eruption.

'Don't swear in front of my children,' said Philip with simmering calm.

She went to kneel down to the children, but something stopped her. It wasn't her place to try to comfort them. She turned to Philip, and there was no trace of the mischief she'd seen in his eyes before.

'Is there anything we . . . ?' Her voice trailed off. What on earth could they do, with their minimal experience of parenting? Even their clothes advertised their own overgrown teenage state – Mark's layered long-sleeved T-shirts, her hastily pulled-on college sweatshirt – and yet her arms ached to comfort the two little children, and it made her feel worse to think she had no right to.

'Don't tell them you're sorry, before you start,' said Philip curtly. 'They might just be kids, but even they're aware of the simple fact that some hooligan was driving too fast and mangled their pet for no good reason other than his own selfish disregard for speed limits.'

Mark mumbled something unintelligible. Carrie didn't want to turn to look at him.

'I'm not even going to talk about the fact that you could have killed Ivor.' Philip gave Mark a terrifyingly black look. 'If there were someone else here to look after these two, I'd take you outside and knock your head off. So unless you're a vet, or are able to bring this cat back to life, I think it would be better if you went. Before I change my mind.'

'Of course, Philip,' said Carrie. 'We don't want to make things worse. But you'll let me know, won't you, if . . . ?' Her voice trailed off impotently. 'Please. I'll be in all day.'

'I'm so sorry,' mumbled Mark. 'I really am . . .'

'Small word, sorry,' said Philip and turned his back on them. Ivor reached up with his arms and buried himself in Philip's thick aran jumper, while Betsy leaned into his side, rubbing his back with her little hand, as if she were trying to comfort him too.

Carrie pushed Mark out of the door before she burst into tears as well.

They stumbled down the path towards the back gate, where Carrie fumbled with the latch, trying to blot out the sound of Betsy and Ivor's sobs. Philip had left the back door open – doubtless they'd be listening to the crying all night. She wasn't sure which was worse – phantom sobbing that Mark couldn't hear, or real sobbing that they both could.

'Hurry up,' she hissed to Mark, who was wandering as if in a trance.

He turned to her, and his expression chilled her with its disconnected panic. Mark seemed little older than Ivor, his eyes blank with something Carrie couldn't share.

Immediately she felt terrible. He'd had a real shock, after all. Carrie thought of all the things she could yell at him about – his driving, his stupidity, his secrecy, his lateness – but the vulnerable, scared look in his face stopped her, and she could only feel a wrench of pure pity.

Had he thought for a horrifying second that he was going to die too, like his parents, skidding off the road and into the darkness, crumpled into the twisted wreckage of his car?

'He was so quick,' mumbled Mark. 'I didn't even *see* the cat. I thought I'd hit him . . .'

The shouting could wait. It always did.

'Come on,' she said, rubbing Mark's arm through the soft jersey and leading him down the path. 'Come on inside. It's OK. You're home now.'

Chapter Twelve

'You're telling me you just went back into the kitchen and made him a bowl of soup?' demanded Lucy. 'And that was it? End of?'

She dunked her Hobnob and popped it into her pink mouth, sucking the hot tea from it before crunching it up. She didn't drip once, even though her quick blue eyes didn't leave Carrie's face throughout the operation.

Carrie was amazed that in a tale that involved a car crash, a dead pet, a livid neighbour and two hysterical children, Lucy had homed in on the photographs.

'Well, more or less, yes,' she said, sorting through the basket of laundry. It seemed pointlessly prim to stop just because Lucy had arrived, given that Lucy saw everyone else's knickers anyway. 'What else was I meant to do? Mark was in shock. After the weeping and wailing next door, I felt like a bit of a bitch, bringing up some holiday snaps. God, those poor kids.' She groaned, just thinking about Betsy's fat little hand on Philip's back. 'They looked devastated. I felt *so* bad.'

'And how did *Mark* feel?' There was more than a trace of sarcasm in Lucy's tone.

'He felt bad too.' Carrie looked up. 'He did. His parents died in a car crash, you know – he was really shaken up.'

And he had been. He had eaten some tomato soup, then gone to bed almost immediately, curled up in a foetal ball. His eyes were shut but Carrie couldn't tell if he was really asleep. She lay with her arms around him all night.

'You'd think that would make him a very careful driver then, wouldn't you?' observed Lucy.

Carrie opened her mouth to say, no, he's an appalling driver, and sometimes I think he's tempting Fate, but she didn't. Mark was getting a bad enough press in the village already. She'd got a very black look from the postman that morning.

'He normally is,' she said instead, turning her attention to one of her shirts. She unbuttoned it and rolled the sleeves down. 'He's normally very careful.'

Lucy's face disagreed. 'So what did he say about where he'd been so late?'

Carrie hesitated. She'd only intended to run the events of the previous night past Lucy so she could dismiss them as nothing. But even though Lucy wasn't exactly putting her mind at rest on that score, there was something cathartic about getting it all out of her head anyway. 'He didn't.'

'What? You didn't ask him what he'd been doing in Swindon? Because there isn't that much, let me tell you!'

'Lucy, he'd just run over next door's cat!'

'Oh, what's a fecking cat?' Lucy made a dismissive gesture with her hands. 'I know where they can get another. I can't believe you didn't give him the third degree about why he's suddenly looking at photos of an ex he's never told you about *and* staying out till all hours! Then I'd have moved onto the cat.'

'We don't have that sort of relationship,' said Carrie, and it didn't console her as much as usual. 'We promised we'd trust each other. Accept that we both had history and leave it at that.'

'Carrie.' Lucy gaped at her. 'There's trust and there's . . . taking advantage. I can't believe you could be so calm! I'd have wanted to know *exactly* who she was.'

Carrie shook her head. 'We agreed we wouldn't get possessive about the past. I mean, I told you – we weren't kids when we met. What's done's done.'

Lucy had listened to the tale of Carrie and Mark's modern romance with more cynicism than Carrie was used to.

'I know, you said. But that doesn't mean you're not allowed to ask questions,' sniffed Lucy. 'Men'll test you.'

'Mark's different,' insisted Carrie. This wasn't how she'd expected it to play out.

'Is he?' Lucy looked almost amused. 'Just because he knows about G-spots? And has his own cleanser? Don't be so sure.'

Carrie didn't like the feeling that she was perhaps getting a glimpse of how the rest of the village saw them. 'You know, it's probably just an overreaction,' she said. 'Mark met lots of people while he was travelling. I don't think she was anyone special.' She chewed her upper lip. 'I mean, he'd have mentioned her by now if she was.'

'Carrie, love,' said Lucy, as if she were talking to a small child, 'that's exactly why he wouldn't have mentioned her.'

She sighed. 'I know.'

'So? Didn't he even try to explain? Didn't he come up with some lame story?' Lucy cocked a cynical eyebrow. 'About half an hour too late?'

Carrie shook her head. 'It never came up, what with the cat and the Gladstones and everything. And there just wasn't a right time for me to ask. I know, I know, I should have said something,' she admitted in a rush. 'It would have cleared the air, wouldn't it?'

Lucy nodded.

'There wouldn't have been any point, though. When Mark doesn't want to talk about something he just clams up. Completely. And it's like the questions just vanish.'

'They don't vanish,' said Lucy. 'You just don't ask them.'

Carrie picked up a pair of Mark's jeans and put her hand in the pockets, checking for loose change. A Boots receipt, a couple of pound coins, a travelcard.

Receipts file, she thought automatically, and put them in her back pocket.

'Did your parents never row in front of you?' asked Lucy. 'Is it that you don't like having arguments, or something?'

'No, I just don't want to go back on the promises I made,' Carrie burst out, finally snapping. 'We agreed, right from the start, that we wouldn't start digging around like this, raking up old relationships. It wouldn't be fair. So I can't start now.' She stuck her hands into her hair, feeling the tension dragging on the roots.

'Carrie, it's not out of order if it puts your mind at rest. It's bloody normal, if you ask me!' Lucy prised another Hobnob out of the packet. 'I know everything there is to know about Chris. I know stuff about him he doesn't even know himself. That's what marriage is about, if you ask me.' She wagged the biscuit at Carrie. 'You get to know the plain, unvarnished truth about each other so well there's no point lying. Now that's where trust starts. Stop me if I try to eat another one of these, by the way.'

'Well, you've known Chris since you were at school. I only met Mark when I was thirty-two. I bet he couldn't *remember* half the stuff I'd want to know.' Carrie felt close to crying, despite her brave words. There was something simultaneously unsettling and comforting about talking to Lucy.

'Do you want a hanky?' asked Lucy, seeing her sniff back a tear. 'Hay fever's a bugger,' she added kindly. 'All these trees you're not used to, eh?'

'No, no, I've got one somewhere.' Carrie searched through her pockets. Slowly, she withdrew the travelcard from her back pocket and looked at it. It had yesterday's date. Mark hadn't been in Swindon at all. He'd been in London.

Her stomach turned to ice. So why had he deliberately told her a lie? Unless he didn't want her to know that's where he was going. And why would he do that unless he had something to hide?

'OK, let's be logical.' Lucy fixed her with a brisk maternal look. 'You think this girl is just someone he met while he was travelling.'

Carrie nodded and shoved the travelcard back in her pocket, not wanting Lucy to fall upon it.

'But your intuition says there's more to it than that?'

She twisted up her mouth and nodded again. Telling Lucy about the travelcard might make this final thing too real. 'It's just a feeling though. Mark's never said anything. It was . . . just the way he looked, when he saw me holding the photo.'

'Well, that's exactly why you've got your gut feeling.' Lucy dunked her biscuit conclusively. 'Female intuition. Helps us spot what they're *not* saying.'

'I don't *want* to be a nagging old wife,' Carrie wailed. 'It was one of my vows! I wrote it myself!'

Lucy laughed and pushed Carrie's untouched coffee towards her. 'You promised that? You divvy. You need to learn how to dig better, love. If there's nothing to tell, he won't mind telling you. If there is something . . .' She shrugged. 'It'll come out anyway, sooner or later. That's the thing about secrets – there's that little bit of you that always wants to spill the beans, deep down.' She made a little scrabbling motion with her fingers. 'Really big secrets, they're always dying to dig their way up to the surface.' She grinned wickedly. 'I mean, we've all got them, haven't we?'

'No!' said Carrie, nearly spilling her coffee. 'No, that's not true. I haven't.'

'Get away,' said Lucy, disbelievingly.

'I haven't,' insisted Carrie. 'Honestly. I've led a very dull life.' She grimaced. 'Maybe too dull, eh?'

'Maybe,' agreed Lucy.

Outside, Carrie heard the clink of milk bottles as the milkman made his delivery next door – one full-fat, one semi-skimmed, one orange juice and yoghurts – then the squeak of the gate and a similar clink outside her own house. Then it was quiet again, except for the chatter of birdsong outside in the orchard.

'Mark was in London yesterday,' she heard herself say. 'He said he was working in Swindon, but I found a travelcard in his jeans. And he promised me he'd make contacts round here, so he could work from home and we could spend more time together in—'

'A London travelcard?' interrupted Lucy.

'Yes, you need one for buses and tubes and—'

'I have been to London, Carrie,' Lucy interrupted. 'I mean, why would he lie about that? You know he goes back to London now and again.'

Carrie hesitated. 'I've found two, actually. I kind of hoped the first one was because he was planning a surprise for me? But he definitely said he was in Swindon again yesterday. Definitely.'

Lucy folded her arms. 'So you think he's seeing someone else?'

'God, no! No, I think it's more because I've put so much pressure on him about having a life out here. Because he thinks I might be jealous of the fact that he can get out, and go back to London to work.'

'Most people would be moaning about having to do that,' Lucy pointed out. She looked hard at Carrie. 'That's not all, though, is it? Hmm?'

'Well, I do sometimes worry that he's . . .' Carrie swallowed and heard her worst fear come out of her mouth. 'That he'd get bored with me, with the life we have. I mean, he's so gregarious, and I'm actually quite shy and dull, really, and I worry that he misses London itself . . .'

She stopped.

Lucy was looking at her with a mixture of sympathy and disbelief. 'You're not *dull*. Don't be stupid! If I were Mark I'd be worried you'd be getting bored of *me*.'

Carrie knew she had to change the subject quickly, or else she'd lose it altogether. 'Anyway, listen. Help me out here. Where can I get hold of two new kittens at short notice?'

Lucy twisted her mouth wryly, then went along with it. 'Funny you should ask me that,' she said. 'I know some going spare. I'll swap you for the real story about what that Philip Gladstone's done with his wife. The pub's a-buzz. It's a good job that cottage doesn't have a patio or else Barbara Purves would be all for digging it up, fancy university or not.'

'He's nothing like that!' Carrie protested. 'I mean, he's a bit odd, but he's perfectly nice.'

He hadn't been that nice the previous evening. Carrie's heart sank at the thought of her mission of forgiveness. Another unpleasant confrontation, but one she couldn't put off.

'Well, all the more reason to get to the bottom of it. Find out for me?'

'OK,' said Carrie, crossing her fingers under the table.

As she was leaving, Lucy hesitated at the door, her basket on one hip. 'Carrie,' she said. 'I know you know I'm a bit of a one for gossip, but . . .' She paused. 'I won't, you know . . .'

'Thank you,' said Carrie. 'Thanks.'

Lucy gave her a brief hug, clasping Carrie to her round shoulder with a sudden, warm movement. It was the first time anyone other than Mark had hugged her in a long time, and Carrie had to bite back tears of unexpected gratitude.

There had been a pot of tea and three mugs on the Rose Cottage kitchen table when she arrived, one large and two very small, but Ivor and Betsy were nowhere to be seen. Philip had offered to make her a fresh pot, and Carrie had accepted, although now he was going to the trouble of boiling the kettle on the Aga and spooning out tea leaves, she just felt worse about intruding.

The pile of history books and opened file pads suggested that she'd interrupted his work too, but he made no reference to it.

'I'm so sorry,' said Carrie, for the fourth time in ten minutes. 'Really. I am so sorry.'

'I know.' Philip glared at her. 'We've been through this. Please stop apologising. It wasn't your fault.'

'Oh God, it probably was. Mark was late, and I'd left him a message and—'

'Your husband was driving like a bloody maniac. He wasn't looking where he was going, he was listening to music so loud I could virtually hear it in the garden, and he came round that corner far too fast. I'm just relieved Ivor didn't run into the road after the damned cat.' Philip's voice didn't rise, but it took on a scary intensity that made the hairs on the back of Carrie's arms prickle.

'I'm furious with him too,' she said weakly. But how furious could you get with someone who looked as scared as Mark had? He'd slunk off to work that morning without even opening his mouth, and she hadn't had the heart to demand to know where he was going. If he were up to anything, as Lucy thought, he didn't exactly look pleased about it.

'You should be.' Philip poured hot water onto the tea leaves, stirred it, and clattered the lid on. 'Much as I appreciate your apology, though, I note he isn't here himself. My children have had a hard enough time of it recently without seeing their cat die too.'

'I know,' said Carrie automatically, then realised she didn't.

Philip raised a dark eyebrow.

'I mean . . . um, with moving and all,' she finished lamely.

'No, you don't. You mean because I haven't moved here with their mother.'

Carrie didn't know what to say. This would be the point at which Lucy would ask straight out, but it seemed unbearably rude.

Philip placed a Durham University mug on the table in front of her. 'Well?'

'It's none of my business,' she stammered.

'I thought everything was common business round here?'

'I think it's important to respect people's privacy,' she said, thinking of her own troubled relationship.

'Well done, Carrie. I'm touched to have such a thoughtful neighbour. Milk?'

She looked up, confused by his sarcastic tone.

Philip's expression seemed innocent enough, but his eyes were glittering like pieces of coal. It was his grey and black beard that made him look almost bear-like. She couldn't imagine him without it. 'That concern for privacy, I mean. Makes me wonder what you've got to hide yourself, seeing as how you're so keen to respect mine. So, tell me. What *is* it you've got to hide?'

He slid into his chair and gripped his mug of tea with long fingers. Carrie noticed the dark hairs growing on the back of his hand, curling up towards his arm. His nails were broad, but clean, and well-kept. She focused on his hands, because she wasn't sure she wanted to meet his gaze.

'I don't have any secrets,' she said for the second time that morning.

'I don't believe that. The Armstrongs, eh? Secret drug users?' he suggested. 'Into wife swapping? On the run from the law? Husband is battling an addiction to Internet war games? Hmm? Witness protection programme? Secret police? Undercover documentary makers from London, sent to spy on us all?'

'None of those things!' Carrie burst out, then realised he was teasing her.

'You're not really married, you're actually brother and sister living incestuously . . .' Philip stroked his beard, thoughtfully, then raised a finger. 'No, no, I know! You've discovered that there's buried treasure in your cellar and you've murdered your way through the family to get the house so you can dig up your Nazi gold?'

'You got me.' Carrie leaned back in her chair. 'It's the Nazi gold. Left here when they evacuated the village. By Goering. He para-chuted in with it shortly after the evacuation.'

'I thought as much.' Philip pushed the sugar bowl towards her, and shut up his files. Carrie automatically read the white labels on the spine: Norse Settlements, Druid Sites, something in Anglo-Saxon script she couldn't make out.

'Is that what everyone's talking about in the pub?' she asked, in a strangled voice. 'Trying to work out who we are?'

She felt a little piqued that Philip, who was even more of an outsider than they were, and wasn't even on Lucy's cleaning rota, should be more informed about the general mood of the village than she was, after a matter of hours. Besides, when had he time to visit the pub, with two small children?

'According to Tony, everyone's trying to work out who the government spy is,' he said solemnly. 'Paul Jenkins is the obvious choice, but I say he's too obvious. Has to be someone much more stealthy. A couple, maybe.'

'But why would there be a government spy in the village? Have I missed something?'

Philip widened his eyes. The whites seemed very bright. 'You want to get down to the pub more. The *government spies* are amongst us to make sure we don't find out why the village was *really* evacuated in 1941.'

'I see,' faltered Carrie. 'And Mark and I – are we . . . do they think . . .'

They? Which *they* would that be? Was this why no one had invited them round for dinner? Were there all sorts of cliques being set up that she knew nothing about?

'No, after Mark's little performance last night, I think you two are off the hook,' said Philip. 'People expect a bit more of their secret service operators. Advanced driving courses, at least. And a bit more sangfroid.'

'Well, yes.' Even though he seemed to have forgiven her, Carrie was forcibly reminded of the reason for her visit. 'That was what I came round about, actually. I really want to try to put things right, though I know the children have had a horrible shock and I can't take that away, but I've spoken to Lucy Ross and she knows someone in the village whose cat's just had some kittens. So I thought maybe I could take, um, you could take . . .' She stumbled, not sure which was the best thing to suggest, wanting to offer some penance, but at the same time, anxious not to seem bossy. 'It's the farm up the valley,' she added. 'The Bowlers?'

There was a pause, in which she could hear an angry banging from upstairs, like a child punishing a toy. Or re-enacting feline death with a Barbie truck and a teddy bear.

'*We* could take . . .' prompted Philip, helpfully.

She looked up, and saw that there was a sort of faint glimmer of encouragement in his eyes. Apparently, she'd grovelled enough, and she felt grateful.

'I don't want them imagining that the next-door neighbours are an ogre and a witch,' he explained. 'Spies, they can live with. But I might need emergency babysitting one day and I don't want them terrified of you. Call it damage limitation.'

'OK, then,' said Carrie. '*We* could take them up to the farm and they could pick out two new kittens.'

'That's a very kind offer,' said Philip, inclining his head graciously. 'And in return, you must attend the ritual burial of Perkins, which will take place this afternoon. I assume your husband will be unavailable?'

'Mark's . . . working away from home today, yes.' She pushed away the thought of the travelcard. Travelcards.

'So.' Philip took a last draining mouthful of tea and replaced the cup on the pine table. 'Are you going to take us?'

'Ah,' she said, turning her mug round and round. 'That's the thing. I can't drive. But I've phoned ahead and sorted out the kittens, if you could drive us up there. And I can make a picnic?' She tried a smile, and looking up, was startled by the intensity of Philip's dark stare. His eyes seemed to bore straight into her mind, past any image she was trying to project, and into the hidden parts of her brain.

The look was so fierce that Carrie felt her skin heat up.

For a moment, she wasn't sure if he was marshalling some particularly stinging words, but then his grey-and-silver beard cracked into a smile, revealing shiny white teeth. 'Come on then,' he said. 'You can tell the kids. Then I think you'll find that'll be your penitence complete.'

Ivor took the news of the new kittens better than Betsy did. He didn't actually burst into tears.

'They won't be the same as Perkins,' she said obstinately, a large tear running down each side of her apple cheeks. 'Perkins came before Ivor.'

'He was a very special cat,' Carrie agreed. 'But just think – you'll be able to pick one each! And they're country cats too, so they'll have lots of fun in your garden. They'll probably tell you all the stories about living on the farm.'

She wasn't sure this wasn't how you were meant to speak to children, but Betsy and Ivor weren't like any children she'd ever met before.

'She's right,' said Philip, helpfully. 'Farm cats make the best familiars, Betsy,' he added with a sidelong glance at his daughter.

'You can't make us forget about Perkins by replacing him,' said Betsy, sticking out her lower lip. She still looked angelic, thought Carrie, even when she was scowling as darkly as her father. 'We're not stupid. We don't just *forget* things.'

'Will they be black?' asked Ivor. 'Will they be a black cat?'

'I don't know. You'll have to choose the ones you like best.' Carrie smiled wildly at him, relieved to have some kind of positive reaction.

'I won't like any of them best,' retorted Betsy, crossing her arms. 'Because they won't be Perkins.'

'That's enough,' said Philip. 'In the car, please, lady.'

She gave him one last scowl, to match his, then got in, doing up her own seatbelt.

Mrs Bowler up at Abbey Farm was, as Lucy had reported, delighted to be getting shot of two kittens, and refused outright to take any money from Carrie for them.

'Didn't know she was pregnant, did I?' she said, gazing pragmatically at her huge tabby cat, curled up in a Walkers crisp box in the main barn, kittens crawling all over her like multi-coloured balls of wool. 'Wondered why she wasn't ratting as well as normal. And we've plenty of rats up here, but I don't need ten cats, now, do I?'

Faced with nine wriggling, pink-nosed kittens, even Betsy couldn't maintain her disinterest, and was now engaged in bossing Ivor around over which they should take home. She was having trouble getting her choices down to four.

'This is a magic cat,' she informed him, setting a tar-black kitten aside with her little hands. 'And this one is nearly magic. We should have these two. And this one – this one is a princess cat. No, no! Stay where I told you!' She hauled the first one, mewing in protest, back to the little nest she'd made out of straw. 'You're coming with us.'

'Want one yourself, love?' asked Mrs Bowler.

'Oh, I don't know,' said Carrie. 'I'd have to ask my husband.'

'I'm not her husband, by the way,' explained Philip with a straight face. 'I'm her neighbour.'

Mrs Bowler looked more closely at them. 'That's right,' she said. '*Your* husband's that maniac with the flashy car, isn't he?'

'Er, yes.' Carrie smiled tightly. 'Word gets round.'

Mrs Bowler gave them both an appraising glance, as if skimming them for gossip, then shrugged. 'Are you sure you won't? They'd be good company for you during the day, while he's away, and they don't take much looking after, being farm cats. I need to get rid of them all.'

'But you wouldn't . . . drown them if no one takes them?' asked Carrie anxiously.

'It's a *farm*, love! I don't keep a cat for a pet up here!' But then seeing Carrie's obvious horror, she added, 'No, well, I daresay we wouldn't drown them, but we've no room. And I'd rather they went to nice folk.'

'You should get one, Carrie,' said Philip. 'I'm sure Betsy would like it if her new cats had a brother or sister next door. I'm going to have trouble keeping her to just two of her own.' He winked conspiratorially, and his face took on the cartoon naughtiness of a pirate.

Carrie dragged her gaze away from Philip's twinkly eyes, back to the barn. Everyone seemed to have cats in St Dee. Philip, Miss

Maxwell, the pub . . . The place was rife with them, slinking round every gate, sprawled feigning sleep in every garden.

'Well, I could, I suppose,' she said, not wanting to sound too much of a pushover. But then, how perfect would a cat look, curled up on her lap next to the Aga, stalking through the shafts of sunlight in her studio? He was right, it would be nice to have some company during the day. And she surprised herself with a sudden longing to do something nice for these strange little children, however obliquely.

'Yes, Mrs Bowler,' she said, 'you know, I will have one. Thank you.'

'Going to help her choose?' Out of the corner of her eye, Carrie saw Mrs Bowler wink at Philip.

'Mrs Armstrong is her own mistress,' he replied soberly.

'Aye?'

Great, thought Carrie, another shoot on the gossip grapevine.

'I think we'll cut out the middle man and leave it for Betsy to decide,' he said. 'Tell me, Mrs Bowler, if you don't mind my asking, how you came to move back? Was this your family's farm?'

While Mrs Bowler was regaling Philip with detailed accounts of her grandparents' beehives, Carrie carefully approached the hay bale where the children were talking intently to the mother cat, who was feigning sleep badly.

'Which ones have you picked?' she asked, crouching down to their level.

'That one and that one,' said Ivor at once, pointing. 'And that one.'

'No, Ivor, *that* one,' Betsy corrected him. 'That's your one.'

'Which kitten shall I take home to my house?' asked Carrie brightly.

'Why are you having one?' Betsy looked suspicious. 'You didn't get your cat run over.'

'I know. But there are so many kittens in this family that I thought it would be nice if one of their brothers and sisters came to live in my house. With me and Mark.'

Betsy stared at her, as if to say, 'And you think Mark won't run over it?'

I'm really not very good at this, Carrie thought, floundering.

'Would you like to choose one for me?' she asked Ivor.

Betsy was silent, and Carrie couldn't tell if she was thinking, or ignoring her.

'Which kitten do you think looks loneliest?' she tried again. 'Which one do you think looks like he needs a big cuddle?'

'That one,' said Ivor, pointing to the smallest of the litter, a gingery tabby hesitating on the edge of the feeding frenzy.

'Oh, yes, he looks like he needs looking after,' agreed Carrie. 'Will you two help me look after him? I mean, you've had a cat before, so you're both experts, aren't you? Will you let him play with your kittens?'

'Maybe,' said Betsy. She poked a white kitten with her finger until it curled round her hand, play-scrabbling with its clawless paws, but she didn't look up. 'If he's nice to them. You have to be nice to cats, or else they scratch you.'

'I'll tell him to be nice.'

'If you're very nice to them, they bring you dead things.'

Carrie blinked.

'With no heads,' Betsy elaborated.

Philip's broad shoulders cast a shadow over the squirming boxful of cats.

'Do you two want to go to see the hens with Mrs Bowler and pick some eggs for tea?' he said, crouching down. 'She'll give you a box for the kittens so we can take them home.'

'Yes, please!' Ivor and Betsy scrambled to their feet and ran out of the barn, Ivor making enthusiastic chicken noises as he went.

'Is that OK?' Carrie said, under her breath. 'Are we forgiven?'

'Well, by Ivor, definitely,' said Philip. 'But Betsy takes a little longer. She's very serious for a little girl.'

'I can see that.'

'Sometimes I think she actually enjoys being cross. Anyway, funny we should come up here – it's one of the farms on my research list,' said Philip, changing the subject. 'Did you know it's one of the oldest? Used to belong to the abbey originally. Domesday Book stuff.

They had all the best grazing rights. Until the Reformation, of course, then the manor grabbed it. Then the MoD grabbed the manor and here we are.'

'That's a lot of grabbing.' Carrie looked down onto St Dee. The houses nestled in the curve of the valley, like sheep huddled in a fold. She could see Oak Cottage and Rose Cottage leaning together, apart from the rest, and the thick, green forest bearing down on the whole village from one side, the white horse on the other.

'So pretty, isn't it?' she said. 'I can't imagine anything violent happening here. And yet you think of the soldiers training, and the explosions on the plain . . .'

Philip laughed. 'Forget the soldier boys, you'd be surprised what they dug up in that wood, years before the evacuation. Prehistoric altars, unidentified skeletons with bits of flint in the skulls . . . One of the theories about the abbey is that it was built to squash the Druid activity in the area. Like a sort of religious police station.'

'And was it?' Carrie turned to him, curious. 'I mean, did it?'

'Yes, and no. Well, we don't exactly know for sure.' He smiled mysteriously. 'My own pet theory is that there's always been some kind of running battle between the Church and the land round here, and not for the reasons they thought. I know some people who'd swear blind to you that this place was on some kind of ley line – what with the Army blowing things up, and the Druids clashing with the Romans, and what have you.' He gave her a dark look. 'Lots of unattached skulls, if you know what I'm saying.'

Carrie snorted, partly to dispel the uneasy feeling creeping over her skin. 'Philip, that's the least likely village conspiracy theory I've heard so far. What, are there UFOs in the wood too?'

'Seriously!' he protested, good-humouredly. 'I'll have you know it's genuine research. You'll find the pub conspiracy theorists stick to the war stories – what the MoD really wanted the land for, Hitler interrogated in the manor, gassed soldiers dumped in a pit in the woods, that sort of thing. Which is narrow-minded of them, if you ask me, since the really good conspiracy theories are the old ones.'

They had started walking back towards the farmhouse, but Philip stopped at a stone wall, and pointed down to where the tumbled remains of the abbey lay, stones scattered like half-eaten fruit cake on the thick grass. 'Never wondered who St Dee was?'

'Um, no.'

'Trick question. There was no St Dee. It's a mangling of the map abbreviation for Sic Locus Dei Est. Meaning "this place is sacred to God".'

'Really?'

'Oh, yeah. There's all sorts of folklore about monks selling their souls to the Devil in return for eternal life, and Druids making living sacrifices in the woods.' He cocked a bushy eyebrow at her. 'All translated into Latin by the monks. You haven't heard the famous tale about the farmer who tried to pull a fast one with the Devil, and the Devil turned him into the chalk horse? No?'

Carrie shook her head. 'I can see I don't get out enough.'

'Well, that's how these things get started – folk not getting out enough.' He turned back towards the farm. 'People have to entertain themselves, you know? And find explanations for things they don't understand properly. Myths, legends, ghost stories . . . But then you discover a whole load of pre-Roman skeletons in the woods, and you have to wonder . . . Come over some time,' he said easily. 'I've got lots of books, not just the dry old religious stuff either. Green Men, folklore, ghosts and goblins . . . It's all here.'

Carrie thought about her own book: the animals scampering through the deserted houses, and the shadows of the forest and run-wild gardens reverting to those ancient forces.

She shivered. Those images had bloomed in her head so easily, almost as if the land itself had seeded them. So many things just popped into her head these days – she seemed able to guess when the phone would ring, or who was knocking on her door. Maybe it was her intuition detoxing after years of city noise and twenty-four-hour distraction blotting it out.

Or maybe it was the ley line.

'Makes a change from popping over for a cup of sugar,' Philip added, with a wink.

'Guess so,' replied Carrie, returning his smile, although as they set off to the farmhouse, she wasn't so sure she was reassured by that.

Chapter Thirteen

M ark sneezed and glared balefully at Carrie over the kitchen table.

In his basket Elvis scrabbled at the old blanket Carrie had folded up, in accordance with Mrs Bowler's somewhat spartan kitten care instructions. His mews were still tiny squeaks, like a baby, and she worried constantly that he might suffocate himself.

'I didn't *know* you were allergic to cats,' she said defensively.

'Not much.' Mark sneezed again, so hard it ruffled the front pages of yesterday's *Guardian*, which lay unread on the table, next to the stack of bills he was also ignoring. 'Just, like, *totally*.'

For once, Carrie didn't feel in the mood for appeasement. Not knowing about Mark's cat allergy only twisted the knife about not knowing about the travelcard. She knew she should mention it, as lightly as she could, but somehow the words wouldn't come. Not yet. Not until she'd made up her own explanation for it.

'You can get antihistamines,' she offered. 'And you might get used to him. Look at him! He's adorable!'

Mark grimaced, then smiled bravely. 'I know he's cute. He's very cute. Our first pet. But you might have asked first.' He sneezed again, and made a faint groan of pain.

She cracked.

'Oh, I'm sorry,' she said. 'It was a spur-of-the-moment thing. I went up to the farm to get some kittens to replace the one you ran over—' Carrie looked up to see if Mark looked guilty at this point, but his eyes were streaming, and he was hunting for some kitchen roll to blow his nose. 'The kids from next door wanted me to get one too. And I thought it would be company for me during the day.' She paused. 'Sometimes it feels like a very big house with just me in it.'

'Pets are a tie.'

'Not really. Not cats. They fend for themselves.'

'What if we wanted to go off on holiday?' he went on, rather resentfully, Carrie thought. 'We'd have to sort out catteries or whatever cats go into.'

'Well, we're not going on holiday any time soon, are we?' she snapped. 'And I've got to get my nose to the grindstone here. It's a good reason for me to stay in.'

'Whatever.'

She paused, her cup halfway to her lips. Mark had got in late the previous evening, had a bath and retired first to his study to 'decompress' with an hour's Playstation driving, and then to his bed, where she'd found him dead to the world at only half past ten, apparently unaware of their new house guest.

And now the tetchy mood in the kitchen was palpable, and obviously wasn't going to get any better until Mark left for work. The pitted kitchen table stood between them like a huge pine barrier. Would this be a good time to ask him when he was next off to London, so she could come with him for a day out, while he was off-guard and unable to think of a good excuse?

Carrie opened her mouth to say it, but the words felt too big in her throat.

Still, surely if he were having an affair in London, he'd be trying to overcompensate by being extra nice to her, not grumpy like this?

This isn't the right time, she told herself. 'Anyway, we could always just get next door to look after him if we did go away. I'm sure Philip wouldn't mind feeding Elvis for a few days.'

Mark had the grace to look embarrassed. 'Philip, is it?'

'Yes. Philip.' Carrie looked over the rim of her cup at him. 'You should be grateful he's actually talking to us at all after what happened. Look, Mark, I have to get on with the neighbours. I'm here all day and it's a small place. They're already talking about us as if we're out-of-town hooligans. I'm trying to fit in. And it would help if you were around too.'

'Sorry,' he sighed. 'I'll make a big effort this weekend.' He ran a hand through his hair, sending it into choppy spikes, and looked more like his normal self. 'I promise.'

'Will you?' said Carrie. 'Please?'

'We'll go to the pub and I'll buy him a drink.' Mark smiled winningly at her for the first time that morning. 'Isn't there a whist drive or something on?'

In his basket Elvis flipped himself on to his side and started scrabbling at an imaginary mouse; Mark twisted his face up and sneezed hard, three times.

'He is cute,' he conceded, wiping his running nose with a rueful grin. 'We'll get used to each other. I don't want my lovely wife to be lonely, do I?'

Carrie got up to hug him. 'Thanks, Mark,' she said. 'And for your information, I'm not allergic to anything, apart from bailiffs and certain brands of sun cream.'

'Well, I'll bear that in mind,' he said, raising his face for a kiss. 'When I bring my pet zebra home.'

'Any other allergies I should know about?' she asked, and for a moment felt dizzy, as if the cosy walls of their relationship had suddenly expanded to infinite space – what else was there she didn't know?

'Ah, well. Isn't the fun in finding out?' asked Mark.

There was a knock on the back door.

Mark screwed up his face and sneezed again.

'Who's that?' he asked. 'This time of the morning? Don't tell me you're having it away with the milkman. That would be very English village.'

The knock came again, more impatiently.

'Seriously,' said Mark. 'Don't they know I'm still here?' He tutted. 'Most indiscreet.'

'Well, at least it'd show how hard I'm trying to get on with the neighbours. I don't know who it is. It might be something urgent. But don't you get up – I'll get it,' said Carrie, pushing her chair back so it screeched on the stone flags.

At first when she swung the door open, Carrie assumed there was no one there, until she realised that her visitors were now sitting on the step, whispering to each other.

'Hello there,' she said, crouching down in a friendly manner to be on Betsy and Ivor's eye level. A cynical voice in her head noted that this was more for Mark's benefit than anything else. Let him see how she'd befriended the children he'd traumatised. Let him see how lovely she looked, looking after children, and how much lovelier it would be if the children were theirs.

'H'lo!' said Ivor. He had a smudge of jam on his pink cheek and didn't smell as if he'd been washed that morning.

Betsy gave her a cool look. 'We've come to let Babbage and Macavity play with Elvis.'

She was holding a black box file tightly shut with her chubby hands, and the box was making scrabbling noises.

Aghast, Carrie noted that it was marked Pagan Sites of Worship. Claws were emerging from the lid like Pandora's Box.

'Well, you'd better come in,' she said, taking the file gently from Betsy's hands before the kittens suffocated. 'I don't suppose they like being carried around in a file much. Does your daddy know you're here?'

'Yes,' said Betsy confidently, marching into the kitchen. She stopped when she saw Mark standing at the table, now packing oranges into his laptop bag, and she turned to face Carrie with outrage on her face. 'We didn't think he'd be here. His car isn't outside.'

'Isn't it?' Carrie looked up from Elvis's basket, where all three kittens were now furiously wrestling. 'Mark?'

'I got a taxi back from the station last night.' Mark ran his hand over his stubbly chin and through his damp hair, then shouldered the bag and grabbed his jacket from the chair. 'Don't say anything. There's a bus out of here in about ten minutes. We'll talk when I get in.' He sneezed again.

'Mark . . .' Carrie began, and stopped.

Betsy's round blue eyes were fixed on Mark with an expression that was positively unsettling.

Mark shuffled awkwardly. 'I, um . . . I'm really sorry about your cat.'

'Perkins.'

'I'm really sorry about Perkins,' repeated Mark.

'So are we,' said Betsy with scary self-possession.

'Good, well, you need to get away, Mark,' Carrie said briskly, wanting him to leave before there was a scene. 'Betsy, why don't you see if the kittens would like some breakfast?'

She followed him out to the door to kiss him goodbye, then said, quietly, 'Are you off to Swindon today?'

'Yes,' said Mark. 'Why?'

Carrie gave him a level look. 'It's just that if you were going further afield, like London, say, I'd have come with you. I wouldn't mind a day trip out sometime.'

Their eyes met, and for a moment, Carrie thought he was going to confess. He looked as if he could barely stop his mouth opening.

But it passed. 'Let's talk about it – plan something properly?' Mark jerked his head towards the kitchen. 'You've got that cat to look after now, haven't you? Phone me if you need anything. And I'll pick up some Allereze.'

He leaned in and kissed her on the lips. 'I love you.'

'I love you too. But Mark . . .' Carrie felt something brush her leg and she looked down with a start.

'Can I have a drink, please?' asked Ivor, tugging on her jeans.

'Leave you to it,' said Mark, and slipped off.

Carrie huffed to herself, but didn't let Ivor see. 'Of course,' she said, leading him by the hand back into the kitchen. 'What would you like?'

'Apple.'

'I don't know if we have apple juice.'

'Ivor only drinks apple,' said Betsy sternly. She turned to Elvis's basket and wagged a finger. 'Play nicely!' she commanded the ensuing kitten brawl. 'Or I'll take you home.'

'Ivor, we have some orange juice or milk,' said Carrie. She was starting to feel out of her depth already, her eyes scanning the kitchen for appliances Ivor might impale himself on. 'Or water? Or, er, tea?'

'Milk,' said Ivor. He plonked himself down on a rug by the kittens and began stroking them with rough baby strokes.

'Does your daddy really know you're here, Betsy?' Carrie poured some milk into the least dangerous cup she could lay her hands on and handed it to him, making sure his chubby fingers were holding it properly.

'Yes.'

Carrie couldn't tell if she was telling the truth or not.

'It's quite early, you know. For visiting.'

Lucy would have a field day with this, she thought. The amount of gossip that could be harvested here from a few innocent questions. Everything the village is gagging to know about Philip Gladstone, here for the asking.

'He's been up for hours,' announced Betsy airily. 'He gets up at five o'clock to write his books. Sometimes he doesn't go to bed.'

'Really? And what do you do while he's writing?'

'I read my books. I sit in his study and keep nice and quiet. Only now I have to look after the kittens too, and they're too noisy for Daddy's study.'

'So he sent you over here to play?'

Betsy didn't answer, but pulled out a kitchen chair and hoisted herself up on it, placing her elbows on the table in the same easy way that Lucy Ross did. 'I'd like some tea, please.'

'OK,' said Carrie, automatically reaching for the teapot. There was something about Betsy's tone that made resistance futile, and yet she was curiously charmed by the prospect of sitting down to chat over the kitchen table with a six-year-old.

'Would you like some breakfast?' she asked.

'Toast, please. Brown bread. Thank you.'

Carrie put the kettle on the boiling plate of the Aga, flicking a nervous glance at Ivor. He was still engrossed in the wriggling kittens.

'Don't worry about Ivor,' said Betsy. 'I've got my eye on him.'

'I can see that.' Carrie held up a selection of cups. 'Which one would you like?'

'The one with flowers on. Your house is the same as ours.'

'Yes, I suppose it is,' said Carrie. How bad was it to pump a child for information? Still, there was something about Philip that rather deterred direct questions. She warmed the pot and put a couple of tea bags in.

'Our house has more books though. And we have proper tea leaves,' said Betsy, peering disapprovingly towards the Aga. 'We always have proper tea leaves.'

'Really? Why's that?' Carrie put some toast on and tried not to feel intimidated. I am the adult here, she told herself, opening the fridge to get the milk. 'Does it taste nicer?'

'Daddy reads the leaves for me. He can tell fortunes. He saw two new cats in my tea cup last week.'

Carrie's hand slipped on the cold milk bottle. She could just imagine Philip gazing seriously into the teacup, pretending to see all sorts of things with his glittering magician's eyes.

'Really?' she said again. 'I must get him to read my tea leaves. I wonder what he'd see?'

'I wonder,' intoned Betsy. She had a very solemn way of talking that Carrie recognised from her own childhood. The long words were straight out of books, clear in her head but unpractised in conversation, with intonations gleaned from eavesdropping on adult gossip. She felt an abrupt pang of empathy with the little girl. She'd spent a lot of time submerging her lonely self in books too.

Carrie took the teapot and the toast to the table and let Betsy butter her own slice, while she sat down opposite. She sensed already that any offer to help would be met with majestic indignation. 'So, shall we call Daddy to let him know you're here?'

'There's no need.' Betsy cut her toast into neat triangles. 'We'll be no trouble. He's working in his study and we're not to disturb him.' She looked up as she bit into one. Carrie couldn't help noticing her beautiful teeth: small, and pearly-white. 'Daddy says you write books too.'

'Yes, I draw books, for children,' said Carrie. Ten minutes, then I'll take them back home, she thought. He can't just let his children wander unannounced into people's houses. Ten minutes is neighbourly enough. 'Picture books.'

'Like storybooks?'

'Yes.' Carrie looked over the table at Betsy, who looked straight back at her. For a children's author, I really am useless with children, she thought. But then she was more of an accidental children's author, when all was said and done. It would make sense to test out Morris on Betsy. If there were any problems, Betsy wouldn't shrink from pointing them out.

For some reason, this scared Carrie more than a dressing-down from Gina and her editor put together.

'Can I see?'

To her surprise, Carrie could feel herself bending to the little girl's will. Where else would they go if Philip was holed up in his study working? She couldn't let two small children roam around the village – anything might happen to them. It was her village duty to assume responsibility until that weirdo saw fit to come and reclaim his children.

And if he panicked that they'd fallen down that well, he only had himself to blame.

'Yes,' she said. 'Of course you can.'

Betsy beamed with delight.

Lucy would have a field day with this shocking display of bohemian parenting, she thought – but immediately decided to keep this to herself. Until she'd had time to remonstrate with him. Presumably there was a good reason for it.

'Well, when you've finished your toast, why don't we bring the kittens upstairs and you can read your book while I do my drawing, and Ivor can play with the kittens,' she suggested.

'You want to keep an eye on us,' said Betsy.

'Of course I do! I don't want anything bad to happen to you!'

'Sometimes bad things happen even when people are keeping an eye on you.'

Carrie swallowed, but Betsy just carried on looking at her with round unblinking eyes. Was Betsy old enough to be doing this for effect? she wondered. Was she trying to freak her out to keep her away from Philip? Weirder things happened.

'Nonsense!' she said brightly. 'You've been reading too many books! Now can you carry your cup of tea? I've got plenty of lovely storybooks upstairs.'

Betsy put down her cup and turned in her chair. 'Ivor, we're going upstairs.'

Ivor's little face turned to hers and Carrie could see panic written on it. 'Are we? Why are we going upstairs?'

'There's nothing to be frightened of.' Betsy turned back to Carrie and whispered confidentially. 'Ivor's scared of the dark. He sees things upstairs in our house. He thinks there's a monster living in our attic. There isn't, of course,' added Betsy, seeing her look of shock. 'There are no such things as monsters. He's just a baby. He doesn't *understand* about old houses like ours.' She finished her last triangle of toast and slipped off the chair. 'Come on then.'

Only now Carrie noticed that she was wearing a beautiful hand-smocked pinafore dress and old-fashioned sandals. The sea-green cotton made Betsy's copper hair even more ethereal than ever, floating around her head in soft curls.

'What a pretty dress!' she said.

'Thank you.' Betsy didn't smile. 'Mummy sent it to me. In one of her parcels. It's a party dress. But I don't have any parties to wear it to. And I don't think Mummy really sent it. Come *on*, Ivor.'

She tugged his jumper and he turned to her with a little scowl. 'Get off me, you.'

'Right,' said Carrie, before a fight could break out. 'Betsy, you carry your cup and Ivor's, and I'll bring the cats.' She scooped up the basket and made her way carefully to the stairs, trying not to think of all the things that could possibly go wrong.

The children's feet clattered across the bare wooden boards of her studio, and Carrie shut the door firmly behind Ivor, limiting the potential hazards.

'You've got a mouse!' he cried, running over to Morris's cage and shoving his pudgy fingers through the bars. 'Hello, mouse!'

Morris scuttled nervously into a heap of straw.

'Do you think he'd like to play with the kittens?' asked Ivor, poking as best he could to dislodge Morris. 'He's hiding! Hide and seek!'

'Don't be silly!' scoffed Betsy. 'They'd gobble him up and crunch his bones like crisps.'

Carrie's imagination filled with terrible scenes of kitten/mouse carnage, and she swept Morris's cage up to safety at the top of the bookshelf near her easel. She could hear him scrabbling in panic, as if he could sense the three hungry farm kittens in their box down on the floor.

I'll never get used to this country way of thinking, she despaired.

The brutality of life seemed that little bit closer to the surface of everything.

'The mouse would run around the room!' hooted Ivor gleefully. 'He would hide!'

'No, I don't think that would be a good idea.' Carrie took down a stack of children's books from the shelf. 'Have you read any of these, Betsy?'

'I don't know.' Betsy began to sort through them, while Ivor lifted the cats up and down, talking to them under his breath.

'So!' said Carrie. 'I'm going to ring your daddy and let him know where you are, and we can all play quietly until he comes to pick you up. Betsy, can you tell me your telephone number?'

'He won't answer,' she said, looking up from an *Angelina Ballerina* book. 'He never answers the telephone when he's working.'

'Well, I should call him, don't you think? In case he's worried.'

'He won't be.' Betsy looked up, with appealing eyes. 'Can't we just stay here and be quiet? Your house is so nice.'

Carrie heard herself say, 'All right. But I need to do some drawing, so you'll have to be quiet. Would you like to draw too? I've got lots of pencils and paper.'

'No,' said Betsy. 'I want to read, thank you.' She rewarded Carrie with a brilliant smile straight out of a Pears soap ad, then picked up another book and buried her head in it. There was something so preternaturally self-possessed about Betsy that Carrie was unable to tear her gaze away immediately, and so she saw the smile curl first into one of triumph, then flatten out into total concentration.

'Don't be so bossy!' Ivor chided one of the kittens. 'You are a bossy boots!'

It sounded like a well-used phrase.

Half an hour passed, the milk van rattled its way back to the village, a few cars drove round the green in the distance, and Carrie abandoned her sketches of Morris and started to draw the children instead; Betsy reading cross-legged, curling her fine coppery hair around her fingers, and Ivor lying on his back letting the kittens roll over him.

She drew them first as children, then as kittens from the village of animals, peering around chairs and batting each other with big paws. But somehow that didn't work: the self-possession was there, but they weren't cute like kittens. There was something more serious about them, more watchful and wise.

Carrie found herself sketching Philip: a sharp-snouted badger in a green velvet waistcoat, working at a desk with a pen and ink. And beneath him, Ivor and Betsy, reading and playing in a jumble of arms and legs.

Two little foxes.

Foxes? Carrie stared at her own pen as if it had drawn them on its own.

By the unused fireplace, Ivor was refereeing a fight between Elvis and his own tortoiseshell kitten, his pale curls glinting in the morning sunlight.

'Don't let them up the chimney, Ivor,' said Betsy, without looking up. 'You know what happened last time.'

Ivor didn't reply.

A look of extreme annoyance passed over Betsy's face. 'Ivor! I'm talking to you. I said, don't let them up the chimney!'

'Betsy? What happened with the chimney?' asked Carrie, intrigued.

Her head spun round. 'Nothing,' she said quickly.

Ivor giggled. 'Up the chimney! Naughty Hazel!'

'Shut *up*, Ivor!' snapped Betsy, but before Carrie could ask any more questions there was a sharp knocking at the front door, making all three of them jump.

'Who's that?' asked Ivor. 'Who's at the door?'

'I bet it's your father,' said Carrie, 'come to take you home for a snack.'

'I bet it's not,' said Betsy, again without bothering to look up from her book. 'He doesn't come out of his study till lunchtime. Not unless there's an incident.' She licked her finger with the utmost delicacy and turned the page.

'Doesn't he?' Carrie wondered anew at Philip's bizarre childcare arrangements. And yet the kids seemed perfectly used to them, so clearly they'd been in place for a while. 'Why don't we go downstairs and see?'

Betsy pouted. 'But we're happy up here. And I'm in the middle of a page.'

Whoever it was downstairs knocked again, but it didn't sound like a father searching frantically for his missing children.

Carrie regarded Betsy doubtfully. How much could go wrong if she left them alone for two minutes? They were perfectly good at amusing themselves. Worryingly so, if she really started to think about it.

'Don't worry,' said Betsy, looking up. 'I'll keep an eye on him. I won't let anything happen.' Her eyes darted around the room, and she frowned. 'We'll be fine here, *on our own.*'

'OK,' said Carrie, feeling told. 'Be careful. I won't be a second.'

Holding onto the solid banister she ran down the stairs, one ear cocked for signs of trouble upstairs, and opened the front door.

Kathleen Maxwell was standing on the step, in a large fur hat and tweed coat. A wicker basket was hooked over one arm, her leather purse, some letters, and, incongruously, a mobile phone visible inside. She looked as though she was just off to run errands in Pimlico.

'Hello, Miss Maxwell!' said Carrie. 'How nice to see you!'

This was more like it, she thought; the neighbour's children playing upstairs, the genuine village ancestor popping round for coffee . . .

'Can't stop. I was doing my rounds and I thought I'd drop this in to you,' said Kathleen, offering Carrie an envelope. 'Some photographs, of the village as it was. They might help you with your book.'

'Oh, thank you. How kind of you to remember!'

'Oh, they're just a few snaps,' she explained as Carrie opened it.

'Of Lily, and Jack, and my parents. I have much larger albums, of course, going back years. I thought, since you didn't know much about them, that you might like to, er, see how they fitted into the village . . .' Her voice died away, as she looked into the hall. 'Gracious, you must have had photographs of your own to get it so . . .'

Carrie followed her line of sight. 'I'm sorry?'

'To get it just the way Lily had it. Even down to that clock!'

'That? Oh, that's so authentic it keeps stopping by itself!' said Carrie. 'It's from a sale somewhere. But thank you. I did try to keep it as authentic as I could.'

Miss Maxwell smiled. 'You've certainly managed that! Even down to the furniture! Did you have it brought back from, ah, Northampton?'

'No, actually we bought it at auction. It's all new. Old new.'

'Uncanny . . .' murmured Kathleen. 'Quite . . . uncanny.'

Carrie wasn't sure whether to feel flattered or slightly spooked.

Kathleen stepped in quickly. 'Anyway, these snaps are from the May Day fete I was telling you about. It was the biggest social event of the calendar – my parents always held a house party, and the villagers . . . well, they took full advantage of the day off.' She pursed her lips, to show she was joking. 'And the half day that followed it, if you know what I mean!'

'Mmm,' said Carrie.

'Jack was on the fete committee, there, you see?' She pointed him out on the back row of a formal committee photograph, taken by the inevitable maypole. 'As the schoolteacher, he had to arrange the children's participation, and Lily was the May Queen one year. I can't even remember if she was the last May Queen we had – I think she was.' She hesitated, as if thinking of something in particular, then said, 'He was a very calming influence, Jack. Very much respected in the village.'

'That's nice to hear,' said Carrie, meaning it. Unlike Lily, Jack's personality didn't exactly leap out at her. 'Did you ever get to be May Queen?'

Miss Maxwell smiled sadly. 'No. No, it would have looked like favouritism. I did ask, one year, and my father was adamant that his daughters wouldn't have anything to do with the May Queen celebrations. I think,' she added delicately, 'it was because we'd have had to be in the pub afterwards, with everyone rather tipsy. I don't think it would have been quite the thing . . .'

'No, I see,' said Carrie. 'Is this your mother?' she asked, looking quickly at the next photograph. Was that Lily next to her?

'Yes, that's my mother at the fete again.' Miss Maxwell pointed to an older, noticeably well-dressed woman, clutching a clipboard to her chest while a crocodile-skin handbag dangled from her wrist. She was smiling as if good humour was being rationed, along with eggs and butter – not, from her sharp cheekbones, that she overindulged in any of the lush local produce. Next to her was Lily, looking quite delicate in a tea dress that hung off her shoulders – it seemed made for a much bigger woman, maybe her mother.

Carrie eagerly scanned her face for clues; her blonde hair was in a grown-up bun, and her full lips were darkened with lipstick, but she still looked very girlish. Paler, though. 'When was this taken?' she asked, wondering if this came before or after Ben, Mark's father.

'It would have been taken just before the big tea started at the fete. They always handed out the prizes before tea. Made sure people stayed around for them and didn't just head off to the Rose and Thorn.'

'Sorry, I meant what year?' asked Carrie.

'Oh, it'll say exactly when, on the back, dear. Mother was punctilious about writing on the back of photographs. She liked to keep everything in its place.'

Carrie turned the photo over, and read 'Lily Armstrong and Self at St Dee Fair, May 1, 1941'. Mrs Maxwell's writing was just as her appearance suggested: neat, and finished, with spiky loops.

'Was she judging something?' asked Carrie. Lily was holding a large silver cup in the crook of her arm, rather awkwardly, as if she was embarrassed.

'Yes, dear, the baking contest,' explained Kathleen. 'Lily had won the cup. That was the second year she beat her own mother.'

Lily's expression was tense and on edge, quite unlike the confident smiling girl of the picture in Mark's shoebox. Had the bloom started to go off her careless beauty already? Carrie studied Mrs Maxwell's acid demeanour and the rosette pinned to the shoulder of her expensive afternoon frock. She looked like the kind of woman who'd make anyone nervous.

'So Lily would be . . . seventeen?' she asked.

'I suppose so. She looks younger, doesn't she?' Kathleen added. 'She had a baby face, Lily. Always used to plait her hair too. Made her look about ten. My mother, in fact, suggested she put her hair up once she was married. I heard her talking about it.'

Carrie's brain whirred. The May before the evacuation. So Lily must have had Ben by then – she didn't look like a woman who'd recently given birth. She didn't look old enough to *have* children.

There was a thud from upstairs and her attention snapped back to the present.

Kathleen jumped. 'What was that?' she asked. Her eyes went to the stairs. 'Goodness!'

'Oh, God!' gasped Carrie, putting a hand to her mouth. 'The kids! I'm so sorry. Will you excuse me? I'm looking after Philip Gladstone's children for the morning.'

'Best get up there before they wreck the place,' said Kathleen. 'How funny that you're doing the same thing as Lily did, looking after other people's children!'

There was another, louder crash from upstairs and a long wail.

'Will you come round again some time? For some tea?' gabbled Carrie, starting up the stairs. 'I'd love to ask you some more about Lily, and the house. You know . . .'

'Of course.' Kathleen flapped her hands. 'Go on, quick!'

Carrie scrambled up the stairs, half-dreading what she was going to find.

Chapter Fourteen

Carrie bounded up the stairs two at a time, hanging onto the banister as she went. The landing above her was in shadow but the door to the studio had been opened, leaving a yellow pool of light spilling out. It should have looked spring-like, but instead it seemed sinister.

Sinister, maybe, because the keening cry was still cutting through the air, and she couldn't tell which child it was: the noise was high-pitched and scared, and it jangled some inherent protective instinct inside her chest. Or were both of them crying now? It sounded like two voices, at least.

'Betsy?' she yelled, her heart hammering as she struggled to reach the top without stumbling. 'Betsy! Did you open this door? I told you not to!'

God almighty, why had she left them on their own? What had she been thinking? You could never leave children unattended for one minute, not unless you were their mother and had some kind of telepathic link to their curious little fingers and brains . . .

Carrie pushed into the room, bracing herself to seem as calm as possible.

'I don't know how it happened,' said Betsy, before Carrie could even frame her first question. 'It wasn't me.'

Ivor, tomato-red with crying, was sitting in the middle of the floor, his sobs temporarily halted by her sudden appearance. When he recognised Carrie's shape in the doorway, he balled up his little fists, pushed them in his eyes and started sobbing again.

'Why is Ivor crying?' asked Carrie, her eyes scanning the room for clues. To her horror, she saw that Morris's cage was right in the middle of the floor. Morris was nowhere to be seen. All three kittens were hunched around the cage, staring motionless into the shredded paper bedding, and as she looked, Betsy's black kitten jabbed a small paw through the wire bars.

'No!' shouted Betsy furiously, scattering the cats with swipes of her hand. 'Bad!'

Then she returned her attention to the book.

How the hell had Betsy got the cage down? The chair was still by the easel and even so, she'd been told not to!

'And why did you bring Morris down from the shelf?' Carrie demanded, lifting the mouse cage off the floor and replacing it at the top of the bookshelf. There was silence inside. Not even the scared rustle of bedding. 'I told you not to!'

Carrie had a bad feeling about Morris. Her own heart was pounding fit to burst, so heaven alone knew how hard a tiny mouse heart must have thumped, smelling cats all around.

Betsy didn't say anything, but turned the page of her book and carried on reading as if nothing had happened.

'Betsy?' Carrie's voice came out sharper than she meant, but Betsy merely finished reading to the end of the page. Then she looked up, her wide eyes round.

'What?'

The calmness in her voice was chilling. It was an adult disinterest, and either Betsy was putting it on like an expert, or she genuinely wasn't bothered.

Carrie smoothed her hair back off her face and tried to suppress her rising tension. There was a strange atmosphere in the room, a stillness that she couldn't put her finger on, as though there'd been frantic action a moment ago, and everything had stopped as she'd walked in. 'Did you move the cage down there, Betsy?'

Ivor took his fists away from his eyes and fixed Carrie with an imploring look. 'Don't leave me alone with her!' he wailed, stretching out his hands. 'Don't leave me alone!' He looked terrified.

Instinctively, Carrie rushed across the room and swept him up in her arms, cradling his head against her shoulder and rocking him back and forth. Ivor turned into a dead weight, collapsing gratefully against her, clinging on with a hot little grip. She glared at Betsy over his head, not sure how to formulate the questions in her head without frightening her into lying some more.

'I didn't *do* anything,' whined Betsy.

'Betsy, I think you need to have a good long think.' Carrie glared at her. 'Then you should tell me what's happened to make Ivor so upset. And I'd like the truth, please.'

Betsy let out a gusty sigh. 'I told you, I didn't *do* anything.'

'But, Betsy, the mouse cage was on the floor. And I especially told you not to bring it down in case the cats . . . in case the cats scared Morris. Didn't I?' Carrie could hear her own voice rising, but she couldn't seem to stop herself. 'Didn't I?'

Betsy looked at her. 'I wouldn't have let the cats get him. Anyway, the mouse was sleeping.'

'Sleeping?' Carrie's skin crawled.

Ivor hiccupped and lifted his head away from Carrie's chest. 'Yes,' he agreed. 'Mouse was asleep. He didn't want to play with the cats.'

'Dead,' mouthed Betsy, when Ivor sank back into Carrie's arms.

'I think it's time for you two to go home, don't you?' said Carrie. Her voice cracked and she had to swallow. 'I think your daddy should be all done with his work now.'

'Fine.' Betsy slapped her book shut and dropped it on the pile.

*

They made an odd procession down the front path: Carrie with Ivor still clinging to her neck and muttering indistinctly in her ear, and Betsy carrying all three kittens in a wicker picnic basket. They were mewing loudly in protest at their makeshift transport and the sulky way Betsy was bouncing it against her leg.

'Why are we going round to the front door?' demanded Betsy.

'Because we are.' Carrie didn't feel able to say, 'Because I want any passing villager to see that your stupid father farms you out to neighbours at all hours of the day, and I know that Lucy Ross and Kathleen Maxwell are liable to come past any minute.'

And yet even as she thought it, part of her felt bad. He was a single parent, after all. And she was still no nearer finding out where the wife was and, indeed, whether Philip deserved sympathy or criticism or what.

She knew she should ask, but somehow that was much harder than bawling him out about his childcare provisions.

Carrie wished she were better at the hard questions.

'He won't hear you.' Betsy sighed and plonked the basket down on the step.

'I have a firm knock.' Carrie rapped on the door of Rose Cottage with considerable force. Like Oak Cottage, it had an old wrought-iron knocker that carried the sound aggressively through the house.

'He says all the hounds of Hades can't bring him to the door when he's working.'

Carrie looked down at Betsy and widened her eyes at her. 'Well, we'll see about that.'

Betsy put her foot on the picnic basket to still the lid, which was under some strain from inside.

Hearing no immediate signs of life, Carrie took a step back. Dark curtains were drawn in most of the windows, giving the house a hungover expression, even though the sun was now glittering on the glass.

Carrie put a tentative hand on the doorknob and turned. The door swung open, letting out a draught of tomb-cold air. The heating didn't seem to be on.

She looked at Betsy, who shrugged.

Ivor was starting to feel very heavy in her arms, and Carrie could feel him dozing off to sleep.

'I've got lots to do,' she said, in what she hoped was a brisk, grown-up voice. 'So we're going to have to go in and find him if he won't be polite enough to answer his own front door.'

Betsy responded by pushing past her and marching in. 'Daddy! Daddy!' she called, but, Carrie noted, not loud enough to disturb him.

Hesitantly, she followed the little girl as she disappeared into the house.

She'd only been as far as the kitchen before, which had been dark, but warm and lived-in. The hall, however, was shadowy, made darker by lots of heavy oak furniture, and it smelled of papery dust and the final lingering traces of fresh paintwork. There were paintings on the walls, with more stacked up along the skirting boards, their gilt frames turned inward as if facing the wall in disgrace, and several religious-looking artefacts hanging by the stairs.

Why do I feel so cross? Carrie wondered, as a fresh feeling of annoyance spread through her. It wasn't just about the children. There was something else. Was it that he had this lovely house and wasn't letting it breathe? That he was shutting out the sun and the light and letting the kids turn into pale little vampire children because he wanted to hide away and work? He'd seemed so friendly on their trip to the farm – happy to exchange waves and brief words over the garden wall since. Was this how real writers were: one person when they were off-duty, and someone completely different when they were working?

'Where's his study?' she asked Betsy, although her instinct told her it was upstairs, where her own study was.

Betsy turned and pointed up the stairs, putting a warning finger on her rosebud lips. Her face looked as pale and waxy as a china doll in the half-light.

'Right then.' Carrie shouldered Ivor and grabbed the banister for support.

'Don't!' said Betsy. 'Don't *disturb* him!'

'I'm afraid he's left me no choice.' Carrie set her jaw. She didn't like talking like Mary Poppins but she was cross. If anything had happened to Betsy while she was balancing on a chair, or however she'd reached that cage down . . .

Carrie ignored the voice of her own conscience reminding her she shouldn't have left them alone while she chatted with Kathleen Maxwell, and instead focused on her righteous annoyance so that she wouldn't be freaked out by the heaven-bound oil-painted angels lining the walls.

The stairs creaked under her determined tread, and what little light was coming in picked out faint cobwebs between the barley-sugar carved rails.

Ivor wriggled nervously in her arms. His body was still vibrating with the occasional smothered sob, and his head, pressed into Carrie's neck, smelled unwashed but not unpleasant. A baby smell, probably full of hormones to trick her into looking after him.

'It's all right,' soothed Carrie, stroking his hair. 'Back home now.'

'Back home, Ivor,' crooned Betsy behind her.

To her surprise, Ivor shuddered further into the crook of her neck.

What *had* Betsy said to him to scare him so much?

She knocked on the study door, not wanting to think about it.

'What do you want?' roared a voice from inside. 'I told you, don't disturb me until the little hand is on the eleven, Betsy! Do you want the witches to come again?'

'The witch has already come, Philip,' snapped Carrie, pushing her way into the book-filled room. 'And I've brought back your children.'

Philip pushed his chair away from the piled-up Victorian desk, his hands gripping the rolled edges like large paws. Like the desk, the chair was big and old-fashioned, more like a throne, with deep red leather padding and brass studs, worn to dullness with age, and it made him look more like a woodland god than ever.

'God almighty,' he bellowed, dragging a hand through his unwashed hair. 'Can a man not get a moment's peace?'

'Don't be melodramatic.' Carrie kept her voice level for the sake of Ivor. 'Of course you can't get a moment's peace! You've got two children to look after! What did you think you were playing at? There's a great big well right outside your front door! Did you tell them to come round to my house? Not that I would have turned them away,' she added, sensing Betsy's presence behind her, and not wanting to make her feel any more unwanted than she already did. 'It was lovely to see them and we've had a most enjoyable morning. But . . .'

She took a breath, waiting for the simmering rage in Philip's eyes to explode into physical force. He looked intensely angry at having his train of thought disturbed, chewing his lip beneath the beard in an effort to control his temper. From the scrawling handwritten Post-it notes littering his desk and discarded cups of coffee, Carrie could tell he'd been right in the middle of something, but that was really no excuse to let his children wander around like stray dogs.

'Daddy, I told her you weren't to be disturbed,' said Betsy, appearing from behind Carrie's legs.

Philip visibly softened. His broad shoulders, bulky in an Aran jumper, seemed to reduce, and the cloud of blackness around him dissipated. He ran a hand over his beard, smoothing down the silver and black curls, and the temper seemed to drain out of him. 'You're quite right. I do apologise. I have a terrible deadline and I'm afraid I let it get the better of me.'

'Carrie made me some breakfast.' Betsy emerged from behind Carrie and stood with her hands crossed. 'But you haven't had any. You should have something to eat. Perhaps Carrie could make you some toast now.'

Philip's mouth twitched under his beard. 'Betsy. You don't invite other people to cook in your house.'

'I don't mind,' said Carrie. 'It's nearly time for lunch.'

'Daddy,' said Ivor, wriggling to get down. Carrie let go of him and watched as he stumbled across the room to leap into Philip's bear-like grasp.

'It's my little Ivor!' Philip hugged him so his small hands were out of reach of the desk.

Carrie shot a discreet glance around the jumbled study. If Philip hadn't got round to hanging all his pictures downstairs it would be because his attention had been taken up with stacking his bookshelves; the walls were lined with books and magazines, files and papers stacked on top of each other, marked in jagged black marker-pen capitals. Most were historical volumes, some were leather-bound and ancient, as if they'd been borrowed from some university library in the last century and never returned.

There weren't many personal touches amongst all the books. On top of one shelf, there were two playgroup photographs, still in their cardboard frames, of Betsy possessively clutching Ivor like an oversized doll, and, in a more ornate pewter frame, a formal portrait of a strikingly beautiful red-haired young woman in a fancy-dress Guinevere outfit: a long, dark green dress with trailing sleeves, the bodice embroidered in gold thread, finished off with a gold chain girdle around her slim hips. Another fine gold chain hung across her broad forehead, making her dark brown eyes seem both exotic and regal.

Carrie tried to guess her age – early twenties? She had a guileless, make-up-free look that would no doubt make her seem a good five years younger than she really was, but even so she could have passed for Betsy and Ivor's older sister.

'My wife,' said Philip sharply. 'Before you ask.'

Something in his tone made any further enquiry impossible. Carrie flushed pink and tore her attention away from the shelves.

'I'm happy to make some lunch if you'd like?' she said, instead. 'I can see you're very busy.'

'We'll all have some lunch,' said Philip firmly. He stood, scooping

Ivor onto his shoulder as if he weighed nothing, and extended the other hand towards the door.

Carrie stepped back. He couldn't have asked her to leave more emphatically if he'd put the hand in the small of her back and shoved her out.

Chapter Fifteen

Philip's kitchen was less dark than the rest of the house, with the large window letting in the morning sunlight. It still felt slightly subterranean, but Carrie had to concede that that might be because she'd spent hours imagining Philip in his storybook guise as a badger, and his two children as tumbling fox cubs.

'Sit down,' said Philip before she could offer to help. 'It's easier – I know where everything is.'

Carrie pulled out a spindle-backed chair, removed a home-made rag dolly from the seat, and sat down, taking in the differences between this and her own identical kitchen.

She wasn't a natural housekeeper, but it seemed Philip was even less inclined to clean. A fine layer of dust had settled on the shelves and the first long cobwebs were appearing where the old beams met the yellow-washed walls. Amid piles of post and old newspapers, an antique milk jug filled with randomly plucked wildflowers stood on the pitted pine table.

'Did you pick the flowers, Betsy?' she asked to fill the expanding silence.

'Daddy did,' said Betsy without looking up from the cat basket by the Aga. 'We took the rest to Perkins' grave.'

'Oh,' said Carrie, feeling told off.

'My daughter has an Ophelia complex,' explained Philip. 'Never happier than when strewing flowers around.'

'Really?' Carrie's brain whirred.

'Like in the book, Carrie. The Shakespeare book,' explained Betsy from the Aga.

'Thank you, Betsy,' said Philip. 'I think Carrie knows who Ophelia is.'

'She's a great reader,' said Carrie, pointedly. 'She spent the whole morning reading in my house. I bet she has a vivid imagination.'

'She does that,' said Philip drily. 'Sometimes a bit too vivid, eh, Betsy? Hmm?'

Betsy pouted.

Should I say something to Philip about Betsy getting the mouse cage down and upsetting Ivor so badly, Carrie wondered. The pair of them were playing quite happily with the kittens now, and Ivor seemed restored to good humour. Betsy was bossing the kittens around, but no more than usual.

They're just children, she thought, sympathy flooding through her. Children who are trying to adjust to a new house, a new village, a new situation, and all without a mother. No wonder they're a little raw around the edges. Telling on them wouldn't help.

She watched Philip opening and shutting the cupboards, trying to find bread and jam, and muttering to himself. And he was adjusting too, under the scrutiny of the gossips.

The best thing I can do is be a friend, she decided. To the kids, first. And if that means being a friend to Philip too, then it's just neighbourly. Maybe he needs some help too. There were too many people all too ready to include the Gladstones in the ever-expanding list of village mysteries.

'How's the deadline going?' she asked.

'Oh, you know how it is.' He put a selection of jams on the table, and raised a warning finger to Betsy, who opened then closed her mouth. 'Trouble is, now people know I'm a researcher I can't get away from the conspiracy theorists. You'll have heard the latest?'

'Tell me. As long as it's not about me and Mark?'

Philip stretched his brown eyes until she could see the whites around the dark irises. 'It's a new one about the manor house. So far we've had a whole selection of Germans in there, but now I have it on good authority that *apparently* it was earmarked as Churchill's own retreat, bunkers and all, which was why the Maxwells did some sneaky deal with the government and evacuated the place without bothering to consult with their tenants. Did rather well out of it too, if what they're saying's to be believed. Not,' he added with another serious twinkle, 'that I recommend believing *all* they're saying in the pub.'

'Seems a bit remote,' Carrie replied stoutly. 'And, I mean, it's nice enough, but it's not exactly Blenheim Palace, the manor house. Is it? Was it, I mean? Anyway, why was it demolished?'

Philip put a large sponge cake and a plate of hatch-marked Aga toast down on the table. He had no toast rack, but the cake looked light and dripped with homemade-looking jam. 'Well, that's the interesting part. Evidence? Traces of Hitler's DNA on the mantel-piece? Barbara Purves – who I think we can both agree knows *everything* – has done some research on the Internet and come up with some story about a secret meeting with the Americans, *before* Pearl Harbor. That's what they were saying in the pub yesterday lunchtime.' He paused dramatically. 'Until Kathleen Maxwell came in. That poor body gets a royal silence whenever she enters a room.'

For a man with two kids, Philip seemed to spend a fair amount of time in the pub, thought Carrie, momentarily distracted. Who was looking after Betsy and Ivor? Were they here, amusing themselves in silence? Letting the house supervise them?

She pushed away the thought, trying to tell herself that it was none of her business, but at the same time conscious that she didn't fancy tackling this dark giant about his childcare.

'Oh. Well, they do that to me and Mark sometimes,' admitted Carrie. 'I suppose it's flattering. Shows you're a hot topic of conversation. But have you met Kathleen? She's very nice, you know, once you get talking. I think she's being typecast by everyone as the big bad posh woman.'

Philip spread some jam on the toast and cut it into precise quarters. 'Ivor! Betsy! Come and have something to eat.' He looked up. 'Just because people are posh doesn't mean you have to believe everything they tell you. How well do you know Kathleen Maxwell? I can't say I've heard particularly great things about the manor house, you know. They weren't exactly popular.'

'Really? In what way?'

'Manor house families are never that popular. Unless they do lots for the community.' Philip folded a whole piece of toast in half for himself and bit into it.

Carrie thought about the photographs Kathleen had brought round. Her mother, presenting prizes at the school; her father judging cattle. The power they must have had in such a remote little village, scaled down over the years to the annual fete. But what control did they really have, by the end? It was a closed world to Carrie, with her childhood of cities and aeroplanes and foreign languages, and she had an uneasy feeling that most of her ideas about villages and squires were based on Agatha Christie novels. 'Well, yes, but . . . What were they *meant* to do?' she asked. 'They gave parties and probably employed lots of villagers and . . .'

Philip washed down his toast with a swig of tea and hacked off a slice of cake. 'We're talking about a very isolated community here, Carrie. Have you ever lived in a village like this? No one really leaves, very few people move in, same families in the same houses for years. The manor house owned all the cottages, and leased all the land to the farmers.'

'Well, yes, but even so . . .' she began, bridling at the tutorial tone.

Philip sensed her response and shrugged. 'Sorry, force of habit.

I'm not being critical, just realistic. That's how it was in rural villages. It would still be like living in quite Victorian circumstances right up until the evacuation – church twice a day on Sunday, horses used on the farms, all the old superstitions observed, everyone's kids educated by one person in the village school . . .'

Carrie opened her mouth to speak, but Philip cocked his head to one side and got in before her.

'Now, that would be your . . . grandfather-in-law, am I right?' he asked, his sharp eyes homing in on her reaction.

She nodded. 'Yes.'

'And he married one of his pupils, I assume? If she grew up in the village?'

Carrie was slightly surprised by how matter-of-fact Philip sounded, laying out the facts like a historian, stripped of the imagined conversations and pictures she'd supplied. When he put it like that, it wasn't quite as strange. And yet . . .

'She was only seventeen. I suppose it was rather scandalous,' she blurted out.

'Mm,' said Philip ambiguously. 'Well, not really. People did marry very young in the countryside. Was she pregnant?'

Carrie nodded. 'I think so. According to Mark, there was always a big "don't go there" sign over their marriage – so I've just assumed there was more to it than met the eye.'

Philip didn't even look surprised. 'Well, there you go. At least she had someone make an honest woman of her. More than lots of girls did. How old was her husband?'

'When they married? Late twenties?' She couldn't help a flicker of distaste run across her face.

'You never have a crush on your teacher?' asked Philip at once.

Carrie blushed. 'Well. Yes. But . . .'

He gave her a playful look. 'Never underestimate the erotic allure of a teacher, Carrie. Even beady old ones like me.'

To her embarrassment, Carrie felt herself go hot and cold. 'But you're not old!' she said, trying to make light of it.

'I'm forty,' he replied ruefully. 'Not old to you and me, but to students . . .'

'Well, I'd rather not be eighteen again, thanks,' she said. 'I'd happily swap some perfect skin for a bit of experience . . . Ah,' she corrected herself, 'that's not quite what I meant!'

'No? Not what you meant to *say*, maybe.' Philip winked. 'No, I know what you mean.'

Carrie realised to her horror that the atmosphere had shifted into something approaching flirtation.

Philip cut himself another slice of cake. 'God, I'm ravenous. Sorry. I've been writing all night. Have some cake. It's very good.'

'Bit early for me, thanks.' She felt the warmth in her cheeks die back. 'Did you make it?'

'God, no. Mrs Bowler dropped it off – you know, from the farm? Wanted to see how we were getting on.' He raised an eyebrow. 'You're not the only female visitor I get. Or the only one concerned about my family arrangements.'

Betsy's coppery head appeared at the other end of the table as she pulled herself up onto a chair. She had waited before coming to the table, obviously sensing that there would be some kind of conflict about her early morning appearance, but unable to resist the lure of a conversation.

Philip gave a frown, but said nothing, and she helped herself to toast.

'So do you often work through the night?' said Carrie. 'You must be exhausted.'

'I try to get most of it out of the way before the kids need looking after. Sometimes I get carried away and lose track of time.' He yawned unselfconsciously, showing a dark pink tongue and very white teeth. 'Still, when the ideas are running, you know . . .'

Carrie suddenly heard her own voice saying, 'Well, if you need some help I don't mind having them for a few hours in the mornings.'

Philip's face brightened. He looked over at Betsy who was eating her toast very demurely. 'How about that, Betsy? Do you think you could go and read very, very quietly round at Mrs Armstrong's while Daddy writes?'

'I hope so,' said Betsy.

Carrie noted that Philip hadn't bothered to do any token demurring. But there was something quite honest about that, and she didn't mind.

'As long as it's just me and Ivor,' she added quietly, almost to herself.

'Of course it'll just be you two,' smiled Carrie. 'Just the three of us.' Did she mean Mark? The incident with Perkins?

'I think we'll all get on very well. You can help me write my stories,' she added. 'Would you like that?'

Betsy nodded enthusiastically, and Carrie wondered what might emerge from Betsy's creative imagination.

'That's very kind of you. I'm not sure what I can offer in return,' he said wryly. 'I mean, if you want to work out some kind of hourly rate . . .'

'God, no!' said Carrie, turning pink. 'Don't be silly. The use of your children as models is quite enough.' She put her hand lightly on Betsy's head. Her hair really was extraordinary. Betsy looked up and gave her a brief, shy smile, turning Carrie's heart over. She just needed more attention so she didn't have to live in her own bookish little world all the time.

I should ask, she thought. I should ask what happened about his wife. This would be a good time.

'Anyway,' she said, steeling herself to drop the first hint. 'That's the point of being neighbours, isn't it? Being able to look out for each other.'

'Indeed,' said Philip and gave her a devilishly attractive grin that stopped any questions right in their tracks.

Back home, Carrie made herself a cup of tea, picked up a squirming Elvis in the other hand, and climbed the stairs thoughtfully, watching the motes of dust spinning in the light. It was curious – eerie, in fact – that the two houses should be mirror images of each other and yet be so different; so much sunlight in hers and so many dark corners in Philip's. Was it down to some tiny angle they were built at, that gave her side more exposure to the sun? Or was it just a lighter, brighter house?

Maybe *he* has more dark corners than we do, she thought, then pulled a face at her own smugness. It wasn't even true. Philip might have a missing wife and two strange kids, but she still hadn't even had a proper chat with Mark about what she'd found out about his own grandparents. Each time she'd tried to draw Jack and Lily into the conversation he'd seemed completely uninterested.

Her mind slid back to the photograph of Astrid and her knowing, intimate eyes, and the travelcard in his jeans pocket. Familiarity had taken away the sting of them, but now she hated herself for neither tackling him about it nor letting it go.

It was ridiculous to elide them, and yet they were two things Mark had deliberately not told her about. Two things he'd wanted to hide from her. Two secrets she'd found out about him almost at the same time.

Just ask him, she thought to herself. If there's nothing to hide, why should he mind?

It'll make a wrinkle, said a voice in her head. It *should* make more than a wrinkle. And who manages to have a wrinkle-free life anyway?

Carrie's stomach quailed a little. All she wanted was to keep things as smooth and easy as they'd been before they moved to St Dee. Just until they were more settled. Then he would tell her. It would be better if he told her, rather than her badgering it out of him.

'There you go,' she said, dropping Elvis into the basket by the window. He trampled round and round, chasing his tail, then curled into a ball and went to sleep.

The sun was falling onto her easel in a stream of light, and Carrie went through her own settling routine, putting her teacup out of spilling reach, moving her sketches so she could see where to start again, arranging her pencils in order . . .

Her attention drifted out of the window and down to the lane, where Barbara Purves was clipping away at the hedgerow with a pair of gardening secateurs, a trug over one arm. Her dangling earrings caught the light like camera flashes, as she worked away at whatever she was harvesting – elderberries? Brambles? Who knew?

Carrie's pen scratched over the paper, as Barbara Purves the bird took shape, tall and thin and definite, stuffing scraps and twigs into her nest. Organising, squawking. Soaring high over the village, observing all the other animals in their day-to-day movements, noting their patterns. When the news came to the village that the humans were coming back, she'd be the first to fly in with it, her wings beating with indignation. She would gather them together, on the village green, marshalling the animals into action . . .

Milly Mouse, thought Carrie, letting her pen move on its own. Of course. It was so obvious: Milly Mouse, looking after all these tiny creatures, letting them run around her home, up and down the stairs.

Carrie paused, taken aback by the pin-sharp images building in her head. Ideas were jostling for space, already formed into pages and lines of text, and it was an intoxicating feeling, like opening one present after another on Christmas morning, and the pile never getting smaller. It felt as though the whole thing could bubble through on its own – it had happened once before when she'd sketched out the whole of her first Morris book in one frenzied evening, then sat back, astonished at what she'd done.

This could be amazing, she thought, as she ripped off the top sheet of her sketchbook and began to map out boxes and flow charts while they were still clear in her mind's eye. A thrill of excitement ran over her skin as her pen moved almost without intervention from her.

As she looked up from the page for a second, Carrie's attention was caught by movement in the lane below and she realised Barbara Purves could not only see her, but was waving at her in cheery greeting.

Guiltily, she waved back, then grabbed her sketchbook and slipped off her chair as if she were leaving the room.

But Carrie didn't leave the room. She slid her back down by the window, next to Elvis's basket and beneath Barbara's line of sight, and carried on drawing while it was all still clear in her mind.

The book would start as the people trudged away with their possessions, leaving the still-warm firesides for the animals to creep into, then, as time passed and they realised the humans weren't coming back, their various characters began to emerge to take on their old roles: the tabby-cat washerwoman, the sociable rabbits in the pub, the elegant dapple-grey horse in the largest stable. And at the centre of it all, Milly Mouse, in the schoolroom.

Carrie paused, chewing her pen for a second. The bells over at Deeting Magna chimed the hour, but she barely heard them, only registered the tall church steeple over the valley as a background detail.

What would come next?

The news that the humans were coming back. New humans, not seen before by the great-grandchildren of the original St Dee creatures.

Who would stare at the newcomers with Betsy and Ivor's wide, curious eyes.

Cautiously, Carrie raised her head to see if Barbara Purves had gone; fortunately, she had. But before she could wonder whether Barbara was in fact heading up her own path, Carrie's eye was distracted by a flash of white in next door's garden where Betsy, with a white broderie anglaise sunhat over her curls, was playing on her own with three dolls, lining them up as if they were at school, obviously telling them a story out of the book on her knee.

Making order out of chaos, thought Carrie, with a twinge of sympathy. Poor bossy Betsy.

She watched as Betsy lectured on, wagging her finger periodically and casting a little shadow over her class. She seemed to be snapping at one doll in particular, with the same look of annoyance on her face that she'd shown the kittens when they'd tried to put their paws through the mouse cage.

The mouse!

Carrie put her hand over her open mouth. How could she have forgotten that?

What kind of mother would I make, she thought, scrambling to her feet.

'Sorry, sorry, sorry.' The words tumbled out of her mouth, though she wasn't sure why or who she was apologising to, as she reached up to lift Morris's cage from the top of her bookshelf. It was very still inside.

Elvis stirred and stretched in his basket, exposing the candy-pink ribbed roof of his tiny mouth, and a wave of guilty panic washed over her at her maternal ineptitude.

Why am I suddenly in charge of all these living things? Carrie wondered. Kittens, mice, children . . .

She opened the lid and poked the straw with her pen. Still nothing moved. Then with a sick feeling building in her stomach, she pushed the straw around, until she found Morris.

He was lying very still – or was very deeply asleep, as Ivor had said. Definitely dead.

Bile rose in her throat, and she fought back an instinct to shove it back on a high shelf and let Mark deal with it. The idea of the decaying mouse corpse made her feel sick, even though it was probably still warm.

A sudden throaty screech from Elvis almost made her drop the cage in surprise and she looked down to see him arching his back and hissing so violently his small body seemed to be vibrating with the effort. Carrie spun round to see what had set him off, but there was nothing there.

Nothing at all. Just motes of spinning dust in the sunlight. She looked out of the window. Betsy had gone.

'Elvis,' she said, trying to reassure herself, 'is it the mouse? Or was it a bird? A bird at the window?'

The kitten backed towards the far edge of the basket, still hissing, its fur almost standing on end.

Carrie's heart was pounding in her chest. 'What?' she said aloud, this time not to Elvis, but to the room in general. For all the times she'd willed the house to speak to her, now she wished it back. Her frantic gaze turned to her easel, terrified she'd suddenly start seeing the pages lift and fall, or the pencils drop from their rest.

Isn't that what you wanted?

'What?'

And then, as abruptly as he'd started, Elvis dropped his back and began to circle in his basket, arching his back and rolling his head to the side.

Just like he did when he was being stroked, Carrie thought to her horror.

She shoved the mouse cage down, grabbed the kitten and made a bolt for the door.

Chapter Sixteen

Carrie debated whether or not to tell Mark about the weird moment with Elvis, but he'd arrived home in a strange mood, and then insisted that they go to the pub – 'to see our friends, right?' – where she didn't feel like revealing such a scary moment to Mark *and* Lucy *and* Chris, who would probably want to go straight back and conduct a seance.

And, she told herself, the comfortingly mindless banter about television and idle village gossip seemed to drain away the spookiness of it. Mark had been in great form – the funny, easy man she'd admired at London parties, secretly amazed he was her husband. A couple of glasses of wine, and she wondered if she'd just imagined it. She did, however, ask Mark to bring the mouse cage downstairs for her 'while he was up there', rather than venture in to her study again that evening.

Several hours later, though, despite the absolute darkness around her, and the unusual silence outside, and the clean, air-dried sheets she'd made up the bed with that evening, Carrie couldn't sleep. She lay very still, but her body refused to go limp when her mind was churning. A series of vivid images jumbled over and over in disconcerting sequences – Betsy and Ivor sitting silently in her studio, Philip working through the night at his heaped-up desk, old pictures of Kathleen Maxwell and Lily and Jack and the village fete, then her own imaginings of people's houses, inhabited by tiny woodland creatures who grew and grew over the years to be people-sized, with clothes over their fur and real emotion in their glittering eyes . . .

And the kitten. The kitten had been staring right at *something* . . .

'Carrie, for Christ's sake, will you either take some Nytol or just go downstairs and read a fucking book? I need to get up in the morning.'

She rolled onto her side. Mark was squinting at her with one eye open a fraction and the other still squeezed tightly shut. He didn't look his best in the middle of the night. But though his words were cross, his voice was more weary than angry.

'Sorry.' Carrie rolled herself over again so she could curl her back into his body, and pulled his arm under her neck. They fitted together well, and she would happily have dropped off, but Mark had made it very clear early on in their relationship that he couldn't sleep so close to someone else. He normally waited until she'd dropped off before reclaiming his own cool space. If he was in a bad mood, he didn't wait.

But now he held her tightly, and Carrie felt grateful for his tenderness.

'How did you know I wasn't asleep?' she asked, nuzzling the hairs on his arm with her nose. 'I was trying not to disturb you.'

'I can tell. You go hot when you're asleep. And you weren't snoring.'

'Oh. I didn't know I did that.'

'Well, you do. Why can't you sleep?' he asked into her hair.

Carrie hesitated. 'I think I'm spending too much time on my own. I think I might be starting to imagine things.'

Mark paused, and for a split second, Carrie thought he was about to say something serious, but instead he pulled her tighter to him, and said, 'Maybe you're not the only one. Maybe I'm lying awake waiting to hear this ghost baby, just to make sure my wife's not going mental.'

'Don't joke. You know I heard it again?' She paused. 'I've heard it several times, actually.'

'I'm not joking. I worry about you. Going mad here on your own without me to keep you sane. You know it was probably one of the kids from next door?'

'Maybe.' Carrie knew it wasn't. She knew what Betsy and Ivor sounded like when they cried.

They lay still, both now listening for an imaginary sound that neither really wanted to hear. Nothing broke the silence apart from the distant hoot of a barn owl but Carrie couldn't stop herself imagining it as a dispossessed animal neighbour, signalling its rage at being evicted from its old home, and that didn't make her feel any better.

'They're really very sweet, Betsy and Ivor,' she said.

He didn't reply, and she went on, encouraged by his silence. 'I really enjoy spending time with them. Looking after them. I really wish . . . It would be so nice to have our own kids. Now we've got so much space for them.'

Silence.

'Mark?'

'Don't, Carrie,' said Mark unexpectedly. 'It's not a good time, all right?'

A heavy stone settled in Carrie's stomach. That wasn't the reply she'd been after. Was he lying awake worrying about work? Or was it her? Were the disappointments in their marriage showing up like ultraviolet light now she wasn't surrounded by London glamour? Kitchen sinks were a long way from sushi bars, or – her mind flicked up a tormenting image – an Australian beach.

The questions multiplied in her head, and she was scared that somehow they'd burst out of her regardless, but her mother had always told her to leave the bed free of any difficult conversations, and she pressed her lips together to keep them in.

Mark sighed, sending a pungent gust of night breath over her ear.

'Carrie . . .' he began, then stopped.

The tone of his voice wasn't reassuring

'What?' She leaned back against him.

He didn't go on.

'Come on, Mark,' said Carrie bravely. 'You can tell me. Is something the matter?'

'It's . . .' She heard him swallow – his lips made a dry, clicking sound. 'Carrie, I'm sorry I haven't been here as much as I said I would. It's a lovely house, and you've made it really beautiful. It's not that I don't like it. Or appreciate the way you've moved here and tried to settle us in. I just . . .' His voice trailed off. 'You know. London. It's been . . . hard.'

'I know.' Carrie seized gratefully on this easy worry. 'I know how much you love London. And I know you need to get your work sorted out.'

Mark was silent, as if he was weighing up his words.

'And you've got friends in London too, that you probably want to see,' she went on, generously. She didn't really have friends in London, just the ones she shared with Mark. And Mark had an address book full of acquaintances and people he went for drinks with – even if none of them really knew him properly, as she did. But in the dark, with his arms round her, it was easy to be generous. 'I don't want you to feel cut off.'

'No, it's important not to do that,' he said, too quickly. 'I need to see other people. I mean, for work, you know, contacts and stuff. As well as friends. But I love this place too, you know. It's like . . . a different life.'

'That's OK, Mark,' said Carrie, even though she wasn't sure that what he'd said was in any way comforting. It only made her wonder what he was apologising for, what doubts he was having that he wasn't telling her. *Friends*. What did that mean, exactly?

But she said, 'I understand it's hard getting started when you're freelance. I didn't expect you to be here every day with me. Anyway,

I need to finish this book, don't I, with as few disturbances as possible?'

Mark hugged her without speaking, but Carrie's relief was tempered by the small voice in her head, remarking acidly on how much easier it was to have her own life in the village without Mark here, messing it up. How much easier it was to play with the kids next door, or chat in the village shop without having to explain in whispers to Mark who everyone was. And know that they'd be whispering about him, and why he refused to join in with the rest of them, why he wouldn't join the neighbourhood watch. How much easier, indeed, it would be to spend time drinking coffee with Philip Gladstone and getting to know more about the village from him. Getting to know more about him, full stop.

Carrie blinked in surprise at herself. Was that a sense of *guilt*? Because surely there was nothing about her friendship with Philip that she'd want to keep from Mark? Was there?

At the same moment, Mark's hand, curled under her neck, began to move in a familiar smoothing rhythm, scooping the curves of her narrow waist and sliding up her ribs, around the slope of her back. His other arm pulled her even closer into his body while his free hand ran down the front of her thigh, stroking with two fingers between her knees.

'So, neither of us are sleepy, eh?' he murmured into the nape of her neck. He wasn't wearing pyjamas and from the insistent stirring in the small of her back, she could tell he wasn't at all sleepy. His fingers traced up the inside of her thigh, pushing under the lace hem of her cotton shorts. 'Can I wake you up a bit more?'

To Carrie's surprise, a powerful, irrational reluctance to be touched swept through her – irrational because it had been a while since she and Mark had had sex, and she'd never pushed him away before. But now something was putting up boundaries that made her skin shrink against his touch as if it was sunburned, and she couldn't explain it.

'I'm going to make myself a cup of Ovaltine,' she said, throwing off the covers and swinging herself out of his reach. 'Do you want one?'

'Ovaltine?'

'Yes.' Carrie pulled on her dressing gown and tied it hard around her waist. 'Listen, you need to get some rest. I won't wake you.'

'Carrie, I can think of something that'll put you to sleep much better than Ovaltine.' Mark sounded amused but annoyed at the same time.

'You, maybe. Not me.'

There was a silence and the room was too dark for Carrie to make out his face.

'Do you want children or not?' he asked, and there was an edge to his jokey tone. 'Because we need to practise.'

'I don't . . . feel like it,' she said, and knew it sounded lame.

Mark was obviously waiting for more explanation but Carrie let the awful silence extend.

'OK. Be like that,' he said eventually, and rolled himself into the duvet.

Carrie hesitated with her hand on the cool iron bedstead, conscious that whatever she said now could smooth the moment over, or leave a scab they'd both pick at later.

Her mind raced but came up with nothing. She hovered awkwardly, feeling the seconds draining away. Why did she never know the right thing to do?

Wasn't it *worse* to say the wrong thing?

So she bit her lip, and slipped silently downstairs.

After the stuffy darkness of the bedroom the air seemed lighter and easier to breathe in the kitchen. Carrie put a pan of milk on the Aga to heat up and sat at the table, her head in her hands.

It was normal to go off sex, she told herself first. And it was normal when a couple who'd lived out of each other's pockets for three years suddenly got their own spaces to feel protective of that. But how can I feel so broody at the same time?

It'll seem different in the morning, she thought, listening to the milk hiss in the pan. It's just night-time when worries get room to expand, to fill your imagination.

She lifted her head. There was so much more that Mark hadn't said.

Idly, Carrie started to doodle houses on the sketchpad lying open on the table. As she drew the tension drained from her shoulders and she realised she was drawing the village again, cottages huddled together in gangs, grouped around the green with the maypole in the centre as though the houses themselves were like the children, circling the pole ready to dance round in patterns.

Would the maypole ever be used again, she wondered, seeing it rise up in her book with mice and fox cubs twining the ribbons. Ivor and Betsy. Lily, and Kathleen Maxwell.

At least I'm old enough to know what's happening, and have some control over my life, she thought, letting the pen move on its own. Not like poor Lily, pregnant at sixteen. Or Betsy, without her mother and dumped in a new place.

The pen stopped. I should have *asked*, she thought, crossly. Maybe Philip wanted to tell me about what happened to his wife. Maybe he wanted me to ask, so he wouldn't have to bring it up.

'God,' said Carrie aloud. 'It's so hard.' Then she bit her lip superstitiously, not wanting to invite anything unseen into another conversation.

As she got up to pour the hot milk into her mug, Carrie's eye fell on the mouse cage, which was where she'd left it, by the back door, and she shuddered, thinking of the small corpse inside. That awful knowing look on Betsy's face when Ivor had told her the mouse was just sleeping. Like she'd already learned to tell white lies to her little brother to cover up sadness.

How long would be it before the flesh started to rot? Or the bones show through the thin fur? Her imagination shrank away from the image. Carrie knew she was prone to leaving unpleasant tasks – rinsing out mouldy teapots, emptying bins, opening bank statements – until they'd multiplied into something much worse.

She cradled her hot mug. She felt totally awake now. Awake and determined to be rational.

Right, she thought to herself, this is one chore you're not going to let get any worse.

She put the mug down, and before she could think twice, slipped on her trainers and coat, opened the back door, and took the mouse cage outside to the garden.

There was a chill in the night air, and she pulled her coat tightly around her as the cold bit into her skin. The moon was nearly full and gave off enough light to see the trowel she'd just been using to plant bulbs in the borders, still stuck in the earth.

The rest of the garden loomed in the darkness, the fruit trees quite sharp in the moonlight. Carrie didn't look down the garden towards the chalk horse, but kept her eyes firmly on the area illuminated by the kitchen light.

'Five minutes,' she muttered to herself, holding her dressing gown shut with one hand and gripping the trowel in the other. 'This'll take five minutes and it'll be done.'

Working as fast and as quietly as she could, Carrie dug a hole in the border, shovelling out the chalky earth until it formed a musty heap that spilled over onto the grass. Then, when she judged she'd dug far enough, she took a deep breath and tipped the contents of the cage, straw bedding and all, into the hole.

Carrie paused. She'd never buried anything before. There was something oddly furtive about the action, as though she might stumble upon other things in the earth, like the plates hidden in the cellar. What else was underneath this soil? What about those prehistoric skeletons Philip had mentioned? How had they first been discovered? By someone innocently planting bulbs, or burying a cat?

She shook herself and began trowelling the earth back on top. Her back ached, and she dropped to her knees on the grass to finish the job as quickly as possible.

When the bedding was covered over, she patted the soil firmly with the trowel and sat back on her heels.

There.

Morris, all warm under the earth. Safe from the cats. Dust to dust. Ashes to ashes.

You'd better hope he was dead and not just sleeping, said the voice in her head. You might have checked first before burying him.

A barn owl hooted somewhere over her head and Carrie nearly yelled aloud with shock.

Stop it, she told herself, scrambling to her feet and looking up at the house, away from her little burial site. The rambling ivy along the back wall was picked out by the moon, so it looked like a rough beard covering the lower storeys. Their bedroom on the first floor was dark, and the light in the kitchen spilled artificially across the grass. On the Rose Cottage half of the façade there was only one window with a muted illumination behind the heavy curtains – she guessed that was Philip, working late in his study.

There were no lights on in the other windows, though now Carrie's eyes had become accustomed to the moonlight she noticed not all the curtains were drawn. There were two windows on the top floor where the moonlight bounced straight back off the new glass. Which rooms were those, she wondered? Betsy and Ivor presumably shared a room on the first floor opposite Philip's at the front: the mirror image, in the floor plan, of her own spare room. Maybe Philip had run out of curtains for the unused rooms.

A cloud shifted across the clear night sky, obscuring the moon and throwing part of the garden into shade, and Carrie blinked, suddenly unsure of what she was seeing behind the glass.

Either it was a trick of the light or a little girl's face was peering out of the window: round, white, indistinct, like that of a sleepwalker.

'Betsy!' breathed Carrie to herself. Poor little girl!

She wasn't sure what the best thing to do was – should she wave? Would that frighten her even more? The thought of Betsy wandering around that dark house like a little ghost, unable to sleep while her father locked himself away in his study, made her yearn with sympathy.

As Carrie stared up at the window, shivering, the cloud shifted again, letting more white light fall over the house. In the darkness it seemed black and white, as though it had slid back to 1941 under the cover of night-time, ready to slip back to the present when the sun rose.

And then the face was gone.

The barn owl hooted again and all at once, Carrie felt very cold and alone in the darkness of her own garden, as though the only souls awake were the animals outside and the simmering presence of Philip Gladstone above her, poring over his ancient maps of the abbey, half with the animals himself.

And above the whole village, that huge white chalk figure, stretching like a giant's handprint across the valley, linking the modern newcomers to the ancient people who'd first struggled to break the soil in the middle of the plain. Dark-hooded monks in the abbey, prehistoric farmers carving out rhythms from the seasons, patterns of existence that were still going on in the rise and fall of the moon, and the blossom and wane of the hedgerows, beneath the superficial concerns their descendants had about library vans and neighbourhood watch.

There was something about the neighbourhood that was constantly being watched.

The clouds shifted again, with a tangible gust of chill, reproving wind and Carrie was filled with a sudden need to be back inside her own house, near Mark's warm body.

Stumbling across the garden, not wanting to look up to the windows for fear of what she might see, she ran back up the path, dropping the trowel in the boot rack inside the back door.

Her mug of Ovaltine was where she had left it on the table, next to the comforting normality of the pink photocopied bus timetable and the stack of bills. Even so, Carrie didn't let her line of sight rise to the inky-blackness of the garden beyond the uncurtained kitchen windows. Gratefully, with shaking hands, she picked up the mug, cradling it and feeling the heat seep into her fingers, allowing her breathing to return to normal while she sank her back against the Aga.

I'll mention it to Philip in the morning, she thought, soothed by the idea of doing something constructive with that unsettling image. I'll tell him I saw Betsy sleepwalking. It could be dangerous. There were all those carved wooden things lying about the place – she could hurt herself.

The Ovaltine spread a trail of reassuring heat down her throat and Carrie began to feel more rational. She managed a wan smile at how ridiculous she'd been about the mouse. Of course the mouse had been dead. It hadn't moved when she'd poked about in the straw, had it? And what was there to be scared of in the garden?

All the same, she left the lights on when she went upstairs and for the first time ever, lay awake feeling grateful for Mark's reassuring snores.

Chapter Seventeen

In the morning, Carrie woke before the alarm, when the sun began filtering through the linen curtains. She knew she'd only managed a fitful few hours' sleep from the soreness in her eyes and the damp sweat collecting between her breasts, but she'd definitely been dreaming. What was that relief she felt about waking up? What had she been dreaming about?

The details slipped away as her mind fruitlessly flapped about for them.

Somewhere in the valley a cock was crowing and the birds were already making a racket in the fruit trees outside the window.

Carrie rolled over to look at Mark, who was still fast asleep, his fist clenched under his head. Fire engines and dustcarts didn't disturb him. Birds and sunlight wouldn't stand a chance.

Even after three years, Carrie still felt a tiny thrill to wake and see a man that handsome lying in her bed, but as the light fell on the pillow, she noticed how much less stressed Mark looked asleep, and it made her realise how the little lines around his mouth and eyes were a new daytime addition.

As she began to slide herself next to him, so she could wake him with a cuddle, Mark stirred in his dream, and muttered something, his brow creasing up with irritation.

Carrie stopped, her ears pricking for words.

'I can't!' he mumbled emphatically. 'No. She won't like . . .'

Can't what?

Mark paused, obviously hearing the reply, then frowned again. 'I've told you. I can't. Not here.'

She froze, half-hoping he'd go on, half-dreading what he'd say next. But Mark's brow smoothed out as he slipped back into sleep, and whatever he was muttering now was lost into his pillow as he rolled over and away from the confrontation.

Any desire to wake him up with kisses evaporated and Carrie sat up straight.

Lucy was right: she was far too naïve. 'Not here? I can't?' Weren't they classic affair words?

No.

No, she told herself, staring blankly at the oak beams above her. No. They're more likely to be IT paranoia words about some firewall or some file he's been asked to sort out. Basic ignorance about Mark's job prevented her from reassuring herself better.

And, her brain argued, at least he's refusing to do whatever it is that's so dodgy.

Carrie looked over at him. Mark looked helpless, wrapped like a larva in the duvet, his long lashes grazing his cheekbone, almost as long as hers. He wasn't the sort to have an affair; yes, he could chat easily to women, but he wouldn't cheat on her. He wouldn't throw away the special thing they'd waited so long to find in each other. She knew that.

Maybe that photograph had just reawoken some memories.

That's not what you were thinking, she told herself.

Silently, she swung her feet off the bed and got up.

Downstairs, lemon-yellow sunlight was drenching the kitchen walls, and the farmhouse clock showed it was ten past ten. Carrie went to wind it, as she did every morning now, but checked it against her watch first. She frowned. It was quarter to eight. And the clock had been working fine when she checked the time last night.

Elvis woke in his basket as she walked about, and mewing, butted at her legs until she picked up his saucer. She scraped out some kitten food for him, then put the kettle on and dropped the last slices of bread into the toaster. Then turned it off. Save them for Mark, she thought. I can always get some croissants from the shop later.

Carrie made herself some proper coffee and began planning her day in her head while she watched the thrushes flit from branch to branch in the apple trees. Breakfast for Mark, Betsy and Ivor arrive, sketch, lunch, get groceries, post letters, work on book, return some of those increasingly terse calls from Gina, her agent.

She smiled wryly at herself. The Routine Queen – so much so that she'd already absorbed Betsy and Ivor into it. Some artist she was. Not what you'd call the most bohemian lifestyle.

Next to Philip Gladstone's melodramatic all-night writing sessions, her own work felt kind of mundane. Scribbling away into the small hours, burning with inspiration, his head crowded with all those details and facts, weaving them into some fantastic, colourful, academic authority . . . Like a *proper* writer.

The sounds of Mark stirring upstairs brought her back to herself. He clattered his way into the bathroom and turned up the shower, setting the boiler into clanking overdrive.

'Things to do,' she said aloud, and went into the garden to retrieve the empty mouse cage.

It lay on its side next to the freshly disturbed pile of earth, bits of bedding still clinging to the bars where she'd hurriedly tipped it out. There was no sign of any mouse resurrection. Would the fresh earth attract a marauding cat? Carrie wondered. She trod it down with her foot and scattered some leaves over the top.

A quick glance up at the house showed that Mark had drawn their bedroom curtains. She could see brief flashes of him as he moved around – white T-shirt, black shorts – dressing himself with absolutely no regard for anyone who might be watching. But it was next door that drew her attention.

Carrie stared, confused, at the façade. All the windows had curtains. Even the ones she had seen uncurtained just hours ago. How could that be?

Don't be silly, she thought, shaking herself. Philip could easily have gone round the house this morning and drawn them.

Drawn them closed – in the morning?

He's a very odd man, she told herself firmly, picking up the cage and pushing away any more imaginative explanations.

The fact remained, however, that she needed a replacement life model.

'I think you should get it yourself,' said Mark in response to her request to set and check the trap.

'Why? Didn't you say mouse-catching's the kind of thing husbands are meant to do?'

'Well, yes. But I might not always be here to do things like that for you.'

'Thanks, Mark,' said Carrie, pretending to look hurt to disguise the fact that she really was hurt. 'Do you have a timeframe in mind for that?'

'No, I just mean . . . What?' demanded Mark. 'I mean, if I'm out at work, or something! You're not one of those helpless housewife types.'

'Maybe I'm just doing it so you'll feel like a proper husband.'

There was a pause and she could tell that Mark was trying to work out how serious she was.

Let him try to work it out, she thought. He ought to be able to read me by now. She met his eyes defiantly.

Mark raised his hands. 'OK, I'll go down there and put the cheese in, but you have to check it yourself, all right?'

'All right,' said Carrie.

He touched her nose. 'You can't be scared of creepy-crawly things. You're a country girl now.'

'It's not the creepy-crawly things,' Carrie protested. 'It's the . . . I don't know, it's the idea of catching something, then putting it in a cage to draw it against its will . . . Why are you looking at me like that?'

'Because you're being silly. Field mice are so tiny!' He smiled at her. 'That's the trouble with you, always trying to make things more exciting than they really are – the spooky house, the village, now evil mice in the cellar . . .'

Carrie looked at him reproachfully. 'The IT geek husband.'

'Yeah, maybe,' said Mark, and stifled a yawn. 'God, sorry.'

'Tired?' she asked, trying not to think about his sleeptalking. There were lots of non-exciting explanations for that.

'Yeah. Rubbish night's sleep. Must be catching it off you. Bad dreams and all that.' Mark ran a hand over his face. 'Anyway, I'd better get a move on.'

'What time'll you be back? I thought I'd cook something nice. Lucy was saying the village shop's going to start stocking Mrs Bowler's chickens. They're so free range they've been in most gardens in the village, apparently.'

'Ace. Shouldn't be too late tonight. Six-ish? Got a meeting with those architects in Devizes. They're going to go ahead with the website.'

'Oh. Oh, right.' He said that as if he'd already told her. But he hadn't.

'Devizes?' she wanted to ask. 'Are you sure about that? Want to change your mind? Devizes? Swindon? Or Clerkenwell?' But she saw the smooth, unruffled silk of their marriage stretching out in front of her, and was too scared to snag it.

Mark swung his laptop bag over his shoulder and stretched out his arms. 'Come here.' He blinked slowly at her, letting his eyes crinkle in a way that still made her stomach twitch.

Carrie walked over and let herself be enclosed in Mark's hug. He smelled of freshly washed clothes, and cologne, and toothpaste. A rush of nostalgia came over her for the days when they'd first met, and how she had changed all her soap powders so she could smell him all the time, even on her own clothes. It took her a while to work out that the smell was Mark's own, somehow, not Unilever's.

'Sorry,' he said, over her head. 'Last night. I didn't handle things very well, did I?'

'Don't,' she began, suddenly not wanting to hear any more. 'There's no need to . . .'

But Mark clearly thought he had something to get off his chest. 'It was stupid of me to apologise for something you weren't even thinking about, so you ended up worrying about it anyway, then jump all over you,' he went on. 'That was really selfish of me. No wonder you weren't in the mood. I just didn't think.' He held her at arm's length so he could give her the full benefit of his remorseful expression. 'I lay awake thinking about it for ages. I'm sorry, Carrie. I'm not the easiest person to live with.'

Carrie bit her lip. 'Well, neither of us are. It's not just you, Mark.'

'And I didn't mean to sound so dismissive about having kids. It's just . . . It's just too big a topic to start discussing like that. You know? Anyway, you're right, we haven't spent enough proper time together lately,' he said. 'Can we put that right? Starting tonight?'

Carrie nodded.

'Forgiven?'

'There's nothing to forgive, stupid.'

'Thank you,' said Mark, and pulled her close to kiss her.

Carrie left the mousetrap for a couple of hours, then, steeling herself to act like an adult, she went down to the cellar to check, hoping there would be nothing.

But already a dark brown Morris replacement was circling furiously in the box, the cheese long gone. She carried the trap upstairs at arm's length, while the mouse's claws made brittle, skittering noises against the plastic, and decanted it into the refurbished mouse cage.

Then she washed her hands furiously.

Betsy and Ivor arrived at her back door just before nine and they all went straight upstairs to her studio. Betsy regarded the reappearance of Morris with some visible suspicion, although Ivor was delighted, and laughed gleefully as Morris 2.0 scurried in and out of his toilet-roll assault course.

'He seems darker than before,' observed Betsy.

'Probably just a trick of the light.'

'And he seems bigger.' Betsy was looking at her sternly over the top of her first Morris book.

Carrie lifted the cage up and placed it very safely on top of her bookshelf. Out of sight and out of harm's way. She got the distinct impression that Betsy wasn't fooled by Morris's unexpected resurrection. 'Do you think so?' she said, trying to sound conversational.

'Yes. I do.'

'Well, maybe he's grown.'

Betsy put her head on one side. 'Maybe he was turned into a different mouse by a witch?'

'Maybe,' said Carrie. 'Though it wasn't me. Maybe he's just changed. Like when people go abroad on holiday they might come back with a tan. Or if they've gone away to a health farm they might come back thinner.'

'Or if they're a soldier who's gone off to war they might come back without an eye, or with one leg.'

'Exactly. Yes.' Carrie sat back down at her desk where she felt more in charge, and picked up a pencil.

'My mummy's gone away,' Betsy said. 'Do you think she'll come back different?' She set her lips in a firm line, waiting for a reaction.

Carrie squirmed and suddenly saw the stupidity of pretending Morris had just been asleep. Had Philip told them his wife had gone on holiday when really she'd died or got divorced or something? It would be very irresponsible of him if he had.

Carrie met Betsy's clear-eyed gaze, not sure what to say. Philip had a nerve. He could at least send a few notes round with his kids.

Maybe she'd run off with someone else. That had happened to one of her own lecturers at college. And if he was always shutting himself up writing, moody, keeping weird hours . . . He looked like an easy man to admire but a hard one to live with.

Then again, there was something kind of fascinating about him. Carrie put her pencil down. 'Well . . .' she began.

'Hazel came back the same,' observed Ivor, suddenly. He was lying on his stomach, playing with the kittens, and Carrie noticed Betsy glare furiously at him.

'Well, she did,' he protested. 'She came back just the same.'

'Who's Hazel?' asked Carrie. A cat? A nanny?

'No one,' insisted Betsy, turning her fierce furrowed brow to Ivor, who didn't notice.

'Hazel's Betsy's friend,' he told Carrie with a sunny smile.

'Really? A friend from home?'

'No. From here.' Ivor squirmed on his tummy like one of the kittens, rolling over with Elvis on his chest.

'Ivor . . .' Betsy began in a very warning tone.

'Shut up, Ivor, shut up, Ivor,' he sing-songed.

Carrie wasn't sure what happened next – whether Elvis was about to scratch Ivor's face and Betsy batted the kitten away, or whether Betsy launched herself at him of her own accord. She just knew that she moved across the room faster than she could think about it, to scoop Ivor out of reach of Betsy's hard little hands and their ringing slaps.

Ivor was silent for a moment, then drew a breath and wailed deafeningly into Carrie's shoulder, sending damp vibrations through her T-shirt.

The kittens scrambled for the safety of Elvis's basket.

With a sulky shrug, Betsy picked up the nearest book and began reading it as if nothing had happened.

Carrie cuddled Ivor to her shoulder and tried to murmur comforting things into his hair, but she felt utterly out of her depth. Maybe if she'd known them for longer she might have been able to exert some discipline, but this was just too much. Pulling aside his pale copper fringe, she saw an angry red hand mark beginning to develop on his cheek.

This was the final straw. Philip was going to have to do some explaining.

'Betsy,' she said, holding out her hand, 'time to go home.'

'Can I bring this book with me?' Betsy looked up at her with wide and innocent blue eyes, the colour of Wedgwood china.

'No,' said Carrie, swallowing hard. 'You can't.'

'I'm right in the middle of a chapter,' muttered Philip, stroking his beard distractedly. 'Could you have just yelled at her and hung on for a bit longer?'

'No, Philip, I couldn't! She *slapped* him!' They were standing alone in the kitchen, but even so, Carrie lowered her voice in case Betsy could hear her. The child had bat ears. 'She just slapped him for no reason. I didn't know what to do.'

And where, Carrie wanted to demand, did she learn that?

Philip was showing every sign of having written through the night again. His beard was unkempt and his dark eyes were hooded, and from the way they were darting about, his mind was clearly elsewhere. Carrie knew that look, because it was one of her own.

'I don't know why she's started slapping,' he said. 'She's never done it before. And she certainly doesn't get slapped here, I can assure you – we've . . . I've never punished either of them physically.'

'I saw her sleepwalking last night,' Carrie added, determined not to let him off the hook. 'She was at the window. Philip, look, I don't mean to pry, but . . .' She swallowed. 'Was there some trauma with her mother? Betsy was talking about how her mummy had gone away. I don't mean to pry, but I need to know. I don't want to upset her by saying the wrong thing.'

Philip stared at a gloomy oil painting of some angels dragging a moribund Christ up to heaven. Then he turned his gaze back to Carrie. 'Have you been up to the church yet?' he asked.

She shook her head impatiently. 'Well, yes, I've been up there to have a look but it's locked. Philip, I don't think this is the right time to . . .'

'Kids! We're going for a walk!' Philip raised his hand in an 'excuse me' gesture and went to search about in the cupboard under the stairs. Carrie half-expected him to pull out a broomstick or something, but instead he dragged out a surprisingly modern buggy.

'Ivor will say he'll walk but he gets tired,' he explained, shaking it out roughly.

'As for you, madam . . .' he said sternly. 'We need to have words.'

Betsy had reappeared with her coat already on. Her face looked pale, but her eyes were red as if she'd been crying. While Philip was struggling with the clasps on the buggy, Betsy took Carrie's hand and pulled her a little way down the hall.

She cast a quick glance to check her father's attention was elsewhere, then said, in a whisper. 'I'm sorry. I didn't mean to do it.'

'You should never hit your brother,' Carrie whispered back, crouching down to her level. 'You should never hit anyone.'

'I don't. Hazel . . .' She bit her lip.

'Hazel what?'

Betsy shook her head stubbornly, bouncing her curls.

Hazel sounded like a right little troublemaker. Carrie made a mental note to ask Lucy whose daughter she was. There were still a few people at the other end of the village that she hadn't met, but if the parents were as bad as the daughter, it wouldn't be long.

If, of course, she was real. If anyone needed an imaginary friend it was Betsy. Carrie had had an imaginary friend of her own for several lonely years; for one miserable term, Esmerelda was the only person she'd spoken to at boarding school for days on end.

'Betsy,' she said, carefully, 'is Hazel a little girl in the village, or is she a . . . a special friend who lives in your head?'

Seeing Betsy's face turned mutinous, she tried a different tack. 'Well, OK. But have you said sorry to Ivor?'

Betsy nodded.

'And did you mean it?'

She nodded again. 'I gave him a hug and a kiss.'

'That's the main thing then. I want us to be friends, Betsy.' Carrie squeezed her small hand. 'And I don't like little girls who hurt other people.'

Betsy's eyes filled up. 'I don't. I *don't* hurt other people!'

'Are we ready then?'

Carrie straightened up as Philip loomed over them. Ivor was jumping from foot to foot with excitement in his red wellies.

'The church!' he squealed. 'Ghosts!'

Philip shrugged. 'What can I say? They're not like other kids.'

Philip let Betsy run ahead as they walked down the road into the village. He seemed slightly ill-at-ease pushing Ivor in the buggy, but perhaps, thought Carrie, that was because it seemed ludicrously cute next to his powerful frame. He had the sort of large hands that could happily have steered shire horses and ploughs across the fields on the other side of the hedgerows.

They walked through the village, past the pointlessly restored red telephone box that no one ever used and the new benches around the green, already dedicated to old families by new residents keen to get their markers in. There weren't many people around, but those they did see waved in a friendly manner. Philip and Carrie waved back. Betsy galloped off down the path, her foxy-red hair glinting in the sun, but never so far that she was out of sight. It was an optimistically spring-like day, and the sun made the village seem chocolate-box pretty.

Carrie's mood lifted, despite herself, cheered by the daffodils by the side of the road, and the lovely symmetry of the cottages. It was weird, she thought, that the village seemed to have such a personality it could affect her as a person could.

And if a village could be harmonious merely from its inhabitants wishing it to be so, then St Dee was a perfect example, right down to its community noticeboard outside the pub, filled with fluttering announcements of neighbourhood watch meetings and pub quizzes.

As if on cue, as they rounded the corner of the green to take the lane headed up to the church, Lucy Ross and Barbara Purves came barrelling out of the pub towards them.

Lucy won the race to impart news by a short head, and the fact that she dispensed entirely with pleasantries while Barbara was still adjusting her face into a 'good afternoon!' smile.

'Carrie, you'll be on the fete committee, won't you? We've decided that to speed things up, we'll basically just get the neighbourhood watch committee to run it, then if anyone else wants to come on board later, they can,' she announced breathlessly, cutting a swift sideways glance at Barbara. 'I thought you could be on the heritage tent with me,' she went on, 'what with your Mark being into computers, I thought he could help us out with the research and printing up some stuff and so on. And with you being artistic, and all. And me being nosy,' she added, 'before anyone says it.'

'Kathleen Maxwell has very graciously agreed to lend some of her own family archive material to start us off,' Barbara interrupted. 'I think if we're going to do this properly, we have to start with the main family of the area.'

'Indeed,' said Philip.

'Would you like to be on the committee, Philip?' asked Lucy, cheekily. 'We could do with an academic like you. Keep us all spelling right.'

Barbara meanwhile tucked a strand of hair behind her ear in a manner that was almost girlish. 'If, of course, you have time, is what Lucy meant to say. We wouldn't want to impose on your publishing schedule.'

How does he know them this well? Carrie wondered. When's he had time to charm them in the pub?

But Philip seemed amused by Lucy's forward manner, rather than annoyed, and gave her a grin that suggested a certain familiarity, as if they'd already exchanged some banter, and got the measure of one another. 'Don't you mean you need someone to do the typing?'

'If you're volunteering.'

Lucy cackled, and Carrie felt irrationally jealous that she and Philip were so at ease with each other. She also noticed that Lucy wasn't in the slightest bit intimidated either by his size or his scholarliness, zoning straight in on the charm that twinkled beneath the beardy gruffness.

'What about Carrie's deadline?' he said. 'She's pretty busy too.'

'Oh,' Lucy flapped her hand. 'She's been busy since she arrived. She's used to it.'

'I'd be happy to help,' said Carrie. 'And if you need any computer stuff done, let me know. I'm sure Mark would love to be involved.'

Barbara and Lucy looked less than convinced.

'Anyway, ladies,' said Philip. 'Let me know what needs doing.' Their attention turned towards the green where Betsy was dancing round the maypole with an imaginary ribbon.

'I hope *they'll* both be in the maypole celebration!' exclaimed Barbara. She pulled out a large A4 notebook from her handbag. 'You too, young man,' she added, nodding at Ivor. 'We need as many children as we can find for the maypole element. I hope we'll have enough within the village. I want it to be the centrepiece of the day.'

'So is it going to be an old-fashioned type of event?' asked Carrie. 'I've seen pictures of the one they had before the evacuation and . . .'

'Have you?' demanded Barbara. 'Where?'

'Oh, er, Kathleen Maxwell showed me some pictures. I'm sure she has lots more.' Carrie spotted Lucy giving her a 'score one!' wink behind Barbara's back. 'Will she be presenting prizes like her mother did?' she added, for good value.

Barbara looked peeved. 'Well, yes, that was one of my ideas. But that won't be the main part of the day, since we don't have the livestock to judge as they would have had then. Obviously plans are in a very early stage, but I'd hoped to have several baking classes, local produce and the like, kiddies' games and so on.

Maybe a pet show. Make it a proper local event. Show people we're a real village.'

'It'll be like the old days. But without the annual bath,' observed Philip.

Barbara beamed with pleasure and Carrie noted the bird-like preening of her neck. 'Paul Jenkins has promised to help where he can with any archive material, if you want to make a start, Carrie. I've given Lucy his number.' She shot Carrie a look that made it clear that she didn't expect Lucy to do very much with it in the meantime.

'Where are you two off to then?' asked Lucy, swinging her big fake Gucci bag onto her other shoulder.

'We're going for a walk up to the church,' said Carrie, guardedly.

'I'm going to bore Carrie senseless with some historical detail,' said Philip soberly before Lucy could say anything. 'She's asked me to explain the religious significance of the valley to the local Anglo-Romano settlers. I'd ask you to come but I'm sure you've got much better things to do.'

Lucy rolled her eyes. 'Well, have fun. I'm running late for Mrs Cooper. I don't know how she gets that place in such a mess. I'd say it was something to do with that lad of hers if . . .' She stopped, sensing Barbara's disapproving glare, then winked at Carrie.

'Later. I'll drop in, get some ideas down on paper, eh?' she said. 'Bye now!'

They watched her swing down the road and turn down to Mrs Cooper's pristine cottage, converted from the old blacksmith's forge, where her cheery greeting was audible.

Carrie turned back to Barbara, who was looking as if she'd just made a sizeable mistake. Her imagination was already sketching the bird Barbara perched on top of the pub chimneys, regretting delegating anything to Lucy with a rueful flap of the wings.

'I'm so glad you're able to help out, dear,' said Barbara, putting a bony hand on Carrie's arm. 'I know I can rely on *you*.'

I wouldn't be so sure, thought Carrie, but she smiled anyway.

'Well, you know where to get hold of me if you need anything, Barbara,' she said. 'Don't want to keep you.'

'Goodbye, Mrs Purves,' said Philip, nodding politely, and moved on with the buggy.

'Well, then,' he said when Barbara was out of earshot. 'I wondered how long it would be before May Day came back to St Dee.'

'Sorry?'

'May Day. It was a huge deal here, for years and years. It's a powerful thing, tradition.' He cocked a bushy eyebrow at her. 'Seems to be dormant then, before you know it, it's stretching out its influence again, luring us all back under its spell . . .'

'Don't,' said Carrie, plucking at some wild hops growing in the hedgerow. 'You make it sound like some kind of curse, not a spell. It's just the village organisers getting everyone together to make cakes.'

'You say that,' said Philip, darkly, 'but it doesn't go away. Look how keen the Purveses are to reassert the squirarchy judging everyone! It's in the blood, this need to be part of an order. Why shouldn't it be in the soil? Like those hops – those same hops you're holding were probably seeded from the hops the monks planted, to make beer in the brewery.'

Carrie looked at the spiky round buds in her hand. 'Really?'

'Really. They don't stop growing because there's no one here to see them. Just like the chalk horse doesn't go away if there's no one there to worship it. It all just goes back into the ground. Waiting.' His eyes glittered with implications.

'Very profound.' Carrie tucked the hops into the hood of the buggy.

They had arrived at the gate of the village church, which had a notice on the board detailing the services at the nearby parishes. It was exactly the same as it had appeared in Jack and Lily's wedding photograph – simple, slightly austere, with a small graveyard behind where time had made the headstones higgledy-piggledy in the ground.

Betsy was already sitting on the new bench outside, her head bent over a pile of daisies on her lap, which she was beginning to string together, piercing their stems laboriously with her sharp thumbnail.

'Will they reopen it?' asked Carrie, keeping one eye on the children. 'Would it have to be re-consecrated?'

'I don't know,' said Philip. 'There was probably some ruling about keeping it in reasonable order, even when the place was evacuated – see, the roof's OK? And the windows? You'd have to ask Paul Jenkins. Ivor? Are you tired yet? Do you want to get in the buggy?'

Ivor stumbled over gratefully and seated himself, pulling at the straps.

'At least they haven't made it into flats, like the forge and the schoolhouse.' Carrie pushed open the gate, letting Betsy run up the path. 'Surely there are people still buried here?'

'I think people even came back to be buried.' Philip gestured towards a section near the back of the graveyard where some dark headstones stood, their inscriptions still freshly legible and sharp.

'Wow. So how come the Army let people back?'

'They probably had to.'

Carrie hesitated. 'Is it ghoulish to go and look, with the kids here?'

'Try stopping Betsy. She loves gravestones. She's got a thing about them.' Philip raised his eyebrows sardonically. 'My own fault. I've tried to get her interested in history, but she's more interested in dead bodies. "How did he die, Daddy? Was it the Black Death? Or the plague?" She's already set up some kind of regular flower arrangement on Perkins' final resting place. We're somewhat morbid in our household. As you've probably worked out by now.'

He let out a low cackle.

'Philip,' said Carrie, taking her courage in both hands. 'I'm happy to look after the kids now and again, but if this is going to be part of their routine, I do need to know some things. So I know what to say. And I'm not being nosy here, just anxious not to put my foot in it.'

Philip met her gaze. He didn't look offended, just rather tired. 'You want some answers about their mother.'

'Yes,' said Carrie. 'If you don't mind telling me.'

He blew out his cheeks and looked down ruefully at Ivor, playing with the beads on the buggy. 'Well, according to the village gossip, I murdered her.'

'And did you?' Carrie tried to keep her voice light but the half-smile froze on her lips when she saw Philip's expression turn blank.

He stretched out his long blacksmith's hands on his knees, staring at them, but not seeing anything.

'You know,' he said eventually, 'sometimes I think I did.'

Chapter Eighteen

Philip and Carrie sat on the large, moss-covered family tomb while Betsy wandered solemnly between the headstones, head bowed respectfully in some silent tribute to her new dead neighbours, and Ivor ran around chasing butterflies.

Carrie was completely lost for words.

'I don't quite know where to begin,' Philip admitted, after a few moments' pause.

'By telling me you didn't actually murder her?' she suggested, only half-joking.

'You know, in all honesty, I'm not even sure I can do that,' said Philip. Then, seeing Carrie's face turn pale, he added, 'Um, no, look. Sorry. You can see where Betsy gets the melodrama from. It's just that I find it very hard to talk about, as you might imagine, and . . . it's not something I find easy to discuss.' He raised his eyes back up, and met her nervous gaze. 'And you must know that I'm only telling you because you do seem to get on well with Betsy and Ivor. This isn't something I'd want to hear around the village, for their sakes, if nothing else. I know I haven't been an ideal dad but I have managed to protect them from . . .' He paused. 'But I've kept them away from other people for too long, I can see that. They need some company again.'

'They're nice kids,' said Carrie, quietly. 'But I think they're lonely.' She stopped, conscious that as a non-parent she had no right to tell him what his kids were or weren't. 'I think they could do with some company, you're right,' she said instead. 'So. Their mother isn't with you any more.'

'You could say that,' said Philip evasively.

Carrie felt the brightness of the sun on her face, and noted the birds cheeping and squawking in the trees around them. The churchyard seemed peaceful but somehow busy at the same time. She was reminded of the loneliness she used to feel on a busy tube platform.

'OK,' said Philip at last, stretching out his hands on the knees of his green cords. 'Giselle was one of my students – a postgrad student,' he added. 'She was twenty-two when we met. I supervised her thesis on sites of pagan worship, and . . . we clicked. I noticed you saw the photograph of her.'

He sounded proud, and Carrie saw no point in denying her nosiness. 'It was hard to miss. She's very beautiful.'

'She is. Incredibly beautiful. I know it's clichéd to talk about people being out of their time, but she really was. She wasn't a modern woman, Giselle. I don't think she suited modern life. She had very thin skin, no shell at all.'

'Was she academic? It's a good way of bailing out of the day-to-day grind,' said Carrie. 'Almost as good as writing.'

It was a get-out for him, in case it was turning too personal, but Philip answered quite seriously. 'You know, not really? I don't know that she was that academic. Not in the way that I suppose I am. I like sifting through history, chiselling away at it. Turning the evidence over to find new angles, new insights. With Giselle it was more . . . as if she just enjoyed sitting in history like it was an atmospheric . . . *bath*. She liked the idea of other times, more than the facts of them. The details. The flavours. You know.'

Carrie was getting a mental picture of Giselle as a sealed-knot-type obsessive, but she wasn't sure it was a flattering image to be forming, so she said nothing.

'I knew she wasn't the most robust of women,' Philip went on, 'but then you don't tend to get Outward Bound types in our sort of field. Didn't want to learn to drive, preferred to write her essays longhand . . . Anyway, cut a long story short, we got married when she finished her doctorate. Giselle was already a few months' gone with Betsy, as it happens. Not that it made any difference. We'd have married as soon as we could, whatever.'

'Had you been together long? When you knew about Betsy, I mean?'

'About a year. Long enough. I know it's not long by other people's standards, but long enough to know.'

'Mark and I, we'd only known each other a few months when we got married,' Carrie interjected. 'My mom and dad weren't that keen, even though they pretended to be. But we knew. We weren't kids. You don't have to have grown up with someone to know they're right for you.'

'Is that right?' Philip looked across at her. 'You seem like you've been together years.'

Carrie shook her head. 'It feels like that. But no, just three years, end of April.'

'Oh,' he said, with an inscrutable lift of his eyebrows.

'Sorry,' said Carrie. 'I interrupted. Go on.'

'So, Giselle . . .' He paused. 'It was like . . . it was like holding a little bird in my hands.' He shrugged in apology for the simile, but went on anyway. 'Little things used to upset her – unexpected bills, phone calls late at night. I wanted to hold her tight enough to comfort, but not so hard that I crushed her by mistake. Christ. That sounds dreadful. But that's how it was. Sometimes I could feel her heart beating in her chest. I was just like anyone would be in that situation – man or woman she brought out this incredible protective instinct.'

Philip twisted up his mouth, ruefully, and stroked his beard with his whole hand, as if he were trying to smooth the rest of the story out. 'In fact, I probably made everything much worse.'

'Was Ivor planned?' asked Carrie, very quietly, guessing. 'Betsy must have been, what, three? That's quite a handful.'

There was a long pause, and her words hung in the air between them like floating blossom. In the distance the milk van drove round the green. It was so quiet that Carrie could hear the clink of bottles. Proper bottles. No cartons in St Dee.

'No. No, he wasn't,' said Philip eventually. 'And she didn't take it well. Now how did you know that?'

'Oh, it happens. Has happened to people I know. One child is just about manageable, two is suddenly a nightmare.' It was Carrie's turn to fiddle with her nails. 'I suppose, if *I'm* being honest, it's one of the reasons I've put it off until now. You just don't know how you're going to react. All those hormones. All the pressure, never having a second to think. I don't understand how people can have kids to hold relationships together. I'd have thought it would be the biggest mental and physical assault course you could put yourself through. And if she wasn't the most practical person, it must have been . . . difficult.'

'Difficult?' Philip laughed, drily, but there wasn't much humour in it. 'It was bloody *impossible*. Betsy went from being calm and loving to . . . God, I don't know, like one of those horror-story dolls that's possessed by the Devil. Ivor cried all the time. Giselle cried all the time. I wanted to cry all the time. The only one of us not in floods of tears was Betsy. It was like being trapped in some hideous Gothic novel. And Giselle just seemed to fade, like she wanted to fade into the background and disappear . . .'

'I can imagine,' said Carrie.

'Can you?' Philip looked at her, his dark eyes intense on hers. 'Really?'

Carrie nodded. 'It's hard work, being a mother. It's not for everyone. People just assume that all women want kids, can cope with kids, then everyone feels bad when it's not perfect.'

'Well, I couldn't imagine. I had no idea.' He stopped and examined his hands. 'In fact, that's just what I assumed. That all women had some kind of switch that tripped when kids arrived. Giselle didn't. She went . . . Well, she went into some other world.'

'She had post-natal depression, do you mean?' said Carrie, more sharply than she intended to.

He had the grace to shake his head. 'That was partly it. But there was more than that going on, I think, looking back. It had always been there – big mood swings, depression. I was stupid, I just put it down to stuff I didn't really understand about women. She started disappearing for hours and hours at a time, and I'd have to drive round Durham looking for her. She could walk for miles, Giselle. Miles and miles, without a coat or anything. Then when I found her, tried to take her home, she'd be foul, like she was someone else. I couldn't take the kids with me in the end, because even Betsy knew something wasn't right.'

'And was she OK with the children?'

'She never tried to hurt them, if that's what you mean.' He sighed. 'But she could be vague. And silent. Kids don't like silence. Well. My kids didn't. They're not so bad with it now.'

Carrie wasn't sure what she could say to that.

Over by the gravestones, Betsy was meticulously redistributing flowers so that some of the older graves, mossy and lop-sided with neglect, had one or two fresh blooms.

'So . . . ?' Carrie prompted, tentatively. 'Did you get help for her?'

'I wanted to,' admitted Philip. 'I was trying to persuade her. But she vanished during Betsy's birthday party.'

'Vanished?'

'Walked out. Disappeared. Got such a head start we never found her.'

'Oh my God,' said Carrie. 'Poor Betsy.' She paused. 'Poor you,' she added with a cautious sideways glance. Philip was staring blankly at the church.

'Three days dragging the river. Weeks of searching. Well, I think they were weeks. I can't remember time passing, actually. I've only got that back since I moved here.'

'But how?' asked Carrie. 'How did it happen? Did she just snap? Was it that bad?'

'I didn't think so at the time, but you know . . . she wasn't living in the same world as me by then. I mean, it was bad enough on a low level – I was right in the middle of a big departmental reorganisation – I know, I know, work shouldn't come first, but the funding for my entire department was basically on the line – and Giselle had been in a low way for weeks. She refused to believe Betsy even had a birthday coming up. Plus, Betsy was being naughty all the time, Ivor wasn't well . . . In the end, I had to sort out the party, keep the assessors off my case at work, deal with Giselle, stop madam over there from tearing the house up, and . . .' He stopped and gripped his beard.

'Get it off your chest,' said Carrie, bravely. 'I'm not going to judge you. Or tell anyone, I promise.'

Philip smiled grimly without opening his mouth. 'It's a bit bathetic, I'm afraid. These things always are in the end. We'd been bickering all day. Little things – she didn't want to get crisps because of the mess crisps make when you mix them with little kids. She couldn't find exactly the right present for Betsy and she cried for an hour. I just didn't know what to do. She wasn't the woman I'd married. I didn't know what had gone wrong, and I couldn't seem to get through to her to help. Then while we were still yelling at one another, about, I don't know, crisps or something, the doorbell starting ringing and the little girls started arriving in our house with their mothers. Giselle got her coat, said she was popping out for more marshmallows and . . .' His voice trailed off.

'Never came back,' Carrie finished.

'No.'

'And she's never been in touch since? No phone calls? No cards on the kids' birthdays?'

He shook his head. 'Well. I've sent them cards on their birthdays.

From her, I mean. Lots of love, Mummy. Kiss, kiss. Ivor can't really remember her too well, but, ah, I don't want him thinking badly of her. Betsy, mind – there's no fooling that one.'

'Well, surely it's better that they don't think she's dead?'

'No. No, they think she's gone abroad to stay with some family in France. But you know my daughter. She reads enough books to have morbid ideas of her own about what I've done with her mother. The beard, you know.' Philip grimaced. 'It features heavily in her reading. I'm sure the child psychologists would have a field day with poor Betsy.'

'Mmm,' agreed Carrie. And so would the rest of the village. She surprised herself with the sudden surge of protectiveness that flooded her chest at the thought of Barbara Purves speculating in the pub about Betsy's unsettling behaviour. 'And what about Giselle's family? Do they know where you are?'

'She doesn't have much family here. I've left details with her sister, and her mother, but they've not heard from her either. And since they blame me for her departure in the first place . . .' Philip rubbed his chin.

'Maybe she'd like it better here,' said Carrie. 'It's not quite the real world.'

'That's what I've been thinking,' said Philip. He turned and looked at Carrie with a quizzical expression playing on his lips, pink beneath the dark whiskers. 'Funny, isn't it? Your grandparents-in-law and my grandparents were next-door neighbours. And yours were the ones with the young girl married to her teacher too. Funny how symmetrical things are.'

Despite the warm breeze now blowing through the churchyard, Carrie shuddered.

Betsy's shrill voice cut through the atmosphere. 'Daddy!' she yelled. 'Daddy! Come and see!'

Philip rose. 'I'm being summoned.'

'Listen, I should go,' said Carrie, pushing herself off the stone tomb and dusting the yellow moss spores from the seat of her cotton skirt. She had a sudden desire to get back to a world where she was in control of the stories. 'I'm way behind as it is. And if there's this meeting tonight . . .'

'Don't you want to see what Betsy's found?' asked Philip. 'Come and say goodbye to the kids.'

Despite herself, Carrie found her footsteps falling in with his long strides.

'What have you got there, Betsy?' he called out while they were still several rows of headstones away. She noted the shift to the carrying lecture-room voice, very different from the intimate supervision tones he'd just been using.

'A whole family tomb,' she announced portentously. 'Look. It's Miss Maxwell's family. All of them. Do you think it's a crypt, Daddy, with steps? Do you think there are rows and rows of coffins down there, in the ground?'

'I don't know.' Philip inspected the imposing sides. 'What do you think?'

'Oh, I think they're all down there,' said Betsy confidently. 'And I expect there's room for Miss Maxwell too?'

'Like bunk beds,' said Philip. 'Like in the seven dwarves' cottage, so there's room for everyone.'

'How does she know all this?' whispered Carrie, as Betsy peered closer.

'Books,' said Philip. 'Don't blame me.'

'Just think,' said Carrie, 'this whole churchyard has been asleep for sixty years!'

'No, it hasn't,' said Betsy, dismissively. 'Haven't you seen the flowers?'

'The flowers?'

'Yes. There's a whole lot of graves round this side that are quite new. There are flowers on them, plastic ones mainly. I like children's ones best, with the little angels and cherubs. Like this one.' She pointed to a very small headstone, a little way apart, by the wall. 'It hasn't got a cherub but the baby was nearly newborn,' she added.

'There are lots and lots of children's graves here, but they're all quite ancient.'

'Poor little thing,' said Carrie automatically. The letters weren't so expensively hewn as on the Maxwells' crypt and she had to crouch down to read the name through the felty moss.

'Matthew Armstrong, born February 4, 1941, died March 3, 1941. Beloved son of Jack and Lily Armstrong, St Dee, much missed twin brother of Benjamin. *Blessed are the little children.*'

Twin of Benjamin?

She stumbled back a little and sat back on her heels. Somewhere behind her, Ivor giggled gleefully, as if she'd done it specially to make him laugh.

Mark's father had been a twin. Mark had never mentioned it. Did he even know? A twin, with a poor dead baby brother left behind in St Dee's silent churchyard.

'Are you OK?' Philip appeared behind her.

'Oh, yes. Yes, just a little winded.' Carrie dusted the grass off her skirt and nodded towards the little headstone. Her hands were trembling. 'That's my husband's uncle. I didn't realise his father was one of twins.' She pushed her fringe out of her eyes. 'Mark's certainly never mentioned it.'

Philip raised his eyebrows. 'Never looked at the birth certificates?'

'Well, *I* haven't, no,' said Carrie. 'Mark's parents died when he was at school, and as far as I know there are no other living relatives.' She corrected herself, 'Well, I know there aren't, otherwise we wouldn't be here.'

'Really?' asked Philip. 'He's never looked into it? That would make some people desperate to find out anything they could.'

'Not Mark,' said Carrie. 'He's not like that.'

For the first time, it dawned on her properly how airtight Mark's little world was. Just him, and her, and all the things around him in the present. No past at all. No wonder he didn't share her fascination with Lily and Jack. What did they mean to him, anyway? They would only pry open his sealed existence.

Ivor wandered up with a handful of wild grasses, which he gave to Carrie.

'No, Ivor,' said Betsy, 'you have to put them on the little baby's grave. Look, like this.' She grabbed the stems off him and started strewing dramatically. Ivor's mouth moved into a letterbox of distress, and instinctively Carrie picked him up to distract him.

'Look, Ivor,' she said, to distract herself as much as him. 'Shall we read these names?'

'"Jacob, loving husband of Joanna, loving father of Jacob, Joanna, Elizabeth and John. Elizabeth, loving wife of Joseph, died in childbirth, aged 23. Loving mother of Jacob, Mary, Joanna, Josephine."' The Maxwells obviously had the dogged British determination to stick with the same four names, thought Carrie, as she parroted the names aloud, joggling Ivor with each name to make him laugh.

On and on, up to a new inscription, the marks still quite sharp. 'Simon, loving husband of Miriam, died September 18, 1991. Miriam, wife of Simon, mother of Kathleen, Josephine and Joanna. Died December 26, 1992. *Always in my thoughts.*'

My thoughts? Presumably that was Kathleen. How sad, thought Carrie, that she was the last one. That she'd had to come back here to bury them alone in some modern hearse, when all the other Maxwells would have been laid to rest with crowds of mourning villagers and black-plumed horses and long tables of funeral baked meats in the manor house.

There were one or two other recent stones nearer the far wall, and Carrie tried to imagine the procession through the abandoned village. That must have been hard for some of the older people, seeing their houses deserted and eyeless, wondering what was stopping them coming back.

'Sheep,' said Ivor, pointing with a stumpy hand out towards the field. 'Lots of sheep.'

'Lots of sheep,' agreed Carrie. Thank God someone in that family preferred living creatures to spooky dead ones. She turned to leave, not sure how to acknowledge what had just passed between them without making more of it.

'Thank you,' said Philip, touching her arm before she could speak. 'I hadn't realised how much better I would feel for getting that off my chest.'

'Don't worry about it.' Carrie smiled. 'I'll . . .' She lifted her hands, then dropped them. 'I'd say I'll forget it, but, you know . . . I'll bear it in mind.' She nodded slightly towards the kids.

'Well, really, you should tell me something secret too,' said Philip. 'That's normally how they run these things in Betsy's books. Bonds of secrecy.'

Carrie wasn't sure how serious he was being, and laughed nervously. 'Oh, God, I don't have anything to tell you! I, er . . .'

My husband's been lying about his whereabouts and I'm too chicken to challenge him about it?

I hear crying coming from your garden, and I never feel quite alone in my own house?

I find you oddly attractive, even though there's something dark about you that makes me wonder whether I can believe everything you tell me?

Philip was looking at her, with one eyebrow lifted as if he could read all these thoughts in her head.

'I'm creeped out by mice even though I have to draw one for my books,' Carrie blurted out before any of the other thoughts could bubble their way to the surface.

Philip raised his eyebrows. 'Really?'

'Yeah. Very stupid of me. Anyway, speaking of which . . .' Carrie made a move to go, and as she did, caught sight of the arched front door of the church, exactly as it was behind Lily and Jack.

At the top of the arch was the strange snake-haired head, worn now a little more with rain and wind, but still there.

Now, though, it reminded her of Philip.

'I'll see you later,' she said, and scrambled down the slope to the village.

Chapter Nineteen

In a village as small as St Dee, there was no chance of slipping under the radar of organisers like Lucy. She dropped by on her way back from her last cleaning job – though Carrie knew it was on the other side of the green – to 'remind' her about the committee meeting in the pub that evening, and so at five o'clock, Carrie made her way down the lane to the Rose and Thorn.

She paused at the tug-of-war photograph in the porch. 1930. The whole village, more or less, lined up on the green, with a younger version of Miss Maxwell's mother and father presiding over the middle of the rope. Everyone's faces had a strange similarity, she thought, but surely that was just because of the men's identical caps, and the same plain skirts all the women wore. Her eyes searched for Philip's ancestors. Just as she thought it was ridiculous to try to identify individuals, she spotted a man who couldn't have been anything other than Philip's grandfather – a huge man, a whole head higher than anyone else, with dark eyes and a thick dark beard. He stared right at the camera, unsmiling.

No one seemed to smile in any of these old pictures.

'Carrie!'

She jumped as Lucy's voice dragged her back into the present, and made her way into the main bar. Over on the table in the corner, Lucy waved to her and made a 'drinky drinky' gesture, which, judging by the accompanying facial expression, Carrie took to mean, 'get a drink in'.

She peered over the dark wood of the bar. Tony was nowhere in sight.

'Hello?' she called into the gloom.

'Be right there, my love,' called Tony from the back room. After a moment, he emerged with a tea tray, laden down with mugs of coffee and a teetering packet of chocolate digestives.

'Mine's a skinny latte!' said Carrie, then changed her smile to a sympathetic frown when she saw the look on his face.

Tony nodded towards the bony figure of Barbara Purves, firmly installed at the head of the table. 'Her idea,' he said. 'The coffee. Or tea. Myself, I'd have thought a nice glass of cider would have helped it all along a bit. Smoothed out the discussions.'

'They need smoothing?'

As if by way of illustration, Paul Jenkins, who was sitting next to Lucy with all the relaxation of someone sitting on a spike, began to cough and make polite noises of demurral, tapping his pen on his clipboard as he did so. Lucy rolled her eyes.

'Let me help you with that tray, Tony,' said Carrie.

'Cheers, my love. I'll get the tea.'

Carrie took the tray over and placed it on the table next to the committee meeting. The main table was piled high with photocopied agendas and important-looking emails.

'So it's critical to get these lists made right now and for me to know they will be adhered to, to the *letter*. I simply don't have time to chase you all for the next three months, not if this is going to get back up to speed properly. Hello, Carrie. Pleased you could make it, I did wonder if you were coming or not,' said Barbara, without drawing breath.

'Sorry, am I late?' Carrie looked round: all the usual suspects were there – Lucy and Chris, Kathleen, Sandra from the shop, Paul Jenkins. 'I thought I was going to be early!'

'No. We're still here from the neighbourhood watch executive committee meeting,' said Lucy brightly. 'This is more fun, though.'

'Not at all. Keeping St Dee secure is a year-round priority for everyone. But to save time, when we're all so busy, I'm running the two together.' Barbara shuffled her papers. 'Anyhoo, Carrie, now you're here we might as well start properly on the fete committee meeting.'

Carrie sat down self-consciously.

'Cup of coffee?' Lucy started to hand round the mugs and biscuits.

I don't think I've ever drunk so much coffee as I do these days, thought Carrie, stirring in some milk as a way of avoiding Barbara's gaze. No wonder everyone's in a state of constant hypertension.

'I've made a list of each volunteer and their field of responsibility.' Barbara began to hand out more papers, going against the current of Lucy's biscuit distribution. 'I am the chair. Paul is our official liaison with any archival material the MoD can provide. Philip Gladstone had kindly offered to furnish me with a list of ancient and modern May traditions in this area. I think it should be our aim to make this first fete as close as possible to the spirit of the traditional St Dee May Day celebration, and to that end, we need to gather as much information, both formal and informal, about the day as we can.'

Barbara turned to Carrie. 'Do you know if Philip is on his way? I hear he's quite an expert on these sorts of traditions.'

'I, er . . .' Carrie was aware of everyone looking at her expectantly.

'Although we don't want it to be some kind of re-enactment, do we?' interrupted Sandra. 'We want it to be fun and modern. It's not like we're living in a museum. We want to have traditions of our own. Make it fun for the kiddies.'

Barbara clicked her pen crossly. 'I hardly think it'll be a re-enactment, Sandra. Rather, us holding a fete at all will be a sort of tribute to St Dee itself. I'd like to hold the sort of May Day festivity that died when the original villagers had to leave their homes.'

Paul Jenkins coughed. 'That's perhaps putting it rather strongly, Barbara.'

'Is it?' Lucy sipped her coffee and looked angelically over the rim of the cup. 'I'd say being *forced out* of everything they ever knew would be a strong way of putting it. '

'It's all about moving on. So shall we, move on, with the meeting?' Paul gave them a tight smile.

Carrie looked between Barbara and Lucy, who looked annoyed to have agreed with each other, albeit accidentally.

'Have you thought about having some people wearing period dress?' she asked. 'I just wondered – it might be a nice idea for me and Lucy to bring some of the history to life for the children, you know, in our history tent? Doesn't have to be elaborate, just pinnies and long skirts.'

'That's a great idea, Carrie!' exclaimed Lucy. 'Isn't it?'

'It is. But it would help us all get through this more quickly if we stick to the *agenda*,' snapped Barbara. 'And I thought perhaps to start us off, Miss Maxwell could give us a flavour of what the day usually entailed, as she's the only one here with any direct experience of it.'

Everyone's eyes turned to Kathleen.

'Then I will open the floor to suggestions,' Barbara added. 'I don't want to dominate the proceedings.'

'Heaven forbid,' muttered Tony and helped himself to more biscuits.

'Well, goodness me, it was such a long time ago,' Kathleen began. 'I'm not sure I can recall everything in the sort of detail you're after, Barbara . . .'

'You must have seen most of the important parts, though, what with your family being so central to the day's events,' Barbara prompted gushily.

Lucy's eyes crossed.

'I do remember that everyone used to end up here by six in the evening!' said Kathleen. 'I hope that's one tradition we'll be upholding in good faith!'

'I was meaning more to do with the rural traditions,' said Barbara.

'Oh. Of course. Well, the day would begin with the farmers bringing the stock in to be judged and all the young women in the village would walk around the green in their new outfits. My father had to choose the Queen of the May, you see – she would be Queen of St Dee, just for the day, and her friends would have to wait on her. That was always great fun. It used to get really rather competitive!'

'Girls, you say?' Barbara made a note. 'How old?'

'I think they had to be unmarried. Usually it was just the girls from the village school, and a few that had gone into service locally and came home for the holiday.'

Carrie thought of the photograph of the school, with Lily shining out from the back row. She'd been like a rose just about to burst out of bud in that photograph. So was it childbirth that had taken away that freshness? Or, as she now knew, the sadness of losing one of her babies? That photograph of Lily holding her baking trophy made more sense now; the deflation, the lack of joy in her eyes.

I should tell Mark, she thought, but then hesitated: another family death. Another relative he hadn't known. She bit her lip. It was so complicated.

Barbara was more focused on the present, however. 'I do have one additional important announcement to make,' she said, pinking slightly. 'I was contacted this afternoon by a journalist, who is very interested in covering the planning and the actual day of the fete, possibly for a documentary on the BBC. And naturally there'll be other members of the local press invited. I've had quite a few interested phone calls about the village already.'

There was a general murmur of surprise.

'You didn't mention this before,' said Kathleen. Her lips tightened very slightly.

'I only took the call as I was leaving the house on my way here.' Barbara pushed a hank of blow-dried bob away from her face, but she couldn't disguise the look of triumph playing on her sharp features. 'He assured me that their presence would be barely noticeable. Isn't that a marvellous offer? Having St Dee on the BBC? And it would be wonderful publicity.'

'Publicity? But what for?' asked Kathleen, as if confused.

'The fete, of course.'

'Well, I'm all for raising money, but do we want *lots* of people traipsing through, peering at everything? I was under the impression it was to be more of a private May Day celebration. For the village, and a few local people.'

'Mmm,' agreed Chris Ross.

'Now you put it like that, I'm not sure I want to be on television,' added Sandra. 'Not all the time. Not without make-up and warning and such like.'

'Och, don't be so boring!' Barbara looked around the group. 'It'll be fun! And don't you want people to see what lovely homes you have? What a wonderful community we're building?'

Paul Jenkins cleared his throat. 'Actually, Barbara, now you mention that . . . While we've tried to give the village as much time as possible to settle into itself, there will come a time when the restoration project management would like to "open" it to the public, as it were. And this would be an excellent opportunity for the public to see St Dee, at its best.'

Everyone stared at him in surprise.

'Isn't that up to us?' demanded Lucy.

Paul Jenkins gave one of his little non-committal shrugs. 'Well, to an extent . . . There were certain things you assented to, if you examine your tenancy agreements carefully. Privacy will be paramount, of course, but it would make sense to hand over any media contact to our press team so we can manage the event properly. In terms of access to the village, and interviews and so on.'

There was a vague murmur as they processed this information and its rather sinister implications.

'But Paul,' said Kathleen, more emphatically, 'do we want St Dee to become a tourist attraction? I mean, on a practical level, where will people park, if they do come in their droves? And do we really want some journalists poking their noses into our lives?' Kathleen looked over at Carrie, as if for backup. 'These London journalists can be terribly persistent, you know, if they think they've got a story. And they'll *want* a story. I'm sure there are plenty of folk who'll be more than happy to hold forth with all those ridiculous conspiracy theories, for a start. Carrie, you would know, wouldn't you, about how these people work?'

Carrie felt all eyes turn to her and she paused, coffee cup half to her lips. 'Well, Kathleen's right,' she said, hesitantly. 'I'm sure they'd want more than just what a nice place it is. They'd be after . . . human-interest angles. People being kicked out and suffering, that sort of thing.'

She thought of her and Mark – the young London couple newly moved to the village, standing out like a sore thumb in the rural community. They'd be on the list, being needled to bitch about the place, then edited to make innocuous comments seem worse than they were. At least they were savvy enough to know when they were being set up. Plenty wouldn't.

Carrie looked at Barbara, opening and narrowing her beady eyes around the group. It wouldn't take much to make them all look faintly insane.

'They might edit stuff so we look a bit . . . you know. Batty.'

'Well, let them run wild with all the conspiracy theories!' exclaimed Barbara. 'There's plenty of those for them to debunk. All that business with Hitler in the manor house, or that story Tony told us about the arson at the abbey. Plenty to go at. All false, of course, but let them find that out for themselves!'

Kathleen's lips tightened even further. 'There was nothing in that, I can assure you! My family would have had nothing to do with the Nazis! I think our reputation locally would make that sound ridiculous to anyone who knew my father!'

'Well, this is precisely why it makes sense to let my media team handle that aspect of the event,' said Paul Jenkins smoothly. 'We can control press releases and make sure none of these ridiculous stories are repeated. I can arrange for some security too.'

'They do say that burglaries go on the rise after them antiques programmes,' added Chris. 'And I still haven't got all the window locks fitted.'

'Are there any other problems anyone would like to raise?' asked Paul Jenkins. 'While I'm here, and we can air concerns? Is anyone in *favour* of this?'

Tony looked awkward. 'I'm not saying a bit of passing trade wouldn't be good for me and Judith, what with the summer season coming up . . .'

'Do we really want the village to turn into some kind of . . . open-air museum?' Kathleen went on. Her tone was very polite, almost kindly, but Carrie sensed a more metallic authority beneath. 'I would have thought, Barbara, as neighbourhood watch chair, that you'd have wanted to keep the privacy of the villagers as a top priority. Is this going to be some kind of legal obligation every year? To open up our houses to the public? Because I don't feel that was made very clear at all at the time!'

'I see.' Barbara paused, then played her trump card. 'Oh dear. Well, if you feel like that . . . It's a shame you're so reluctant, Kathleen, because you were really the one the journalist wanted to speak to. About your family and how far they go back round here. I mean, you know so much more about it than anyone else, and I thought you'd be able to explain so well what a wrench it was to leave? After all, it was your father who negotiated the sale of the land back to the ministry and set the wheels in motion. As it were.'

There was a long pause, while Carrie and Lucy admired Barbara's timing. Carrie watched as a variety of expressions flickered across Kathleen's face, but none managed to disturb the dominant one of serene confidence.

'Well . . .' said Kathleen, pretending to consider. 'I doubt you'd be able to stop them coming now you've piqued their interest . . . And I daresay I am the most qualified person in the village to talk about life here before the evacuation . . .'

'Fine,' said Barbara before she could change her mind. 'Now, I thought we'd have a cake stall and an orange-squash stand, and put the proceeds towards a general village beautification scheme . . .'

While Tony excused himself to tend to the first evening customers, Barbara steamed mercilessly through the points on her agenda, allocating the history tent to Lucy and Carrie, putting Sandra in charge of a baking tent, finding volunteers to liaise with a local brass band, to trace a vintage public address system, to run a pet competition.

'Which brings me finally to the topic of the May Queen,' she concluded.

'Ah, that's nice,' said Tony, returning with fresh coffee. 'Will it just be for the kiddies?'

'No,' said Barbara, looking over her glasses. 'I don't think we ought to be encouraging that sort of attention, do you? You read such awful things about pageant queens.'

'Oh, come on, Barbara,' protested Sandra. 'I hardly think kiddy fiddling's high up on the list of St Dee's war crimes, do you?'

Carrie thought about Philip. He'd probably have something to say about it. She wasn't sure if she was fascinated or creeped out by the way he seemed to be able to extend a finger and turn over the dark side of every pretty detail of the village, with a twinkle in his eye all the while.

Kiddy fiddling. What constituted the end of childhood in a community like this anyway? Did you lose your innocence at nine, in the farmyard, or at nineteen, when you finally moved out of the village's cotton-wool clutches?

She thought of Lily, and pushed away the image in her mind.

'Are there enough children anyway?' asked Sandra.

There was a general murmur of agreement.

'How many children are there in the village?' asked Carrie, suddenly thinking of Hazel. 'Apart from Ivor and Betsy?'

'There's the Wilson sisters, up in Holly Cottage – Emma and Caroline, they're about sixteen so there's no way they'll want to do this,' Lucy replied immediately. 'That Kieran Cavendish – he's about nine, now he's a kid who wants a good . . . Um, then there's Jill Parker, she's about twelve. Katie Murray? She wouldn't thank you for reminding her she's seventeen, not twenty-five. And that's it, as far as I know . . . What? What?' she demanded, as Chris's eyes bored into her.

No Hazel, thought Carrie. She didn't even have to ask – there was no way Lucy would have left someone out. So Hazel really was a little imaginary friend. Poor Betsy.

'Now, I think we should open the May Queen competition to all the ladies of the village that would like to enter.' Barbara looked round the table. 'I'll assume that'll include all those present. Show willing, ladies!'

'Who will judge it?' asked Kathleen. 'Traditionally, of course, my father used to crown the May Queen. She used to be invited to be head of the table at the dinner up in our barn in the evening,' she added. 'Everyone had to dance attendance on her, and then she went up to the chalk horse to lay the flowers. A procession of torch light.' She sighed. 'So atmospheric!'

Lucy gave Carrie a pointed look over the bar table.

'Was there something you wanted to share, Lucy?' asked Barbara, spotting it.

'Oh, nothing. My granny was telling me about those dinners.' Lucy paused, then winked at Carrie. 'More about what everyone used to get up to afterwards, mind! Up in the woods?'

Kathleen looked as if she'd been poked with a stick. 'Maybe that's what some people in the village . . . might have got up to. But certainly not anyone from the manor house! Besides,' she added, with a sweeter smile, 'I didn't think the vicarage would be privy to that sort of knowledge.'

'Oh, I'm not saying she *went*,' said Lucy innocently. 'Just that my grandad got quite a lot of business round February time. Font-and-altar-related. If you know what I mean.'

Carrie managed to suppress a snort at Lucy's unconvincing display of innocence, then remembered that Lily's son, the one buried in the churchyard, had been born in February. February 4th.

That would have made hers a May Day baby too.

Lily! Carrie felt her heart quicken, as if she'd caught a glimpse of her in the mirror behind the bar. Her imagination scrabbled for the details. How had it happened? One glass of cider too many at the manor-house feast? Jack's schoolmasterly restrain worn down by her childish enthusiasm, carried away by the dancing, and the chance to behave like pagans for one evening of the year?

Had it been amongst the trees, in a patch of wild flowers? Had it been her first time?

Carrie's mouth twisted in frustration that so much detail just vanished into speculation, the moment she felt her fingertips touch the hem of Lily's dress.

'I wouldn't know about that,' Kathleen was saying. 'I just remember the splendid May feast, with all the long tables, all decorated with leaves and flowers. We were allowed to stay up until ten o'clock!'

Barbara coughed. 'According to Philip Gladstone, who has kindly supplied me with some notes on the May traditions locally, the May Queen was chosen by the Jack-of-the-Green.' She looked up from her clipboard. 'The Jack-of-the-Green being the young man of the village dressed up in a costume of leaves and branches, to represent the woodland spirits.'

'Well, yes,' said Kathleen patiently. 'But my father told him who to pick.'

'And who's going to be the Jack-of-the-Green?' asked Carrie, though she suspected she already knew the answer to that one.

'Philip Gladstone,' replied Barbara. 'He's even volunteered to make his own costume!'

'Philip!' exclaimed Sandra. 'I don't see him being handy with a needle, do you?'

But Carrie wasn't surprised at all.

After the meeting broke up – when Kathleen excused herself with a headache, and Barbara had to leave to liaise with someone about a marquee – the others headed for the bar, where Tony offered them all a free drink.

'Oh, go on, just a quick half,' wheedled Lucy, when Carrie pulled on her coat. 'I need some moral support with this lot and their stupid theories . . .'

'Shut up,' said Sandra, good-naturedly. 'It's solid gold this one, I swear. I heard it from someone who overhead Paul Jenkins on his mobile last week.'

'No!' said Carrie, despite herself. 'What?'

'Well, apparently, St Dee's got the same type of layout as some of the Normandy villages, so they wanted to use it for training the American troops before the landings. Which is why they had to get everyone out, top secret, like. But . . .' Sandra opened her eyes very wide. 'Something went wrong and they had to bury a whole squadron in the woods, so as not to cause a security alert! Said they'd gone missing in action!'

'Are you sure the dates work?' sighed Chris.

'And they're all still buried in the woods?' echoed Lucy.

'And what would Paul Jenkins be discussing this for?' demanded Carrie, but no one paid her any attention.

'Have you been in there recently?' asked Sandra, rhetorically.

Lucy shuddered. 'No way. Gives me the creeps. I'll tell you who has though,' she added, pointing her finger.

'Who?'

'That Philip Gladstone.' She nodded to underline the suspicious nature of his movements.

'Oh, but that's for his research,' said Carrie, leaping to his defence.

'Research into what?' demanded Lucy. 'Eh?'

'Research into pagan rituals and early Christianity round here.' Carrie finished her drink, then realised all eyes were on her. 'What? You knew that. That's why he's helping Barbara with the May Day – he's an expert on that sort of thing.'

'Convenient,' crowed Sandra.

'Convenient for what?' Carrie spluttered. 'Since when has this village been convenient for anything?'

Sandra merely raised her eyebrows cartoonishly. 'You tell us, Carrie. You tell us.'

'You're getting carried away with yourselves,' Carrie retorted. 'Anyway, I've got to be off. Mark's meant to be home by six for his dinner.'

'You've had that, love,' said Tony, taking her glass. 'It's gone quarter to eight.'

'What?' Carrie looked at the clock above the bar. 'But it says it's ten to . . .'

'Carrie,' said Lucy, shaking her head, 'you've never noticed that the clock's stopped in here?'

'Won't keep time,' explained Tony. 'I never know whether it's gaining or losing or what.'

'Not yours as well,' said Carrie in surprise. 'My kitchen clock does that.'

Lucy nodded. 'That'll be the soldiers. Trying to turn the clock back.'

'I've got to go,' said Carrie, and grabbed her bag.

A few lights were on in the houses around the green, and the old-fashioned lamps lit the path well enough for Carrie to quicken her step. She rounded the corner, her eyes searching for lights on in their house, and immediately she spotted Mark's car parked tight up to the gate outside.

Typical. The one night when he was back when he said he would be, she was late. He'd love that.

But as she got closer, Carrie saw Mark's lanky frame leaning against the gate-post, one hand holding his phone to his ear, and the other clutching his forehead in a gesture she recognised at once as his 'very stressed' pose. As she watched, he squeezed his forehead even tighter, and leaned his whole forearm onto the stone post.

Who was he talking to? She stopped and without thinking, stepped onto the grass verge so she could get nearer without her heels drawing attention to her steps.

Mark's voice carried in the stillness of the evening air, pushed even louder by an irritation Carrie could make out from a distance. Instinctively, she stopped, knowing somehow that she was intruding on something – that this was a call he didn't want to take in their house.

Don't be ridiculous, she told herself. It could be anyone. If the mobile rang while you had precious reception in St Dee, you answered it quickly before it cut out again.

She strained her eyes to make out his expression, but his hand covered his face.

'No, I won't,' he was saying. 'I can't! Are you listening to me at all? Or just hearing what you want to hear, as usual?'

There was a pause in which Carrie felt her heart beating up in her throat. Those were almost the words he'd been muttering in his sleep. She leaned back against the wall, feeling, without thinking, the nubbly cushions of the moss between the stones.

As usual. How usual were these conversations? How well did you have to know someone to nag them about their arguing style?

'No, you're so wrong – I didn't cancel this evening because I'm running away from the problem,' Mark went on, in a voice she hadn't heard him use before. He sounded more transatlantic, less media London. As if he had shifted into being someone else in his head. 'I cancelled because I don't have anything more to say. I've told you,' he whined, 'you can't just come back and . . . No, I don't want to start . . . Look, Carrie's really happy here. I could be really happy here.' Another pause. 'I *could*. I am.'

What? Why doesn't he sound more sure? agonised Carrie. Why does he sound like he's trying to convince himself?

There was a longer pause, in which Mark tried to interject, but failed several times. 'Look . . . Look . . .' he kept saying, then, 'No, listen . . . No, listen . . .' Eventually, he forced his way back into the conversation by snapping out his words and refusing to stop.

'No, you have to listen to me now. What you're doing really isn't fair.' His tone was tight, whiny – unfamiliar. 'It's a part of my life that is over. Over. It's been over for years, and now suddenly . . . Well, I know. And don't you think I'm sorry about that? You know it's not something I . . . No, not like this.'

What *was* it? wondered Carrie, her thoughts scattering like shattered glass.

'Astrid, I don't want to talk about this on the phone!' snapped Mark.

Astrid. Carrie stared at Mark, seeing him as a stranger all of a sudden.

It was her. The woman in the photograph. He'd been seeing her. He'd cancelled a date with her this evening.

I don't want to hear any more, she thought, panic tumbling over her. I don't know what I'd do with the knowledge if I had it. I'd have to do something, like getting a loose thread and yanking it to see the whole dress fall apart.

Silently, slinking like one of the kittens, she stepped back from the wall, and down the garden of Rose Cottage. Philip's path was overgrown with grass, unlike her own neatly gravelled and bordered path, and she made no sound as she went. Carrie's legs felt twitchy with tension, as if they wanted to run away with her, not just into her own orchard but up the grassy valley to the chalk horse and further, into the forest. A sick feeling rose up in her throat. No matter where she ran, she couldn't get away. Before she knew what she was doing, she had slipped through their front garden, round to the back, then headed towards the little wall that separated the two back gardens.

Somehow, now she was within reach of her back door, rationality prevailed and she felt a rush of calming hormones spread through her system.

If I slip in the back, I can be there making supper, in control, when he gets in, she thought with a cool logic. Then *he* can tell *me* what's going on. If he doesn't . . .

If he doesn't, I'll have to ask him.

She stopped, chilled to the bone.

Something moved in the grass on the other side of the garden, over by a big apple tree, and she jumped out of her skin.

It was Betsy, sitting cross-legged on her own, surrounded, as usual, by books. In the dusk, her skin looked even more pearly than normal and her red dress glowed against the overgrown foliage around her. She was talking to herself, but though Carrie could see her lips moving, the sound didn't carry.

Carrie put a hand to her chest, and when Betsy looked up, she felt obliged to speak. 'Betsy, you gave me a shock. What are you doing?' she asked. 'Hiding out in the grass at this time of night?'

Betsy just gave her an inscrutable stare and said nothing.

Carrie wasn't sure why she felt the need to explain herself to Betsy, but she did. 'I'm just . . .' She nodded towards her back door. 'Picking some herbs for supper.' Maybe it's myself I need to be explaining to, she thought, distractedly.

Betsy didn't reply. Instead, she put a finger to her rosebud lips and opened her eyes to shush Carrie.

'What?'

'I'm *hiding*,' hissed Betsy.

'From Ivor?' Carrie looked round. She needed to get into the house as soon as possible, so there was at least some semblance of dinner action, but Betsy had an even more weird air about her than normal, and after what Philip had said about her mother, Carrie wasn't sure she should leave her alone. Shouldn't leave Ivor alone, more to the point.

'No.' Betsy rolled her eyes. 'Ivor's inside, with Daddy and the cats. I'm hiding from *Hazel*.'

Hazel? The sound of a car door slamming signalled the end of Mark's conversation, and Carrie darted an anxious look back down the path.

Betsy's face clouded over. 'Is that Mark?'

'Yes,' said Carrie, reluctant to leave Betsy on her own, but anxious to get inside. 'And I need to get on and make his tea. It's a bit late to be playing outside, isn't it?'

'Hazel doesn't like Mark,' Betsy informed her. She pressed her lips together and picked at the grass. 'She told me he's bad.'

Carrie shuddered. 'Betsy?'

The evening air was very still and the sound of Mark's key scraping in the lock was clearly audible.

'Betsy? Where does Hazel live?'

Betsy looked at her very seriously. 'Here.'

'Here in the village? Or here in your house?'

'Carrie!' She could hear Mark's footsteps now, on the cool stone flags of the kitchen. 'Carrie, are you in?'

Betsy said nothing, but her eyes moved around the garden, and narrowed. Carrie spun round but there was nothing to see.

'There you are! Hello, Betsy!'

Carrie jumped as Mark's hand slid round her waist.

'Hello, Betsy!'

Without speaking, Betsy got to her feet and stalked into the kitchen.

'Oh dear.' Mark sighed. 'I'm rubbish with children.'

'You ran over her cat,' Carrie reminded him.

'Yeah, there is that.' He rubbed his face reflectively. 'But I don't think I'd be much good anyway. Not everyone's cut out for nappies and responsibility,' he said. 'Anyway, why don't I smell chicken? I thought we were having a fabulous free-range roast, and a quiet evening in.'

'Um, we are,' said Carrie. 'I just got a bit . . . behind. I was down at the pub, at a village meeting.'

She turned and went into the kitchen. After the strange moment with Betsy, her mind was full of the conversation again. Astrid. That whiny voice.

Say something, say something!

Mechanically, Carrie took an onion out of the vegetable basket and started chopping it up, end first so she wouldn't cry.

Mark followed her, and took a bottle of wine out of the fridge, pouring them both large glasses.

He set hers down in front of her on the pine table. 'So what's the latest then?' he asked. 'Anything I should know?'

'We're having a May Day fete, so Paul Jenkins can show off his heritage thatching. If you want to rehabilitate yourself back into the community, you could offer to do something on your computer for them.'

Carrie was surprised at how easily her brain grasped at the apparent normality of the situation. Apart from the huge glass of wine he was now sipping, Mark was showing little sign of having had a stressful conversation only moments ago.

Was he so good at this that she'd never noticed?

'Could do,' he said, with none of his usual rancour about village life.

If I hadn't seen him just now, I'd never have guessed, thought Carrie, mechanically smearing butter on the chicken. What else have I missed?

'You OK?' he asked, peering at her.

Carrie wiped her eyes with the back of her hand. 'Fine, yeah. I was up at the church today,' she began, wondering what the best way was to break the news about his long-lost uncle. 'Have you been up there?'

'Nope.' Mark was unpacking his bag. 'Should I?'

'Well, there are lots of very old gravestones up there.' Carrie paused. 'Did . . . Did your dad ever mention having any brothers or sisters?'

Mark looked up and shook his head. 'No, it was always just him. Said that's why he had such a bloody boring time at home. Couldn't wait to get away.' His expression changed. 'Why?'

'Well, I think he might have had a twin brother,' said Carrie. 'There's a little headstone up there, for a boy called Matthew Armstrong, twin of Benjamin, son of Jack and Lily.'

'Oh.' Mark blinked and sat down. 'No, he never mentioned it. Really? Shit. Are you sure?'

Carrie nodded. 'Do you want to go up there and see it?'

'In the morning.' Mark looked surprised. 'No one ever said anything about that. I don't even know if Dad knew. A brother?'

'The baby was only a month old when he died,' said Carrie. 'And he died before the village was evacuated, so maybe Lily wanted to leave her sadness behind?' She paused. 'It would explain why poor Lily looks so sad in that photograph. She did leave part of herself behind in the village, like your grandad said. Well, if you can *really* leave something like that behind.'

Mark suddenly looked very pained. 'Listen, I think I've got a migraine coming on. It's been a long day. I'm going to go and lie down for half an hour, OK?'

'OK,' said Carrie. 'Then are we going to . . . have a chat?' She smiled. 'Like we said we would this morning?'

Mark tried to force his mouth into a smile, but it didn't work. 'I'll see how my migraine goes, OK?'

When she looked into the bedroom an hour later, the glass of wine was empty and Mark was either asleep or pretending to be. When she looked in again a few hours later, he'd taken off his clothes and slipped under the covers.

Chapter Twenty

'You look better this morning,' Carrie observed as Mark covered a slice of toast in marmalade (local, made by Mrs Cooper, bought from the shop).

'Do I? Don't feel it. Think I'm getting your insomnia,' he said guardedly. 'What are you doing today, then?'

Carrie hadn't had a good night either and she felt worse at the thought of them both lying sleeplessly, each faking oblivion for the sake of the other. Too many things going round and round in her head; too many of them things she didn't really want to think about anyway. She wondered what had kept Mark awake. Exactly the same thoughts probably.

'Lucy's coming over to talk about the history tent this morning. We're going to look through the archive material we've already got and make some collages. You know, big sheets about the farmers, and weddings, and village customs. That sort of thing.'

'How long's that going to take?' He boggled his eyes at her. 'I thought you were meant to be working on the mouse? Hey? The mouse? Remember him? Your little mouse employer?'

'Nearly finished,' said Carrie. 'Anyway, I want to be involved in the fete. It's going to be a really good way of bringing everyone in the village together. Most people are offering to help out now, one way or another.'

'Apart from me, you mean.'

'Yes, apart from you. I could put you down for dressing up as a farmer, if you want?'

'Er, I don't think so, Carrie.'

'Oh, go on. I'm going to be dressed up as a schoolteacher?'

A flicker of Mark's old good humour crossed his face, and Carrie's heart lifted. 'Well, in that case, I might volunteer to be a lord of the manor, if the position's not been taken? Would I get to have my wicked way with the village wenches?'

'No,' said Carrie. 'It's not that kind of village.'

He raised his eyebrow caddishly.

'Well, you might have a chance with this one. But that's your lot. Anyway, I've already volunteered your IT skills. I just have to find out what needs to be done.'

'Fine,' said Mark, finishing off his toast. 'Let me know.'

Carrie chewed her lip, and while she was thinking how she could bring up what she'd overheard the previous night, her mobile rang, with an unknown number.

It rang twice, then the reception cut out.

'I get such lousy reception here,' she said, seizing the chance. 'How about you?'

'It depends,' said Mark. 'I reckon the Army switch signal blockers on and off. There's another one for the pub, eh?'

'I mean, sometimes I call your phone and there's no reply at all,' she went on. 'And sometimes you can be standing outside and it's as clear as a bell.'

She stopped and looked at him. He was stirring his tea round and round and round. 'Mark?'

Mark stopped stirring. 'Weird, isn't it?'

His expression was so innocent, she knew she'd have to ask if she wanted answers. And that would mean admitting she'd eaves-dropped, *and* worked herself up into paranoia, and . . .

'Are you going up to town today?' she heard her voice ask.

'Which town?' said Mark, too quickly, and when their eyes met, she knew he could see the doubt in her face, because he looked away almost immediately. 'Devizes, since you ask. Want anything?'

Carrie shook her head.

'Want to come with me?' He looked at her closely. 'Have a day out?'

That wasn't quite what he was asking though, and she knew it.

'Love to, but I can't,' she said. 'Lucy's coming round, and the kids from next door . . .'

'Fine. Listen, I might walk up by the church before I go,' he said casually. 'See this family mystery for myself.'

'Shall I come too?'

'No, you're OK,' said Mark. 'I, er . . .' He seemed to struggle for words. 'I'd quite like to see it for myself. It's quite a . . . thing to get my head round. You know, finding there's more of my family than I knew I had.' He chewed his lip. 'If we hadn't come here, I'd never have known, would I? If the village had never been reopened.'

Carrie looked at him and saw genuine confusion in his expression, struggling with his habitual 'whatever' attitude. But he'd said it aloud, rather than just pushing it aside. That was something.

'But now you do know,' she said, and came round the kitchen table to hug him for that alone.

Lucy arrived half an hour later, with two big carrier bags of photographs, letters, old maps and assorted scraps of memorabilia, gleaned from Barbara Purves' door-to-door appeal.

'Not a lot to show for hundreds of years of so-called history, is there?' said Lucy as she unpacked the finds under Carrie's impatient eye.

'What were you expecting?' asked Carrie. 'Roman sandals?'

'Well, something more interesting than school certificates,' snorted Lucy. 'And boring letters.'

'Oh, I like the letters,' said Carrie. There were one or two about the evacuation, another about a successful home birth, carried out at the same time as a successful calving. The calf got two more lines than the baby. One resident had included a set of First World War medals; more than one had sent along yellowing school leaving certificates, fragile but still kept crisply flat.

Carrie studied the cursive signature with a flip in her stomach: 'Jack Armstrong, BA. June 1938'. The scene flashed into her mind like a screen being turned on: the school hall smelling of hay and summer grass, the scrubbed-up children waiting in a line, Mrs Maxwell, bored in a smart hat, presenting the certificates, Jack perspiring in his heavy suit, Lily somewhere at the back of the class, watching the children, sweets at the ready in her pocket . . .

'Are we going to do this on the computer then?' asked Lucy, dumping the final photograph album on the table. She turfed Elvis off the nearest chair and settled herself, automatically looking for the biscuits.

'Not if I can help it. Well, not to begin with, anyway.' Carrie put the certificate down, opened her biggest sketchpad and uncapped a black pen. 'It'd take ages to scan this lot, so I thought for now we'd just see what we've got, sort it out into collages, then Mark can scan them all later, and do something clever with them.'

'Good for Mark,' said Lucy, in suspiciously neutral tones. 'Nice to see him getting involved.'

'Well, he's very busy,' said Carrie. 'And it's quite personal for him. He doesn't know very much about his family, so it's like I'm finding out about his past at the same time as he is.'

'So . . .' Lucy leaned forward. 'Heard any more crying from next door? I was talking to someone else the other day who reckoned that their auntie had come home crying when she was a little girl, saying that she'd been . . .'

'Are you going to be working here all day?'

Carrie and Lucy looked over to the back door, where Betsy was standing with her hands on her hips. Ivor stood next to her, holding a plastic carrier bag, which, from the scrabbling, Carrie guessed contained the kittens.

'Betsy,' she said, 'you can't just put the kittens in a bag. And you must knock!'

'Well?' She looked accusing. 'What about me and Ivor?'

'Come on in,' said Carrie. 'Lucy and I are both going to be working in the kitchen this morning, yes. Would you like to sit down here with us?'

Betsy paused. 'Yes.'

Lucy groaned under her breath, as Betsy marshalled Ivor towards the cat basket. 'You didn't say you had the Addams family round.'

'I'm looking after her and Ivor anyway,' whispered Carrie. 'They're really very sweet, but I'd rather have her where I can see her.' She raised her voice so Betsy could hear, though she had a feeling that Betsy's ears could pick up whispers from ten feet away. 'Do you want to go upstairs and bring some books down?'

Betsy sighed elaborately. 'I've read everything. Ivor will be fine to play with the cats. What are you doing?'

'We're looking through some old pictures of the village before everyone had to leave, and making displays for inside the tent. Would you like to see?'

'Maybe,' she replied, studying Carrie's antique flour bin with exaggerated interest.

Lucy tutted.

'Well, it's going to take us a while, so if you want to go and get yourself some books, you can. And if you want to give us a hand, you can do that too,' said Carrie, briskly. She'd learned that Betsy liked to be asked twice, and sometimes she played along, and sometimes she didn't. 'Ivor, if you want to put the kittens in the basket with Elvis, I'm sure they'll be much happier than they are in that bag.'

'OK!' he said with a huge, unworried smile. It was bizarre, she thought, that Betsy could be so moody and Ivor so sunny. They were like the forecasting weathermen on Barbara Purves' weather house;

one in the sun, one in the shade. Her heart twitched protectively for him.

'Can I get you anything, Ivor?' she asked, watching him stroke the cats with his chubby hands.

'No, thank you.'

'At least one of them has manners,' muttered Lucy.

'Don't worry, Ivor, I'll go upstairs,' she heard Betsy say with solicitous care.

Once she was sure Ivor wasn't going to burn, scald or impale himself on anything, Carrie turned her attention back to Lucy's haul of material.

'Are these new?' she asked, picking up one of the bundles of pictures stacked up against the teapot. Some were so old they looked as if they'd been printed from silver mercury plates. 'Where've they come from? I haven't seen them before.'

'Those? Yeah, they're mine actually. I went to see my gran at the weekend, and she told me about a whole lot more stuff in a box in Mum's shed.' She raised her eyebrows as Betsy's feet trotted up the stairs. 'You really don't mind her going up there on her own? What about him?'

Carrie shook her head. 'She's fine.' She didn't add that Morris 2.0 was safely hidden out of Betsy's curious reach. 'Anyway, Ivor won't go up on his own.'

'You seem to know them pretty well.'

'They're nice children. Just not used to company.'

'And the father?'

Carrie looked up and met Lucy's curious gaze. 'Much the same. Anyway. These photographs . . .'

Lucy grinned, as if to say, 'I'll find out anyway.' 'My grandad was a bit of an enthusiast, according to Mum. Amateur historian, sort of thing. Nothing pervy, mind,' she added, defensively. 'There was no "can I take your photo, little girl?" funny business.'

Carrie sifted through the photographs, dividing them into piles of church outings, weddings, Christmas celebrations and, inevitably,

May Day. Every person in them stared nervously back at the camera – there was none of the ease that modern people had with being photographed. Plus, Carrie reasoned, the vicar was on the other side of the contraption. You wouldn't want to be seen having too much fun.

'Mum was telling me he used to be into photographing old customs before they died out, you know. That's why there's so many of the May Day,' Lucy explained. 'Green Men, the wood party, that sort of thing. Can you see? The ones with everyone covered in flowers? They even put flowers on the horses. I don't know what half of them are meant to be, to be honest. I think Gran noted stuff on the back, but not on all of them.'

'The wood party?' asked Carrie, stopping at a photograph of thirty or so shifty-looking youngish people, arranged around a grassy hillock, all bedecked in flowers and their best clothes. Some of the men were blurred, which suggested that the vicar had taken rather a long time to get his shot. Or that his sitters weren't entirely sober. 'Why didn't you mention this at the meeting?'

'I didn't really know about it, to be honest. Mum told me when we got these out of the shed. Oh, apparently people used to go into the wood after the May Day and get pissed and get up to God knows what else. It was meant to be some sort of ritual offering to the woodland gods originally, the May Queen laying flowers on the chalk horse, but you know how these things end up.' Lucy grinned cheekily. 'Drinking, fertility rites, young men and women, make your own entertainment . . . I'm kind of hoping that's one tradition they'll carry on, know what I mean? Look, here's one of your house.'

Carrie peered at the faded print. With no people in the foreground to date it, the effect was eerie: the fronts of Oak Cottage and Rose Cottage seemed virtually unchanged, with the same trees growing in the background, only slightly smaller, and the same sweeping view over the valley dominated by the white horse. Apart from the cars now parked outside, there was practically nothing to tell the reincarnated cottages from the old.

It's like the houses have gone back in time, she thought, the walls repainted authentic colours, the roofs restored in the old ways – even the inhabitants are just newer shoots from the same old roots. In fact, it was as if the whole village had been artificially grafted back to life in some huge laboratory experiment.

'So was your granny telling you about this May Day orgy?' she asked, to dispel the creepiness on her skin. 'I can't imagine the vicar condoning that sort of behaviour!'

'Oh, I don't think he was invited. Anyway, she was quite a goer in her time, my gran, before she married the vicar. I tried to get some more gossip out of her, about Lily, for you, but I don't know. Poor old thing, she can't remember a lot,' said Lucy. 'Mind's gone, you know. She'll talk for hours about the kind of milk bottles they used to get their milk in from the farm, but if you ask her about her own wedding day . . .' She shrugged. 'Sad thing is that she used to be *incredibly* nosy. You think I'm bad? She was one of them – what do you call it – mass observers, during the war.'

'Mass what?' It was wrong, thought Carrie, that even now she assumed that nothing went on out here, that girls like Lucy would know stuff she didn't. Then again, she reminded herself bitterly, it seemed there was no end to the stuff she didn't know.

'Mass observers. Well, legal nosy-parkering, that's what my mum reckons. We never even knew Gran was doing it, not for years. You really haven't heard of it?' Lucy gave her a close stare, to check she wasn't being patronised. Carrie shook her head.

Satisfied she wasn't, Lucy went on, 'It was some kind of national archive, of how people behaved, what they thought about stuff. Kind of like big brother is watching you, but voluntary. Gran kept a diary of what happened in the village, and sent it off every so often to London. I think with her being the vicar's wife, she had a good idea of everything that was going on.'

'She wrote everything down? Like what?' asked Carrie, intrigued.

'Oh, I don't know. What people thought about rationing, how many people were getting married, that sort of thing. She wouldn't talk about it for years, you see. I don't know if it was meant to be all hush-hush, or if she just liked having her own secrets, like Grandad did being the vicar, or what, but we only found out about it when she started getting a bit rambly. Kept asking us if we'd seen her diaries.' Lucy paused in her photograph-separating, and looked down at the picture in her hands. 'Look, spooky – here they are on their wedding day.' She sighed. 'We showed her this, and she thought it was my mum. Poor old thing.'

She passed Carrie a photograph of a man who couldn't have been anything other than a vicar in his day job – all solemn eyes and lugubrious expression, even at twenty-something – and a small, sharp woman whom Carrie immediately placed in her imaginary animal St Dee as a vole. She carried a massive bouquet of white chrysanthemums in front of her like a riot shield. Like every other bridal couple, they stood at the studded oak door of the church, beneath the curling, faintly sinister watch of the Green Man.

Lucy, noted Carrie, had inherited her grandmother's quick, dark eyes, and none of her grandfather's looks whatsoever.

'So between the photographs and the diaries and the church, it sounds like they had the village pretty much covered,' said Carrie, placing the photograph carefully on the wedding pile. It certainly made her version of Lily's character more credible – even given that she wanted to believe it more. 'I bet nothing got past them.'

''Spose so,' said Lucy, without a trace of self-consciousness. 'Then again, it's amazing what you can keep quiet if you really try. Even in this place.'

'Oh, come on,' scoffed Carrie. 'It's not. Even I know about Mrs Baker's brother's drink-driving thing.'

'How do you know that?'

'Um, how do I know that?' Carrie thought hard. 'Oh, Philip told me.'

'Philip, eh?' Lucy jiggled her eyebrows. 'Now there's a tale and a half. The man with the wife under the patio!'

'Shh!' said Carrie, but Ivor was lying half-in, half-out of the cat basket, oblivious to the conversation. She looked nervously over her shoulder, just in case Betsy had floated ghost-like into earshot.

'Have you found out what happened to his wife yet?' asked Lucy, leaning forward, her eyes glittering with curiosity. 'If, of course, there was one in the first place? I bet you do know. You two are thick as thieves.'

Carrie was shocked to feel a tug of power that for once she knew something Lucy didn't.

'Go on, you can tell me.' Lucy's face was encouraging, and for a moment, Carrie was tempted to win herself some serious points. After all, she never had very much to offer by way of return gossip, and didn't Lucy have the key to finding out more about Lily?

'It's not gossip,' added Lucy, persuasively. 'I mean, it's better to know, so we don't put our feet in it with him.'

Carrie met her gaze. That much was true. And it wasn't fair that everyone was speculating about Philip, spreading those awful rumours about his wife, when really he'd done well to hold his family together . . .

'Well,' she began in an undertone, 'he's a lecturer at Durham University, as you know, specialising in paganism and folklore, and he's here to finish a book on Druids and the early Christian church. And he met his wife, Giselle . . .'

Suddenly, Carrie heard the words coming out of her mouth and stopped herself, shocked. What was she doing? It would be betraying a trust Philip had put in her for the sake of his children, who were right here in her care. And more than that, Carrie realised she didn't want to see the look on his face if he found out she'd dished up his secrets so easily over tea and biscuits, instead of keeping it a private confidence between the two of them.

A confusing mixture of emotions surged around her chest, and she blushed.

'What? Don't you trust me?' Lucy looked offended.

'No, no, it's not that,' stammered Carrie. 'It's just that . . . he didn't exactly go into details. I wouldn't want to give you the wrong idea.

They're separated, Philip and his wife. He's looking after the kids.'

Lucy made an '*and* . . . ?' face.

'And that's all he said,' finished Carrie.

'So why isn't that freaky girl in school? She's old enough.'

'Betsy? She's not freaky,' Carrie protested. 'She's just . . . shy.'

Lucy tipped her head in sarcastic disbelief. 'She needs to get into school, that one. Make some real friends. I've seen her round the village, talking to herself. And I mean this kindly, but people are saying things.'

'Like what?'

'Oh, like she's not all there. No, come on, Carrie, don't look like that – I'm just telling you what people have told me.'

'Well, you can tell them they're wrong!' fumed Carrie. 'Are people saying Betsy's . . .' She fumbled for the right word. 'Disturbed? Because there's nothing wrong with her. Lots of kids have imaginary friends at her age, especially kids who spend a lot of time alone.'

'She has an imaginary friend?'

'Hazel isn't imaginary.'

Carrie and Lucy both jumped so hard that photographs scattered everywhere on the table.

'Betsy!' gasped Carrie. 'You mustn't do that!'

'Do what?' Betsy calmly helped herself to a biscuit from the plate.

'Creep up on people!'

'People creep up on me all the time,' she replied. 'Hazel's always creeping up on me. I tell her not to, but she does it anyway.'

Lucy looked over Betsy's head and looped her finger in circles.

'Well, that's very rude of Hazel,' said Carrie. 'You should tell her to stop it.'

'I have. She won't,' said Betsy, sadly.

'Well, now you're here, would you like to help us?' asked Carrie, feeling out of her depth.

'How?'

'Yeah, how?' repeated Lucy, clearly narked at the lost opportunity to probe further about Philip.

'By sorting out pictures.' Carrie looked appealingly back at her, then dropped her gaze to Betsy, who was now pushing the photographs idly round the table top. 'You're going to be in the fete, aren't you? In the maypole dancing that Mrs Purves is organising?'

'That,' said Betsy, scornfully. 'It's *obligatory*.'

Lucy gaped at her and Betsy's eyes darted nervously between their faces, her expression suddenly vulnerable.

'What? What? Did I say it wrong?' she asked. 'I read it. I know what it *means*.'

Carrie felt the tremor of uncertainty in Betsy's voice. That self-possessed maturity was misleading, acquired like her vocabulary, in a darkly silent world of words, gobbled down alone.

'You said it perfectly,' she said, touching her hair. 'Anyway it should be a lot of fun,' said Carrie. 'I wish I was allowed to do it.'

'You can if you want,' said Lucy. 'Barbara's running short of kids. There aren't enough to go round. Literally. Ha!'

'Oh.' Carrie could almost hear Mark scoffing about how the place had become a retirement home, and she felt defensive. 'Well, I might just do that,' she said. 'It's a fertility rite, after all, isn't it? Should really be the married ladies doing it, not the kids.'

'Daddy says May Day is all about sex,' observed Betsy, conversationally. 'He made Mrs Purves go really red when she came round to talk to him about the fete. He told her that the maypole was,' – she paused this time to make sure she got the word right, '*phallic* and that the May Queen should really be a virgin.'

Lucy and Carrie both stared at her this time.

'Betsy, would you like a glass of milk?' spluttered Carrie.

'No, no,' said Lucy, holding up a hand, 'what else did your daddy say to Mrs Purves?'

'He said May Day was really called Beltane and it was a Druid festival that the Romans celebrated here too.' Carrie noted that Betsy was using her own version of Philip's patient lecturing voice. 'He told her that the men and ladies would go into the woods and do fertility rites. On the horse.'

'What?' Carrie suppressed a snort of laughter at the thought of Barbara's face. 'He was making that up, surely, to get a rise out of her!'

'No, I've heard that,' said Lucy. 'It's just a fancy name for the wood party, I reckon. My mum reckons half the village was meant to have been conceived on that horse before they put a stop to it.' She winked. 'Riding the white horse, if you know what I mean!'

'Betsy, I'm not sure it's really the sort of thing you should be listening to,' said Carrie faintly.

'Oh, Daddy tells me all sorts of things like that. It's *history*,' replied Betsy, with a superior look. 'Daddy was going to help with the English customs tent, but Mrs Purves decided he'd be better helping them make the Green Man outfit. Can I have another biscuit, please? Thank you,' she said, helping herself without waiting for a reply.

'Do you want one for Hazel?' asked Carrie.

'Don't be silly, Carrie.' Betsy tutted. 'Hazel doesn't eat biscuits.'

'Right,' said Carrie. 'Silly me.'

By lunchtime, Carrie and Lucy had made three huge posters that covered every inch of the big pine table.

'That's the best one,' said Lucy, crossing her arms in a satisfied fashion. 'Something for everyone on there.'

Carrie had drawn a map of the village over several sheets of paper, from the village green at its heart, radiating out to the hill farms, and the chalk horse, and the crumbling remains of the monastery, and Lucy had Blu-Tacked photographs round the edge, drawing them into place with long red felt-tipped arrows.

Thanks to the vicar's obsessive archival instincts, nearly all the houses featured, along with the pub, the church, the blacksmith's, the little shop, the schoolhouse and the post office. Only the manor house hovered like a ghost on the edge of the page, its ivy-covered frontage and sweeping drive left pointing at nothing in the living village.

'Poor Kathleen,' sighed Carrie, drawing the final line linking the manor house to its empty space on the map. 'She's gone from being the queen of the village to being the only one with nothing to come back to.'

'You don't think she's acting like the queen of the village now?'

Carrie acknowledged that this wasn't far off. 'Well . . . Rather her than Barbara Purves. I feel a bit sorry for her.'

'Don't feel sorry for them,' snorted Lucy. 'They were quick enough to sell up and leave, despite all that hand-wringing about being here for generations. The other day Gran was telling me some tales you wouldn't believe about those hunting parties they had. Oh, God, don't get me started, Carrie.'

'But . . .'

'People shouldn't ride roughshod over the rest of us, just because they've got the biggest house. No disrespect, but it's much easier for her to sell you some rose-tinted version of what it was like here before the war. There are things she doesn't even know about. And I don't mean outside lavs.'

Carrie looked over the table at Lucy's face tensing with the effort of not letting rip in front of Betsy. Maybe Lucy was right – what did she know? While she instinctively wanted to defend Kathleen, who had only ever been kind and charming, what did she, as an outsider, know about what it had been like here with no electricity or baths? Just what people had told her. She felt awkward, and ignorant of these invisible threads of family resentments. It wasn't her place to start tripping up over them.

'Well, none of us know, do we?' she said lamely.

Betsy had stayed at the table with them, quietly looking through the pictures with a solemn expression. Eventually even Lucy forgot she was there, and the conversation ebbed and flowed around her, wandering from Barbara Purves' neighbourhood watch rotas that always seemed to pair her with the relatively attractive new doctor, to Sandra from the shop's fibroids, to Chris's ongoing stress from Paul Jenkins' heritage guidelines. Now, though, Carrie was glad Betsy was there to act as a gossip breaker.

'See, Betsy? There's the school where you would have gone,' said Carrie, pointing to the school on the map. 'Can you find me another photograph of it?'

'There's no need to talk to me as if I'm Ivor,' huffed Betsy. 'I'm not a baby.'

'OK, OK.' Carrie put up her hands jokingly.

'Here, have a look through these,' said Lucy, passing her a handful of photographs. 'Anyway, Carrie, I meant to ask – what are you baking for the competition?'

'A sponge cake. And scones.'

'Scones.' Lucy looked thoughtful. 'Can I get away with entering M&S ones, do you think? I'm really pushed this week and Chris is going into Devizes soon.'

Carrie pretended to look shocked.

'I could freeze them,' suggested Lucy. 'What do you think?'

'I think Barbara will be running tests to make sure there are no shenanigans of that nature.'

'You reckon?' Lucy's expression suddenly shifted from cheeky to concerned.

'What?' said Carrie.

She nodded towards Betsy and Carrie swivelled in her seat.

Betsy was staring at the photographs, laid out in front of her like playing cards, and was moving her mouth slowly, as if she was talking to herself.

'Betsy?' said Carrie sharply. 'Is something the matter?' She leaned nearer to see what Betsy was fixated on so intently; one picture was of a prize day one summer in the 1930s, with the entire class arranged outside the school, Jack, like a large bat in his gown, book-ending one side, and the vicar at the other, hands tucked into his sleeves; another was of Lily looking deeply unhappy with Kathleen's mother; another was of an unspecified May Queen, her dark head wreathed in green leaves.

'Please may I be excused?' gabbled Betsy, sliding off her seat before Carrie could say anything.

'Honey, if there's something the matter . . .' she began, concerned, but Betsy was already clattering across the kitchen. Then she was out of the back door and the soft grass muffled her footsteps, and Carrie didn't know where she'd gone. There was no slam of the door in Rose Cottage.

'Strange little girl,' said Lucy, not without sympathy. 'That's the trouble about living out in the middle of nowhere. If you've no friends, you've no friends.' She paused, significantly. 'Apart from the ones in your head.'

Carrie looked out of the window, not listening, but remembering.

Chapter Twenty-one

The right moment to tackle Mark about his phone conversation never came. Instead the atmosphere seemed to settle back over the traces like snow, covering the jagged edges of her panic with easy, day-to-day routine until Carrie wondered if she hadn't over-reacted, after all. There was nothing in Mark's behaviour that suggested that it heralded some great crisis; he kissed her more, he told her he loved her more, he left for work each morning, but was back at home by six, and he was taking a new interest in the village that went beyond visits to the pub. Even Philip noticed that Mark was around more.

'I saw your man talking to the Purveses about the fete yesterday,' he'd said, when she brought the children back round after lunch. 'Bit of a turnaround, isn't it? What gives?'

Carrie shrugged. 'I don't know – the little gravestone in the churchyard? Finding out there's more here than he knows?' She smiled. 'I don't care, really. Feels nicer.'

And it hadn't taken a huge row, she thought, shuddering at the damage that might have caused. For nothing.

The weather turned warmer at the end of April, bringing the first froths of blossom into the fruit trees early, and one morning Carrie took her easel into the garden and began work on her anniversary present for Mark: a sketch of the house, with tiny little clues to their relationship, woven in like a proper old painting. Red roses around the door for love, a pair of doves hiding in the eaves for fidelity, seashells along the path to represent their travelling together.

Carrie bit her pencil, wondering what could symbolise Mark's IT skills. Blue teeth somewhere?

She jumped as a familiar small presence made itself felt next to her.

'What are you doing?' asked Betsy. She was holding a large slice of cake in one hand, and a couple of books under her other arm.

'I'm drawing my house,' said Carrie. 'It's going to be a present for Mark.'

'Why?'

'It's our wedding anniversary this week.'

'Oh.'

'We've been married for three years.'

Betsy settled herself down, then squinted at Carrie, screwing up her blue eyes against the sunlight. 'What's he going to give you?'

'Oooh, I don't know,' said Carrie. 'I don't want anything really. Some new paintbrushes? What do you think would be nice?'

'He should bring you a deer's heart. In a carved box. Or some red roses,' said Betsy solemnly.

'Roses would be very romantic,' Carrie agreed. 'Not sure about the deer's heart though. Bit messy, don't you think? Anyway, I don't know where he'd get one.'

'In the woods. There used to be deer in the woods, Daddy says, and all kinds of wild beasts. Unicorns and griffins. And bears.'

'He's very keen on those woods, isn't he, your father?' Carrie sketched in the ivy around the windows, noting how it darkened into blood-red, then faded back up to green as it climbed the walls up to their bedroom window. There was something beautifully neat about Oak Cottage that appealed to her sense of proportion. Her plan was to collage shards of shiny photograph onto the pencil drawing, to make the fairy-tale cottage a real home. The windows would be real, she decided, and the door.

'Does he ever take you and Ivor on nature trails up there?'

'No,' said Betsy. 'He says they're no place for children.'

'Really? Why not?'

Betsy didn't reply, but chewed her lip and looked thoughtfully up at the house, checking it against Carrie's drawing.

I've never met a child who was so happy with being quiet, thought Carrie, watching as Betsy tipped her head from one side to the other, in thought. It almost looked as if she were listening to a conversation Carrie couldn't hear. A shiver ran over her skin. Was Hazel there with them now, chattering away? About her?

Betsy looked up at the windows, then across to her own bedroom and frowned.

'Is your daddy working today?' Carrie asked to break the silence. 'He must have nearly finished his book now.'

'He's working on some May Day things for Mrs Purves' tent. Are you going to be a May Queen too?'

'I think we all are,' said Carrie. 'Even Mrs Purves, I should think.'

Betsy looked solemn. 'You know the May Queen is meant to be *sky-clad*?'

'I beg your pardon?'

'Sky-clad.' Betsy's eyes rounded. 'Daddy says the May Queen was meant to go into the forest *sky-clad* to make the offering to the gods.'

Naked? Carrie tried to remember where she'd seen the term sky-clad before – in one of Philip's pagan books? Betsy dropped her voice to a whisper, and said, 'Does that mean she wore clouds? Like a tutu?'

Carrie realised Betsy's embarrassment stemmed from being caught out in ignorance, rather than anything else, and she grabbed the chance to cover up some of the child's innocence for a change.

I should speak to Philip, she thought. It's just not suitable, the things he discusses with Betsy. In fact, it's getting creepy.

'I should think so,' she said. 'Isn't that a lovely idea? Wouldn't you like to be wrapped up in great big fluffy clouds, like big towels of sky? You could have lightning for a headdress, and big hailstones in your ears like diamonds.'

Betsy smiled, dimpling her soft pink cheeks, then her smile faded as she turned her gaze back to the house and tipped her head again, her brow wrinkling.

'Are you looking forward to the maypole?' Carrie asked. 'That should be fun. Mrs Purves was telling me that she's making a list of all the children in the village so she can have a special dancing class the night before, so you all know what to do.'

They were running seriously short of suitably picturesque children, and Barbara had unwillingly extended her age range to 'below twenty'. Even so, Lucy had pointed out, rather unhelpfully, that would make about five dancers. Barbara was 'looking into it'.

'Betsy?' she probed when there was no response. 'Won't that be fun to meet some new friends?'

Betsy twisted her head away so Carrie couldn't see her face. 'I don't need any new friends,' she mumbled.

'Oh, we all need new friends,' said Carrie, keeping her voice brisk even though she wanted to scoop the stiff little girl into her arms and cuddle her. 'We all need people to chat to, and play with. Even grown-ups.' She paused, not sure where the line was between wanting to help and hurting Betsy's feelings by prying.

'I have lots of friends to play with,' insisted Betsy.

'Like Hazel?'

Betsy didn't answer.

'Betsy?' Carrie tried. 'I haven't met Hazel. Would I like her, do you think?'

There was a long pause. 'No.'

'That's a shame,' she said, trying to sound neutral. 'Why not?'

'Because . . . Because she cries, and says horrible things.'

Carrie looked up at Rose Cottage, the mirror image of her own house. Or was it the negative image? She tried not to let her increasing twitchiness show. 'Then you should tell her to go away.'

'I have done. She doesn't want to.'

'Then you'll just have to make some new friends, won't you? So you don't have any time to play with her.'

'You don't have many friends,' observed Betsy.

'I do!' Carrie almost laughed at the indignation in her own voice. 'I have Lucy, and your father . . . and, um, Miss Maxwell.'

'That's not a lot.'

'It's enough. Anyway,' said Carrie, 'I'm married to Mark. He's my best friend. When you're married, that's all you need.' She looked at her picture house. 'It's the two of you, against the world. A team. A . . .'

She stopped, shocked at her own tactlessness.

'You'll find that too, one day, when you get married!' she added quickly. 'When your handsome prince comes along and gallops off with you on his white horse.'

'That's just in stories,' said Betsy, disparagingly.

'Not always. Mark came along and galloped off with me.' But even Carrie knew how lame she sounded, so she let a silence fall between them.

'Carrie . . .' said Betsy, slowly, then stopped.

'What, honey?' said Carrie, looking up and down at her house.

'Carrie, do you ever wake up in the middle of the night?'

'I do sometimes, yes.' Whatever had been causing her to wake feeling weary had got worse recently, to the point where whatever she was dreaming about actually woke her up. Most nights now she found her eyes snapping open, usually between three and four, often grasping at the edges of a dream that felt too vivid to forget, but which slipped out of her head before she could remember why, leaving her slick with night-sweat.

This happens a lot, thought Carrie, staring at her sketch. It happens most nights, around the same sort of time. No wonder I feel sleepy in the afternoons.

'Sometimes I wake up because I think I hear something in the room,' Carrie went on, forcing a light tone into her voice. 'But then I put on the light, and I realise it's only a moth fluttering about. Or sometimes a little bird at the window, or something like that. Nothing to worry about.'

'I wake up in the night,' said Betsy. 'And I can't get back to sleep.'

'Then you should go and see your daddy in his study! I'm sure he'd be happy to let you sit in one of those big chairs and read until you were sleepy again.'

'It's very dark.'

Betsy looked away, but not quickly enough to hide the shiver of fear that crossed her small face, and Carrie remembered her own childhood terrors of cupboards and mirrors that might show someone else's face if you looked in them after midnight.

Even now the cottage sometimes spooked her with its unexpected creaks and shadows. How much scarier for little Betsy in that creepy house and only Philip and his stupid folk tales for reassurance!

'Betsy,' she said, extending her arm, 'can I tell you a secret?'

Betsy nodded and leaned a little nearer.

'If you say to yourself, "There's no such thing as ghosts! There's no such thing as ghosts!" when you're walking around the house at night, it makes a little bubble around you. And no one can get in and hurt you. Not even when it's really dark and creepy.' Carrie widened her eyes to show how much she meant it.

Betsy's interest turned to a curious pity. 'But Carrie,' she said, 'there *are* no such things as ghosts.'

She looked up at Carrie and gave her a patient, chilling smile.

A cool breeze blew over Carrie's skin.

Betsy sank back onto the grass with a thud and she began to play with the wooden box of pencils, stroking the colours and putting them in rainbow order.

'Have you finished your book?' she asked.

Carrie's pencil stopped shading in the roof. 'Which book do you mean? The one with the mouse?'

'The one with the animals living in our houses. I saw it, on your easel,' Betsy added, helpfully. 'I saw Daddy like a badger, and me and Ivor like fox cubs. And Mrs Purves like a great big bird.'

'Betsy, have you been peeping in my studio?'

She pouted and didn't say anything.

A thought began to unravel in Carrie's mind, like an old carpet unrolling and showing itself to be unusually colourful.

'Actually, maybe you can help me,' she said. 'I don't know how the story ends, that's why I'm having trouble with it.'

Betsy's face illuminated with new interest, though she tried to look casually at the pencils. 'Tell me the story, and I'll tell you how it ends.'

'Well, the people have to leave their homes, just like we did here, then, when everyone's gone, the animals creep in from the woods, and leave their sets and their nests and come and live in the houses. And no one knows, because the village is sealed off from everyone else, while the Army practise with their tanks over the hill. Then, one day, the animals hear that the people are coming back.' Carrie paused. 'I've drawn that page – they have a big meeting in the pub, all the cats and badgers and mice and birds. The birds are sitting on the beer pumps, and the cats are sitting on barstools with their paws just like *this*. Like Elvis sits on the Aga. But . . . I don't know what happens next.' She shrugged. 'What do you think? The animals will have to go back to the wood, I suppose.'

'The animals stay,' said Betsy, very definitely.

'But what about the humans?'

'They stay too.'

'They can't all stay, Betsy! There'd be no room in the houses, would there?' Carrie looked up to check the distance between the date plaque and the stone door lintel, then drew it in. 'They'd be bumping into each other on the landings.'

Betsy looked up at her with a strange expression on her round face. 'Why not? Why would the animals want to leave their nice houses? They just find a way to stay there, so the humans don't notice.'

'Even the cows who've moved into the vicarage?'

She fidgeted. 'I don't think Daddy would notice a cow if it was living in our house. Not if it didn't want to be seen.'

Carrie stared at her, but while a distant alarm bell was ringing in her brain, her imagination was already seeing pages of cows and chickens blending into the panelled walls and seagrass floors of the cottages, while the modern-day humans sailed past with their mobile phones and iPods, oblivious to the way the woods had come into their houses for ever.

'Betsy, you're so clever!' she said, putting down her pencil so she could clap her hands. 'That's the perfect way to end the story!'

'Is it?'

'It is! Will you help me draw it?' Carrie was already seeing the maypole in her head, with the human children dancing around with ribbons in their hot hands while the mice and chickens scampered around outside their circle, unseen.

'Maybe,' said Betsy.

'Is that your daddy at the window?' Carrie added, seeing something move in Rose Cottage. 'Shall we ask him to come down for a cup of tea?'

Betsy shaded her eyes, then frowned. 'No, that's not Daddy.'

Carrie looked up. There was nothing at the window. She brushed away the flicker of unease, buoyed up by the excitement of seeing an end to her book at last. Probably the shadow of a passing bird on the glass. 'It must have been the clouds. Do you want to run up and ask him in, anyway? I think we could all do with a tea break. I'll go and put the kettle on and you try one of my horrible scones.'

Reluctantly, Betsy put down the pencils and got up.

Carrie flipped over the sketchpad and started drawing quickly, before the pictures in her head faded away.

'Go on,' she urged, as Betsy dragged her feet on the grass. 'I'll be two ticks. Tell him I've been practising for the cake show, and that there are two flat but tasty sponges that need eating up.'

Brilliant, she thought, turning her attention to the page as it filled up nicely with idea after idea. Maybe things weren't as bad as she thought.

'Can I come in?'

Philip peered round the kitchen door, then let himself in without waiting for a response. Betsy and Ivor followed close behind, Betsy carrying a spotted biscuit tin and Ivor wearing a pair of yellow wellingtons.

'These are my seven-league boots,' he announced, and marched over to the cat basket where Elvis was asleep.

'Sandra does a very good shortbread,' said Philip, nodding at the tin. 'You're not the only one practising. Cup of tea for me, please, and one for madam here. Betsy?'

Betsy put the tin on the table, a little too forcefully, and jutted her lip ominously. Carrie detected the lingering notes of a sharp exchange of words.

'I told Daddy we were having a nice time *on our own*, but he wanted to come over,' she said.

'Only because Carrie invited me,' replied Philip. 'Madam.'

'Do you want to go and read upstairs?' asked Carrie quickly. 'You can have a look at my book on the desk, if you want. But don't touch the paper, OK! Or Morris!' She tugged on her ears. 'I've got my super-sensitive ears on and I can hear every tiny step . . .'

Betsy nodded, and spun on her heel.

They listened to her feet stamping up the stairs, the cross sound echoing off the beams.

Philip shook his head. 'You know, she won't go upstairs on her own in our house? And I can't keep her from running around in here. What've you got up there? Magic beans?'

'Something like that,' said Carrie. She wondered what it was that Betsy was so drawn to upstairs – Morris? Her books? The house did feel very different to Rose Cottage. Maybe it was just that her house had fewer shadows and fewer spooky oil paintings. Or maybe, between her and Lily, it had more of a feminine atmosphere altogether?

'Why won't she?'

Philip shook his head. 'Don't know. It used to be just Ivor, but now neither of them like going up there unless I'm with them. Anyway, all set for May Day?' he asked, with a twinkle. He had a devilishly attractive twinkle. Distractingly so.

'Just about.' Carrie busied herself with her tea. 'I've got the posters done for the tent, Lucy's getting some more bits and pieces from her granny's house, and Barbara's finding me a costume.' She looked up. Philip's smile was still twinkling in his eyes, and Carrie couldn't stop herself returning it. 'A costume, if you will. Apparently I have to dress up as a pre-war farmer's wife to sit in the tent and tell people about farming.' She pulled a face. 'What do I know about farming? I barely know where eggs come from!'

'I'm surprised she's not asking you to do your hair up in pigtails and find a yoke from somewhere.'

'Have you finished the leaflets?'

'Just about.' Philip pulled a wry face. 'I've had to tone it down a bit. Some of the details weren't suitable, according to Mrs Purves.'

'So I hear. Betsy was telling . . .'

'What Barbara doesn't really understand is that you can't pick and choose which quaint customs happened round here.' He took another biscuit. 'She doesn't like the fact that there was more monkey business going on in that wood than in Soho on a Friday night – and most of it was perfectly sanctioned! Well,' he added, seeing the disbelief on Carrie's face, 'until the Middle Ages, anyway.'

'What exactly have you told her that she's so horrified by?'

'Oh, well, she's very happy with the prancing around the maypole and the Jack-of-the-Green costumes, but she's not so keen on the fertility rituals in the woods, let us say. Very puritanical attitude, that woman.'

'Well, there will be children at the fete,' said Carrie, faintly. 'And we are talking about very ancient rites, aren't we? Surely the abbey must have cracked down on the, er, wood festival.'

'Tried to.' Philip winked. 'Don't believe all they tell you about monasteries, either.'

'Is nothing round here the way it looks?' asked Carrie, only half-joking.

'Only you, I think.'

'Only me,' she repeated. It wasn't a reassuring thought.

Chapter Twenty-two

Mark refused to give her any clues about her anniversary present, but Carrie was so pleased with the way her painting had turned out that she didn't even pester him.

The night before, she let Mark go upstairs to bed first, then when she heard the bath running, she threw aside her magazine and hurried through to the kitchen.

It had to be perfect for the morning. Carefully, she removed the canvas from its hiding place below the sink and set it up on the table, surrounding it with milk bottles full of wild flowers from their garden. Then she laid out two plates, two cups and saucers and two bowls from Lily's untouched dinner service, ready for the full English breakfast she was going to make him in the morning.

Carrie stood back to admire the effect.

The house in the painting looked peaceful and warm, the sort of family home she'd always wanted to live in.

That's our house, she thought, proudly. Our house.

She waited, holding her breath, and realised that she was almost anticipating a response, some echo from the fabric of the house itself.

Her eyes slid fearfully to Elvis, asleep in his basket, half-expecting him to leap up again.

But he slept on, undisturbed, and Carrie took a deep breath, turned off the lights and went up the stairs to bed.

She had only been asleep for an hour or so when the dream started, finally breaking over her like a storm that had been brewing on the edges of her consciousness for weeks.

She was standing at the foot of the hill, looking up at the chalk horse, which seemed bigger and whiter than ever, stretching its sinewy legs with barely contained power. It glowed from under the ground like a lightbox, but as she got nearer, without feeling herself move, it turned back into its familiar chalky texture, and she realised that the light was coming from flaming torches stuck in the ground around its perimeter. The torches were burning orange with wisps of black smoke around the edges of the flames and the flickering light made the shadows move and swoop around her.

Carrie felt a wave of nausea grip her stomach and she looked down at her arms. They were cradled as if she was holding a baby, but instead of a baby, she was holding garlands of flowers from her garden: overblown roses, and lilies with pollen seeping onto her clothes, and sickly sweet honeysuckle. Without knowing why, she leaned down and placed the flowers on the nose of the horse, which was shrinking and expanding trippily so sometimes she could see the whole thing, and sometimes it seemed bigger than the whole valley. There was a distant cheer, but she couldn't tell where it was coming from, or who was making the noise, just that it was all around her and coming closer.

Then Carrie felt herself being dragged backwards so the horse got smaller and smaller, and real panic took over her body, although her arms and legs felt leaden and bound. From the unreal glow around the horse, she was plunged into thick green darkness, with leaves and branches and roots all around her, and from the earthy, rotten smell alone, she knew she was in the heart of the forest. She couldn't see anyone, but she had the certain impression that she was surrounded by living things, breathing things, moving around her inert body. She tried to struggle but her arms and legs seemed to be sinking into the ground, just as the movement around her increased.

Carrie tried to call out for help, but her mouth felt as if it was full of leaves. Yet it wasn't choking, or unpleasant, but felt more as if she was being absorbed by the forest, sucked in by a greater strength whether she liked it or not.

Suddenly a broad face loomed over her, with dark eyes glittering out of the shadows, and thick hair tangling wildly all around his face.

Philip Gladstone.

'Philip!' she shouted, her chest flooding with relief, but no sound came out of her mouth. 'Philip, help me!' she tried again, uselessly.

Then, to her growing horror, she saw that Philip's face was turning dark green, and leaves were sprouting from his beard, which was roiling and growing of its own accord. When he opened his mouth to speak, more leaves shot out like green flames and Carrie realised he was turning into a Green Man.

'Lily,' said a voice that wasn't Philip's. It seemed to come from all around her. 'Lily.'

It was hundreds of voices.

Carrie looked down at her legs and saw hands creeping up her shins and knees, pushing her skirt over her thighs. Dirty hands, white hands, delicate hands, big hands, some with rings, some with bruises. She couldn't see the arms they were attached to, and she struggled, trying to free her own hands to push them away. But she couldn't move, and the hands continued creeping up her thighs, pushing her bare knees apart until her long skirt was around her waist, and Carrie looked down and saw to her shame that she wasn't wearing any knickers.

She marvelled at how long and slender her legs were, and how her skin was pearly-pale against the glossy leaves, but although she wriggled, the hands carried on invading her until she could only see knuckles and fingers and nails covering every inch of her legs, like a mermaid's tail made of skin.

Carrie threw her head back into the leaves that now seemed to be moving around her head and wept as the hands made her skin tingle and crawl in equal measure.

'Lily, Lily,' hissed the voices, like wind shifting restlessly through trees. 'Lily, Lily, Lily . . .'

Then she was moving upwards, very quickly, being shaken roughly by some new force, and when she opened her eyes, Mark was holding her by the shoulders and she was in bed, not in the woods at all.

She almost burst into tears.

'Carrie? Carrie, for God's sake, wake up!'

Instinctively, she pulled herself free and sat rocking on the edge of the bed. The duvet was wrapped tightly around her legs and both her pillows were thrown onto the floor. Her water glass lay shattered where she'd knocked it off the bedside cabinet.

Carrie was shocked to find that, despite the adrenalin still pounding through her veins, she was trembling with arousal, and when Mark put his arms around her, she felt a powerful need to be touched and held, but the hot shame still made her wriggle under his touch.

'Are you OK?' he asked, stroking her hair. 'You were making the scariest noises. Was it a nightmare? Tell me – you'll feel better . . .'

She buried her head in the soft warmth of his old cotton T-shirt, and the familiar scent of his skin began to smooth down her ragged nerves.

'I was up in the woods,' she murmured, pressing her forehead into his shoulder. 'On the horse. It was . . . it was some kind of May Day thing. I think.'

As she spoke, she could feel the edges of the dream begin to soften and slip away from her, and already Carrie knew she couldn't find the right words for the paralysing fear that had pinned her to the ground. That was still vivid around the edges of her consciousness, making her skin shiver as the memory of the leaves and the building terror flickered in and out of her mind's eye, but, in a way she couldn't put into words, that force was still out there, in the dark, night-time woods, and she didn't want to speak it aloud.

'May Day? Well, that's understandable, given the amount of time you've been spending going over all those spooky old books. Do you want to tell me about it?' asked Mark, circling the small of her back with his palm. His voice was so familiar it made her stomach clench with relief. 'Would that help?'

'No,' said Carrie.

'Shall I just hold you then?'

'Please.'

Mark curled himself around her, tucking her arms under his, and she lay with her eyes wide open in the dark, feeling the arousal drain away from her body, to be replaced with an exhausted sort of calm.

That can't be right, she thought. I shouldn't be more aroused in a nightmare like that than I am lying next to my own husband.

Tears swelled against her closed eyelids. It's delayed relief, she thought, listening to the distant hush of the wind in the branches of the trees, the ticking of the pipes.

Next to her, Mark's breathing turned back into the first stages of what would, in five minutes or so, become rasping snores. Carrie knew she wouldn't be able to get back to sleep, but she held on to the comforting familiarity of his grunts and sniffs until the light started to creep around the edges of the curtains and morning came.

She must have fallen asleep for a few minutes before the alarm went off, because the next thing she knew Mark was waking her up with a breakfast tray.

'Happy anniversary!' he said, holding out a cup of tea, and Carrie struggled up to a sitting position.

'Happy anniversary to you.' She turned her face up for a kiss. 'Oh, I was going to make you a proper wifely breakfast. Sorry. Your present is in the kitchen, did you see?'

'I did.' Mark looked moved. 'It's lovely. Kind of, um, spooky, but a lovely thought.'

'Spooky? Why spooky?'

'Oh, you know . . . the mixture of the real bits and the drawn bits, and the people and shadows, you know.' Mark snuggled back into bed with her. 'Don't ask me to come out with any of your art criticism, Carrie. You should know by now it's not my thing. But I get the general message, and I really like it. It must have taken you ages.'

'Good,' she said, distracted by what he'd said. Where were the shadows? More to the point, which *people* did he mean?

Mark buried his nose in the soft part of her neck and removed the cup of tea from her hand, then moved the hand onto his own back.

'Oh yeah?' said Carrie. 'And where's my gift, before we get into that?'

Mark stopped nuzzling, and gazed up at her.

'I've got something for you,' he said, seriously, 'but you can have it tonight, over supper.'

'Not now?'

'No. I have other gifts for you now, but of a more physical nature.'

'OK,' said Carrie, and slid back down the bed, relieved beyond words at the eager way her body responded to his.

Mark didn't say where he was going when he left, and Carrie, not wanting to spoil their anniversary, didn't ask.

She showered and dressed, then got out the hammer and a nail to hang up her painting in the kitchen, in pride of place next to the dresser.

'There's nothing spooky here,' she murmured to herself, examining it in the fresh morning light. What had he meant? She stared at the windows, wondering if there'd been some trick of the paint she hadn't spotted. If the house had inserted some ghosts into its own portrait, Carrie would have been freaked, but not completely surprised. But there was nothing. Nothing she could see, at any rate.

All in all, it was a good day: she made a sponge cake in the Aga that didn't come out like a pancake, and Gina, called to say that her publishers had paid the delivery money for Morris, and she'd already wired it into her account. Philip seemed to be having a day out with Betsy and Ivor, as no one came round, and even Lucy only put her head round the door briefly to pass on the news that Margery Stephens from the terrace had been rushed into hospital with a suspected heart attack, which Lucy herself diagnosed as merely acute indigestion, brought on by too much baking.

So, free from human distraction, Carrie was able to climb the stairs to the studio and spend the rest of the afternoon drawing the final pages of her St Dee book. The work absorbed her, as she let her imagination twist and illuminate Betsy's idea until it filled three intricate pages. Oak-coloured otters crept unseen along the dark panelled skirting boards of Kathleen's house, while buttery cows blended into the walls of her own kitchen, as she washed up at the sink, unaware of the blue tits hiding in the large vase of wild flowers behind her. The countryside had crept into the old houses, and everyone lived together.

It was a nice idea, she thought, leaning back from the completed page. Philip should approve, with all his ideas about the land and the people influencing each other.

At her feet, Elvis tensed, wriggling with concentration, then pounced on a daddy-long-legs, ripping it to shreds with unnecessary force.

Still a wild farm cat, underneath the silky fur.

At five o'clock, Carrie took a long bath and washed her hair, taking more care with her make-up than she would have done for a night out in London. She slipped on a simple black dress and painted her toenails a glossy ruby red because she knew that her long, delicate feet were one of Mark's favourite bits of her.

Forty years, Jack and Lily were married, she thought, twisting her thick dark hair into damp curls. That was a long time. Thousands of suppers, hundreds of birthdays and Christmases and New Years. Will Mark and I manage forty years?

She heard the sound of his car in the lane outside the house and rushed barefoot down the stairs to light the candles on the kitchen table. He had offered to take her out for a meal, but she'd pointed out that it would mean one of them not drinking, or a taxi back to the middle of nowhere that would probably end up costing more than dinner.

Besides, she thought, shaking out the match, somehow she wanted to include the house. It was just as much part of their future – it meant settling down, dealing with problems, facing up to each other.

She stood back from the table. With the candles around the plates, and the fresh flowers in the centre, it must have looked pretty much like Lily would have had it herself, before electricity or plastic or television.

It would be so easy to go back to that, she thought. One storm to cut us off, blow down our power cables, block our roads with ancient trees . . .

'Hi, honey!' called Mark from the hall. 'That smells amazing!' He came into the kitchen, shrugging off his jacket and turning off his mobile before dropping it casually into his bag. 'And you look amazing,' he added, and slid his arms around her waist.

Carrie felt her cheeks turn pink.

'I hope so,' she said. It was so nice when Mark turned the full beam of his attention onto her. It made her feel giddy.

'I've brought champagne,' he murmured into her neck, 'and I've booked the honeymoon suite upstairs.'

'You're confident!' Though her brain was yelling at her to take good moods where she found them, Carrie wondered why he was turning off his mobile like that. Was he making a *special* effort for their anniversary?

Damn it, this is what happens when you listen to Lucy, she thought angrily.

'What?' said Mark, sensing her tension.

'Oh, nothing.' Carrie gave him a brilliant smile, which she knew he'd spot as fake a mile off. 'Just happy.'

'Well, that makes two of us,' said Mark. 'I'm very happy. And I'm going to open that champagne now. I have lots to celebrate.'

Carrie looked closely at him as he ripped off the foil and opened and shut cupboard doors, in search of glasses. Happy wasn't the word. He seemed positively euphoric. If his breath didn't smell totally innocuous, she'd say he seemed drunk already.

Enough, she told herself sternly, and opened the fridge to get the starters.

'You know what my problem is?' said Mark, finally leaning away from the table to place the empty half-bottle of dessert wine next to the two champagne bottles they'd already despatched.

'Where do you want me to start?' Carrie tipped back the last of her wine. 'You're just too perfect?'

'No. Well, that as well, but no.' He pointed at her, slightly off-centre. 'My problem is I never know how lucky I am until it's too late. But I intend to change that right now. Carrie. I don't tell you how lucky I feel to be married to you, but I really am. Lucky.'

'Oh, honey. I feel like that too!' A warm feeling spread through her.

'And I've got a present for you. Hang on, hang on there.' Mark got to his feet somewhat unsteadily, and reached into his jacket pocket. When he brought out a small box, Carrie's heart hammered in her chest.

'Oh, Mark, you didn't need to . . .'

'No, stop!' he said, putting a finger on her lips. 'Stop. Open it.'

She held his gaze for a moment, then flipped open the lid. Held in the crease of thick red velvet was a diamond and sapphire ring: one small diamond circled by sapphires, like a jewelled forget-me-not. Carrie could tell at once that it was old, and as she carefully lifted it out, the candlelight sparkled in the stones and glowed through the fragile filigree setting. It felt heavy, though it was delicate, as if it had been made strong to withstand years and years of wear with a wedding band.

'Mark,' she whispered, 'it's beautiful.'

'Does it fit?' he asked. 'Aren't you going to try it on?'

Carrie hesitated, though she couldn't say why. There was something curious about it, something familiar, as though it was a distant déjà vu from a dream.

It's just the wine, she told herself. Stop looking for spookiness where there isn't any for once.

'Go on,' he said. 'See if it fits.'

She saw the eagerness in Mark's eyes, and any reluctance melted away in a sudden desire not to let him down.

The ring slid onto her engagement finger and fitted with her wedding ring as if it had been there for ever. She looked down at it, glittering against her skin, and her arms goose-pimpled. It wasn't her wedding finger any more. It was someone else's.

'I didn't get you a proper engagement ring at the time,' said Mark. 'And I wasn't sure about giving you this one until now.'

'This one?' Carrie caught his eye, and saw him blink carefully, as if he'd practised what he was going to say next.

'It was my mother's,' he said.

'Your mother's?'

He nodded. 'And I think it was Lily's before that too. It's been in the family for years. Mum was wearing it when she died. I never thought I'd want to see it on anyone else's finger, which is why I didn't propose with it. I didn't want you to be tied onto that chain of unhappiness.'

'Oh, Mark, don't think of your family like that,' Carrie began. She fidgeted with the ring, but it felt stuck on her finger.

I'm on now, it seemed to say. On, and you're not getting me off.

'But I do,' said Mark. 'That's what it feels like for me. Unhappiness. But when I met you, I knew you were a fresh start, someone totally new. I wanted to draw a line under everything in the past and start again, and I have. We have. I know I haven't been trying hard enough lately, but from now on it's just you and me, here in this house. I don't ever want to look back, because . . .' He stopped, choked.

Carrie pushed her chair back to go over to him, but he held up a hand. 'No, let me finish. I have to say this. I've done some things in the past that I'm not proud of. You deserve someone far better than me, I know that. And you're right, I do have a habit of walking away from things. But I don't want to do that any more.'

'You don't have to,' said Carrie, shoving her chair aside. She moved quickly round the table and wrapped her arms around him, wanting to comfort the small child she saw in his face. 'You don't have to, Mark.'

'I should have supported you more when we moved here,' he said, sounding close to tears. 'Well, now I will. I promise, Carrie. I will. I want this to be a happy house.'

'I know, I know,' she said, soothingly. 'I know.'

They swayed slightly together, Mark with his arms round her legs, Carrie with her lips against his forehead.

She wondered where the surge of emotion had come from; it was so unlike Mark's normal detachment that it transformed his whole body into someone different. When he turned vulnerable like this, it moved her almost painfully. He must have been going through his mother's things to find the ring, she thought. Poor Mark. That must have brought everything back. For that alone, she was touched, even if the present itself maybe didn't give the message he thought it did.

Still, he wanted to stay. He'd said all the things she'd always hoped he would – and it gave her the nerve to take her own step into the difficult unspoken land between them.

'It would be nice, wouldn't it, to have a baby here this time next year?' she murmured, tentatively, into his hair.

Mark didn't reply, which she took to be a positive thing. Normally he cut the conversation off right at that point.

'Or maybe we should wait a day or two. Hmm? Apparently, babies conceived on May Day were considered lucky,' she went on, smoothing the short hair, now flecked with one or two silver strands amid the dark chestnut. 'They were gifted from the gods. Special children.'

She looked out of the window, towards the chalk horse. The darkness in the kitchen left little reflection in the glass, and the pale outline stood out in the moonlight. Always there. Watching.

Carrie dropped a kiss into Mark's thick hair.

'I think our children would be special children anyway,' she murmured, more to herself now. 'They'd be so wanted. So loved. I've waited so long. Waited so long to find the right man. But it was worth it, wasn't it? Waiting to find each other like we did.'

'I don't think I'd be very good with kids,' muttered Mark.

'Oh, no one thinks they are until they have them.' Carrie rocked him gently. 'Don't you think I'd be a good mother?'

'You'd be a great mother. But I don't know if I'd be a good enough father.'

'You would. You'd learn. Everyone has to learn, Mark.'

They swayed and stroked in silence, listening to the house creak and the candles sputter as the wax burned down.

'Can't it just be me and you?' he said, quietly.

Carrie paused. He sounded like a small boy. 'It'll always be me and you,' she said, firmly. 'But I'd like it to be us.'

Mark said nothing, but buried his face deeper into her stomach. After another ten minutes of silence, Carrie blew out the candles and led him up to bed.

Chapter Twenty-three

It was only in the morning that Carrie realised that she'd forgotten to take her pill.

She looked at herself in the mirror, cheeks still flushed from making love until about three in the morning, her hair in wispy ruffled curls from where Mark had tangled his fingers through it and then, this morning, pushed his face into her neck to breathe in her sleepy unshowered smell before he left for work, as though he couldn't breathe in enough.

That had been better than any expensive dinner or diamond eternity ring.

She smiled at herself, still tingling at the memory of his fingers and lips on her skin. Mark had been trying so hard, wanting her so much she could feel his desperation barely held back. Then when he finally came, Carrie saw tiny tears beading along the edges of his closed eyes, and she'd kissed them away, running her lips along the sheeny hollows of his neck and cheek bones until his breathing returned to the same rhythm as her own.

They'd hardly said a word, but for once, Carrie didn't feel she was biting words back, or wanting to spill them out to fill a silence. They'd just been silently close.

She smiled at her glowy reflection in the bathroom mirror. I can't let my own stresses and fears get in the way of making us happy, she told herself. That's just destructive.

For a second, she hesitated, then she tucked the blister pack of pills back behind her moisturiser, yesterday's little orange pill still safe in its capsule.

The village shop was quite busy – there were four people waiting for the fresh bread to come out of the French bread oven – and Carrie had to queue before she could pay for her basket of groceries.

This is what it's meant to be like, she thought warmly, scanning the noticeboard advertising gardening services and second-hand bikes, alongside posters about the May Day fete and rotas for neighbourhood watch meetings. A real community, supporting itself. Making its own bread, even if it did come par-baked in a van from Swindon.

Ahead of her, a middle-aged couple were debating the probability of the conspiracy theory that had taken root as easily the most popular: the whole missing regiment buried in the wood, now taking on baroque new twists.

'They were using the village for D-Day training,' a man was insisting. 'Then gassed them, by mistake, with a secret new poison they were developing! Wind went the wrong way, ended up killing the lot of them. Had to bury them in the forest, so as not to give away training secrets.'

At the till Sandra scoffed. 'Couldn't they just have dug 'em up after the war finished?'

'Not if they were radioactive. And the land too.'

'It was the act of a vengeful God,' intoned his wife, primly. 'After what's been done to the sacred land here, in the name of paganism. We're Christians,' she added.

'And then they kept the village during the Seventies as an IRA interrogation centre,' the man went on. 'So no one could hear any screaming. That's why the houses weren't knocked down – they weren't used for target practice. There were people *still being held* in them.'

Sandra rolled her eyes at Carrie. 'That's a new one on me.'

'Where did they do that?' asked Carrie, innocently. 'I mean, whose house do you think . . , ?' She pulled a face. 'Not mine, I hope!'

The couple looked at each other. 'Well, I don't know exactly which houses . . .' he muttered. 'But I've definitely read about it on the Internet!'

'Well, you learn something every day,' said Sandra diplomatically. 'That'll be nine pounds eighty, please.'

When Carrie reached the counter, she let her eyes drift across Sandra's wine selection as she rang up her purchases. It wouldn't hurt to have another romantic evening in tonight, she thought. Tempt Fate a little more . . .

'Ten pounds nine, please, Carrie,' said Sandra. 'Nice night last night?'

She handed over her Switch card and blushed. 'Sorry?'

'Your wedding anniversary, wasn't it?'

'How did you know that?' Carrie demanded.

'Ah . . . We know everything.' Sandra frowned, and stabbed at her Switch machine again.

'Well, we had a very nice evening, thank you,' said Carrie. She was about to carry on smugly when she realised Sandra was having trouble with her card. 'Is there something wrong?'

'Sorry, Carrie, your card's not going through. Machine's refusing it.'

Sandra handed the Switch card back and Carrie stared at it, confused: there should be plenty of money in the current account, since Gina had just paid her delivery money, and even if all their direct debits went out at once, that still didn't go near their overdraft limit.

'That's weird,' she said. 'I can't think why it wouldn't. Is there a problem with the machine?'

'I don't think so. Mind, you can't trust computers, can you? I'll try it again,' said Sandra, rubbing the back of it on her apron, but Carrie could tell she was humouring her.

Carrie's cheeks began to warm up as the machine refused the transaction again. Embarrassment gave way under a tide of panic, as visions of credit-card fraud swept through her mind in a series of lurid documentary images. Had Mark left his card behind in a bar in London? Had they cloned it at a garage? People could run up huge debts in minutes using those things, and hadn't she read recently that banks weren't honouring them any more?

The hot flush turned cold on her skin. They really couldn't afford to lose that money, not while Mark was still freelance.

The machine squeaked ominously and Carrie stared unseeing at the display of breath fresheners on the counter.

How? How had it happened? It had to be something to do with Mark – she'd barely left the village in weeks, and never used her card on the Internet any more. He could be so careless. And he was the one going out in London, having a drink, hanging out in trendy bars where criminals lurked . . .

'Nope,' said Sandra. 'Not going through.'

'Oh, God. How annoying.' She swallowed. Her bagged-up groceries sat between them, and the embarrassment returned. 'Um. You don't take Visa yet, do you?'

'No.' Sandra looked curious. 'Not yet, sorry.'

'OK, OK. It's not a problem. Let me write you a cheque.' Carrie scrabbled in her bag for her chequebook. Behind her a couple she recognised from the pub were hovering discreetly, and she cringed. As if she didn't know this was how rumours swept round the village. 'I'm sure it's just a problem with the Switch machine. I *know* there's plenty of money in the account. I've just been paid.'

Sandra murmured something about paying her later, and Carrie tried to stop herself gabbling.

If the account was empty, then a cheque would bounce anyway, wouldn't it? And how humiliating would that be?

'Nuts,' she said, holding her head up. 'My chequebook's at home. Why don't you serve these people, and I'll pop back in two minutes with some cash instead?'

'You do that, love,' said Sandra and Carrie was horrified to hear the kindness in her voice.

Outside, the breeze cooled Carrie's cheeks as she hurried across the green, trying not to think about the conversation that would be breaking out behind her in the shop.

It just shows how you've let yourself get cocooned out here, she told herself sternly. With no bank in the village, she never bothered to check the balance of the joint account, and since her days revolved around painting, child minding and pottering around the house, she barely spent any money anyway, apart from paying the bills.

I'm turning into a Victorian housewife, she thought, complete with village shop humiliations. This has to stop right now.

It took eight long minutes to be connected to a human operator at her bank, and even then, nothing they said made sense to Carrie.

'You're saying our account is overdrawn by how much?' she asked, incredulously.

'Two thousand, seven hundred pounds and fifty-nine pence.'

'How?' She stopped and made her voice drop down to its normal pitch. 'No, that's impossible. Are you sure it isn't a computer error?'

'It's all here on the screen, madam. Do you want a mini-statement?'

'Yes, I do.' Carrie realised her hands were shaking. 'I think my card must have been cloned. Do I report it to the police? Should I cancel the cards?'

There was a long pause. 'Well, let me run through some recent transactions, Mrs Armstrong. There's a cash withdrawal of five hundred pounds yesterday from a cashpoint in Sloane Square, another five hundred the day before, and the last card purchase was . . . plane tickets with British Airways? Does that ring any bells?'

The blood drained from Carrie's face and she felt light-headed.

Elvis slinked in and leapt onto her lap and she stroked him absently. Sloane Square? Plane tickets? How dare someone steal a life she'd like to be having?

'Mrs Armstrong? Are you still there?'

'Yes,' she croaked. 'Yes, I am.'

I'm still here, she thought, wildly. I'm still here in this remote village, trapped, with no money, and I don't know where Mark is. I don't know where Mark is.

'Do you want me to cancel the cards and freeze the account?'

Carrie heard her voice say yes, and it sounded firmer than she thought possible. It sounded like her mother's.

She was trying Mark's phone again, walking around in small panicked circles, when she heard Lucy let herself in.

'Mark, it's me, I've been ringing you all morning! Call me the second you get this message,' she said to the answering machine, motioning Lucy to sit down.

'You look dreadful. What's happened?' asked Lucy, automatically putting the kettle onto the Aga.

'Someone's cleared out our bank account.' Carrie let out a shuddering breath and sank onto a spindle-backed chair.

'No!' Lucy put her hands on her hips. 'And that's why your card wasn't working in the shop?'

'How did you know that?' said Carrie, through her hands.

'Oh, I popped in there just now. That's why I came over, to see if everything was OK. Sandra was saying how awful it was, how banks were so . . . Carrie, are you crying?'

'Yes, yes I am!' Carrie wiped her eyes with a tea towel. 'I'm *mortified*! And I feel so *helpless*, stuck out here! At least in London you could go round to a bank and demand to see someone!'

'I can drive you into Devizes if it'd make you feel better?' offered Lucy. 'But I don't see how it would, really. What's done's done. Here, have a biscuit. You need some sugar inside you.'

'I just feel so *violated*,' moaned Carrie. 'Someone hacking into our account, taking money I've earned and spending it on, on *plane tickets*! And God knows what they did with the cash!'

'Have you called the police?'

'Not yet. The bank's checking out the withdrawals. I have to get a crime number. What? What are you looking like that for?'

'Nothing.'

'What?'

'Well.' Lucy poured the hot water into the teapot. 'Far be it for me to tell you what's going on, but . . . Before you start getting the police involved, are you absolutely sure it's been stolen?'

'What do you mean by that?'

'I mean, have you checked with Mark?'

Carrie almost laughed. 'What would Mark be doing, cleaning out the bank account? And we're not going on holiday any time soon, so it's not like he'd be buying plane tickets.' She paused. 'Well, he might be. We've . . . we've been getting on a lot better recently. He might have booked them as a surprise break. An anniversary treat or something.'

'But would he have cleaned out the money as well?' asked Lucy. 'Surely he'd have told you if he needed cash for something.' Then her face darkened. 'Or . . . well. Actually, forget that.'

'Forget what?' Carrie's relief evaporated.

'Oh, nothing.'

'Lucy, don't just say things like that and then stop.'

'Well, it's just that . . . You don't really know what he's been up to recently, do you? Being in London when he's not supposed to be. Not answering the phone. I mean, it might be that he's been planning some kind of surprise for you, taking you away on holiday. Or might he be taking . . . someone else?'

Carrie met Lucy's blue-eyed stare, expecting to encounter the feverish glitter of gossip, but saw genuine sympathy in her eyes. And for a second it rattled her, that these people felt sorry for *her*, for her city ways, and her absent husband, and her lack of children – all the things they probably gossiped about idly in the pub, using them as soap opera ciphers, without knowing the inside workings of her and Mark, what made them what they were. If they knew that, how could they possibly feel sorry for her?

Yet at the same time, she realised that Lucy had unerringly put her finger straight on the terrible doubt that had been worming its way from the back of her mind right to the front.

'No,' she said. 'No, I can't believe that. I mean, he was so lovely on our anniversary. We even talked about having a baby.'

We? But had they? Or had it just been her?

Carrie's mouth dried.

Lucy pushed the teapot towards her and didn't say anything.

At that moment, the telephone rang and she jumped.

'Well, answer it,' said Lucy. 'It's probably Mark.'

'Yes, it probably is,' said Carrie. She shoved her chair away from the table and walked as calmly as she could to the phone.

'Hello?' she said, coolly, in case it was the bank calling back.

'Hey,' said Mark. 'What's with all the missed calls? Is the house on fire?'

'Oh, Mark, I've been trying to get hold of you all morning,' said Carrie, relief flooding her body at the sound of his voice. 'I had to cancel the cards. I think someone's stolen them – they've cleared out our account. So don't try to pay for anything with Switch.'

'What? You froze the account?'

'Well, I had to! Someone's been siphoning off five hundred quid a day! And plane tickets!'

A police siren obscured Mark's response.

'You're in London, are you?' said Carrie, fighting back resentment.

'Yes, I'm meeting someone about, you know, borrowing some software. Look, Carrie, can't you speak to the bank again? We can't just freeze our accounts. I can transfer some money from my savings account this afternoon.'

'No, listen to me, Mark, I *had* to freeze the accounts!' She widened her eyes at his attitude. 'It's fraud! I'd just put my delivery payment in there! I've got to phone the police next, so they can . . .'

'Don't phone the police!'

'What? Are you *high*? I've got to get a crime number!'

She turned round and saw Lucy pouring two mugs of tea.

'Don't phone the police, Carrie,' said Mark.

'Why not, for God's sake?'

'I took the money out. It was me.'

She turned back to face their wedding photograph, hanging on the wall over the telephone table, so Lucy wouldn't see her face. 'You did *what*?'

'Calm down. There's a perfectly reasonable explanation.'

'Hit me with it.' Carrie tried to breathe deeply. Maybe the plane tickets *were* a surprise anniversary gift. It had been a while since Mark had been abroad. Maybe he had itchy feet.

Maybe he was bored.

Maybe . . .

She swallowed and pushed the painful doubts away.

There was a long pause, in which Carrie heard various London street noises, and realised she didn't feel nostalgic for the city at all. In fact, she hated it, and all the scary uncertainty round every corner.

'Oh, look. I can't explain now,' said Mark. 'I'm meeting someone in ten minutes. We'll discuss it when I get back.'

'No, Mark!' she nearly yelled. 'I want to know *now*! What's going on? Just tell me!'

'I can't talk to you when you're hysterical,' he snapped. 'We'll speak later.'

Carrie hung up before he could, her hands shaking. All her suppressed fears bubbled up to the surface, stinging her inside.

'So?' asked Lucy.

'Mark took the money out,' said Carrie, in a wobbling voice. 'And he didn't have a good explanation ready.'

'Oh,' said Lucy, and looked down at her cup.

Carrie had intended to spend the rest of the day working on the collages of material for the history tent, but she couldn't. Her mind refused to be distracted, and instead she found herself searching the house for Mark's box of photographs. She wanted to see this Astrid again. See what it was that she seemed to be competing against.

She told herself it was a fair enough exchange for his betrayal of her trust, but deep down, she knew it was more to do with tearing back the curtain of his past, to face her growing certainty that someone from that well-guarded place was coming back to spoil everything, and it would all be her fault, for turning a blind eye. Her instincts were so strong these days that she was more afraid to examine where they were coming from than she was of ignoring them.

Predictably, the box was nowhere to be found, and she sat on the bed staring at the wall for fifteen long minutes, while the ominous feeling inside her stomach expanded and contracted, as if it was struggling to get out.

Mark must have hidden it. Which meant that he didn't want her to see – and that he knew she would look.

Carrie looked up at the old beams crossing above her, and felt sick.

This had been her only fear about Mark, that she wouldn't be interesting enough for him, that whatever it was about her that had been so different would eventually wear off, and he'd look for it again in another woman's conversation, or smile, or bed. His feet would wander, as well as his eyes.

She fell back against the pillows, too devastated even to cry.

At seven, she heard the familiar rumble of Mark's car pulling up outside, and the butterflies in her stomach started rising as soon as the engine stopped and the door slammed.

She breathed deeply, as his steps crunched up the gravel path, and his key grated in the lock.

I'm going to be calm about this, she thought. It doesn't have to turn into a row. We can talk about this like adults.

Even so, she didn't get up from the kitchen table.

'Hi, Carrie,' called Mark from the hall.

Carrie looked around the kitchen, trying to imprint it all on her mind; how perfect everything looked before she opened the box that would tear everything to broken shreds.

'Carrie? You OK?'

She looked up, and saw her husband standing by the kitchen door, tall and handsome, and nervous-looking. He was holding a large bunch of flowers that had obviously come from a London florist's, and not a petrol station.

'Here,' he said. 'I bought you these.'

He handed her the bouquet and she stared at them disbelievingly. 'Well, now I know you really have done something wrong,' she said.

Mark's face fell. 'Don't be like that. I wanted to bring you some flowers. You deserve treats. What happened to our new start, eh?'

Carrie looked at the tightly budded roses, fashionably throttled with tropical grasses and raffia, and realised that she preferred the messy flowers from her own garden. They actually smelled of roses.

Her own garden. For how much longer?

'Mark,' she said quietly, 'why did you take all that money out of our account? In *cash?*'

The bank had called back and given her a list of all the withdrawals, and in her head she saw Mark's movements around London in the past ten days: Sloane Square, Liverpool Street, Waterloo, Broadwick Street. She'd only asked about withdrawals, not purchases made on the card. Her imagination had already filled in dinners for two, and fancy knickers, and hotels. She didn't want some faceless call-centre worker itemising her husband's infidelity to her.

'Hold on. Aren't you even going to let me get my coat off?' he asked, and she knew he was stalling for time. And that if it had been for something reasonable, he would have told her by now.

'OK,' she said calmly. 'I'm going to put these in a vase, and then

I want to know what's going on. I don't care how bad it is, you have to tell me.' She gave him a hard look. 'Didn't we promise not to have secrets?'

'Yeah. We did,' said Mark. He tried a smile, but it didn't work. 'Look, let me get changed first, eh? I need a shower.'

Carrie turned away from him and walked over to the sink, making her heavy feet move despite themselves. Mechanically, she stripped off the sodden tissue paper and snapped the ends of the stems as she listened to Mark jog up the stairs, then move around, his feet making the bare floorboards squeak.

What was he doing? Hiding the evidence? Checking his pockets for incriminating bus tickets or phone numbers?

I've been so stupid, she thought, staring blindly out of the window into the orchard. How can I be married to someone I don't know at all? How could we have lived together for three years, and me know so little about him?

Something moved in the garden next door, catching her eye.

Betsy was there, dancing around in her red dress, swirling like a poppy, deep in her own world. She looked as if she was practising for the maypole.

Upstairs the boiler clanked, which meant Mark was running the shower.

He's washing off the smell of her, thought Carrie, her hands moving the stems around in the vase. He's washing away the smell of London. Her feet itched to run upstairs and slap him in a frenzy of rage, hands blurring furiously through the air like Betsy's had, but the dead weight in her legs kept her anchored.

The clanking stopped, and it annoyed her that he'd be wrapping himself in towels that she'd hung out on the line to dry, when he didn't care how much fresher the laundry smelled now it wasn't being rinsed with London water. He'd never wanted to be here, and now he was going to take it all away from her too.

Stop it, she thought. Stop it.

The flowers were all arranged, and she lifted the vase and carried it over to the table. Then she sat down and waited for Mark's feet to come padding down the stairs.

He took three minutes, according to the farmhouse clock above the door. For once, it was showing the right time.

'Right,' he said, rubbing his still-damp hair. 'Let's talk about this, shall we?'

Carrie simply nodded. He looked so boyish still, with his glasses on. She could feel the fragile balance of her marriage in her hands and wanted so much to protect it. But she knew she had to ask the questions, and she felt sick.

'OK, first of all, don't worry about the money,' said Mark, sitting down at the table and spreading his hands. 'I was going to transfer every penny from my savings account, but I guess the bank didn't do it as quickly as they said they would.'

Carrie stared at him. 'That's not the point. Why did you take the money in the first place? What do you need it for? And why didn't we talk about it first?'

'Well, it *is* the point, really. I didn't mean there to be a problem about cash flow.'

'No, you mean you didn't want me to find *out* about whatever it was you needed the money for!'

'Well, no, actually, I didn't!' snapped Mark. 'But, more importantly, I didn't want you to be worried!'

'But you didn't mind risking me being humiliated in the shop? When my card was refused? Or what if the phone had been cut off because the cheque bounced? Or what if . . .'

'Carrie, did any of those things happen? Apart from the shop,' he added, hastily. 'But that would look like a bank error. I'll make sure they think that, anyway.'

Carrie's mind skimmed over the ludicrous idea of Mark trying to charm Sandra, a woman he'd barely bothered to speak to since they'd moved in, and realised he'd almost succeeded in throwing her off the point. 'Oh, for God's sake, Mark,' she spluttered, 'don't you ever think about the consequences of things *before* they happen?'

'You sound like someone's mother when you say that.'

'You make me *feel* like your mother sometimes!' The tension rose from her stomach into a tight knot, high up in her chest. 'You're the one running round London having a good time, while I'm here, trying to make this our home, *and* working! I don't know where you are, I don't know what you're doing half the time . . .'

'Carrie . . .' said Mark, warningly.

But the tension that had been building in her for the past weeks had finally found somewhere to go, and it surged out of her like a burst pipe. Anger made her words sharp and they echoed through the quiet house, bouncing off the beams.

'What am I meant to think? Can you imagine how I felt, thinking someone had stolen all our money and not even able to leave the house? I was going mad! I didn't know what else of ours they had, whether they were stealing our identity and doing God knows what!'

'Well, if you could *drive*, you could have gone into Salisbury and had this little scene with the bank manager. Oh, but you can't, can you? You've never bothered to learn.'

Carrie's jaw dropped. 'What?'

'You're very passive-aggressive, Carrie,' said Mark. 'I mean, it's all very well getting jealous because I'm going back to London and working from there, but isn't this what you wanted? The cottage with the roses round the door? Is it my fault you can't get in the car and get away from it? I thought you *wanted* to stay here for ever, dressing up in old clothes, and investigating my family, and snooping around the church like some old biddy with the rest of them.'

'Mark! That's not fair,' she gasped, 'and it's absolutely not true. You've never shown any interest in living here. You haven't even *tried*.'

'Oh, come on! What is there to try? Morris dancing? The neighbourhood watch?' He rolled his eyes. 'Carrie, it's turning into some kind of living history museum! That's why so many old people have come here to die. I had no idea it was going to be like this. Or that you'd want to get so into it.'

Carrie clenched her fists until her nails dug into the soft skin of her palm. 'It's not boring! It's *fascinating*! Do you really not have *any* interest in all the stories? Where all the people went? Real people, like us? The chalk horse – you were so interested in that when we first came here,' she finished plaintively. 'Weren't you?'

'It's all just stuff, Carrie,' said Mark, tersely. 'It's all dead. Get over it.'

'Are you saying you regret coming here?' she demanded. 'Because let's get all this out in the open!'

Mark opened his mouth, then stopped, and closed it again. When he spoke, his voice was softer. 'No. I don't regret coming here, but I didn't expect it to be like this. I mean, we didn't come here to be in some historical reconstruction! We came here to . . . to start some kind of life *together*.'

'Mark, if that's true,' said Carrie tightly, 'then why are you spending so much time in London?'

'Because at least there I know I've got some sort of purpose, and I'm not just playing a part in your fantasy Midsomer Murders world!'

They glared at each other, temporarily winded by the other's unfamiliar anger.

He's jealous, thought Carrie. He's jealous. But of what? The time I spend with the village? Or the fact that I might be making friends?

'Mark, I understand why you're not interested in all the gossip and cliques, but there's more to it than that,' she tried. 'This village has so many stories buried in it. And they're not just facts in books. They're people.'

Mark twisted his mouth up in frustration. 'Carrie, you might enjoy getting involved in digging up the past in this village, but have you ever stopped to think that maybe I don't want to?' he demanded. 'Don't you think I might have enough to deal with, coping with the fact that it's my family you're digging up and I don't know them any more than you do? And I *can't*. I *can't* get to know them now.'

Carrie froze, as if he'd slapped her. 'Mark, I didn't mean to . . .'

'I wanted this to be a fresh start,' he said, his hands stressing the words. 'I wanted this to be about just you and me. Nothing from the past to spoil things. And instead . . . Instead, it's all just a massive headfuck.'

Carrie looked at him closely. Surely this couldn't just be about the village? He looked as if he was about to burst his veins with the stress of holding in whatever was fighting to come out next. She swallowed and made her mouth form the words, even though she wasn't sure she was ready to hear what he might say. 'Honey, whatever it is, just tell me. You can tell me anything. It's what we promised when we got—'

'No! Just leave it, will you?'

He made to storm out, but Carrie grabbed his arm. 'It's this Astrid, isn't it? You're seeing her, aren't you? In London. That's why you've been going back. Don't deny it. I *heard* you! I heard you talking to her!'

'I don't want to discuss this any more,' he said icily. 'You don't know what you're talking about.'

Then Carrie knew he was, and she wanted to be sick.

'No, Mark, don't walk away from me! You've got to tell me what's going on. Right now.'

'I don't *have* to do anything.' He wheeled round and glared at her. 'You have no idea how much I have to deal with right now.'

'Oh, don't be such a *brat*!' said Carrie. 'That makes you sound so childish and immature.' *Why are you being so weird?* she wanted to yell. 'Do you really believe I don't understand about your family? Do you?'

'That's what it feels like.'

'Then you obviously don't know me very well.'

He stared at her and the silence swelled up between them.

'And you don't know me at all,' he said, after what seemed to Carrie like an hour.

There was an agonising moment, in which one of them could have spoken, said anything, to stop the awful drifting sensation, but the only sound in the old house was the ticking of the hall clock, and Carrie's mental eye saw it sweep away the chances to bring the situation back.

But I want to know you, she thought, I've been trying to know everything about you, even the things you don't tell yourself, but some lump in her throat, some fear of saying the wrong thing, stopped her speaking.

'OK, that's it. I don't have to stay here and listen to this.' Mark swept his jacket off the chair where he'd dropped it and started looking for his keys.

'That's right. Just run away if you don't want to answer any tough questions,' said Carrie. 'Like you always do, eh? Off you go. Move on.'

'You have no idea the stress I'm under,' snarled Mark.

'The sort of stress that makes you buy plane tickets? What did you do with the cash, Mark? Where did that go? On a hotel room? Up your nose? *What is it that you aren't telling me?*'

He flinched at the harshness of her words.

'Are you going to leave me for her?' she demanded, finally giving way to her darkest, cruellest thought, letting her panic bubble out of her like black tar. 'Is that it? Are you setting up, ready to go? Did you come back to get your bags?'

As the words left her mouth and became real, Carrie could feel the rage inside her dissolve into terrible, acidic fear. Now she'd asked, he'd have to reply.

Mark looked as if he were about to say something, then stopped himself with a superhuman effort and turned to leave.

'Where are you going?' Carrie asked, wishing immediately she'd said, 'Don't go!'

'I'm going somewhere I can think,' he said, in a voice that almost broke, then before Carrie could respond, the front door slammed and he'd gone.

She sank onto the nearest chair. At least he hasn't taken any bags, she told herself, trying to be brave. But it sounded hollow in her ears.

Chapter Twenty-four

Carrie waited up on the sofa all night for Mark to return, picking mindlessly at the tassles on the cushions as the clouds shifted across the sky and the night darkened, then began to pale into dawn. She was too angry and too miserable to sleep, and she couldn't bring herself to lie there in their double bed – the idyllic iron-framed fantasy bed. She barely noticed the clock stop at ten past four as she worked over the few words he'd thrown her, trying to imagine what she could have said differently to stop the door slamming.

That wasn't the only reason she couldn't face the bedroom. Though Carrie refused to admit it to herself, at the back of her mind she knew she didn't want to go to sleep and have the chalk-horse nightmare again, not when she was alone in the house, with no Mark to hold her if the leaves and the forest started to creep through the paler security of her dreams again with their invasive dark green shoots. The house had got rid of Mark, and was only waiting for her.

The stopped clock didn't strike the hours, and time blurred. As the adrenalin slowly cooled to thick dread in her bloodstream, Carrie began to feel trapped, as though something was draining her of energy. The framed photographs of Lily leaped out at her now she was in the silent room on her own, and she could feel a sense of disapproval almost radiating out from the house itself. She and Mark had let this place down. After all their efforts to bring it back to life, too. But in the end they were two selfish, modern individuals with no idea how to steer their marriage when it hit choppy water, living in a traditional family home, using the nursery as a spare room and storming away from each other at the first sign of trouble.

But then again, she thought, flicking cushion fluff onto the floor, was Lily's own marriage any better, just because they stuck it out? At least she and Mark had some smiling photographic evidence that their marriage had been happy once. How many rows were embedded in the mortar and beams of this house already? What echoes of Lily's own relationship, lingering in the nooks and crannies of the house as well as running through Mark's blood? In many ways, Lily and Jack were still here with her. Even though she lived in her house and slept with the living product of their marriage, she'd never know the real secrets of Lily's life. A silent and secretive family had made sure those secrets had stayed safely contained.

Outside, something screeched, sending Carrie's nerves into a jangling mess, then screeched again, much nearer the window, and her hand shot out to the remote control, to turn on the television and reconnect herself to a world of reassuring plastic celebrity.

Then, with a deep breath, she turned it off. I've made a commitment to this life, she thought, and I should stick with it.

Carrie sat back on the sofa and let the silence of the house fall back again like a blanket, while her ears turned subconsciously to the clicks and shifts of the old wood as the temperature dropped during the night.

Am I the only person awake in the village now, she wondered? If I climbed up on the hill, up to the chalk horse, would there be any other lights on in St Dee? Is anyone else sleepless, or are they all tucked up in their new old-fashioned beds, dreaming about cakes and jams and brass bands?

She wondered if Philip was awake next door, working on his book. Drawing all the spooky myths and faceless monks, and green forest men into his study like a pied piper, then disabling their darkness and pinning them down with logic. He would understand about her dreams. He'd probably even have an explanation for them.

For a wild moment, Carrie considered going round there, certain he could slot her fears into some reassuringly logical place, but as the shadows of the dream memory slid around the edges of her consciousness again, Philip's face hovering a breath above hers, she found herself blushing with half-remembered shame, and knew she couldn't bring herself to tell him exactly what she thought had happened.

There was something about Philip that didn't bear thinking about too closely.

Where has Mark gone? she wondered, deliberately twisting the knife in her own side. The realisation that she had no idea where he'd gone, and knew no one to call, made her feel panicky. Had he gone to her? Was he sleeping by the side of the road in his car – or was he in her bed? Carrie tried to make herself angry, but she only felt acid jealousy eating away her heart, and a dull, aching fear that he wouldn't ever come back.

Though she wrapped herself in one of the throws on the sofa, sleep didn't come, and she watched the sky lighten gradually as the night turned into early morning, and the birds started to wake and chirp. Panic slowly curdled into a strange sleepwalking calmness. There are things I have to do today, thought Carrie, and she was comforted by the idea of a routine.

May Day. I was meant to get up at dawn to wash my face in dew. I'll never be the May Queen now. She pulled on her thick cardigan and went out into the garden.

The sky over the valley was clear and blue, and there was an unseasonable warmth in the air already. Carrie drew in a deep lungful of clean, grassy air and felt something lift around her heart. She closed her eyes and carried on breathing in, imagining the light filling her up from the inside. She held her breath for as long as she could, then let the air rush out of her, trying to imagine all her pain rushing out with it.

But when she breathed again, the heaviness returned, and she closed her eyes again, this time against the thud of pain.

No, she thought, refusing to let it. There's nothing here that can't be fixed. Nothing.

There was a little dew on the leaves of the first roses, but not enough to wash even Betsy's face. Carrie stroked the rasping leaves of a climbing rose and remembered how happy she and Mark had been, planting and teasing each other. He can't hate this place so much when we have some good memories already, she thought. Carrie ran her fingertips across the leaves, feeling the coldness of the water, then slowly touched her face with her wet fingers, stroking her nose, her eye sockets, her cheekbones with the dew. It felt as though she was anointing herself with tradition, taking some kind of protection from the land. Committing herself to it.

Goose pimples sprang up along her arms, and she couldn't tell if they came from the cool breeze that blew her fringe into her eyes, or from some sudden coolness inside herself.

The back door to the Gladstones' kitchen was open, and Carrie could see movement. Philip, in a dark blue shirt, rolled up at the sleeves to expose his hairy forearms, seemed to be making himself some breakfast while the kittens ran round and round on the step. He was moving quite quietly, and the radio wasn't on, indicating that he might be the only one up so far.

Should I go and invite myself in? she wondered. I shouldn't. I probably look a wreck.

And why should that matter? Women whose husbands have left them generally do.

Then it struck her that Mark really had walked out, and she couldn't even phone his mother to see if he'd run home, so she had no way of finding him till he decided he wanted to be found, and her knees almost buckled underneath her again.

Oh God, she thought, looking back in desperation at the ivy-coloured walls of her lovely country cottage, how am I going to get through today?

Carrie rubbed her sore eyes and gazed at Philip's kitchen with longing, torn between needing some company and wanting to stay huddled on the sofa at home, so the unreal half-dream of the night wouldn't have to solidify into reality.

Philip solved the problem for her by spotting her through the kitchen window. Carrie's pulse quickened as a broad smile broke out from beneath his beard, showing his strong white teeth, and she knew she'd have to tell him what had happened. There was no point trying to cover it up; he drew private thoughts out of her like a magnet.

She raised a hand in greeting, and for a moment, resisted the lure of his warm kitchen. But it was useless. Her feet started moving before she could tell herself not to.

At the window, Philip put a finger to his lips, pointed upstairs in explanation, and beckoned her in, but as she got closer, walking self-consciously through the wet grass in her wellies, his expression changed to one of concern and the bushy eyebrows creased together.

'Good God, you looked like a ghost out there. I was going to say you were up early, but are you not very late to bed instead?' he asked, too surprised by her dishevelled appearance to drop his voice.

'Both,' said Carrie. 'I mean, I don't know any more.' She put her palm up to her mouth as the lack of sleep finally caught up with her, making her voice wobble dangerously.

'Come on in.' Philip swept her into the kitchen, and pulled out a chair. Neither of the children was about and the table was strewn with papers and notes, and dirty plates. He pushed everything aside and put his own mug of tea down in front of her. 'Get some hot tea inside you. You look shattered. What's the matter?'

Carrie said nothing. She couldn't. The tears were too close to the back of her eyes.

'But, ah, you don't have to tell me if you don't want,' said Philip quickly. 'I can just make you some toast instead?'

'That would be nice.' Carrie put her elbows on the table, cradled her head in her hands, and steeled herself. She had to tell someone.

'Mark's walked out on me,' she said, and waited for the rush of misery to engulf her.

The clock ticked in the silence. The misery didn't come. She sat up. The world still didn't fall in.

Philip didn't say anything, but pushed the sugar bowl nearer her mug. Carrie spooned in two teaspoons and stirred hard, making a whirlpool of strong tea.

'He's been taking money out of our bank account, seeing some woman, some ex. Her name's Astrid, she's unbelievably gorgeous. He's bought airline tickets.' She watched as the cats ran in from the garden, the fur on their legs spiked into fringes by the wet grass. 'Maybe that's where he is now,' she added, her voice tightening. 'Heathrow.'

'You don't know where he's gone? You've phoned his family? Oh, you can't really, can you? Sorry.'

Carrie shook her head. Maybe it was Philip's practical response that was making her so steadfast.

'Friends?'

She shook her head again. 'He doesn't really have a best friend.' Her mouth twisted mirthlessly. '*Me*, I thought.'

'Did he take a bag with him?'

She shook her head again.

'Then he'll be back,' said Philip confidently.

'I don't think so,' said Carrie. 'He seemed pretty desperate to leave.'

'I think he'll be back by lunchtime.' Philip gave her a dark look. 'There's a world of difference to men like Mark between running away and leaving someone.'

Carrie stared at her tea. But then Giselle had just walked out too. No bag. Nothing. And she'd never come back.

'So, start at the beginning. How long has this been going on?'

Carrie took a deep breath. 'I've had some suspicions for a while, to be honest.' Honest with whom? Philip? Or herself? 'For a few weeks, at least. He's been sneaking off to London when he said he was working round here, and he started paying bills so I wouldn't see the phone calls on his mobile, and . . . little things.' She didn't mention her 'instincts', the whispers of intuition around the edges of her consciousness that had sprung up like wild hops in the hedges round the house. That would make her sound paranoid. Yet they'd been the strongest clue of all, and they'd been right.

'And?'

'And he's . . . he's been in touch with some girl he used to go out with. Making phone calls outside the house.' She shivered. 'I've been stupid. I hoped it was my imagination making things up.'

'But you tackled him about it?'

She nodded. 'Last night. My card was refused at the shop so I called the bank and we were overdrawn. He'd been taking the money out, so I . . . I needed to know.'

'And did he admit it? That there was something going on?'

Carrie twisted her mouth. 'Sort of. He said it wasn't what it looked like. So I knew there was someone else then.'

'Have I got this straight – you accused Mark of cheating on you and stealing your money, he confessed all, and yet *he* was the one who stormed out in a rage?' Philip looked incredulous. 'Carrie, what is going on in your head? *You* should have kicked *him* out!'

'Well, part of it *was* my fault,' conceded Carrie. 'He hates the way I'm letting the village take over my whole life, and maybe it is a bit tactless of me, getting so into what's really his family. I mean, he didn't even know his father had a twin brother who died here, for one thing, and—'

'Do you mind me speaking plainly?' Philip interrupted.

'No,' sighed Carrie, 'go on.'

'Mark wants to bloody well grow up. I don't know what this is really about, but he's acting like a spoiled kid. If he wants to storm off, let him. Get the locks changed today.' He made a dismissive gesture with his hand. 'I'll do it. Christ, I'll get Chris Ross round to do it. I don't know why you put up with this nonsense.'

Carrie stared at him. There was real annoyance in his dark eyes, even though he was making an effort to control it. Her loyalty racketed back and forth like a pinball; instinctively, she wanted to defend Mark against these people who barely knew him, but at the same time she was angry. Angry because it was Mark's own fault they didn't know what he was really like. And she wasn't even sure *she* knew any more.

'He's not . . . He's not like that,' she stuttered.

'Isn't he? He should think himself bloody lucky to have a wife like you.' Philip lifted his shoulders. 'And as for the village taking over . . . God almighty! I'm sorry to tell you this, but he's pissed off a lot of folk round here, with his smart-arse comments, not wanting to get involved, telling Tony what he 'should' have in his cellar. They might not say so to his face, but he's got no fans in the village. And I'm not just saying that because he ran over my cat. Although that didn't help, I can tell you. Selfish little . . . Sorry. I'm sorry, Carrie.'

'Is that what they say? Are we really unpopular?' Suddenly, the tears rushed back up Carrie's throat and flooded the corners of her eyes, as she felt her whole world tremble beneath her feet. So the people, the friendships she'd made, were as fake as the restored telephone box, looking solid but really as flimsy as the worst London filmset? 'So does everyone think we're just townies?'

Philip shot his hand across the table and covered hers. 'Not you, Carrie. Not you.'

She looked down at the dark hairs covering the back of his broad hand, and felt the warmth of his fingers gripping hers.

'Everyone thinks very highly of you. Even Barbara Purves.'

'Not much good if they all hate Mark, though, is it?'

She raised her eyes and was startled to meet Philip's fierce gaze boring into her face. 'Is it?' she added weakly, to put some words between them, into the charged silence building over the table. Her heart beat faster, high up in her chest, and she realised her throat was very dry.

He spoke quietly, but with force. 'I can't say I really know Mark, but I don't think you'd fall apart without him. If he wants to run off, let the bugger go.'

'Let the bugger go where?'

They sprang apart as if an electric shock had shot through their fingers.

Betsy was standing by the table in her long white May Queen dress, her arms folded and her head tipped to one side in enquiry. If she hadn't looked so nosy, thought Carrie, she'd have been a dead ringer for one of the oil-painted angel children lining the stairs.

'How many times have I told you not to eavesdrop?' roared Philip.

'I wasn't eavesdropping,' Betsy protested. 'You just didn't see me. Why is Carrie here? It's too early.'

'That's rich, given the hours you and Ivor turn up at my house,' said Carrie, as flippantly as she could manage.

'And where has Mark gone?' demanded Betsy.

'Mark?' Carrie tried to look confused.

'Mark,' said Betsy. 'I saw his car drive away last night. I wasn't spying,' she added, with a defensive look towards her father. 'I couldn't sleep and Gillian told me to look out of the window.'

Philip sighed and held out his arms so Betsy could climb onto his knee. 'I thought we had a talk, Betsy. Didn't we say that Gillian was just in a dream? Like Hazel.'

Betsy climbed up, but scowled. '*You* said that. But *you* don't have them in your room at night, do you?' She turned back to Carrie. 'Is he the bugger?'

'Betsy!'

'I like your dress,' said Carrie, in an effort to distract her. 'But won't you get it dirty if you put it on so soon? The May Queen parade isn't until later.'

Betsy sighed elaborately. 'It doesn't matter. I'm not going to be the May Queen anyway. I won't be chosen.'

'Oh, you don't know that.'

'I do, though.' She looked hard at Carrie, with her father's piercing expression. Carrie blinked, unsettled by the sharply focused, grown-up eyes gazing out of the soft baby face. 'You're going to win it,' she said. 'Gillian told me. You're going to be the May Queen, Carrie.'

'Right, that's enough,' said Philip, lifting her off his knee. 'Enough of that. If your imaginary friends are going to give you tips, then I'd like you to ask them for racing tips for your daddy, OK?'

'But . . .'

'But nothing. Have you had a bath this morning?'

She shook her head sullenly, and on cue, a high-pitched squeal announced that Ivor had woken up.

'Well, we can't have a smelly May Queen, can we?'

'No,' Carrie agreed. 'Did you wash your face in the dew this morning?'

Betsy shook her head.

'Well, then. I did. So I'm bound to win.'

'No, you're bound to win because Gillian . . .'

'Betsy, that is now more than enough. Go on, upstairs.' Philip looked at Carrie apologetically. 'Take no notice.'

'Who's this Gillian?' she asked curiously when Betsy was out of earshot.

'Another of her imaginary friends.' Philip raised his hands. 'I know. I was hoping she'd grow out of them but they seem to be multiplying.'

'She told me about Hazel being in her room, telling her things,' said Carrie slowly. 'She doesn't sound very nice. Do you think maybe it's time to talk to someone about it?'

'A psychologist?' asked Philip. 'Or . . . a parapsychologist? Would you . . .' He hesitated. 'Would you talk to her? She's much more open with you.'

'I'll try,' said Carrie. Despite her heavy mood, she managed a small smile. 'She's a lovely little girl.'

'I know,' said Philip ruefully. 'We'll see you later, will we? What time does your tent open?'

'I've to be there at half ten, in full costume, as supplied by Barbara.' Carrie looked at her watch. 'Though I don't think they usually choose May Queens dressed up as schoolteachers.'

'Well, good luck,' said Philip, adding, with a twitch of his eyebrows, 'although apparently you don't need it.'

'We'll see,' said Carrie. She got up, surprised at how calm she was feeling now. But it was more like standing in the eye of a storm whirling just out of reach, than real peacefulness.

'Look, if Mark comes back and you want me to . . .' Philip ran out of words, but Carrie knew what he was saying.

'Thanks,' she said. 'I'll be fine.'

Philip said nothing, but smiled back sadly. His white teeth gleamed in the dark curls of his beard, but there was no twinkle in his brown badger's eyes.

Chapter Twenty-five

Carrie let herself back into her silent house. She showered, washed her hair, then put on the long floral-sprigged Laura Ashley dress and apron Barbara had unearthed from someone's mother's wardrobe, all the time trying not to listen out for the phone or the front door.

Let him come back in his own time, she thought, dividing her hair into plaits in front of her oval dressing-table mirror. I'm going to enjoy today, at least. I'm going to see St Dee through Lily's eyes, just the way she did before she left it. It'll be easier without Mark here to spoil it.

She stopped, halfway through pinning up one side of her hair. What a weird thing to think. And yet the idea of seeing the village slip back in time made the butterflies rise in her stomach, because maybe, somehow, it would tell her what had happened to turn Lily from that smiling May Queen into the crushed shell in the pictures. What had happened to her other baby maybe, or why she'd married stolid Jack.

Carrie stood up to get the full effect of her costume in the long cheval mirror opposite the brass bed.

It was eerie. Eerie to look at herself and see herself slid back in time, along with the rest of the room reflected in the mirror behind her – the authentically handmade brass bed, the antique dressing table, the garden flowers in a jug on the chest. The tea dress flattered the long curves that were usually hidden in jeans, and with her hair up and her feet bare, she looked years younger. But older at the same time, as if the girl reflected in the old mirror could easily have lurked in the background of one of the faded village photographs, carrying a basket of eggs and kowtowing to Mrs Maxwell.

Carrie stared at herself. A ripple of apprehension ran over her skin in case something, someone, appeared behind her in the mirror.

Wasn't that another May Day thing? Looking in mirrors at midnight to see your true love's face reflected next to yours?

She held her own gaze purposefully, but the corners of her eye skated around the thick wooden beams, the gauzy curtains now being lifted by a faint breeze, the untouched white cloud of her bed behind her . . .

Carrie's ears twitched. It was the child crying again, but faint, very faint, just on the furthest edge of her hearing. A high-pitched note of distress, the frustrated bleat of a baby who wouldn't sleep, grating on her nerves. She gripped the bed rail, her body freezing. In the light of day, the shrill keening was even more horrific, but more than fear, she was swept with a terrible angry frustration.

'Stop it!' Carrie heard her own voice yell. 'Just stop it!'

The sound stopped.

She took a shuddering breath, then bolted from the room, almost falling over herself to get downstairs.

In the kitchen, Carrie turned on the radio, and drank a scalding cup of tea until her pulse returned to normal. She checked over her bag of stuff to take to the tent, fixing her attention on the routine: the cakes in tins for the judging, her sun cream, lip gloss, mobile phone, keys.

Mobile phone. Lip gloss. Sun cream. Modern things.

What else, she thought, wandering through to the sitting room, pushing back thoughts of where Mark might be, what he might have to say when he came back. What have I forgotten? Her eye fell on the photograph of Lily on the mantelpiece, blooming like a cherry tree in her May Queen regalia.

She picked it up. Did I move this down here? she wondered. I really am going mad.

Superstitiously, Carrie didn't look too closely at Lily's eyes, but focused instead on what she was wearing: a loose white dress, and a foamy diadem of cherry blossom over her thick blonde plaits.

I should really have some flowers for my hair, she thought.

She put her cup down on a bookshelf and walked out to the back garden, picking up her secateurs from the dresser as she went. The sun had come out, making the few lingering dew drops glint like diamonds on the leaves. There wasn't a huge amount of choice, but she clipped some small rosebuds to tuck into her pinned-up hair, and twisted some supple laurel branches into a sort of crown, threading some daisies in between.

She peered over the bushes into Philip's garden to see if he had anything worth appropriating, and was surprised to see that someone had already been at the wilderness with bigger secateurs than hers. Most of the bigger branches had been lopped. And then she spotted something else that turned her stomach over: standing in a thick border of tall grass, on the other side of the garden, was a little girl who definitely wasn't Betsy – blonde, slight, pensive, wearing a pretty cream dress that caught the weak morning sunshine. She seemed both substantial and yet transparent, silent, looking at nothing in particular, as if she was waiting for someone. Waiting for Betsy to come and play?

Carrie's skin crawled. Was this Hazel? Was she the little girl who fell down the well?

What if all the houses gave up their old residents on this seance-like recreation of their May Day celebration, letting them fade–up into vision on the village green, passing amongst the curious visitors and dressed-up locals? She stumbled a little on the grass. When she looked up again, the girl had gone and Philip's wild garden was empty.

Don't be ridiculous, she told herself. 'Hello?' she called out. 'Hello? Are you lost?'

But there was no answer.

Carrie rubbed her face. Was this spooky village starting to get to her? Had she reached so far into the past lives of the houses, with her blind yearning to know their secrets, that she was actually stepping back into them?

The silence around her was broken only by birdsong and the distant rumble of cars arriving.

Too jittery now to hang around, Carrie ran in, collected her bag and left for the fete.

Chris Ross's men had already set up the various tents around the village green, along with some old-fashioned tannoys, which were playing test fragments of old brass-band music through authentically crackling speakers. The maypole was glossy white, and long red, blue and yellow ribbons hung from the top, looped and tied halfway down, ready to be plaited. Clear morning sunshine intensified the bright green of the grass and the cloudless periwinkle blue of the sky, until the paintbox colours seemed to vibrate with energy.

Suddenly feeling dizzy, Carrie paused and put a hand on a nearby seat. Breathe deeply, she told herself, it's just lack of sleep. And stress. And no supper.

She blinked, to see if the mad colours were just her imagination. They weren't. Even the hanging baskets outside the pub were jumping with feverish brightness, red busy Lizzies fighting with pink fuschias and streaky variegated ivy. It was as if the whole village was determined to be as ultra-life-like as possible, and in doing so it looked more like a film set than ever, an effect enhanced by the first few early tourists peering into houses like awkward extras.

Carrie's eye ran along the line of cars parked round the edge of the green, but there was no sign of Mark's. Already there were twice as many cars as usual, and a few people starting to set up chairs and picnic baskets behind the roped-off areas. A curious defensiveness spread through her, at the thought of their little village being invaded by rubberneckers, strange cars parked around their green, day trippers taking photographs of their homes and speculating about their ghosts.

She tried to get up, but her legs wobbled and deposited her back down on the bench with a thump.

Fine, she thought. I'll just sit here for a moment.

The 'fete personnel only' area of the green was already bustling with women setting out bunting-draped stalls; Carrie counted a bottle stall, a cake stall, two long trestle tables full of spindly plants in small pots (how smug was that? she marvelled; 'my garden is so abundant that I can sell off the excess'), a book stall, and a couple yet to be piled high with wares. In between were a raffle, an old 'Hit the Ferret' game, and a tent in which Anne Barker would be telling fortunes with playing cards.

Carrie wondered if Paul Jenkins had helped them to make it all look so authentically pre-war. The fabric bunting, and old-fashioned streamers, and everyone in hats and long skirts – the shades of previous May Days could walk undetected here, like the cows in the background of her books.

Maybe there's a shade of me, she thought, walking around, in a version of my life where Mark hasn't left, and everything is going right, and I have a baby, and . . .

Suppressing a shudder, Carrie filled her lungs with clean air and held it in for as long as she could.

I have to get on with today, she thought, and slowly stood up. The ground felt firm beneath her feet, and she turned and walked towards the tent with 'The St Dee Story' tacked above its open door.

Inside, the tent smelled of flattened grass and damp earth – a green, secretive smell that triggered flickers of recognition from her nightmares. Carrie stared fully at the old posters of houses she only knew in their new reconditioned state. Funny, that she should be in here explaining the village to outsiders while her connection to the village was driving away from both her and St Dee, even now.

If I were superstitious, she thought, toying with an old milk bottle from the village dairy ('very small but fully functional until 1941'), I would think Lily was trying to make me as miserable as she ended up. Reaching out from the cracks in the floorboards to make me feel her misery. But subtly, like arsenic in the wallpaper.

'Carrie? Are you OK?' asked Lucy. She was dressed as a farmer's daughter in a checked shirt and long apron, but with more honey-tanned cleavage on show than Barbara Purves had deemed suitable when she'd dropped in with her clipboard to check up on them. Five cake tins underneath the table proved that either Lucy was taking the baking very seriously, or she'd sensibly decanted any shop-bought cakes into battered tins.

'Carrie,' she said again. 'I said, are you OK?'

'What? Oh, yeah. I'm fine,' replied Carrie automatically. She didn't feel that fine. She wondered if she had a temperature. She certainly felt flushed.

If I can just get through today, she repeated to herself, it'll work out. If I don't make a big deal of it, he'll come back. As long as only Philip knows, when he comes back everyone can carry on as normal. Not hate him any more than they do already.

'You look really peaky.' Lucy peered more closely at her. 'What's happened? Is it Mark? Did you get that business about the money sorted out?'

'Um, yeah.' Lucy knew. It was naïve to think she wouldn't put two and two together. 'I haven't slept much.'

'That's not what I asked. You had any breakfast?'

She shook her head. 'Don't feel like it.'

Lucy dropped her voice to a discreet but very obvious whisper. 'You can tell me. You're pregnant, aren't you?'

Carrie stared at her. 'What? No!'

'You've got that look.' Lucy nodded. 'Don't ask me how I know. It's a country thing.'

Carrie's throat tightened. No. That would be too mean. That would be the final, meanest blow.

'I'm not,' she managed. 'I'm just . . . Got hay fever. Makes my eyes water.'

Lucy looked as if she didn't believe her for a moment. 'You could try taking those flowers out of your hair, in that case.'

'Well, the grass in here isn't helping.'

Lucy gave her a 'don't give me that' look. 'So, Mark?' Lucy persisted, unable to contain herself. 'Did he have a good explanation? Where's he got to this morning? I know Chris could do with some help on the heavy lifting.'

Carrie fanned out the photocopied leaflets about the history of St Dee. 'Can we talk about that later, please?'

'I'm only trying to help,' said Lucy, looking hurt.

Carrie bit her lip. 'I know.'

'Hello? Hello?'

They both looked up sharply as Kathleen Maxwell's familiar regal shape peered in the door of the tent.

'Oh, look, it's Lady Muck,' said Lucy, in an undertone. 'How nice of her to drop in.'

Carrie nudged her under the table. 'Don't be mean.'

'Are you open yet, ladies?'

'Of course, come on in,' said Carrie, nudging Lucy under the table.

'I couldn't resist,' said Kathleen, beaming from underneath her large straw hat. She was also dressed up, in a neat pea-green pre-war suit and white cotton gloves. Carrie noted that it didn't look like a costume on her, and suddenly felt awkward in her borrowed frock. 'I rather wanted to have a peek before all the ravening hordes appeared, what with there being so many of my own bits and pieces in here.' She made a vague gesture to her photographs, which took pride of place under the grand heading 'Village Social

Life'. Barbara had been very specific about that, according to a scornful Lucy.

'What do you think?' asked Carrie. 'Bring back memories?'

'You've really made a wonderful display. Quite brought the old village to life.' Her gaze drifted round their posters, then she sighed with nostalgic pleasure when her eye fell on Carrie's milk bottle. 'Oh, I remember those! The dairy used to deliver milk to the manor in our own special churns.'

'Naturally,' said Lucy.

'Your grandmother would have popped down there for the vicarage milk,' said Kathleen, graciously. 'I'm sure she'd have had her own special . . . receptacle.'

Carrie glanced back and forth between Lucy and Kathleen. Lucy's expression was bordering on rude.

'Is she coming along today?' Carrie asked, to break the tension. 'Your granny?'

'She is,' said Lucy. 'Chris is going to get her. She's very excited about coming back. First time she's been back in twenty years. Since she buried my grandad, in fact.'

'Oh, do come and find me,' said Kathleen. 'I'd love to say hello. It must be over sixty years since I last saw Phyllis. Goodness. Sixty years! I wonder if she'd recognise me?' she added with a self-deprecating smile.

'I'm sure she would,' said Lucy. 'You're the spitting image of your father. Very distinctive *genes*, the Maxwells.'

'Thank you!' beamed Kathleen. 'Still, must get on, lots to do! Barbara has me judging practically everything today. She's got printed-out score sheets for everything from dogs to rock buns.' She rolled her eyes good-humouredly and smoothed down the thick double strand of pearls at her neck. 'Don't forget the May Queen parade is at ten thirty! I hope you're both going to take part!'

'We'll be there!' said Carrie.

Lucy smiled with tight lips.

'You will make sure you leave someone responsible in charge of the tent though, won't you?' Kathleen added. 'There are so many precious things here, and . . .' She pulled a face. 'You really can't trust anyone, can you? Especially with so many *outsiders* milling around . . .'

'I'll ask Barbara herself to step in,' said Carrie, and smiled until Kathleen swept off. 'What did you mean by that?' she demanded when she was out of earshot.

'By what?' Lucy was fiddling crossly with the old farming instruments table.

'Being so aggressive.' A sudden dizziness overwhelmed Carrie, and she had to grab the edge of the table to support herself.

'Carrie?' Lucy moved swiftly to catch her, and pushed her into a chair. 'I'm worried about you.'

'I'm fine.' Carrie motioned for the bottle of water by her basket. 'I'll be fine.'

'You're not,' said Lucy. 'I've got my eye on you, madam.'

'Would all May Queens please gather by the maypole?' Barbara's voice came bellowing through the tannoys, warping slightly as she shouted too loud. 'By the maypole? All May Queens, please. The selection will take place in five, I repeat five, minutes!'

'That's us,' said Lucy.

Carrie pulled a face. 'I'm not sure we should, you know. We're married. The May Queen should be a little girl, like Betsy.'

'Have you been in that local traditions tent?' demanded Lucy.

'No. Why?'

'Because you're really starting to sound like Philip Gladstone. Come on.' She gave her a friendly nudge. 'It's just a bit of a laugh. Stop taking it so seriously. We're just going to be closing for a few minutes,' she informed the middle-aged couple browsing the photos. 'Would you mind popping back later?'

A sudden, powerful reluctance to go anywhere near the May Queen parade overwhelmed her. 'Lucy, I don't want to do this, I think I'll just stay here where it's shady.'

Lucy turned to her. 'You have to, Carrie. It's a *village* thing.'

At that moment, Barbara Purves appeared at the door, dragging her husband Ron behind her. He looked deeply annoyed to be missing the parade of village talent.

'Come along, ladies,' she trilled. 'Ron's volunteered to look after the tent while you join us on the green!'

'See?' Lucy turned to Barbara. 'We were just about to come over!' She reached behind the stall and picked up an elaborate headpiece of shell-pink rambling roses. 'I made it from my old wedding whatsit,' she explained, seeing Carrie's reaction. 'Fabric. Saves them dropping later on in the pub! Come on.'

And she dragged a reluctant Carrie out of the tent over to the village green, so crowded now with people that there was barely any green visible.

An odd assortment of womanhood lined up next to the maypole, perfectly illustrating St Dee's curious population. Lucy and Carrie, along with Sandra and a couple of women Carrie had barely met, stood next to one awkward teenage redhead and a pair of dark-haired twins Lucy didn't recognise.

Lucy was scowling at them. 'Ringers,' she whispered to Carrie, her breath gusting hotly against her ear. 'Sue Coolidge's grandchildren. Never been here before in their lives. I wonder if Barbara'll disqualify them?'

'Lucy . . .' Carrie began, but the bright sunlight was making her eyes ache again. Maybe I do have hay fever, she thought. Everyone around her was decked out in floral arrangements – how did people still know how to make them? she wondered. Was it some countryside knowledge that was passed down in the blood, like knowing when it was about to rain or how to make scones without measuring anything?

'Well, if they win, I'm saying something.'

Carrie stared into the crowd, her eyes searching, despite herself, for Mark's familiar face. He wasn't there. She knew he wasn't.

'Where's Betsy?' she wondered aloud.

'Dunno. Oh no, there she is.' Lucy pointed across the green, where a furious-looking Betsy was running at full pelt, coppery pigtails bouncing with the effort. Carrie went cold. Running behind her was the blonde girl she'd seen in Philip's garden.

'Lucy,' she said under her breath. 'Lucy, can you . . .'

'Shh!'

Carrie fixed her gaze straight ahead in an attempt to stop the swaying in her head. Beyond the crowds, and the cars, and the stalls selling ice creams and seedlings, she could see the chalk horse, gleaming under the sunshine.

When she looked back, the blonde girl had vanished, and Betsy was pushing her way through the crowd of onlookers to get to the maypole. Seeing Carrie, her face lightened up and she waved.

Weakly, Carrie waved back and motioned to the space next to her.

You've got to get a grip, she thought. You mustn't let Betsy see you're upset by it. You have to be strong for her.

'We bid a traditional St Dee welcome to the Jack-of-the-Green!' announced Barbara through the tannoy. 'Please welcome him in from the forest!'

Behind her, the visiting brass band burst into 'The Floral Dance' and there was a ripple of applause and laughter from the crowd. A procession of men and lads from the village had been making their way unseen out of the forest, and were now halfway down the hill, dressed in green and hefting branches at shoulder height as if they were spears. Bouncing above their heads was a tall green tower of branches, like an eight-foot-tall lighthouse of leaves, and as it came nearer, Carrie realised that there was someone inside it.

The crowd parted to let the procession through and slowly, slowly the tower of leaves rustled towards the maypole.

'The forest has come to the village,' announced Barbara, reading off her card. 'Jack-of-the-Green has come to choose his queen!'

Without warning, the vivid emerald of the village green brightened in front of Carrie's eyes, bulging and receding like the sheets billowing on her washing line and the people disappeared. The sky too seemed to race up to meet her face, too blue to be real, and she was overwhelmed with a dark, resinous smell, like tree roots and rotting pine cones. It filled her nose and she coughed in panic.

'Lucy . . .' she muttered, but no words came out of her dry mouth.

Carrie heard her name being called, and looked up, making her head spin. She could see the little girl again, white-faced, white-haired in the crowd, looking straight at her without blinking. Her face was sharp, focused in the blur of everyone else.

'Carrie!' Lucy was gripping her arm, and instinctively she struggled to shrug it off. 'Carrie!'

There was someone behind the girl now. A tall woman, with long blonde hair in plaits down the side of her face. Carrie's stomach turned to stone. Was that *Lily*? Was she seeing Lily now too? Out there in the crowd? Was the old village coming to life, moving around behind the oblivious new residents? Could anyone else see this, or just her?

The procession had stopped in front of them, although the cheerful brass-band music played on. It sounded manic in Carrie's ears, too bright, too sharp. Too real.

She closed her eyes, hoping to wipe the image away, but when she opened them again, Lily hadn't gone, and there was another crowd of people around her. A second fainter group of villagers, over-lapping with the familiar faces like a double-exposure photograph: children running about, burly men in rolled-up sleeves, everyone wearing thick coronets of leaves around their heads, fading in and out of the light. The faces beneath the crowns were unclear, apart from Lily, who continued to stare. Carrie thought she could hear bells, like sleigh bells. They were watching. Watching us, she thought, panicking, as we watch the procession come down from the hill, welcoming whatever it is into our village.

'Carrie!' said a deep voice. 'Carrie!'"

'Our May Queen!' Barbara's voice crackled over the top of the racket. 'Carrie Armstrong has been chosen as the Queen of the May!'

The tower of greenery advanced on her, and now it was close

Carrie could see dark eyes sparkling through the circles cut through the leaves. They glittered at her, and she couldn't tell whether they were wicked or laughing. Were they both? The resinous smell of bark and damp intensified until the air felt too thick to breathe in her chest.

'So, Carrie,' said the voice inside the tower. 'You're my Queen of the May! The forest has come to the village and claimed a queen!'

Carrie's thoughts were coming in short, staccato bursts of clarity. Philip. She knew it was Philip Gladstone in there. But without the familiar face, his disembodied voice sounded eerily like she imagined a Green Man would sound: rumbling, and teasing, and vaguely threatening. Confident that he was at liberty to indulge the darkest human instincts while concealed beneath the traditional disguises. Like all the men in the village had been on May Day – landowners, gardeners, farmers, teachers, servants and masters.

Carrie stared at him, aware of the applause rippling around the green, but unable to speak. She swayed, but her feet felt rooted into the ground.

'Well, then?' said the treacly voice that was Philip and yet wasn't. 'Does this make you feel like a proper local girl at last?' He paused and the leaves rustled. 'Are you going to come into the forest with me? Are you going to fulfil your duties, and make sure all the crops flourish and there'll be lambs on the hillside?'

The crowd of faint villagers seemed to have moved nearer, fading in and out just behind Philip. And Carrie couldn't see Lily any more. She couldn't see any women at all, just the men in their open shirts, eyes obscured by the leaves around their heads, some tall, some short and stocky, some old, but all standing shoulder-to-shoulder like a brawny wall of darkness, advancing on her.

Terror gripped her insides, and Carrie knew it was way beyond what she should rationally be feeling. These weren't her own emotions; they belonged to someone else. Was this how Lily had felt? Was she picking up the lingering remains of something left behind, unresolved by the evacuation? Or was she just, all of a sudden, properly understanding the sinister spirit of the woods, invited into the village by people who once understood the power of the dark trees but now imagined it was all pretty maypoles and chalk horses?

Carrie widened her eyes to stop herself falling. That wasn't Philip in front of her either. That was the darkness he'd tried to pin down with research, the animals hiding in the houses, the mysteries of the sacrifices and the shattered Roman bones, the capricious gifts of fertility and death.

The colours vibrated in front of her, and the sound of the brass band seemed to turn into stabbing colours in her head, and with it all swirling too fast for her to focus, Carrie felt her legs buckle underneath her, and everything went black.

As she fell, in slow motion, the panic of her dream rushed back into her head, and she tried to scream and scream to stop it happening again.

The first thing Carrie smelled when she came round was musty, crushed grass, and she knew she was in one of the spare tents. Then she smelled Anaïs Anaïs, and knew that Lucy was looking after her.

Cautiously, Carrie opened her eyes.

'I didn't realise I had that effect on women,' said Philip Gladstone's voice, ruefully, and someone laughed.

'Carrie?' That was Lucy.

'I'm fine,' she said, struggling to get up. But her arms felt weak and she slipped back.

'Don't get up.' Lucy pressed a glass of water to her lips. 'Have a sip of this.'

Carrie sipped the water gratefully and looked round. 'Sorry,' she said. They were in the programmes and marshals' tent, although none of Barbara's gang of marshals were in sight. Just Lucy and Philip, now out of his leafy prison, but still looking like a forest man with bits of twig and leaf in his hair.

Mark wasn't there. Her heart sank under a wave of fresh misery as her brain refreshed her memory.

'Don't do that again.' Lucy wagged a finger at her. 'Barbara didn't have that scheduled. You've held up the dog show. And she asked me to give you this.' She passed over a crown of silk flowers, and Carrie shuddered.

'What?' demanded Lucy, ramming it on her head. 'Suits you.'

'Thanks,' mumbled Carrie. It hurt her scalp but she was too weak to move it.

'I did tell you you weren't looking right,' said Lucy. 'I'm going to go and get the St John's Ambulance woman.'

'No, don't,' said Carrie. 'Don't . . . it's nothing. Just the pollen. Or the sun. It's nothing serious, honestly.'

Lucy regarded her cynically. 'You mean, you want to keep whatever it is to yourself?'

Carrie closed her eyes and didn't answer.

'Well, fair enough,' said Lucy. 'I've got to go and pick up my gran off Chris, but I'll be back in two minutes. Philip'll stay with you, won't you, Philip?'

'Of course.'

'Two minutes.' Lucy wagged her finger.

Carrie listened to Lucy rustling her way out of the tent, and felt her limbs turn heavy and sink into the ground. She was exhausted, but at least felt more like herself, as if the torrent of emotion that had surged through her on the green had left only the bare essentials of her own self behind.

'Carrie?' said a voice quietly by her ear.

She turned her head and came face to face with Philip, who was crouching down beside her as if she were Betsy, ill in bed. His face was drawn with concern, and there were bits of leaf in his curling beard. He smelled green.

'I'm sorry,' he said. 'I didn't mean to scare you. Well, not into fainting, anyway.'

'You didn't,' said Carrie, closing her eyes again so she didn't have to look at him.

I might have gone up to the forest with Philip, she realised. If he'd been on his own. Shame and lust and fear and fascination. All presented in the excuse of tradition. No wonder the whole village used to go insane on May Day.

'It was weird, in that Jack-of-the-Green costume,' he went on, in an undertone. His tone was conversational but Carrie could make out a hesitancy, as if he was confessing something that only she would understand. 'I didn't feel . . . like me. And you'd think after all the years I've spent on this sort of tree worship . . .' He paused. 'I understood more in ten minutes than I've done in ten years. It felt like there was something coming alive.'

Outside, the band was still playing, and faint fete sounds of dogs barking and children's giggles drifted in to fill the silence.

'I know,' said Carrie. The hard ground seemed to be yielding like padded velvet beneath her, cushioning her, drawing her down.

A cool, broad hand stretched out and laid itself flat on her forehead. 'Maybe it wasn't the most tactful thing to do, to choose you as May Queen . . . in the circumstances.'

'If you mean Mark, forget it.'

'I wasn't going to. But it was Kathleen Maxwell who insisted,' he went on. 'She reckoned since Lily was the last May Queen, it was only right that you should be the first new one. Barbara wanted to pick Betsy. Said it was traditional to have a proper maiden.' He paused. 'Inasmuch as she knows anything about those traditions. I mean, yes, it's traditional, but suddenly, when it's your own little girl, you see all that sort of thing a bit differently. Not that I imagine that's what Barbara had in mind, of course.'

Betsy? A sharp horror cooled Carrie's blood, and she finally knew, quite clearly, as if the idea had been dropped whole into her head like a pebble, how Lily's stem had snapped. Something, someone, had taken full advantage of the May Queen's traditional sacrifice – not that any good had come from it. The village hadn't been blessed with crops – it had been destroyed. Who had it been though? Carrie shuddered. The man she married? Or more than one man?

She looked into Philip's brown eyes. Badger's eyes, knowing and ancient. He moved his hand from her forehead to hold her hand, without speaking, and she knew he was dangerous. Not necessarily in a bad way, but still. He was part of the forest, understanding its rituals and silent growth. Not bound in like the villagers.

'Philip,' Carrie began, 'Philip, I think I'm seeing things today. I saw Betsy's imaginary friend. Hazel. I saw her in your garden . . .'

He shook his head. 'Carrie, I don't think you're feeling . . .'

'No!" she insisted. 'No! And I saw the old village, out on the green! They were . . .'

Before she could go on, Lucy reappeared, pushing a very old lady in a wheelchair through the flap in the tent.

'Don't get up,' she commanded, but Carrie was already sitting up, and tentatively rising to her feet with a wobble.

'You should take it easy,' said Philip, holding out a hand to support her.

'I know,' said Carrie. 'But, Philip, I mean it, I saw . . .'

'Carrie, let's talk about this later. When we're both in jeans and T-shirts and feeling more modern?' Philip made to go. 'I'll leave you to it,' he said to Lucy, who was looking predictably curious. 'I left Betsy and Ivor helping Sandra with the ice-cream stand.' He pulled an amused face. 'I think Betsy may have found her vocation in life. I'll come back for you later. Let me know if . . .' His voice trailed off, but Carrie knew what he meant.

'I will,' she said.

Chapter Twenty-six

'He seemed like a nice young man,' said Lucy's grandmother to no one in particular. 'Bearded. Your grandfather had a beard. In his youth. I didn't like it. Bishop did though. Made him look like an Apostle.'

'I know, Gran. You've said. Many times.' Lucy rolled her eyes at Carrie. 'Carrie, this is my gran, Phyllis. Gran, this is my friend, Carrie. You remember, she's living in Oak Cottage?'

The old lady screwed up her face in the dim light of the tent. 'Lily?'

'No, Carrie.' Carrie extended a hand and felt thin bones beneath the papery skin. Nervously, she reduced the pressure of her handshake for fear of snapping them.

'*Carrie* lives in *Oak* Cottage,' said Lucy, very slowly and loudly. 'Where the *Armstrongs* lived.'

'Oh. Them.' Phyllis leaned forward to peer more closely at her, with dark eyes that seemed sharper than the feebleness of her voice. 'Don't look like one. Looks more like one of them Maxwell brats. You could always tell them. Narrow eyes and a tea set on the dresser.'

'Gran,' said Lucy. 'This is *Carrie*. She's not even related.'

'My husband – *Mark* – is Lily and Jack's *grandson*,' explained Carrie.

'Lily and Jack,' repeated the old lady. Her eyes were darting back and forth between Carrie and Lucy and the space over Carrie's shoulder. 'Are they here then? Where's Lily?'

'No, Gran, they're both dead,' said Lucy, briskly.

There was another pause. 'No, they're not,' chided the old lady. 'I've just seen them both, Lucy. In the pub.'

If Carrie hadn't been so thoroughly freaked out she would have dismissed it as old-lady rambling, but now she wasn't so sure.

'They died a long time ago,' she added, more gently than Lucy had.

'I want to be buried in the church, when I go,' said Phyllis. Painfully, she turned her head back to Lucy. 'They owe us that much. Being buried in our own churchyard. Can't keep us out of that. Eh, Joyce?'

Lucy rolled her eyes, and stage-whispered, 'Joyce is my *mum*. See what I mean?' She leaned forward. 'Is there anywhere in particular you'd like to see, Gran? Any of your old haunts?'

'Take me to the Rose and Thorn,' said Phyllis decisively.

'Not the church? You don't want to see Grandad's old church? I think they're opening it for the day,' she added to Carrie.

'I saw enough of that place when I were alive,' sniffed Phyllis. 'Let's go to the pub. I'm sure this one fancies a drink, eh?'

Carrie stared at her, not sure what to say.

'You're still alive, Gran, you daft old thing,' said Lucy. 'Come on, then, I'll take you to the pub. Fancy a drink, Carrie? I mean, your majesty? Bit of brandy's probably the best thing for you. Unless . . . ?' She raised a quizzical eyebrow.

'Brandy would be lovely,' said Carrie.

They pushed the wheelchair past the cake stand and book stall across the green towards the pub. The little village green was so busy now that Lucy had to weave her way through the crowds, marching defiantly through the viewfinders of several home videos.

Phyllis chattered as they went, remarking on how nicely they'd done the gardens, and what a shame it was that there wasn't a bakery there any more, but as they neared the pub she fell silent, and appeared to retreat into her own thoughts.

'What'll you have, Gran?' asked Lucy.

'A port and lemon.'

'Carrie?'

'Oh, er . . . some lemonade, please.' Tony was making authentic gallons of the stuff in honour of the day.

'As well as that brandy. When Tony finds out about your funny turn, I'm sure he'll send it out as medicinal.'

Phyllis gave her a sharp look. 'She's fine with lemonade, Lucy.'

While Lucy went inside to get drinks, Carrie pulled the old lady's wheelchair next to a table beneath a large umbrella. She felt a little self-conscious beneath the gaze of several tourists, taking snaps and cooing over the period pub details. Barbara, holding court by the post office, was having her picture taken by several photographers, and clearly loving every moment of it.

'Do you remember the May Day celebrations?' Carrie asked.

'Oh, I do,' said Phyllis. 'You always remember the best times as you get older. They get sharper, but you can't remember what you had for dinner yesterday.'

'I'm glad to hear that.' Carrie watched a couple walking along, giggling as they lifted their linked hands over obstacles rather than separate their fingers, and she felt an sharp pang of jealousy, like a knife beneath her ribs, that turned at once back to a dull ache.

'They used to get up to some wild business on May Day.' The old lady's eyes shone beneath the thinly plucked remains of her eyebrows. 'Everyone in the village too, not just the bad 'uns. You'd be surprised. Alfred was always being told to get it stopped. He'd have letters from the Bishop during Easter, telling him to make sure he preached a good few sermons about the evils of paganism and letting the Devil into your home, put the fear of God in all the young 'uns before May Day. Never worked, mind. You can't preach much against nature, I told him.'

Carrie got the impression that Phyllis would have told Alfred quite a lot. She wasn't the vicar's wife she'd been expecting.

'What you do mean, wild business? You mean . . . in the forest?'

'What do you think I mean, my love?' Phyllis cackled. 'What do young men and women get up to when they've a day's holiday, and nothing to do, and plenty of cider around? You young ones now, you think you've done everything for the first time, but let me tell you, you haven't!'

Carrie stared at her, shocked. Fortunately, Phyllis's tongue was only starting to loosen up.

'Now you, for instance, you'd have had to watch out.' She winked.

'Sorry?'

'As May Queen. The May Queen was the one who was meant to make the offering to the horse, you see – the flowers. But she had other duties too.'

'What?' asked Carrie. A rolling sense of déjà vu began to creep up the back of her neck, lifting the hairs.

The eyes crinkled up, as if Phyllis was amused by Carrie's innocence. 'Well, the story used to be that way back, she'd have to couple with the Jack-of-the-Green. Up in the woods! They used to say it were one of those Druid traditions, that and the big bonfire. Well, everyone likes a bonfire, if you know what I mean! And some people took it upon themselves, as you do, to do their bit for the harvest as well. Oh, there were some right goings-on. Not that I took part.' She looked sad, as if being the vicar's wife had seriously curtailed her social life.

Carrie held her breath.

'Stopped for a while though, when Gerard Maxwell had the manor,' she went on. 'He didn't like it. Very religious man, he was. Big church-goer, always setting up this, that and the other – temperance unions for the farm lads, Sunday schools, what have you. Now, his lad, though, Simon . . . couldn't have been more different. Parties all the time, folk up from London, roping everyone in the village in to skivvy for them.' Her face darkened. 'Well, they were her friends, of course.'

'Whose friends?'

'That wife of Simon's. Snooty woman, Miriam was. He brought the class, she brought the cash, that's what they used to say in the pub, though Alfred didn't like to hear a word said against them. She came from London, you see, never really liked it here. Didn't go in for the fusty old history, just the connections and the nice house.'

'I know they used to have a big party for May Day, didn't they?' Carrie prompted gently.

Phyllis was silent.

'Phyllis?'

The old lady's eyes had unfocused and her hands, bent with arthritis, were twitching in her lap.

Carrie touched her hand. 'Are you all right?' she asked, concerned. 'Can I get you some water?'

She blinked, as if she wasn't sure where she was. 'Lily?'

'No, I'm Carrie.'

The old lady suddenly grabbed her hand with a surprising force. 'I'm sorry, dear,' she said. 'So sorry.'

'For what?'

'I thought it was for the best. If you'd just come to me, I'd have helped you.'

'I don't know what you . . .'

'You know I've thought about it for the rest of my life,' she said, milky blue eyes piercing into Carrie's fearful face. 'How scared you must have been! Nice girl like you! And being too afraid to say anything to anyone.' She almost spat out the words. 'Oh, Lily, I did the best I could. And I'm sorry for Jack too, letting everyone think he'd taken advantage. When all he did was to act like a gentleman.'

She sank back in her seat and Carrie could see the tears welling up in her eyes, spilling into the folds of loose skin. 'It was an awful business. Awful. Every day, watching you get older and wiser and seeing that lovely, lively girl die . . .'

The blood hammered in Carrie's chest. She didn't know what

to say, to prompt more answers without breaking the fragile memory.

'I never told Alfred that I'd been to see Miriam. He'd have been livid. But I told her. I told her about you, and about all the other little bastards I'd watched Alfred christen. Some he wasn't allowed to christen. Some he'd buried – too early, poor little shrimps. God knows what there was about those Maxwells, but they couldn't even sire healthy bastards.'

Carrie's eyes widened.

The old lady was breathing hard now. 'S'pose it was partly my fault the place got evacuated. Government wanted this place for some secret war business, and Simon couldn't get out fast enough. I reckon Miriam threatened to divorce him, you see, take all her money away. Too many, too many to be kept a secret, and that could never be allowed to happen to the Maxwells. Oh no.'

'No,' breathed Carrie. Did Kathleen know any of this, she wondered? Or was her family history just like Mark's: gleaned from photographs, and stories, and other people's memories? A little girl, listening behind the door, eavesdropping on servants to find out what was going on in the village her parents lorded it over.

She'd come back just as ignorant as the rest of them, in other words, to a gaping space where the solid grandeur of her childhood had been.

'Can you forgive me?' The old lady put her clawed hand on Carrie's. 'Can you?' Her tone was pleading. 'I thought I'd done it for the best. I didn't know what else would happen, but I couldn't not say anything. I couldn't keep it to myself, that would have been wicked! At least you had a little money, and a home, and a man who loved you. At least you had that. And then that business with your baby.' The hand squeezed, suddenly strong. 'I know it wasn't your fault. But Jack . . . he stood by you, didn't he? I know Jack wasn't . . . wasn't what you might have wished for, but he was never cruel, was he?'

Around them, the tannoys piped brass-band music, and the sun beat down on the freshly cut green. Neat and tidy.

'You were happy, weren't you, Lilian?'

How do I know if Lily was happy, thought Carrie? How do I know how else things might have turned out? But what would it achieve to hurt this old woman now?

'Yes,' said Carrie, stroking the papery skin. 'I was happy enough, Phyllis. You did the right thing. You did the right thing.'

Phyllis closed her eyes, and a faint smile appeared on her face.

Chapter Twenty-seven

When Lucy had returned with the drinks, something had shifted in the old lady's mind, and she'd come back to the present day, albeit rather vaguely.

'You're putting on weight, Joyce,' she remarked tartly to Lucy.

'It's Lucy, Gran. Joyce is in Florida. On holiday. She did your hair before she left, remember?'

'No.'

Carrie didn't mention the strange, rich story she'd just heard. She wanted to be on her own, somewhere where she could digest it, and set everything in the proper order in her mind.

'I, er . . . there's something I need to check on at home,' she said, when she'd downed her lemonade, then the brandy Tony had sent out 'with his congratulations'. 'Would you excuse me?'

Lucy gave her a meaningful look. 'Come back out when you've checked your house,' she said. 'Or I'll pop over to make sure you're OK.'

'Goodbye, Phyllis,' said Carrie, crouching to take the old lady's hand, but she was somewhere else again, her eyes flitting back and forth between the old three-pointed roadsign and the electric gaslight.

Carrie excused herself and began to walk back through the village to the coolness of her own kitchen, where these fragments of truth about Lily might combine into some sense. The bright spring sunshine had turned hot, without warning, and she still wasn't sure she felt completely well. The crackling of the tannoys in particular was starting to give her a migraine.

As she crossed the green, weaving through the chattering tourists and boasting locals gathered about the various stalls, she caught sight of the little blonde girl again, accompanied by a tall blonde woman, and she stopped dead. Or were they the same ones? They were both eating ice creams and laughing in a very real way, although there was obviously some tension on the face of the mother, who kept looking around her, scanning the crowds.

So not ghosts after all. Not Lily and the little girl in the well. But Carrie's initial relief was swiftly replaced by a new shock. It had to be Astrid. A few years older, a woman now, but obviously Astrid.

Here! In her village. In St Dee. Real, finally.

Carrie felt her knees buckle again, but a determination to find out what was going on gave her unexpected strength, and she began striding over.

As she did so, out of the corner of her eye, she spotted Mark, running towards them.

Let him run, she thought. Let him explain this. An unusual fierceness filled her, as if she was looking down on herself from outside. I'm going to deal with this myself. If he has another woman, let her explain before he gets a chance to.

The woman looked up when she realised Carrie was walking directly towards her. Her face was hard to read: defiant, but tired at the same time. She wasn't the careless girl in the photo, but she was still striking, her blonde hair partly hidden by a wide black silk scarf, tall enough to carry off a scarlet linen tunic and cropped trousers with uncrumpled elegance.

Carrie got there before Mark did. 'Hello,' she said. 'You must be Astrid.'

'I am,' said the woman. She didn't sound surprised. She didn't sound Scandinavian either, as Carrie had imagined she would – she was Australian. 'Carrie?'

'Yes. Yes, Mark's wife.'

'I know that,' she replied, almost offended at the assumption she didn't.

They looked at each other, and Carrie realised she didn't know what to say next. She wanted to feel surging rage, but she didn't. She felt numb.

'And you know who this is?' Astrid went on, slipping her hand onto the child's shoulder.

Carrie shook her head, unable to take her eyes off the pale hair, shimmering in the sunlight.

'This is Mark's daughter, Rowan,' she went on, before Carrie could reply.

'Astrid! Wait, let me tell her!'

They both turned, as Mark stumbled to a halt.

'Carrie,' gasped Mark. His face was ashen, and beads of sweat glistened on his forehead from running. 'Carrie, I . . .' He glared at Astrid. 'I *told* you. You promised . . .'

'Mark,' snapped Carrie, and nodded towards the little girl.

Astrid put a protective hand on the child's head. 'Quite. I'll leave you for a moment,' she said, sounding more vexed than anything. 'Mark's got a lot of explaining to get through. I can't believe he hasn't told you anything before now. Well, I can, but . . .'

'I was going to tell . . .'

Astrid lifted an angry finger. 'No, you weren't. That's why I came here today to sort all this out. And it's typical of you that when I get here, you've done one of your usual runners, and it's your wife I end up finding!' She gave him a final glare and turned back to Carrie. 'Don't let him off the hook,' she said warningly. 'Come on, Ro, let's see the donkeys,' she said, in a lower voice to her daughter, and led her away.

Carrie folded her arms across her chest for comfort and waited.

'Carrie, let me explain all this,' Mark panted, trying to get his breath and his dignity back. 'It's not what it looks like.'

'She's your daughter?' It didn't sound any more real even when she said the words aloud. 'Mark, I don't understand what's going on.'

'Neither do I. Not really.' Mark pushed his fingers into his hair and closed his eyes. He looked exhausted.

'But she is your daughter?' Carrie asked again.

He spoke without opening his eyes. 'She's my daughter, yes.'

'And what's she doing here?' Carrie couldn't believe how calm her voice sounded, even though inside she felt as if everything was fragmenting into tiny pieces, too small to ever stick back together. 'What's Astrid doing here? Astrid – the woman you haven't seen for years?'

There was a long pause. The band by the green finished playing, and a polite ripple of applause broke out. Carrie felt as if she were standing on a film set, listening to some actor delivering lines. Nothing was connecting inside her. Nothing looked real.

'I never actually said that,' said Mark.

'Oh, for *God's sake!*' snapped Carrie.

Mark rubbed his face.

'You saw the photos of Astrid,' he said, eventually. 'We met while I was travelling through Australia. Years ago. We were together nine months, a year? If that. Astrid had a job to get back to, I didn't. I wanted to keep travelling, I was nowhere near ready for marriage. She was special, yes, but we were never going to get married.'

He ran away, in other words.

Carrie put her hands to her mouth because she didn't know what else to do with them, and wanted to cover her face somehow.

'Please say something, Carrie,' begged Mark. 'Anything. Just don't look at me like that.'

She gazed at her husband and realised that he'd become so familiar that she'd almost forgotten how to see him at all. Looking at him now was as if a tissue-paper page had been lifted away from a photograph: she noticed the lines of stress around his eyes, the beginnings of crêpe-iness on his cheeks. Too much coffee. Too much stress. Too little sleep. The boyish looks were there, but weariness and stress were beginning to wear them away.

'Mark,' she said, barely aware that she was speaking his name out loud. 'Oh, Mark.'

He'd turned into a completely different person while they'd been living here, and she'd done her best not to notice. Or rather, he'd shown her who he really was. All the time, she'd been trying to see the man she married, even when he wasn't there any more. All the time she thought he'd been her husband, he'd been this little girl's father.

'You must have been laughing at me inside when I was trying to get you to talk about having a child,' she said, angrily. 'The *months* I wasted trying to think of ways to talk to you about it . . . You already *had* a baby. And now . . .'

Tears sprang into her eyes, and she had to move her gaze away from Mark, towards where the little girl was playing with Betsy, making chains with the fat daisies that had escaped mowing on the 'wildflower' sides of the village green. In her pinafore and with her pigtails and her milky white skin lit by the sun, suddenly it was Betsy who looked like a ghost, not the other child. Astrid stood a few feet away, making a call on her mobile, but keeping a watchful eye on her little girl.

Mark's eyes flickered up, like a dog expecting a kick, not a pat on the head.

'Carrie, you have to believe me when I say that I didn't even know she existed until about four months ago. I honestly had no idea. I've been a bag of nerves ever since. It's been driving me completely insane, wondering what to do. I thought I'd sorted it.'

Carrie was still watching the little girls, trying to control the twist of longing in the pit of her stomach. Was it already too late now?

And there was no point even wondering if Rowan was really his. She reflected Mark like a mirror: she laughed with his dark blue eyes, and his mobile mouth, even if it was set in a pale Scandinavian face, surrounded by Astrid's white-blonde hair. A mixture of their genes that she could never come between. Proof that there had been someone before her. Proof that was impossible to hide in a shoebox and pretend it never existed.

Carrie stroked her forehead with her hand as Rowan carefully placed a daisy chain around Betsy's neck. Betsy looked excited to be playing with an older girl at last, instead of her baby brother, and glowed with delight at the attention. A real friend, not like Hazel or the other ghostly little playmates in that house.

'When did they arrive?'

'Carrie?' said Mark, sounding more worried.

She didn't turn her gaze from the girls. 'Rowan was in the garden this morning. She gave me a real shock. I thought she was Betsy's imaginary friend. I thought she was the ghost from next door.'

'I don't know. About half an hour before I got back, I reckon. Look, don't start that again. There was never a ghost next door,' said Mark, impatiently.

'No,' said Carrie, squinting at him in the sunlight, 'all the ghosts were in our house. Funny, huh.'

'Carrie, are you listening to me?' demanded Mark. 'I didn't know about Rowan until Astrid tracked me down in London. Carrie, please listen to me, will you?'

'Mark! I need to borrow the May Queen, if you don't mind.'

Carrie knew it was Philip without having to turn round; his broad shadow had fallen on the grass in front of them, and she could sense his bear-like presence behind her. A cool breeze ran over her hot skin, though there was no wind around, and she smelled the green forest.

'It's not a great time, Philip. I'm trying to talk to Carrie about something private,' snapped Mark. He sounded very London to Carrie's ears.

'On the village green?' Philip raised a dark eyebrow. 'You haven't spent a lot of time here, clearly.'

'Philip,' said Carrie. 'He's right. Could you give us five minutes?'

He looked at her inquisitively from beneath the crown of twisted leaves that had replaced his green tower. He looked more like an affable Bacchus now than a menacing forest. Even so, there was something about him that . . . Carrie pushed the thought away.

'Everything OK?' he asked.

'Yes,' she nodded. 'Everything's fine.'

Philip held her gaze for a beat without speaking, which conveyed his concern better than words, but then nodded curtly at Mark and stretched out his hand to Betsy. 'Come on, madam,' he said. 'Do you want a donkey ride?'

'Can I bring my friend?' she asked, tugging at Rowan's dress.

'Why not? Plenty of donkeys to go round.'

Betsy grabbed Rowan by the hand and began to march her away. Rowan looked up at Astrid sitting on a bench a few feet away, who nodded agreement, but Mark was still staring at Carrie as if their whole relationship depended on not letting her out of his sight.

She watched as Philip approached Astrid, and said something that made her lift her head and smile up at him. Then she got up and followed the girls towards the donkey rides, her willowy frame tall enough to reach Philip's shoulder.

'Oh God, I can't believe this is happening to me,' moaned Mark. 'I mean, I'd make a really crap father. I don't know what to do . . .'

Carrie looked at him. He was right. He would make a useless father. Unless something snapped him out of believing the world revolved around him. 'Mark? Why didn't you tell me as soon as you found out?' she demanded. 'What was the point in keeping something like this a secret?'

'I couldn't. I just . . . couldn't tell you.'

'But why not? Didn't you think I'd notice the child support payments leaving our joint bank account? Anyway, what did you think I was going to do, for God's sake? Run away? Leave you because of something that happened years ago before I even met you?'

Mark met her furious eyes. 'I don't know. I didn't know what you'd do.'

Carrie looked at him and realised that while she knew, without even having to consider it, that she would have stood by him no matter what, maybe he didn't. Maybe they just didn't know each other well enough to risk a crisis like this.

'But *I* would have risked it,' she heard herself say aloud. 'Better to take a risk than to let someone you love feel so . . . untrusted.' Something pinched inside her chest and unconsciously she put her hand over it to try to soothe it away.

'Carrie, when we got married, didn't we say we'd leave the past in the past? And I didn't even know this was there!' Mark pushed his fingers back into his hair. 'I mean, it's such a headfuck! It was bad enough for me, finding out I'd . . . got a child.' He sounded awkward even saying it. 'And not a baby either, a little *girl*. Who looked exactly like I did. God. When I saw the photos I couldn't believe it. I thought it was a wind-up. Then when I met her, I knew it was for real . . . I think it was the worst moment of my life. And I just didn't know what you'd do.'

'How can it be the worst moment of your life?' Carrie whispered. 'Finding out you had a child?'

He wiped his hand over his face, then raised his eyes to hers and his expression was pleading. Carrie was horrified by the helplessness in Mark's face. 'When it's not with the right woman? It was you I thought of first. Not me. Not Astrid. *You*. You were so excited about moving here, and starting a new life. Wanting a pretty house, and a cat, and kids of our own. You wanted everything to be perfect, and, you know, I did too. For the first time in my whole life, I thought, *right*, I'm finally ready to settle down. Then suddenly . . . this! I didn't want to spoil everything for you. For us. I just . . .' His voice trailed away.

'You just wanted it all to go away,' Carrie supplied the words he didn't want to say.

Mark sighed. 'Yes. Yes, maybe I did. Is that a really awful thing?'

'It's awful that you didn't think about Rowan before all that.'

'I know. I know. But she wasn't real to me, and you are.'

Carrie said nothing. But instead of thinking of herself, and what it might mean to have this reminder of Mark's past suddenly dropped into their marriage, she couldn't stop thinking about Astrid. Presumably she'd spent the previous eight years imagining that moment, when Mark finally faced up to the life he'd run away from and met his daughter. How had that gone in her head? Did she know him well enough to guess his reaction?

Did she know him better than Carrie herself did?

'How did you take it when Astrid told you?' she asked.

'Badly. I didn't know if she wanted some big reunion.' Mark paused. 'She told me I was being selfish. She didn't know I was married, obviously. That shocked her, that I'd settled down. Are you angry?'

Carrie looked him in the eye. 'Angry about Rowan? No, of course not. I'm *angry* that all the time I've been trying to make the perfect life, in the lovely house, with the orchard and the cat, you've known this secret was there, festering away, undermining everything. Would you have told me, if Astrid hadn't come here today? Would you have let me build our life here on a *lie*?'

'I was scared that if I told you, there wouldn't *be* a life.'

Carrie swallowed. She sank onto a bench, and after a diffident pause, Mark sat down next to her.

'Why did Astrid get in touch now?' she asked.

'Rowan had been asking questions, about her father. And Astrid was going to move to London, and she thought maybe it was time to involve me.' He grimaced. 'She thought I might have grown up enough to take some responsibility, were her exact words.'

'And have you?'

Mark took her hand. Carrie pulled it away, then relented and let him slide his fingers between hers. 'I don't know. Maybe. I've got different responsibilities now. You, for a start.'

'For what it's worth, Mark,' she said, wishing she didn't have to tell him things he ought to know, 'I'm not the sort of woman who'd try to insist on coming before an eight-year-old girl.'

Mark winced. 'I know. But, Carrie . . . You know I've never really had a family before. After Mum and Dad died, I decided I didn't need one. But you're my family now, and you've made me so happy, these last few years, I just couldn't bear the thought of letting anything spoil that. I know that's cowardly. I'm not proud of thinking it, but I'm trying to be honest with you here.'

'And the money?' She wanted to give him every chance to be honest, because if he couldn't manage that now, there really wasn't much point in going on. 'The plane tickets?'

Mark let out a long sigh. 'OK. Astrid called me, just before I lost my job. At first . . . At first I was kind of excited. I wanted to see her, I can't lie about that. And . . . we had a great evening out. Nothing happened,' he added. 'Honestly, nothing happened. And then she called me the next day, wanting to meet again. She said she had something to tell me. I was so distracted, with her, with you, with this St Dee thing – I screwed up something badly on the system I was meant to be fixing.' He passed a hand across his forehead. 'That's why my contract wasn't renewed. Then I met her, and she told me we had a daughter.'

Carrie knew without being told which night that had been: the night he'd curled around her for comfort like an exhausted, hunted animal. 'I should have guessed it was more than just the job,' she said softly.

'How? How were you meant to know?' Mark shrugged, as if he could shrug off the weight on his back. Then he straightened up. 'I saw her a couple of times after that. We talked about what I ought to do – what *we* ought to do. She didn't want me to meet Rowan until she was sure I wasn't going to run off again, but it wasn't as easy as that, was it?'

'No. And yes.'

'Carrie, look . . . Maybe I didn't do the right thing. But I did the best I could, OK? I couldn't talk about it to anyone. It just went round and round in circles in my head. I was snappy with you, I was snappy with Astrid, I hated myself. All I knew was that I didn't want it to spoil what we had, or be the kind of useless father that would let Rowan down. Everyone would lose. In the end, I reckoned the best thing I could do would be to give her a fresh start, so that's when I bought the plane tickets and gave Astrid the cash. I'm sorry it was yours. I just couldn't get hold of mine that quickly. She was going to go to America. I didn't realise she'd change her mind and come and find me, did I?'

Carrie said nothing.

He let his head hang so she couldn't see his eyes. 'I know I haven't been the ideal husband because, you know? I don't really know what that's meant to be like. But you've been the ideal wife, ideal for me, and I knew I'd never find anyone like you again. I wanted to be on my own till I met you, and now I hate the thought of . . . I just felt that you didn't deserve to have everything ruined by a mistake I didn't even know about.' He snorted.

'Don't call her a mistake,' said Carrie. 'And you don't know how bad a father you'd be, not if you don't even try.'

They sat without speaking, staring out towards the green at the *Trumpton*-ish scene that carried on unfolding even as their marriage was turning into something unfamiliar. Children were leading dogs around in a circle, while Kathleen Maxwell stood on a presidential box, writing on her official judging clipboard, and the tannoys crackled announcements that faded in and out of intelligibility in waves, as if they were floating in from a different time altogether.

Carrie was acutely conscious that every single word that either of them spoke now would swing the course of the rest of their lives, and she felt overwhelmed.

Where are my instincts now? she wondered. What am I meant to do? Out of habit, she wondered what Lily would do, then pushed the thought away: poor Lily. Lily did what she was told. Buried one screeching baby here, never spoke of it again, moved away with his living twin and made the best of what she had.

'Carrie, can we start again?' Mark's voice was quiet, and serious in a way she'd never really heard before. He hadn't sounded so serious when they'd made their marriage vows.

She let his words hang in the air between them, real words amid the crackle of the tannoy and the drifting music. Philip was over by the welcome tent, talking to Astrid while Betsy and Rowan squealed in delight on their donkeys, decorated with flowers on their tails and soft noses. Ivor was up on Philip's broad shoulders, his coppery head twisting from side to side like a lighthouse, solemnly trying to take in everything that was going on.

When he saw Carrie, he waved his fat little hand in her direction and shouted something, banging Philip's head and bending to speak in his ear. Philip rolled his eyes, and waved too, at Ivor's instruction.

No, she thought. I don't want to start again.

'Carrie?' repeated Mark. 'Can we start again?'

She lifted her hand and waved, smiling, at Ivor. 'No,' she said.

'What?'

Carrie turned on the bench so she could look straight into Mark's bewildered face. 'We can't just start again. You seem to think that you can keep on starting again indefinitely. And we can't, Mark. No one can. You *can't* just wipe the slate clean each time. Life doesn't work like that.'

'Carrie, are you saying that we . . .' Mark let his voice trail off, but his fears were written plainly in his eyes, even if he couldn't put them into words.

What *am* I saying? wondered Carrie. She turned away, and looked back out onto the green, letting her gaze drift around the crowds of people. Kathleen was handing a third Victoria sponge from the cake stall to Barbara Purves, who seemed to have taken on a role as lady-in-waiting while Kathleen did the rounds of the stalls. She knew, without having to hear, what Lucy would say about that.

'I suppose I'm saying can I trust you? Can I honestly believe you won't try to run away from me too, if we have a child and it's suddenly too much for you to deal with?'

'Carrie, I swear to you I would do my best. I'd do anything to make you happy,' said Mark.

She tried to see herself on her own in St Dee, marooned in the green valley without a car, stuck in the house alone with a tiny, screaming baby, and no one to hold her when she ran out of patience and energy. How would she manage if Mark never grew up? How would she manage if Mark turned out not to be the man she hoped he was?

But as Carrie tried to summon up the images in her mind, the house was full of light, and the crying baby was in a tree-shaded pram in the orchard. And she was rocking it in her arms, the comforting smells of old wood and linen rising from the cellar where the washing machine was on.

And she knew she would cope whatever happened. There was something in the house that made her strong, and rooted in a way that perhaps Mark might eventually come to share. Until then, it was enough for her to face up to pretty much anything. She had a home, even in this strange village where nothing was exactly as it looked.

She pressed her palms over her eyes and saw Lily's bright face, surrounded by the flowers of her May Queen crown. She couldn't picture the dried-up old lady any more.

'Mark,' she said, taking her hands away from her face. 'I don't want to start again. I want to carry on with what we've got. You and me. And Rowan is part of that. Here.'

Mark didn't speak. He simply turned and laid his head on her shoulder, curling his arms around her waist. Carrie put her arms around him, and spoke into his hair. 'Don't think it's going to be easy,' she said. 'But if we're really honest with each other . . .'

'I will be.' His voice was muffled. 'I promise you.'

Carrie looked into the distance, feeling her heart pump in her chest. Gradually, as she breathed deeply, it slowed to a calm, controlled pulse.

*

Towards the end of the afternoon, Carrie found Betsy sitting on the grass, eating a chocolate cornet outside the history tent, where Philip was explaining about the headless Roman skeletons to an elderly couple in travel sandals. She strongly suspected he was adding a little poetic licence to some of the gorier details.

'I like Rowan,' Betsy informed Carrie. 'Is she coming to live in your house?'

'I don't know. She might come and stay now and again.'

'That would be nice,' said Betsy. 'She can do extra*ordinary* daisy chains.'

Carrie sat down next to her and was moved by the easy way Betsy leaned against her side, the warm skin of their bare arms touching. It was the biggest compliment the odd little girl could pay, and she appreciated it. 'Can I tell you a secret, Betsy?'

Betsy immediately stopped licking her ice cream and regarded her with round eyes. 'What?'

'When I saw Rowan talking to you today, I thought it was Hazel.'

Betsy looked scornfully up at her. 'How silly!'

'Silly?'

'Yes, silly. Hazel looks nothing like Rowan.' Betsy returned her attention to her ice cream. 'Hazel has red hair, like me.'

'Does she? Oh. Maybe it was Gillian I thought I saw, then?' Carrie watched Sandra shepherd a group of tourists towards the refreshment tent with an expression of grim entrepreneurial determination, while Betsy crunched up the final end of the cornet.

'No, silly. Gillian's *much* older than Rowan,' Betsy went on, daintily licking her fingers clean like a kitten. 'She's a grown-up with lovely long skirts. They *swish*.' She demonstrated with her own fancy May Day pinafore. 'I hear them swish at night.'

Carrie looked down at Betsy, understanding finally beginning to stir in her mind. 'You hear them?'

'Yes, in my room. There's a picture of her in there.' She nodded backwards towards the history tent, and her brow furrowed.. 'Maybe she's younger than you.'

Carrie's skin crept a little. 'And what does she look like?'

'She's quite tall, and very pretty, and she has bee-yoo-tiful golden hair' – Betsy stroked her imaginary sheets of hair on either side of her head – 'and she always says, don't worry, don't worry, when the owls hoot outside my window.' She frowned. 'She doesn't say much else, though. Not to me. Sometimes she gets cross with the other little girls when they're naughty. She gets very cross with Hazel sometimes. And the baby who won't stop crying. Ivor doesn't like the baby either. That's why he doesn't like going upstairs.'

Betsy stopped, then looked up at Carrie, very seriously. 'Can I tell you a secret, too, Carrie?'

'Of course you can.' Carrie swallowed back a lump in her throat. 'You can tell me anything, sweetheart. Anything at all.'

Betsy looked around to check that Philip's attention was still with the elderly couple, then she leaned up on her knees and cupped her hand around Carrie's ear.

'Gillian lives in *your* house,' she whispered, her breath hot against Carrie's skin.

Of course she did. If anyone had been in need of Lily's doting child-minding, it had been Betsy. If any child had a longing for attention strong enough to pull spirits back into a house, it was her.

Carrie widened her eyes at the little girl, then beckoned her nearer, so she could whisper back. She pushed a thick curl of ginger hair out of the way, marvelling at the shimmer of colour, and the pale delicacy of the tender skin behind the small ear.

'I know!' she said.

Betsy's eyes widened too, and she put her white hands over her mouth in delight.

Carrie put a finger on her lips. 'Secret,' she said.

Betsy nodded. 'Secret.'

Carrie put her arm around Betsy and squeezed her. Maybe with more real-life attention the other presence in the house would fade into the background again, like the cows blending happily into the skirting boards in her illustrations. Maybe it was too much to ask that they leave altogether. Maybe they had no choice. So long as you knew they were there.

'Where did you get that ice cream?' she asked.

'Sandra's got a stall by the tombola. She has five different flavours, plus sprinkles.'

'Come on then.' Carrie got up and extended a hand to pull Betsy to her feet. 'Shall we get another one?'

'Yes, please!'

Carrie watched as Betsy galloped towards the tombola, her arms windmilling happily. Living in an empty, sterile house wasn't what she wanted. And now the tiny, crying baby and the sad mother had bridged that silent chasm, between the abrupt end of their story and the beginning of hers and Mark's, perhaps they'd stop trying to get her attention.

She looked towards the ice-cream stall where Mark was making – or doing his best to make – conversation with Paul Jenkins. Paul had removed his jacket in deference to the festive atmosphere, but his tie was as straight and perfectly knotted as ever. They were holding their mobile phones up in different directions, waving them around, obviously discussing the erratic reception.

Barbara and Kathleen won't let them build a mast, she thought, automatically picturing the outrage at having St Dee 'spoiled' with modern technology.

Carrie smiled to herself. I really am thinking like a villager now, she thought, turning towards Sandra's ice-cream stand, decked out in period bunting with Sandra herself scooping away in a striped pinny, wiping her brow with the back of her hand as she added up the prices in her head.

The green was no different from the way it had been at the start of the morning, and yet everything had shifted, very subtly. Brass-band music still crackled from the tannoys, but now Carrie could see trainers beneath the costumes, and caught the occasional jangle of text messages. Lucy, helping Sandra with a bulk cornet order, had whipped off her long skirt and replaced it with her familiar skintight jeans, although she'd left the smocked top, now unlaced and hanging flirtatiously off one golden shoulder.

Carrie looked up towards the chalk horse, caught in furious mid-gallop on the hill. We're just an overlay, she thought suddenly. A modern overlay of jeans and cars and computers, a temporary filter of life over the ancient valley, like the faint cows and horses on my easel. Lily's past, the evacuation – it was just a scratch on the surface of what's happened here, and will be here when Mark and Lucy and Barbara and I have faded into the skirting boards of our houses, floating up and down the stairs with everything else that's still here.

But somehow the thought didn't bother her. Somehow it made her feel more settled than she ever had been in her life.

Carrie stopped and took off her shoes, so she could feel the grass between her toes, and headed off towards the ice-cream stand to buy as many scoops as Lucy could fit on one cone. And then she was going to share it with Mark.

POCKET
BOOKS

Constance & Faith
Victoria Routledge

Hannah Marshall never thought she'd return to Linton – a Cumbrian town riddled with exhausted coal mines and permanently overhung with rain cloud

Ten years later, seeking refuge from a jilted love affair, she finds that little has changed. The rain pours ceaselessly, her mother is still railing against the injustices of the world, and her bewitching grandmother Dora and her circle of fearsome matriarchs continue to rule the town.

But now, seeing through adult eyes, Hannah begins to understand the web of grudges and old secrets that have ensnared her hometown – and the unspoken scandal that surrounds her turbulent family.

As she faces up to her own demons, she's forced to confront the past, and the hidden truths that have scarred her life, her family and the very town itself.

'A fat, plot-rich novel . . . a diverting fable about daring to look back' DAILY MAIL

ISBN-13: 978-0-7434-1520-0
ISBN-10: 0-7434-1520-5
PRICE £6.99

POCKET
BOOKS

Rococo

Adriana Trigiani

Makeover specialist Bartolomeo Di Crespi is all his name
suggests – stylish, sophisticated, a legend in his own time.
From the Mediterranean to Manhattan his taste reigns
supreme. When the renovation of his hometown church
comes up for tender, Bartolemeo assumes only he can do
justice to the task ahead. But the local pastor, Father
Porporino, has other ideas . . .

Captivating, hilarious, bursting with effervescent life, as
fanciful as flocked wallpaper, *Rococo* is a comic masterpiece
with a heart of goldleaf from Richard & Judy favourite
Adriana Trigiani.

'With her usual deftness and lightness of touch together
with a delightfully charismatic hero, she has created an
exuberant and stylish story'
INDEPENDENT ON SUNDAY

'Yum yum – if novels were food, this one would be fudge.
A joyous blend of Italian-American warmth and whiplash
New York wit' THE TIMES

ISBN-13: 978-0-7434-9588-2
ISBN-10: 0-7434-9588-8
PRICE £6.99

POCKET
BOOKS

The Mercy of Thin Air
Ronlyn Domingue

In 1920s New Orleans, Raziela Nolan is in the throes of a
magnificent love affair when she dies suddenly in an
accident. Immediately after her death, she chooses to stay
between – a realm that exists after life and before
whatever lies beyond it.

From this remarkable vantage point, Razi narrates the story
of her lost love, and life, as well as the relationship of Amy
and Scott, a young couple whose house she haunts almost
seventy-five years later. Their trials compel Razi to slowly
unravel the mystery of what happened to her first and only
love, Andrew, and to confront a long-hidden secret.

'Fans of *The Lovely Bones* and *The Time Traveller's Wife* now
have another classic . . . a wonderfully powerful depiction of
true, heart-wrenching love and the grief experienced when it
is lost.' EASY LIVING MAGAZINE

'Superbly constructed, this is a story about the power of
first love and the potency of memory. Ronlyn Domingue
is a first-class writer' IRISH EXAMINER

'A truly original voice and a truly original story'
Jodi Picoult

ISBN-13: 978-1-4165-1125-0
ISBN-10: 1-4165-1125-3
PRICE £6.99

POCKET
BOOKS

Goodnight Nobody
Jennifer Weiner

For Kate Klein, semi-accidental mother of three, the
unsolved murder of a fellow mother is the most
interesting thing to happen since the neighbours cracked
their septic tank. Up until then life in suburbia has been
distinctly underwhelming. Her once-loving husband is
hardly ever home. The supermums on the playground
routinely snub her and her days are filled with empty
routine. At night, most of her orgasms are of the do-it-
yourself variety.

So, from 8:45 to 11:30 am on Mondays, Wednesdays and
Fridays, when her kids are in nursery school, Kate
launches a murder investigation of her own. With the help
of her best friend, carpet heiress Janie Segal, and former
flame, Evan McKenna, she is drawn deep into the dead
woman's double life. Suddenly suburbia is not so ordinary
after all . . .

Engrossing, suspenseful, and laugh-out-loud funny,
Goodnight Nobody is another unputdownable, sparkling tale;
a quick-witted mystery with a great heart and a narrator
you'll never forget.

ISBN-13: 978-0-7434-6895-4
ISBN-10: 0-7434-6895-3
PRICE £6.99

POCKET
BOOKS

The Dream House
Rachel Hore

Everyone has a dream of their perfect house – in the heart of the countryside, or perhaps a stately residence in the middle of a wonderful city?

For Kate Hutchinson, the move to Suffolk from the tiny, noisy London terrace she shares with her husband Simon and their two young children was almost enough to make her dreams come true.

Space, peace, a measured, rural pace of life have a far greater pull for Kate than the constantly overflowing in-tray on her desk at work. Moving in with her mother-in-law must surely be only a temporary measure before the estate agent's details of the perfect house fall through the letterbox.

But when, out walking one evening, Kate stumbles upon the beautiful house of her dreams, it is tantalizingly out of her reach. Its owner is the frail elderly Agnes, whose story – as it unravels – echoes so much of Kate's own. And Kate comes to realize how uncertain and unsettling even a life built on dreams can be: wherever you are, at whatever time you are living, and whoever you are with . . .

ISBN-13: 978-1-4165-1099-4
ISBN-10: 1-4165-1099-0
PRICE £6.99

**POCKET
BOOKS**

This book and other **Pocket** titles are available from your local
bookshop or can be ordered direct
from the publisher.

0743415205	Constance & Faith	Victoria Routledge	£6.99
0743495888	Rococo	Adriana Trigiani	£6.99
1416511253	The Mercy of Thin Air	Victoria Routledge	£6.99
0743468953	Goodnight Nobody	Jennifer Weiner	£6.99
1416510990	The Dream House	Rachel Hore	£6.99

Please send cheque or postal order for the value of the book,
free postage and packing within the UK, to
SIMON & SCHUSTER CASH SALES
PO Box 29, Douglas Isle of Man, IM99 1BQ
Tel: 01624 677237, Fax: 01624 670923
Email: bookshop@enterprise.net
www.bookpost.co.uk

Please allow 14 days for delivery. Prices and availability
subject to change without notice